Love and Carnage

By Dick Clifton

Also by Dick Clifton

The Missing Years

http://bit.ly/themissingyears

The story opens in the Western Desert a short while before the June 1942 advance by Rommel, which took the Axis to the outskirts of Alexandria.

Basil Holden, using a patrol truck from the Long range Desert Group as a taxi, is about to blow up a petrol dump deep in the desert and many miles behind enemy lines.

Although only 22 years of age, nearly three years of active service have endowed him with a maturity not often found in one so young. The special duties he undertook, invariably in enemy territory, had developed his natural self-reliance into a sense of leadership which was to prove invaluable in the days to follow.

"What beautiful prose, even the opening line was one I had to read then reread just to savour the lyrical nature of your writing. This quality is continued throughout the chapters that I read. Wonderful stuff."

Carl Ashmore - www.authonomy.com

"I like books that take me away from my everyday world and transport me to a different one. And this does that very well by moving me back in time to WWII and into a POW camp. You have a great writing style. I'm glad you wrote this in third person; that's a much more sophisticated style of writing than first person; gives the story depth it wouldn't have had if you'd written this as just another war memoir. This is what I call a "plane book"; one I could sink myself in so deeply if I read it on a plane I could forget I was 30,000 miles up in a metal cage. It's a good read."

Burgio - www.authonomy.com

Copyright © 2014 by Dick Clifton All rights reserved.

First published in Great Britain in 2011

Neath blazing sun and pale moonlight
remote and far away.
When winds are high a mournful
song is heard by night and day.
The ghostly spirit wanders,
away from haunts of man.
Who knows what memories linger
in an empty petrol can.

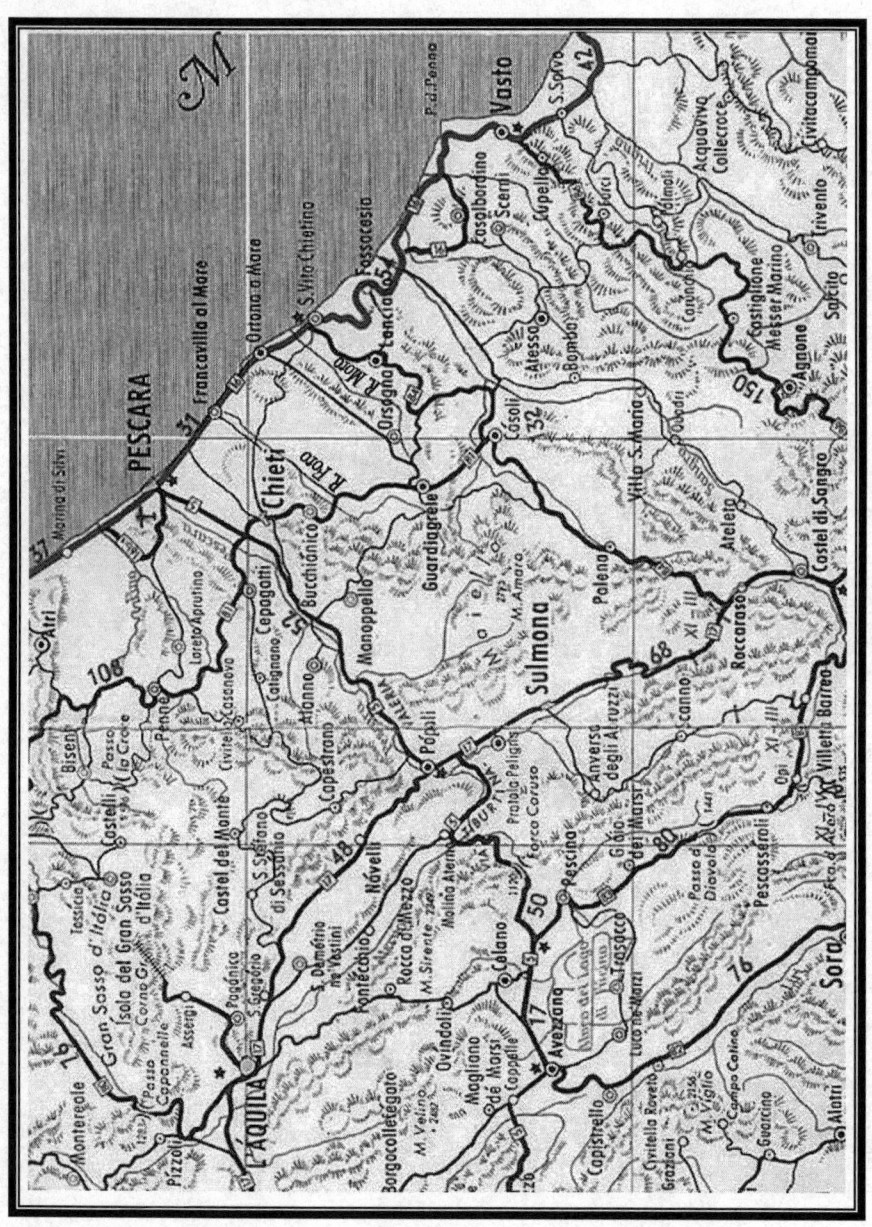

CHARACTERS

Families

Angelo Tocco: Working with Partito d' Azione.
- **Filomena:** Daughter. Courier for Giorgio

Michele Zerella: Land owner and wine producer
- **Vincensina:** Wife.
- **Giuseppina:** Daughter
- **Mario:** Son. Ex Captain of the Alpini regiment. [Giulia]
- **Caterina:** Vincensina's mother. Old and nearly blind.

Ernesto Battistero: Employee of Michele
- **Donnina:** Wife
- **Lucia:** Daughter
- **Dora:** Eleven year old daughter.
- **Gianni:** Son

Vichi Antonio (Il Maresciallo): Donnina's father.

Concetta Castello: Widow
- **Carina:** Daughter.

Ida Di Lorenzo: Has a second name, Hannah, which she prefers not to use.
- **Roberto:** Eight year old son.
- **Konrad Brucker:** Uncle by marriage. A German spy named Konrad poses under other names (Marco, Jim), but generally known as the Sicilian.

Pasquale Bartolino: Ex Mountaineering guide.
- **Carlotina:** Pasquale's wife.

Enrico Mattoni: Friend of Ernesto Battistero.
- **Pasquale:** Son

The 'Leaf Men'

Giorgio: Oak leaf
Francesco: Sycamore leaf
Il Topo: Beech leaf

The Partisans

Alan: Released P.O.W. Turned Partisan.

Paul: Released P.O.W. Turned Partisan

Capitano Luigi Vincenzo:

  Tina: Daughter. Courier for Francesco.

  Pamela: Wife

  Tania: Sister

Sgt Major: Ricardo called Il Tiranno a play on his real name. Florio di Tirane.

Donnola: Ex Army friend of Gianni Battistero

Gianni Battistero: Known as Lepre [See Battistero family]

Grillo: 2nd in Command of Scolopendre

Lama: Expert with a knife.

Lombo:

Migale: Leader of the Scolopendre.

Proco:

Young would be partisans

Carlo: Grandson of Pasquale Bartolino known as Guerriero.

Leopoldo: Self proclaimed leader of young group under protection of Captain Vincenzo.

Alfonso:

The Germans

Oberst Ludwig Von Hoffmann: In Command of Garrison in Santa Stefano

Hans:

Hauptmann Karl Schmitt:

Oberleutnant Wolfgang: Officer in charge of a raiding party.

Oberleutnant Schmidt: Appointed to liaise with Italian civilians in Santa Stefano.

Maximilian Braur: A Sentry.

Otto Spach: Interrogator.

British Officers
Lt Philip Cargil: Officer sent to help with a drop of arms
Lt Sandy Flood: Officer sent to assist in demolition
Archie: A Flt Lieutenant shot down and trying to return to Allied territory

Other Characters
Abbondio Monk: Probationer.
Alberto: 10/11 year old Staffatino Child Courier.
Anna: Wife of Ercolene. Raped and murdered.
Antonio: Son of Nazario and Anna.
Baldino Domenico: Charcoal burner.
Carlo Loriano: O.V.R.A. Officer.
Cortesa Giovanna: Radio operator Known as Favilla.
Donna Ricci: Elderly widow
Don Pezza: Senior Monk
Eric Spink: Released P.O.W. Friend of Robin.
Emma: Wife of Nazario.
Francesca: 10/11 year old friend of Alberto, also a child courier.
Garguillo: Pawnbroker. [Only mentioned, not met.]
Geoff: S.S. Man on mission to liaise with Partisans.
Giafranco: A guide for Topo.
Gino: A guide, friend of Michele.
Guido: The name used by all the Guides
Gordon: Ex Partisan claims to be a released P.O.W.
Jock: Released P.O.W.
John: Released P.O.W.
Max: Wounded German waiting repatriation.
Nazario: Alan and Paul's protectors
Peter: Released P.O.W.
Petra: Wife of Sergio Ferucci.
Robin Parsons: Released P.O.W. Called Kiwi by Eric.

GLOSSARY

Babbo: Daddy

Conca: Large copper urn used for collecting and storing water.

Dopolavoro: A centre organising recreation and cultural activities for workers.

Fonte: Fountain

Gefreiter: German corporal.

Ginestra: Ginesta. (Gorse)

Guerriero: Warrior.

La Locale: Term used indicating place for entertainment, or rest; bar, club, restaurant etc.

Nummer drei: Number 3

OVRA (Ovra): Opera di Vigilanza e Represione Antifascista (Political Police of the Fascists.)

Paese: Town. (In this story it is the name of the town.)

Podesta: Administrative head of a community

Rastrellamento: Combing out.

Ribello (Pl: i): Rebel

Maremmano: A breed of working Bovine.

Nonno: Grandfather.

Nonna: Grandmother.

Ribelli: Rebels. (The common name for the Partisans.)

Sale-Tabac: Store licensed to sell salt and tobacco.

Signora: Mrs

Staffettini: Children acting as go-betweens for the partisans and their families.

Tedesco: German

Tedeschi: Germans.

PROLOGUE

Despite the intense heat of the Italian summer, it was cool inside the car which sped silently along the road, which had been a narrow track that twisted and turned as it passed stunted trees, isolated stone cottages and serried ranks of olives towards the hills that limited the horizon.

It was all so familiar, the parched valley, the blue sky and the grey mountains which marched steadily into the distance. Only the steady drone of a tractor performing the age old task of the oxen was new.

When the middle-aged couple in the car left it to follow a well remembered woodland path, it was as if the years between had never been. The remote hill village frowning over the end of the road, looked much the same as it always was. Across the valley to their right, the escarpment with its cluster of poplars silhouetted against the sky hadn't changed; yet somehow, as, hand in hand, they climbed, the slanting way seemed to be steeper than it used to be. They were glad to rest on a stone seat, worn smooth with use on the wall of a derelict house.

The gaunt ruin nestling among the trees had once been a home. Now only the outer walls remained and a tree had grown through a window. The clear area on which the house once stood had been snatched back by the forest and the encroaching growth of nature shrouded the fallen masonry as if to hide it from the face of men.

Nearby cool sweet water still trickled from an iron pipe before making its way as a small rivulet to a stream which tumbled down the mountain side to join a larger stream in the valley. Just visible, part obscured by trees, some new looking roofs amid the old, in the village half a Kilometre below, looked strangely out of place.

Refreshed after a short rest, they continued their climb towards a grass covered slope where a new house had been built.

CHAPTER ONE

The focal point of the little hill village, they would refer to as La Villa, was the square. The men would meet at the locale as the little bar was known and the women at the communal water fountain. There was no dopolavoro, the nearest being in Paese a small town, some 12 Kilometres away in the valley.

Sunday would find the little square crowded with the stalls of itinerant traders, who despite the scarcity of commodities seemed always to have plenty to sell.

Here the men from outlying homesteads would come to buy the non essential items such as cigarettes or tobacco at the Sale-Tabac and the women to fill their great copper urns with water and wash the family linen in the ancient stone trough whose time worn sides received the ice cold spring water which gushed from three iron pipes, rust pitted with age yet smooth with use, which protruded from the living rock.

As if oblivious to the weight of water bearing down on their cercine[1], they would dawdle back to their homes taking every opportunity to linger and chat with any friend they met on the way and exchange the latest piece of gossip or pass on tit-bits of news they had heard in the village. It was a pleasant relief from the monotonous and often lonely pattern of their lives, it mattered not how long it took for time had no meaning in the even tenor of their days.

Here too came Filomena as the first grey streaks appeared in the sky to herald the dawn. She preferred to fetch her daily supply of water before her father (Angelo) left the house to work in the fields. Before the women came with their washing and their gossip; less they disturb signals left there from time to time by her contacts. Few knew of her work as a courier for the Partito d'Azione or "Pi di A" as her father referred to it. Even he was not aware of her involvement.

Pausing only to curtsy in respect for the Madonna figure mounted on a wall, that had once been the wall of a church before it collapsed during an earthquake many generations ago, she made for the fountain opposite. The sight of an oak leaf nestling in a crevice as if deposited there by the wind brought a sigh of relief from the young girl. Relief that the signal for danger was not there. An ivy leaf would have been a warning to stay away, to avoid all contact with the 'Leaf men' as they were known.

---

[1] A small ring of soft material to take the weight of the Conca

There was something strangely disturbing about the man Giorgio she would have to contact, yet she suddenly felt absurdly pleased that it was an oak leaf that had been left at her station and not one of the leaves used by her other contacts.

With practised ease, she brushed the leaf away as she stooped to fill her urn and smiled whimsically as she recalled a pair of penetrating grey eyes. There was a stern quality in them. They seemed able to read her most intimate thoughts, compelling her to return their gaze when she wanted to look away, wanted to escape the mixture of fear and excitement they instilled in her.

Thoughtfully she lifted the heavy urn (or *conca* as she would call it) to her head, adjusted the cercine and humming a snatch of *'La Stell' Alpina'* made her way out of the village towards her home. Carrying the heavy copper urn on her head as countless others had done before her, she paid no heed to the increasing gradient, as with the sure footed grace of her kind she avoided the large boulders which lay about the surface of the path. Pausing only to listen to the music of the water tumbling from the iron pipe her father had placed to tap a spring, she couldn't help wondering why no one had ever asked her why she went all the way down to the communal fountain when she had such a wonderful supply near her home. Allowing herself a quiet little smile and murmuring, "If they only knew." she went on her way.

. . . .

While on her way back from her frequent visits to the fountain Donnina Battistero liked to stand arms akimbo, as was her wont while exchanging the bits of gossip which were her joy. It never occurred to her to set the burden down, as if she didn't notice the weight, or if she did, was ashamed to show it. She would linger to chat at the doorway of her house high on the outskirts of the village and throughout the longest and most intimate discussions, the conca remained aloft. Later, as if the fetching had been no task at all she would splash her water about with a carefree disregard for economy. There was plenty at the fountain which had never, in living memory run dry. If it was down a steep slope, which would have to be climbed on her return and half a kilometre from her home, what did it matter, she was used to it. Had it ever been suggested that Ernesto, her husband should undertake this heavy chore, she would have laughed her scorn and declared that men were not built so strong as women folk. To her, the idea of a man fetching water would have been absurd.

Donnina was a practical woman, not given to fanciful musings, yet the feeling had been with her all day. It was with her when she woke and stayed with her in the grey light of the dawn as she packed the basket of food which her daughter Lucia would take to her husband, Ernesto, later on in the day. The vague undefined sensation remained with her in the heat of the early October noonday sun; an unreal feeling as if something was missing, or about to happen. It was still with her in the late afternoon as she trudged up the narrow path towards her home. Not since she was a girl in her teens had she experienced such pleasurable anticipation, 'yet,' she mused, 'there is no reason for it; there has been no news of note since the armistice.' "I'm getting as bad as Nonna Ricci with her omens" she muttered. Then rebuked herself for being a fool and laughed aloud. A remarkably joyful laugh it was and infectious too. All who knew Donnina knew the sound of it.

. . . .

Nearly three years had gone by since Gianni had heard that laugh but it remained fresh in his mind. Remembering it brought an almost boyish smile to his face as he murmured to himself, "Won't be long now, I bet it's still the same." Lengthening his stride and pausing only to make the sign of the cross where a figure of the Blessed Virgin stood on a pedestal in a niche cut into the living rock, he ascended the steep winding track that led to the village. Stopping to light a cigarette he watched a group of small boys who, with all the boundless energy of the young at play, shouted lustily as they tumbled down the narrow stone clad steps which was the street between the houses.

Gianni was in no hurry now, everything looked exactly as he remembered it; nothing had changed. The same lazy smoke curling from open chimneys as the women stoked up their fires preparing to cook the evening meal. Inhaling deeply, he allowed his gaze to wander over the dilapidated cottages, each on its own terrace and leaning towards it's neighbour; as if reluctant to be alone. Concetta, lingering at the door of her home might never have moved since last he saw her. The tableau as she chatted with her friends could have been eternal. Even the dog sprawled in the shade, oblivious of the chickens which foraged around him was still there. The sight of a cat, crouched and ready to spring on the dog's tail brought a twinkle into his eyes. Nonna Ricci, sitting at the door of her cottage, her arthritic, but still deft, fingers smoothing the wool as she spun it into yarn was as much a part of La villa as was the tiny church which held pride of place on the emerald slope overlooking the village.

It was Carina, the daughter of Concetta, who saw him first. She had entered the village from the top end as was her habit when lengthening shadows told her it was time to bring her turkeys home, for it was Carina's task to tend the turkeys which lived in the tiny back yard of her home during the night.

"It's Gianni - it's Gianni." she cried.

Hearing her excited call Gianni cast his eyes in her direction. The long crook the girl employed to control her flock rested on her shoulders for she knew each bird intimately and she preferred to rely on a soft 'Tag-tag-tag.' It was a sound the turkeys knew in the voice of one they could trust. Hearing it they would cluster round her feet and jostle one another in anticipation of the grain that custom had taught them to expect.

As children, Gianni and Carina had spent many a day in the sparsely wooded gullies which split the surrounding slopes. The turkeys would scratch around there without getting into trouble and find in the stunted bushes the tiny grubs and insects they loved to eat. Now, ignoring her charges, which alarmed by her cry of greeting scattered noisily in all directions, Carina ran down the narrow way towards Gianni, who seeing the lissom figure, the gentle curve of her young breasts straining against the fabric of her dress and the deep brown eyes, eager with welcome, was, suddenly glad to be alive.

The commotion made by the bewildered turkeys galvanized the dog into action and sent the cat streaking off in search of sanctuary. The excited barking silenced the wagging tongues at Concetta's doorway and the prospect of excitement, for in this isolated locality every happening was of moment, drew people to their doors; then out on to the street whence they hastened towards a friend who had returned. Each eager to embrace him.

In a trice, Gianni was surrounded by gabbling voices, as, with everyone trying to talk at once, they escorted him to the door of his home. Scarce able to believe her son was back, Donnina snatched him from the throng, pulled him indoors and hugged him with a fierce possessive joy, as if afraid that even now he might vanish. Then between laughter and tears she scolded him.

"You naughty boy, why didn't you write? How could I know whether you were alive or dead?" The words came out in a rapid torrent as she added, "Why didn't you come home sooner? Where have you been all this time?"

Temporarily at a loss for words, she bit her lips and stood back to gaze silently at her son who could only grin sheepishly back at her. Now it seemed Donnina could scarcely do enough for him as she hastily placed a tin bowl on a chair, splashed water into it and delved around for that piece of soap she had made from pig fat and wood ash lye. Then, having thrown a couple of handfuls of pasta, some maize and a few beans into the massive iron pot suspended over the open fire, she hovered bright eyed and watchful as she tried to anticipate his every need.

Soon, the noise that floated through the windows set on either side of a crude wooden door told something of the din within as friends and relations crowding through the entrance crammed the small room with their presence and bombarded Gianni with their voices as they watched him eat.

To the frustration of Donnina, they all seemed to be more interested in giving him their news than hearing how he had changed into civilian clothes and caught a train from Brescia to Milan to escape from the army. His adventures during the riots in Milan when the people of that city rose in their anger, attacked the jackbooted overlords and took possession of their equipment were brushed aside. He tried to tell them how they had sought out the Fascists and paraded them through the streets. How he had caught a bus in to the country then walked for days, keeping to the foothills of the Apennines and the little used tracks of the forests. Of his fears that the Germans would catch him and press him into one of their labour battalions, or worse that he would just disappear, as so many had, and how pleased he was to be home at last. But their news was starved for fresh ears. He had to be told all about the various births, deaths and marriages that happened during his absence.

They insisted on telling him about the prisoner of war refugees, released from the camps that had been their home since being taken prisoner. How they had fled into the hills, swarming in their hundreds through the villages, exchanging oddments of clothing and Virginia tobacco for food and civilian attire to help them on their long trek south. How many had joined the rebels, while others had found refuge with families that kept them hidden. Meanwhile fleet-footed youngsters scampered through the forest, down the winding paths and along the goat tracks which led to the grassy slopes above the village, as they carried the news of Gianni's return to land workers, charcoal burners and shepherds alike.

Ernesto heard the news from Alberto, a ten year old boy of the village. Alberto was one of the Staffettini. A name given to the children who acted as go-betweens for the partisans, or ribelli, as they were usually called in the mountains and by the people in the villages and surrounding areas. Even before the boy spoke, Ernesto knew something had happened, he knew it by the way Alberto came running over the freshly tilled soil in the valley, eyes bright with excitement and breath so short. He must have run all the way.

It was the time Ernesto always looked forward to, the half hour he invariably gave himself before starting the long trek up the winding path to the house called Casa dei Pioppi; the home of the Zerella family who employed him. After spending the day in the wide valley beyond a brook known as La Fossa[2] which followed the depths of a gully on the edge of the fertile valley, he liked to enjoy the shade of a stand of oaks; especially on those days that had been very hot. He usually saved a small bit of the hard cheese from the basket Lucia, his daughter, brought him during the day and, watched solemnly by the magnificent pair of matching Maremmano oxen, would chew it slowly to savour the flavour.

The oxen were Ernesto's friends who worked with him. He knew their faces as he knew the palms of his hands. Because they were his friends he could talk to them; understand them as, in their way, they understood him. He would call them by name and tell them that they were both beautiful but were wrongly labelled, because Bruto had a more handsome face than his mate Bella. The beasts, hearing his voice would rub their heads against the rough home spun of his jacket or muzzle soft noses into well loved hands, no doubt hopeful of the titbits that could sometimes be found and thankful that the day's work was done; that they too could enjoy the shade of the trees and contemplate the cool drink that would be theirs when they reached the stream at the bottom of an escarpment which would have to be climbed before they could rest.

Hearing the news made Ernesto happy, but it also made him begrudge the time he was wasting in the shade of those trees. He wished he didn't have to make the long trek across the valley. The time consuming climb up the winding path to the house of his employer on top of the escarpment, where the oxen were stabled. Then, there was the grooming, the feeding and the bedding down for the night. All of

---

[2] A natural ditch or furrow usually with a stream at the bottom

which he usually enjoyed doing. Now, he wanted to get home and see his son.

CHAPTER TWO

Casa dei Pioppi, remote from the little hill village, lay at the end of a track overlooking an escarpment which rose from the cultivated slopes below. The poplars which gave the house its name effectively hid it from view so that it generally went unnoticed by the casual passerby. From its windows, the village called La Villa could be plainly seen cascading down the mountain side on the opposite side of the valley.

The home of the Zerella family for many generations had an air of prosperity, despite a dilapidated exterior. The quality of the wines produced there had given birth to a life style unknown to the less fortunate neighbours, who not only looked to Michele, the head of the family, for casual employment but also for advice and protection.

Michele now in his earlier fifties could still remember the hardships of an earlier war which had left him the legacy of a limp. Even more vivid was his memory of a recent trip to the Brenner Pass, where it was said that survivors from the Russian front had arrived and were being entrained. There had been no news from the Don for an age; only rumours, terrible stories of massacre and defeat. He had hoped to see his only remaining son Mario among the survivors. The disturbing sight of closed and shuttered railway wagons, said to contain wounded; too pitiful for the populace to see, had filled him with foreboding and a disappointment hard to bear.

Then had come the collapse of the Fascist government and the so called armistice which had been swiftly followed by an invasion of German soldiers who pillaged and robbed indiscriminately, leaving the people in fear of their presence. Reprisals were common place and there were few who had not experienced the loss of a friend. Victim of the German wrath.

During his frequent visits to La Villa, Michele would stroll through the narrow main street as he made his way to the central square exchanging a friendly nod with everyone he met; Fascist and Antifascist alike, but taking care never to say anything that might sound even remotely subversive. Spies were everywhere and with the Fascists there was the danger that even members of the family could not be trusted; though it would be true to say that this risk applied more to town folk than country. It was not unknown for sons to betray their fathers and daughters their brothers. It seemed, those who who wore the black shirt or followed the dicta of Fascism had loyalty only to their Fascist leaders and the Germans.

Invariably, while on his way through La Villa to meet Angelo, Filomena's father, who he suspected of being involved in clandestine meetings, Michele would spare time to chat with Donna Ricci - he had a great compassion for her. She had lost her son during the 14-18 war and her husband very shortly afterwards. They said it was consumption; it must have been a great blow, yet no one had ever heard her complain about her lot.

Michele and Angelo were friends of long standing; they had served together in the war to end all wars and it was Angelo who had carried Michele to safety when he sustained the wound that gave him his limp. Together they would make their way to Renzo's bar, or la Locale, as it was more generally known.

Inside la Locale the air hung heavily with the lingering odours of tobacco smoke, stale wine and perspiring bodies. Like all the buildings of La Villa it was built of stone and in appearance was the same as all the others. Originally it had been a dwelling, now it was practically a second home for the men of the locality; it was the nearest thing to a dopolavoro that the place could boast.

Behind four walls and out of sight of the prying eyes of strangers passing through the village, the simple peasant folk could feel secure. Paese and the teeming cities where a man might not know his neighbour were a long way off. Here there was no need to walk in fear, to dread the labour battalions. Surely, they thought, La Villa was too remote and too insignificant to attract the attention of the Germans and too high up the mountain to become involved in a mechanised war.

Surrounded by their friends, the men could relax and enjoy a game of cards or just discuss every day things. The state of the weather, the poor crops or the merits of their live stock; in a word, be themselves.

Ostensibly, Michele and Angelo had come for a drink and a chat, but in reality to exchange news and pass on information of interest. It was during one of these meetings that Michele's suspicions were confirmed when Angelo said,

"The Evasion group is looking for a guide and overnight sanctuary for the prisoners of war they are escorting across the line to safety."

"I know just the man," Michele replied, "I'm sure he would do it, he is a mountaineer and knows every conceivable track in Italy. As far as sanctuary is concerned, you can use my stable. The vacche won't mind and Ernesto can be trusted not to talk."

A few days later, Angelo asked Michele if he would look after two released prisoners of war for a few days and introduced him to Giorgio, a tall, stern looking man with such cold grey eyes that he felt uneasy when he looked into them.

"You realise that you must never mention this to anybody, who is not one of our agents. Even with them, it is best to be cautious." Giorgio said with one of his rare smiles. It was a smile that transformed his face and somehow invited confidence. Then, he added. "But I am sure you know that."

Michele relaxed, although willing to help whenever he could, he was reluctant to put members of his family to the extra risk involved in a stay of more than one night. However, he agreed that the two men could come to the house under cover of night; for a visit only. The proposal could then be talked over.

So it was that Robin Parsons and Eric Spink came to Casa dei Pioppi. The bedraggled appearance of the two half starved men filled Michele with pity and he quickly agreed that providing there was no objection from the other members of his household they could stay. It meant extra work for his wife, Vincensina and daughter, Giuseppina; washing and mending the vermin ridden clothes, preparing a bed in the stable and catering from a very limited supply of food, but they were used to toil and didn't mind. The sight of the two men bathed and dressed in clean, ill fitting clothing, enjoying a simple meal was reward enough.

Later that evening, during the daily ritual of prayers, the rich baritone voice of Robin blended harmoniously with the clear soprano voice of Caterina. Despite her age, Caterina's voice had retained its superb quality. Mingling with the lighter voices of Vincensina and her daughter as they sung a well remembered hymn, the sound produced brought joy to their hearts and tears to the eyes of Michele. It was a long time since such a masculine voice had been heard beneath his roof and it reminded him of his missing son.

News that the planned trip through the forward area to the Allies position had been abandoned until the whereabouts of new outposts created by reinforcements in the German forward lines were known, was brought to Michele by Filomena.

The intended few days stretched into weeks and each day brought added perils as the Germans, who usually kept to the small town in the valley, began to visit the village; congregating there and spreading ever deeper in to the countryside in a never ending quest for food to supplement their dwindling rations. Sometimes they would come as patrols with their Fascist friends, combing out deserters, as they considered the one time soldiers of the disbanded army to be, and young men, very often mere boys, to press into their labour camps. Inevitably, men like Robin and Eric, for there were many, who had been released from prisoner of war camps, hiding in friendly houses or roaming aimlessly around the countryside, fell in to the net from time to time. Notwithstanding Badoglio's command to give succour whenever possible, the penalty for harbouring the enemy was swift and severe. Invariably, those helping these men were hung; then their house would be blown up as an example.

Because of the increasing German activity the presence of Robin and Eric in the house during the day imposed a risk to Michele's family, which was unacceptable. Following a suggestion made by Robin, the two left the house each morning, keeping out of sight in one of the many small ravines which abounded in the area. The lavish coating of trees and undergrowth on their steep sides gave excellent cover and made discovery unlikely. Only after night had fallen and he was satisfied that the coast was clear would Michele descend to the area where the two were hiding and escort them back to the house.

The day that Filomena brought the news to Michele that a new evasion route had been formed, was, despite the approaching winter, hotter than usual, but she refused the proffered refreshment and rest in the shade and said,

"Babbo is not at home and I must return to attend to the stock. However I will come back this evening to say goodbye to Robin and Erico," she paused and added as if it was an afterthought, "If I don't get back, in time to see them, wish them luck for me."

"Of course," Michele replied, "Am I to take them to Angelo?"

Filomena smiled and shook her head.

"No, you have to take them to La Villa, Giorgio will meet you near the Sale-Tabac and take them to the assembly house." Then, her eyes sparkled as she added with a grin, "When the clock strikes ten-thirty or whatever - anyway, about that time."

Michele chuckled, he knew what she meant. The village clock was not only incredibly inaccurate, it also had a habit of striking times that did not always match the position of its hands. Becoming more serious, he gazed at the ground, then, back to Filomena before replying.

"I understand, I'll warn them to be ready." Then turning to Vincensina, he said, "Get a meal ready and some food for travelling, I shall bring those two up earlier than usual; they have a long march ahead."

"No! Leave them where they are," Filomena cut in, "Giorgio was specific about that. You are to take them to him. They must not return to the house. He said it was important that you follow his instructions implicitly. I will come with you, tonight, just to bid them safe journey."

Vincensina smiled briefly as she continued the task that occupied her, the news that her guests would be leaving that night brought a sense of relief, tinged with some sadness as she realised she might never see them again. She had grown to regard the two, almost, as family and wondered if she would ever know now why Erico always called Robin, Kiwi. She wished their Italian was good enough to ask.

Michele found Robin and Eric sheltering from the sun in a secluded area beneath a large rock which jutted out over a brook. It was a place that Robin had dubbed, *'Sotto il tufo[3]'*.

"You should take more care," he greeted them crossly, "I could hear your voices from a long way off, the track to La Villa is near here and if the Tedeschi hears you he will come looking," he looked at them sternly, "I wasn't sure where to find you until I heard your chatter."

Seating himself on a flat stone beside the brook Michele took a blackened terracotta pipe from his pocket, examined the stem and dropped it into the water.

"That's no good," he said getting to his feet, "just a minute I'll cut a new one."

Returning to his seat he quickly shaped a piece of cane-like stem cut from a nearby bush, blew through it to clear the residue of sap and pith, then, carefully fitted it to his pipe and sucked noisily through the new stem a couple of times, then, taking a battered tin from his pocket proceeded to fill the bowl of his pipe with a coarse home cut tobacco. "That's better," he remarked. "by tomorrow night you will be safe with your friends. All is arranged and I will take you to your guide tonight." A grin creased his features and his eyes sparkled as he spoke and Robin wondered if he had some private joke. "We meet him at ten - thirty," he continued. "Not when the church clock in the

---

[3] Under the rock.

village thinks it is, that clock's time is always different to everybody else's." then added, "You will not be returning to the house."

"What is your plan if we get separated?" Robin asked.

Using a stick Michele deftly drew a series of lines in the soft bank of the stream, looked at the map he had drawn and pointed to a spot on it. "If that happens, look for a man carrying a switch made from an oak sapling. He will be along this path leading down from the Sale-Tabac. Go to him as the clock strikes the half - hour, not a moment before and say 'it's late', he will reply 'have you seen my uncle'."

"How can we be sure it's the right man? Supposing we arrive after the clock has struck?" Eric protested.

"Seems clear enough to me," Robin rejoined, "but you have a point," then turning to Michele, "what do we do if we arrive late?"

Michele regarded the two men quietly for a moment, as if weighing them up, before replying.

"The same pattern, but you say 'it's very late', instead of 'it's late'. But anyway, we are unlikely to get separated."

Eric frowned, he had an uneasy feeling about the project and left to his own devices would have preferred to remain under the protection of Michele rather than risk re-capture in an attempt to pass through the forward lines.

"If we do get separated, how can we be sure it's the right man, that someone hasn't taken his place?" Eric grunted the words out.

"That would be our hard luck." Robin retorted. He felt irritated. Close association and too many weeks spent with Eric's prevarications had made him that way. He was tired of the delays, the eternal excuses to stay at Casa dei Pioppi and other houses that had given them refuge. He felt trapped.

Although the younger of the two men Robin was the more mature. Life on a remote farm in New Zealand had bred in him a self assurance that was evident in everything he did. His desire to meet the evasion people and attempt to cross the line conflicted with a sense of loyalty which was the essence of his being and forbade him to desert his friend.

"Surely you don't want to stay here forever," he chided.

Eric flushed. "No sense in taking stupid chances," he replied hotly. Then added lamely, "Our forces won't be much longer, they are only just across the Sangro."

"We hope," Robin retorted, "they could be months yet."

Robin could feel himself being dragged into an argument which had been waged countless times before and would lead nowhere.

"If that's your attitude - stay here and rot." he retorted angrily. Even as he spoke, the anger melted. "What do you intend to do?" he asked more kindly.

Eric stared at the ground as if by some magic a solution would manifest itself. Meanwhile, Michele looked on with a puzzled air. The tone of the voices told him they were quarrelling in some way and he was beginning to feel worried.

"We can't hang around forever," Robin continued, "you know the dangers as well as I do." Exasperated by the continued silence of Eric, he spoke angrily, "What's the matter with you? 'Struth mate! . . . You know what they would do to Michele and his folk if we were found near the house, let alone in it."

Eric shuffled his feet self consciously.

"I suppose you are right," he muttered and instantly felt better for it.

. . . .

Inwardly cursing the brambles clutching at his legs and the heavy undergrowth which found its way between his toes, Konrad Bruckner carefully picked his way towards the low murmur of voices that had attracted his attention. He had to strain his ears a little to catch the phrases of the softly speaking Italian, but had no difficulty in following the gist of the conversation. His pulse quickened as he realised that some of the words were English. 'At last,' he thought, 'these weeks of hardship will be rewarded. At last I will be proved right. There is an escape group operating in this area.'

Hoping to get a glimpse of those talking below, Konrad cautiously left the protection of the trees and approached the edge of the gully so that he could peer into its depths. To his disappointment a large outcrop of rock effectively hid the people who were talking from view.

Turning over in his mind what he heard, Konrad slowly retraced his steps as he tried to sort out the best way to use the information he had gleaned. He wished he had managed to hear where they were supposed to meet.

Before emerging on to the track, he carefully checked each way to ensure that the German soldier he had seen earlier that day was not in view. This was no time to be picked up as a refugee. No one seeing him would have realised who and what he was. Even his closest friends would have found difficulty in relating the proudly arrogant and ultra smart Gestapo officer they knew with the barefooted, unkempt figure he presented. Only a few high ranking officers and associate agents knew of his existence and he had no wish for time wasting delays at this stage. Although the house Konrad lived in and worked from was in the village it was easily reached unseen by a seldom used woodland path. Nevertheless, it was a rule that no matter how urgent the reason, he never went there during daylight. Smiling wryly to himself as he realised that while deep in thought, weighing the pros and cons of breaking the rule, he was absent-mindedly tidying his clothes, he crossed the cultivated area and headed for a narrow path through the woods that would take him to the back of the house. Suddenly, his mind made up, he muttered out loud,

"It's not worth the risk."

Thinking, 'I will have to trust Nummer drei to get the information away in good time. They are used to seeing me in the village and won't take any notice if they see me talking to her.' Konrad chuckled and changed direction as he headed for the steep narrow streets of La Villa.

CHAPTER THREE

The late November mid afternoon sun and the lack of wind gave a balmy quality to the day as Hans strolled along the sun baked path, avoiding the ruts made by centuries of bullock carts, as he tried to keep beneath the shade of the overhanging trees. 'How time flies,' he mused, 'it seems as if it was only yesterday I left home.'

The memory of his mother weeping and protesting that he was too young to go to a war that was nearly over came vividly to mind. At eighteen he felt a man and could not understand that to her, he was still the little boy she had fed and clothed with a mother's care as she watched him grow.

The journey by lorry and train from Frankfurt had faded in to a distant memory, so that it seemed as if he had always been in Italy, yet it was only two weeks since he had said his goodbyes.

Full of eagerness and the excitement of great adventures, he had joined his field station two days earlier. The sight of dilapidated and worn uniforms shocked and dismayed him. Haggard, tired faces seemed to be everywhere. There was an air of depression, sharp contrast to the high morale he had read about in the papers. The men seemed generally dispirited and kept grim silence refusing to discuss and reluctant to believe the rumour of a break through by the Allies. Rations were at an all time low and there was little left to rob in the surrounding countryside.

He felt pleased to be away from the camp for a while, away from the taunts of some who seemed to delight in reminding him that soon he would have his first taste of gunfire and he wondered how he would comport himself. Bombing in his home town was an experience which had taught him the meaning of fear and how to control it, how to hide his innermost feelings so that others would not be aware of his shame; but the forward area would be different; an unknown thing, kill or be killed. He prayed he would not fail the test, that he would serve with the courage that befitted a German soldier, that the mixture of excitement and trepidation he felt would not melt into abject fear when the time came.

The sight of a man grooming a powerful black horse turned his thoughts to the strange behaviour of the Italians, he found it difficult to understand why such a strong and fit looking man of military age should be content to stay at home instead of fighting for his country.

Hans loved horses and the sight of such a magnificent animal, so like those on his uncle's farm, reminded him of his mission to commandeer a horse owned by peasants living in a small stone house a stone's throw from the village. Jauntily whistling a snatch of *Lili Marlene* he hurried on his way.

. . . .

There was little opportunity to relax in Filomena's busy day, she took enjoyment where and when she could and the sight of turkeys scratching for bits filled her with pleasure. Living as she did with her father, Angelo, she lacked the companionship of a mother and the sharing of so many chores both inside and outside the house, so feeding the stock and caring for the few sheep that were left made a welcome change from household routine. It gave her time to dream, to remember those village fiestas of her childhood and wonder whether they would return when the war was finished. Time to relax from the dangerous missions she sometimes undertook.

"*Cavolo, Cavolo.*"

Startled, Filomena turned, her deep brown eyes widening with apprehension upon seeing the grey green uniform.

Hans smiled as he noted the slim, graceful girl and called again, "*Cavolo.*"

The word was badly pronounced and difficult to understand and the smile, for all its boyish charm, did nothing to allay her mistrust of the Tedeschi; the feared and hated traditional enemy of Italy.

Overcoming her fears, Filomena walked towards him. The years of fetching water in the great copper urn balanced on her head, as was the custom, had given her a deportment that would have been the envy of many a débutante or cat-walking model.

Although a little taller than the average Italian girl, to Hans, Filomena seemed tiny; even smaller, and certainly more delicate than his 13 year old sister. Not that there was any similarity between the blonde child in Germany and the beautiful brunette teenager, approaching twenty. He felt warm towards her and wished he could speak Italian, that his stay in the area could have been long enough to get to know her.

Suddenly realisation dawned on Filomena, this German thief was trying to say *Cavallo,* (horse,) not *Cavolo,* (cabbage) someone must have told the Tedeschi about the horse hidden in the stable. In desperation, she said,

"*Morto.*" Then, as he didn't appear to understand, she tried, "*Kaput! - kaput!*"

With a deft swoop she scooped up a turkey and offered it to him with a placating smile.

"*Nein! Nein! Cavolo.*" Hans repeated the words impatiently and pushed the girl to one side as he looked about for the horse.

Filomena, thoroughly worried now grabbed his arm in an effort to delay him.

"We are not rich, the horse is all we have," she pleaded.

The lump she could feel in her throat made speech difficult and she could feel her eyes brimming with tears of frustration as she tried to make him understand. She told him that the horse was the nearest thing to a pet she knew. Forli had always been around, as a child he had been her dearest friend; the one she could confide in; the one who shared her secret thoughts.

Hans, unable to understand what was being said, looked at the tearful face and felt embarrassed. He guessed she was pleading with him and was uncertain how to proceed without making an enemy of her. He didn't want her to think ill of him but his orders were to commandeer the horse. With a brusqueness born of emotion, he pushed Filomena roughly aside, so that she nearly fell and made for the stable which was built on to the house.

It was dark in the stable, the air heavy with the acid-sweet odour of rotting hay, reminiscent of those boyhood holidays when his Uncle Wolfgang had allowed him to groom and walk his horses.

Hans looked in dismay at the animal. Possibly powerful in its day, the elderly work horse had long since passed its prime. The sluggish movement as he led it from the stable and the lack-lustre eyes told their own story. Long days hidden from sight, may have contributed to the poor condition, but Anno Dominni had also left its mark. The only sign of life was a whinny of pleasure at the sight of Filomena.

Clutching the German's arm, Filomena desperately tried to separate Hans from the horse.

"No! - No! - No! He is old," she protested tearfully.

Disappointed with his prize and irritated by her insistence, he broke free and pushed her away so hard that she fell to the ground. Horrified by his action and not fully understanding his emotion or the reason for it, Hans released the horse, which stood meekly by, so that he could use both hands to help the girl to her feet. He wanted to apologise and didn't know how, so held her close as he looked into the tear stained face and tried to ask whether she had hurt herself in the fall.

Somehow the feel of the young Germans arms about her was soothing, it was as if he was not the enemy, as if he didn't wear the hated Tedesco uniform. She felt secure and strangely serene as she allowed him to hold her for a brief while before easing herself gently out of his arms.

Startled by the turbulent feelings that had beset him, Hans could only look dumbly at the girl as she quietly led the horse back into the stable. He would have liked to tell her the horse was safe, that he would come back to see her as a friend, but was tongue-tied and knew no Italian words to help. Unable even to smile, he made a stiff, self conscious bow, turned abruptly on his heel, waved awkwardly, and hurried away.

Without a further glance, Hans retraced his steps down the track he had climbed such a short while before. Then, he had been happy and full of confidence in his ability to carry out the simple task he had been set. Now, as the realisation that he had disobeyed an order from his commanding officer came to him, his pace slowed. Hesitating, he turned and started to walk back up the track, only to turn again as he tried to think of a plausible excuse for returning without the horse, but thoughts of the Italian girl kept interfering with his reasoning.

Walking very slowly now, he dolefully ruminated on the consequences of his action. A reprimand seemed the least he could expect, worse, they might shoot him for disobedience in the field. The thought brought him to a halt and he could feel himself trembling. Yet, somehow to return for the horse was unthinkable, furthermore, his inability to speak the language would thwart any attempt to persuade the girl to flee with her horse so that he could say the house and stable were empty.

Eyes cast down, furiously trying to sort out the confused mixture of ideas which filled his mind, Hans continued on his way. Suddenly he remembered the horse he had seen when climbing the track earlier. In his mind, he saw again the proud carriage of its head, the elegance of a well turned stifle. 'Here is a horse even Uncle Wolfgang would be proud to own,' he thought.

With the possible solution of his problem came a sense of alert efficiency. Happy now and with pulse racing, he quickened his step, his mind filled with the task ahead and the congratulations that would surely be his when his commanding officer saw such a fine animal.

Moving forward as quietly as he could Hans rounded a bend in the track immediately above the place where he remembered seeing the horse. To his dismay it was deserted. At first he wondered whether he had made a mistake, whether it was further down the track he had seen the man grooming the animal, but was sure he recognised the tree where it had been tethered. 'Why didn't I take it when I had the opportunity' he thought ruefully and leaving the track descended the grass slope to examine the area more closely. Horsehair clinging to the bushes and scattered on the crushed grass beneath the tree left him without further doubt as to the accuracy of his memory. Disconsolately he gazed about him, vainly hoping to see his prey. All the anxieties he had experienced earlier returned and a feeling akin to panic assailed him, he stared at the empty place, as if by so doing the man and his horse would miraculously re-appear.

. . . .

Capitano Mario Zerella tethered the horse he affectionately called Nove, being the last digit of his army number, to a tree and taking the ancient hat he wore from his head, fondly smoothed the feather which proclaimed him one of the Giulia[4] and descended the steep wooded slope to a place he remembered well, where water trickled from a pipe protruding from a crevice in the rock. Filling his hat he returned to the horse and grinned at the impatience to slake its thirst.

"Won't be long now Nove," he said affectionately and gave the animal a pat, "tonight you sleep in a stable, but first we must make sure there are no Tedeschi up there."

The horse looked at him and pushed its great head into his shoulder.

"Enough of that," Mario laughed, "come let's smarten you up, it will help pass the time and keep you from getting bored."

As he worked, the sleek black coat took on an added sheen which showed up the many scars marring its natural perfection. Scars which

---

[4] Elite Alpine regiment.

were a constant reminder of the blood and ice in the snows of the Ukraine as step by step, night and day, man and beast made their weary way west. A small element in a wave of misery. Regiments - Battalions - Companies – Platoons, fighting the sub zero temperatures. Frozen dead on a red carpet of snow lay in their wake.

There was hunger, great, great hunger, the all pervading stench of gangrene and the enemy; always the enemy following with their tanks and their guns and their hate. Ruthless in their determination that none should escape.

Somehow the man and his horse had stayed together sharing such shelter as could be found, the body heat of the animal keeping its master warm during those brief, so brief, rests in the snow. Only Mario's training and experience ensuring that both survived that terrible retreat.

There were pitifully few left after the massacre when the platoon he was with was trapped in a deserted village where they had gone seeking refuge and possibly food in the empty houses. A doctor, a mule handler, who wept over the death of his mule and himself. When the firing started he had given the horse a slap so that it ran out of the village.

Gratefully the three accepted shelter and food from a woman whose men folk were away with the soldiers, as she explained in halting Italian. They subsequently learned that all except she had fled the village when the warring armies passed over it. She had stayed so that her men folk could find her when they returned, and survived by foraging for food in the empty houses, which the rapidly passing army had not had time to loot.

When Nove returned to the village, lame and near exhaustion, some three days after the massacre, Mario announced that he would leave as soon as the horse was fit.

The combined efforts of the doctor and the mule handler restored the animal back to health; meanwhile Mario went daily into the snow to dig for grass and the mosses to be found beneath its surface.

The long, long trek back to Italy was a blurred memory of unnamed villages, kindly people and remote houses.

When, at last, they reached the small township in the heart of the Dolomites where Umberto - the mule handler, had his home, Mario readily accepted the family's offer to stay a while and rest. Together they watched the doctor descend the winding mountain road toward Cavalese and the valley below.

Footsteps on the track above disturbed Mario's reverie and he anxiously watched Hans make his way toward the thick scrub that hid him from view.

"See those poplars across the valley, that's where you'll sleep tonight," Mario told the horse, who regarded him solemnly as he continued with, "come we had better stay out of sight until dark, but tonight my friend a stable, clean straw and a feast of oats and hay." Then adding thoughtfully, "I hope nobody is staying there." he quietly led the horse to a point on the wooded slope where the trees grew more thickly. Satisfied they were unlikely to be seen, he tethered the horse and settled himself down to rest while he waited for the coming night.

With his back cushioned by his saddle which he had propped up against a tree, Mario watched the horse graze. It was a pleasing sight and he felt relaxed as his mind idly drifted along in a mixture of past memories and the coming re-union with his family and friends.

He could feel his eyelids getting heavy and idly wondered whether Lucia still lived in the village, whether she was still unmarried. Whether Ernesto her father was as great a rogue as ever, and he smiled whimsically as he recalled evenings spent at the Battistero home with Ernesto playing his fisarmonica [5] so loudly that he completely drowned the voices of his wife, Donnina and his two daughters, Lucia and Dora.

Those days before the war had disrupted their lives seemed so long ago. "Such a long time ago" he muttered to himself and shook his head half heartedly to fight off the growing torpor which assailed him, "Such a long l-o-o-n-g . . . ."

Suddenly he was awake, instantly alert his heart pounding as if he had been rudely shaken and he wondered what had disturbed him. Nove had stopped grazing and was standing with head up and ears pointed forward in that interested way horses have when something attracts their attention.

With an instinctive movement toward his service pistol Mario rose to his feet. The shadows had lengthened considerably during his sleep and he felt angry for having slept so long. Then he saw the German

---

[5] Accordion

soldier he had seen earlier examining the place where he had groomed the horse. From the security of the screen of trees Mario watched, hoping that curiosity only had caused the German to leave the track. There was no way Mario could leave the thicket without being seen and he had no intention of giving up his horse without a fight.

With accustomed care he slid back the safety catch of his gun. Something in the thicket behind Mario stirred, possibly a bird or other small creature. It was sufficient to catch the attention of Hans and Mario cursed beneath his breath as he saw him look towards the thicket.

Hans gazed at the clump of trees, he was sure he had seen a movement and the possibility of the horse being there filled him with excitement. Drawing his Luger from its holster, he approached the thicket. Now that time for action had come he felt nervous and tense. The gun felt heavy in his hand. Then, he saw Mario.

"*Hande hoch!*" His voice sounded shrill in his ears and the blood seemed to have drained from his face.

The sound of a single shot split the silence with its horrid noise. For a brief instant all was still as if even the insects had stopped moving. Somewhere a dog barked, distant and ethereal. Then came a great whirring of wings as birds rose in alarm from nearby trees.

In the still air, the sharp sound of the shot carried across the valley.

"What was that?" Eric spoke nervously

"Sounded like gunfire," Robin replied, "probably some farmer having a go at bunnies for dinner. Anyway, it's nothing to worry about. Too far away to be a threat."

Feeling neither pity, nor regret, only anger and the frustration of a soldier sick of killing and weary of seeing young lives wasted Mario approached the inert form of Hans.

. . . .

Leading Nove by the reins and fighting his desire to break into a run, Mario made his way along the poplar lined track. Despite his determination not to hurry, his pace steadily increased and it was only by exerting great control over his emotions that he was able to slow down. As if sensing his excitement, the horse whinnied, it sounded unnaturally loud in the still, night air.

"*Zitto*[6]." Mario spoke softly. In immediate obedience to the command the horse came to a halt.

Motionless, black shapes in the shadows thrown by the trees, man and horse waited, ears straining to catch the slightest sound. When satisfied no one was about, Mario moved forward, slowly now, towards the lighter area ahead where the track came to an end at the clearing where Casa dei Pioppi stood, stark and gaunt against the moonlit sky. Somehow, the house seemed larger than Mario remembered it. Otherwise nothing had changed. The old bullock cart with its broken shaft still stood in the lean-to against the barn. Even the haystacks alongside seemed the same.

The old cart brought back memories that brought a smile to his face. He remembered riding in it as a boy, lost in a world of dreams and oblivious to the jolting caused by the rutted track. The long leather thong slack in his hands and the rawhide whip, forgotten across his knees.

He remembered too how Domenico, his grandfather, sitting beside him, would say, '*this old cart is no good my boy, I will build a new one.*' or, '*the old cart is so old nobody knows who built it.*' It was Domenico's great ambition to build a new cart, but somehow, there never was time. Then, one day, shortly before the outbreak of war, Michele said, '*The harvest is in, we have winter before us. I'll give you a hand in building that cart.*'

Somehow, Domenico had aged by that time, nevertheless, it was Domenico who selected and felled the trees single handed and it was Domenico who lopped the branches from those sturdy oaks.

What a task followed; Mario grinned as he recalled it. Such a cutting and banging and planning and fitting, it seemed endless, but at last the cart was finished and Michele decorated it with coloured wheels and flowers. There had to be a new yoke for the oxen too, Domenico had insisted on that. This was his cart and it had to be right.

A fleeting shadow of sadness crossed Mario's features as he recalled that his grandfather never used the cart; he died before the winter snows subsided.

Were it not for the faint traces of light showing dimly through cracks in the heavily shuttered windows the place would have seemed deserted.

---

[6] Don't speak.

Abruptly, his reverie was broken. The silence of the night was disrupted by loud barking, interspersed by menacing growls as a yellow shape hurtled from the lean-to towards him. Mario chuckled,

"Leone! You old fool."

The dog stopped in its tracks at the sound of a much loved voice, sniffed the air, then, with a yelp of pure joy leapt at him, contorting itself and emitting shrill cries of welcome. Mario stooped to greet the wildly excited dog.

Then the door of the house opened, framed against the dimly lit interior was the unmistakable outline of Michele.

"Who's there?" The well remembered voice came clear to Mario's ears. A huge lump in his throat made speech so difficult he could only sob the words out.

"It's me - Mario - your son."

Suddenly Mario was surrounded as people erupted from the house and thronged about him, it was as if every member of his family had turned out to welcome him home.

Mario's sister, Giuseppina was there, with Vincensina, both laughing and crying at the same time as they vainly tried to reach him.

Vincensina trembled as she anxiously scanned her son's face and tried to kiss away the lines of suffering that only she had seen. Lines which had not been there before and made him look so much older than his years. Desperately she held Mario close, so close he could scarcely breathe; the words she wanted to say trapped in her heart and unable to reach her lips.

Ernesto was there too, in the stable settling the oxen down for the night; looking quietly on, the half smile Mario remembered so well hovering on his lips.

Even Vincensina's mother, Caterina had come out. Walking with the aid of a stick and led by Filomena she was brought to his side as the others gave way to let her by. She put out a frail hand to touch him and Mario realised that his grandmother was now nearly blind,

"I thought I would never see you again," she blurted out. "When will this awful war finish?" Then burst into tears.

Filomena smiled shyly at Mario, then taking Caterina by the hand said kindly,

"Come, the night is cool, you can talk later in the warmth of the house."

Telling the beads she constantly wore, their familiar shape comforting her, Caterina began to pray "*Ave Maria - Gratia Plena. . . .*" as she allowed Filomena to help her back to the house.

Mario watched them go, unable at first to place the girl, then something in the way she turned her head struck a chord of memory and he realised that the child he had known at Angelo's house had developed into a graceful young woman and he wondered what she was doing there.

Everyone seemed to be talking at once as each tried to embrace him and ask the questions that were on all their lips.

Michele looked at his son, noting the faded and worn clothing, part uniform and part civilian, which did nothing to detract from the authority of his bearing. In his mind, he was fighting the desire to tell his son of the occasional overnight visitors. His fatherly instinct and love wanting to trust him, his duty towards his friends in the group, and past experiences, warning him to take care. Suddenly, his mind made up, he said,

"Come, we will stable your horse," then, taking Nove by the bridle, he added, "Come Lad, you will want to help and there are things I must say to you which can only be said in private."

Mario relaxed, he had sensed the tension and a boyish grin, which looked strangely out of place, creased his features.

"Of course, the sooner the better, in any case it is dangerous to stay out here too long."

Watched by the pair of oxen which were housed in the stable, Ernesto forked hay into the manger and fresh straw into a corner where the horse could lie down while Michele motioned Mario toward one of two rush bottom chairs and said,

"Be seated, make yourself comfortable."

Mario grinned and replied,

"I'm not so tired that I can't wait till we go in," then shrugged nonchalantly and sat down.

The feel of the chair beneath him took him back in time to the days, when, as a small boy, he had watched Papa milk the cow whilst sitting on one of those two old chairs they kept in the stable. It was an odd sensation, as if he had never been away, as if all that had happened had been dreamt.

Michele looked at his son for several moments in silence, perhaps sharing some of that same feeling, then, choosing his words carefully, he said,

"You must promise not to tell anyone..."

"Of what?" Mario cut in.

"Of that which I am about to tell you." replied Michele.

"Is it a secret?... Political maybe?" Mario, suddenly alert, looked his father straight in the eye and in a sharp tone of voice said, "Are you harbouring prisoners of war?"

For a moment Michele was nonplussed, he could only nod dumbly.

"Normally only overnight. Promise you will never breath a word outside this house."

"Of course not, I'll swear on it if you like." Mario replied quickly.

Michele embraced him. "You are my son, your promise is enough," he said, then paused and added, "there were two of them, but they have left the house. I have to meet them tonight and take them to their guide at the appointed time. All is arranged and I won't be gone long."

"A dangerous task, so be careful," Mario replied, frowning, "I'd be happier if you left that sort of thing alone."

Michele grinned happily and rose from his chair saying,

"I must leave very soon, it is almost time." Then, noting the worried expression on Mario's face. "Don't look so worried; we are few in number and very careful, which makes the work safer."

"The fewer that know, the better," replied Mario "so remember that."

Michele looked fondly at his son, pleased that he should be so concerned for him and placing an arm round his shoulders, he turned towards Ernesto and said,

"Time you went home Ernesto, it's getting late. Donnina will be wondering what's happened to you."

Ernesto nodded in reply, and opening the door of the stable for Michele and his son to pass through, said,

"I'll just give the horse a rub down, then go...."

"No need for you to do that Ernesto," cut in Mario, "I'll attend to Nove."

"Don't be silly, it's a pleasure," Ernesto retorted as he embraced him. Then giving Mario a push in the back, added, with that quiet smile of his, "Do as you're told boy."

It was pleasantly warm in the house. A great pot hung from a hook above the fierce flames which cast shadows on the plain, undecorated walls of the living room and absorbed the dim light emitted by two small lamps; one placed on a heavy wooden chest in the corner of the room and the other in a niche in the wall, illuminating a stone figure of the Madonna which held pride of place there. The shadows were so heavy that it was difficult to see the faces of those who were not near the fire.

Caterina sat in her usual place beside the fire, just listening to what was going on as Vincensina busied herself stirring something in the pot which gave off an appetizing aroma; which mingled with that of the ginestra blazing on the fire.

Michele glanced at his watch, looked at Filomena and said, for the benefit of Mario,

"How time flies, it's getting late. Come I'll see you home." Then, turning to Vincensina, "I need to go to the Sale-Tobac and Filomena's house is not far out of the way."

"I'll come with you." Offered Mario.

"No you're tired, and anyway it wouldn't be fair to the others. They will want to hear your story . . . I won't be long. I promise."

CHAPTER FOUR

In the dim light of early morning, Angelo and Filomena could just make out the figures of Giorgio and Gino, wearing a white sweater, walking down the lower slopes towards the distant range of mountains which lay beyond Paese. Barely visible in their darker clothing were the blurred outlines of Robin and Eric following some fifty metres or so behind. Surreptitiously wiping a tear from her eyes, Filomena said,

"I do hope they are going to be alright," she gave a wan little smile, and added, "I hope Giorgio will be safe."

"Of course he will, it's not the first time he has made the crossing, and I don't suppose it will be the last." Angelo replied, giving her a fatherly hug. "That's strange, I thought there were to be four in this group."

"There should have been, but one of the other two got kicked in the back by a *vacca*[7] the other day and was too badly injured to attempt the long march he would have to tackle today. His friend didn't like to desert him."

"I can understand that," Angelo replied, "A pity, it won't be long now before the snow comes and an injury like that takes a while to heal. They will probably have to wait until the Spring for the next trip."

Suddenly, Angelo felt really proud of his daughter, he looked at her fondly and said,

"I didn't know you worked with the Leaf men and knew Giorgio, though I did wonder when I saw you at Michele's yesterday. How long has this been going on?"

"Nor I you," she replied, laughing now and ignoring the question.

They watched until the figures could no longer be made out. Then, turned and hand in hand made their way back to the house. It was a long time, not since she was quite a small girl, since her father had held her hand like that. It was a nice feeling that made her feel protected.

. . . .

Pausing every now and then to think, Mario made his way along the well remembered path to La Villa. The sound of Michele's voice

---

[7] Vacca (Vacche- plural) Bovine that has had calves.

warning *'Don't trust anybody until you really know them. Some still have strong feelings for il Duce'*, echoed in his ears. Haunting him with its insistence, as he battled with the desire to tell everyone he had finished with the army and didn't care what happened to Mussolini. The desire, he knew was stupid, and he rebuked himself for being childish. Over-riding this, was a yearning that filled his heart as he tried to calculate how long it was since he vowed he would return and the girl in his arms had said she would wait.

"Was it three years or four?" he asked himself.

The memory, undimmed by the passage of time, of a tearful face, remained clear in Mario's mind and he longed to see it come alive with laughter once again. The love that had sustained him during all the hardships of the long trek from the Ukraine could not be denied and he broke into a run, shouting "I'm coming Lucia, I'm coming." then slowed to a walk and rebuked himself again, this time for being an adolescent fool.

The narrow village street seemed longer than he recalled, as watched by the curious eyes of children from the balconies and doorways of their homes, he trod the familiar cobbles that paved its uneven surface. Even the smells of cooking which pervaded the evening air seemed to be different from those he remembered. Disappointed, Mario looked about him, hoping to see a face he recognised. Nonna Ricci was there, had there ever been a time when she wasn't? Otherwise, there were only children to be seen. Then, realisation suddenly hit him. Of course, it would be the vendemmia, everybody, except some of the women who would be busy preparing the evening meal would be away harvesting the grapes. He hoped Lucia would be home. He wanted to see a face that he knew and was tempted to knock on one of the doors and enter, as was the custom of the place, but didn't want to risk the delay of being invited to sit at a table and share the meal being prepared for the folk still working in the fields.

The heavy iron knocker, decorated with the head of a wolf, reminded him of the day he had taken Lucia to Gubbio, how they had visited the tiny church on the spot where St Francis had placated the wolf. He had bought that knocker as a souvenir for Ernesto, who had laughed over the gift, saying, *'What do I want with a useless thing like that? Everyone will know where I live, if asked they'll be saying he lives in the house with a wolf for a knocker.'* Nevertheless, he lost no time in fitting it and spent the rest of the day standing across the street with a contented smile on his face admiring the new appearance of his door.

Chuckling over the reminiscence, Mario lifted the knocker and reached for the latch, then changed his mind and hoping it would be Lucia who opened the door, waited. Although only moments passed, it seemed an age before he heard a voice call out "Who is it?" Grinning now in anticipation, he replied "You will know me Donnina, when you see me."

"It's Mario - It's Mario, Oh Mama, oh Mama I know it is." There was no mistaking Lucia's voice, nor the excitement in its tone.

Hoping her voice wouldn't betray the news Ernesto had given her the previous night, Donnina said in a tone that tried to simulate scorn,

"Don't be foolish girl . . ."

Before Donnina could finish what she was saying, Lucia had opened the door and was there, transfixed on the threshold, a smudge of flour on her cheek and tears of joy in her eyes. For a brief while, neither spoke as, lost in the ecstasy of the moment, they gazed unbelievingly at each other. Then they both tried to speak at once and her words,

"They thought you were dead but I always knew you would come."

Were drowned by his,

"How I have longed for this moment."

Shaken out of her usual calm, Donnina stopped what she was doing and hurried after her daughter, wiping her hands on her apron as she went.

"Why didn't you write?" she demanded accusingly, her voice harsh with the emotion of the moment, "We thought you were dead," then in a softer tone, "Come in Mario."

Donnina wanted to embrace Mario but the two were clinging to each other so tightly that she realised they had no eyes or ears for anyone but each other. Philosophically she returned to her task.

Vaguely aware that Lucia's cheeks were wet, Mario kissed away the tears and held her close to him, so close, she could hardly breathe. He had almost forgotten how soft and warm she was, how silken her hair could feel when it brushed against his arms. As from a distance he could hear Donnina's laugh, followed by her voice calling,

"Plenty of time for that . . . come eat, the polenta is spread and will spoil." but he couldn't bring himself to pull away.

"Do you still love me?" Lucia whispered, leaning her head back to see him better.

Mario could feel her trembling and wanted to say "More than ever," but the words wouldn't come, he could only nod.

Lucia would have liked to hear him say yes of course I do, but the nod was answer enough. Taking both his hands in hers, she laid them against her cheeks, then, without letting go, led him into the house.

"Ernesto won't be long." Donnina said, embracing Mario and handing him a glass of wine, "He'll be glad you've come to see us."

"I saw him yesterday, I expect he told you. Does he still play the fisarmonica? . . ."

"Oh Mama, why didn't you tell me?" cut in Lucia.

"He asked me not to, he thought it would spoil the surprise." Donnina replied, with a smile, then, shook her head, and said in reply to Mario's question,

"He has changed, he doesn't play it very often now. It's the war, you know how it is, nobody has any heart for celebrations," Then she brightened, "He did play when Gianni arrived home. Perhaps he will play again tonight. Tonight is special." Then, indicating the table. "Eat now before it spoils."

Picking up a fork, Mario grinned across the table at Lucia and started to cut a path through the polenta spread on its scrubbed surface. It was a game that children play; seeing who could eat their way to the opposite side first. Lucia smiled happily and picking up her fork, followed suite, directing her path towards Mario so that it would join his.

Engrossed in what they were doing, neither of them noticed the entrance of Dora, Lucia's eleven year old sister, until they heard her giggle and say "they are making a road of love."

It was already dusk when Ernesto returned, he had a worried frown on his face and looked agitated. Without a word, he hurried through the room, ignoring everyone in it, and made for the rear entrance of the house. Sensing something was wrong, Donnina followed him,

"Are you alright?" she asked.

"I don't know. . . .The Sicilian came asking Michele for refuge and shelter for the night. Michele wasn't very happy about it and said he doesn't think he is genuine. Neither do I for that matter."

"What do you mean - not genuine?"

"I don't know, he doesn't look right. Something about him, I can't put a finger on it. Michele is suspicious as well - he was quite brusque, told him there was no room."

"Did he go away? Why are you so worried?"

"I thought he might have followed me."

Trying not to show her concern, Donnina smiled and said,

"You worry too much; the Sicilian has been around for some time now. Why should he follow you? You're jumping at shadows." Then laughed with an assurance she didn't feel and added, "Did Michele say anything?"

"Well yes, he reckons his Italian is too good. He doesn't sound like the Italian soldier returning home to Sicily that he claims to be. You know what I mean, no odd words of dialect, everything grammatically correct. More like someone who has learned our language in a school. Furthermore he thinks there is just a suspicion of blonde roots in his hair."

"Perhaps he is English."

Ernesto shrugged his shoulders and said,

"Maybe."

Taking his arm, Donnina said,

"Come and sit down before that lot in there has eaten everything."

"Hallo Mario! Welcome to my table, how nice it is to see you here." Ernesto greeted Mario. Then, seating himself, looked around and said, "Where's Gianni?"

"Gone to see his true love - his true love - his true love."

There was a mischievous twinkle in Dora's eyes as she danced round the table singing the words.

Everyone laughed, including Ernesto.

"Who's that?" he asked. "Carina?"

While Ernesto ate, Donnina hovered nearby ready to serve the extra ladle of minestra that she had prepared to go with the polenta. She regarded him thoughtfully, as wedging a monster size loaf of her own baking against an ample bosom; she took hand to blade and handle to draw the fearsome knife through the sweet wholemeal bread. To her eyes Ernesto looked tired, but then, he always looked tired these days. 'It's the war. When will it end?' she mused.

It was Lucia who broke the silence that had fallen while they ate.

"Will you be going out Papa?" she asked as her father drew his chair from the table to be nearer the fire.

Her voice sounded flat, toneless, there was no trace of interrogation in it, as if it had been said for the sake of something to say.

Ernesto deftly rolled a cigarette, the coarse crudely cut tobacco spilling from the ends as he did so. Then, leaning forward, took a small brand of ginestra to light it.

"No I think I will stay in tonight, maybe I'll play my fisarmonica. Apart from when Gianni came home, it seems a long time since I played it. Now with Mario safely home, we really do have something to celebrate." Then giving Lucia a knowing look, added, "don't you think so?"

So saying, he rose from his chair and took the instrument off a hook on the wall, brushed the dust from it with the sleeve of his shirt and lovingly fondled the stops.

"Get out a bottle of wine Donnina. Not our every day stuff. One of the bottles Michele gave us. Tonight is special." The smile, as Ernesto spoke, cancelled out the tired lines and made him look younger.

The small room was soon filled with sound, as Ernesto fingered the stops of his instrument. The table was pushed to one side and despite the lack of space Mario and Lucia started to dance. They were quickly joined by Donnina, half doubled to accommodate Dora, who happily made up her own steps as, joining the fun, she giggled in enjoyment.

The dancing didn't even stop when the door opened and Gianni walked in.

"What's going on?" he exclaimed

Then, seeing Mario, dancing with Lucia squeezed himself between them to administer an enthusiastic embrace.

"Bravo! I heard you were home," he said, with a grin spread over his face, "you didn't lose much time coming to see my sister."

Before long, the door opened again as first one neighbour, having heard the music popped in, then another and another until being no more room in the house, they spilled out into the street. Mario started to laugh, almost hilariously.

"What's making you laugh like that?" asked Lucia suppressing a surge of laughter herself.

"When I came through the village, there was nobody about. Look at them now." Mario replied. "Where did they all come from?"

Although very pleased to see so many friends of his come in to share their festivity, Ernesto had no intention of watching them guzzle down the fine wine he had put out for the occasion. With a sly wink at Donnina and a movement, almost of sleight of hand, he removed the bottle and put a barrel of his own brew in its place.

"That will keep them happy," he said and poured a glass for himself.

. . . .

Keeping a safe distance behind, Konrad watched, with some dismay, Giorgio and Gino, followed by Robin and Eric, enter a gorge. He had expected them to follow the low path towards the river Sangro and thought, that if they were using a new route, his message would be wasted. Quickening his steps he hurried forward, but could see no sign of the party when he arrived at the point where he had last seen them. They seemed to have disappeared without trace.

The presence of rebels in the area was well known and he wondered whether there was a connection between them and the route organisers. Whether it would be worth the risk involved in entering the gorge in an attempt to contact one of the groups and pretend to be a soldier trying to get to his home in Sicily. However, after further careful thought, he decided that they would be unlikely to know anything more than who to contact and were unlikely to divulge even that to someone they didn't know. Furthermore, there was the risk they would want him to join them. The opportunity to infiltrate one of the groups had been offered before, but it was a temptation he had always resisted. Though irritating, they posed no real threat to the German Command and the task of exposing the people operating the evasion route was more important.

Disappointed, he turned and made his way back. By the time he reached the valley below La Villa it was late in the afternoon and the voices of workers returning from work merged with the sonorous creak of bullock carts rumbling over the well worn tracks as they entered the narrow cobbled street of the village. Settling himself on a log in the fringe of woodland above La Villa, Konrad, tired and dispirited waited for darkness to fall. He was angry with himself for having indulged in a long and fruitless adventure that had wasted a day and a half and led nowhere.

Gradually the noises subsided until only the occasional clack of a wooden sandal or distant shout of *Buona sera* could be heard. When Konrad eventually moved the sky had clouded over and a light wind stirred the trees bringing a chill to the air, as if to remind him that the long summer was nearly over. He shivered and stretched his cramped limbs which had grown stiff with inaction.

"Is that you Konrad?"

Ida's barely audible voice coming out of the darkness sounded strained; there was a worried note in it. Suddenly alert, his fatigue forgotten, the German reacted swiftly. Every fibre of his body now vibrant with energy, he quickened his pace. Ida was standing in the doorway. Konrad looked at her keenly.

"Is there a problem Hannah?" he demanded, the huskiness of his voice betraying his lack of sleep.

"Don't use that name. It's not safe," Ida said angrily as she opened the door and stood to one side to let Konrad pass. "People here don't know my uncle married a German girl and I have a German second name."

"Which you should be proud of," retorted Konrad.

"They know me as Ida di Lorenzo. It's better that way. I don't like that German name and have never used it and never will." She continued, her voice over-riding his.

"What's worrying you?"

"You can hear the music and the goings on in the street. Any moment someone could burst in and invite me out to join in the fun. You know how it is. The people think I live alone with Roberto. They don't know you live here; they believe you are a Sicilian soldier named Marco trying to get home."

"Then I'll go straight to my room, get me something to eat. Don't come in. Leave it outside my door I want to pray . . . keep Roberto away. I want a quiet half hour so make sure that kid of yours doesn't come sneaking around." Konrad's words were abrupt to the point of rudeness.

Ida was beginning to feel impatient and it showed in her voice when she said,

"Where were you last night? I waited up to let you in."

37

Ignoring the question, Konrad entered the room and locked the door behind him.

By the time Ida had prepared the meal, Konrad had finished his work with the radio and packed it away.

"You can bring it in now," he called out, "I have finished with my prayers." He had a contented look about him.

"Feeling better?" Ida asked, then, noting his happier appearance she placed the tray of food on a stool by the bed and added, "Prayers are wonderful, good for the soul and they always bring peace."

"*Ja!* Much better."

Alone in his room, his immediate duties finished, Konrad felt unbelievably tired. All the energy that had come to his aid when danger seemed to threaten had gone from him.

"I will feel better when I've had a wash," Konrad muttered to himself, then cursed as he remembered that the only water available was in the main room of the house. 'Perhaps when the risk of visitors has gone.' he mused as, feet still on the floor, he relaxed back on the bed.

Konrad was still in the same position when Ida came to collect the used dishes. Receiving no answer to her knock, she tried the handle. Surprised to find the door unlocked, she opened it and crept into the room. Smiling, she gently lifted the sleeping man's feet on to the bed and threw a blanket over him. For a brief moment she stood looking at him, wondering why he was so insistent that no one, especially Roberto, other than her, should enter that room. Why she wasn't allowed to make the bed unless he was there.

"This room needs a good clean," Ida muttered as she picked up the tray; the bowl of minestra was untouched. Then whispering, "Sleep tight Konrad." she left the room as silently as she had come.

CHAPTER FIVE

October merged into November and now those great jagged crests towering over La Villa were hidden more often than not by a fine white mist which rose from the valley at night and seeped through the forest causing every tree to drip with moisture. Then, clung obstinately to the summit until the sun and winds united efforts sent it away.

Falling leaves now carpeted the woodland paths with their variegated hues. Paths which, ever since the day of the armistice, young men of the village walked to come home and refugees used seeking sanctuary. They came in dribs and drabs by various routes. From the north, where it was said the German masters dictated their will through Mussolini. From the south where the now hated Tedeschi had consolidated themselves along that line they called the Winterstellung. From, the east and from the west where every major town had it's Nazi cell, where the secret police, the dreaded OVRA of the old regime were busy re-establishing themselves in a network which included even small towns and villages in its grasp.

With few exceptions, veterans, who had altered almost out of recognition and boys who seemed scarcely to have been away settled back to the life they had known before their routine was interrupted. Content to be free. Free from the discipline of service life and the horrors of combat. Content just to be at home.

Here, there was no hurly burly waking of the day, just a gradual transition of darkness into light. A sleepy awareness that the night had gone, that the first grey emissaries of dawn had come. Nobody minded if the dawn brought another day, it was the pattern of living; life was like that. Only the crowing cocks could be expected to voice a protest. To the people of the area it was the rhythm of being.

Not so Mario and Gianni; they had formed a routine of going to Renzo's bar to enjoy an hour together over a glass of wine and listen to the general conversation. Having a common interest they would discuss their plans for the future and extol the virtues of their beloved girl friends. To hear them talk, you could have been forgiven if you thought nobody quite like those two girls had ever existed.

They were surprised there was so much talk of the war, for they had had enough of it. Enough of the lying - the deceit - the perversion of justice. They were weary of the endless restrictions, regulations and requisitions. They were disappointed too that the armistice had not brought the peace they desired so desperately.

Sometimes, even though battle weary, they would, in despair, talk of joining the rebels. Such was their feeling of guilt, for doing nothing; but this was tempered by a reluctance to leave their loved ones.

Finally their minds were made up when, one afternoon towards the end of November, Mario, while grooming Nove, heard a noise that sounded like an explosion. He had heard too many, not to be mistaken. He dashed out of the stable and looked down the valley. A mushroom of smoke was rising from a distant house. Calling to Michele, he shouted,

"It looks as if Ercolene is in trouble, I think his house might have been blown up"

Quickly saddling the horse, he strapped on his service pistol. Then, mounted and beckoned to Michele, who had come running out of the house, to join him on the horse.

"You're taking a chance riding Nove in daylight," Michele cautioned.

"Can't be helped, speed is the essence."

What they saw when they arrived horrified them. Ercolene swung on a rope from the branch of a tree. A note pinned to his waistcoat bore the legend HA PROTETTO UNO DEI NEMICI[8]. Close by, Anna, Ercolene's wife, lay, half naked, sprawled on the ground. What disgusted Mario most, was that she had obviously been raped before they killed her.

"You had better get the cart Ernesto," Michele said, as Ernesto, having left his work in the field, joined them. "We can't leave them here."

"Take the horse, it will be quicker," suggested Mario.

While Michele, seething with anger, was cutting Ercolene down, Mario tenderly re-arranged Anna's clothes in an effort to restore some of her dignity.

It was with heavy hearts they returned with their burden to Casa dei Pioppi. As in all rural areas throughout the world, where everybody knows everybody else, Ercolene and Anna were friends; friends, with whom, they had often shared a glass of wine. On their arrival at the house, they found Alberto, who had seen them returning, waiting.

---

[8] He protected one of the enemies.

"Run and fetch Don Umberto" Michele said to the boy. "They will need the final rites and a decent burial."

"I'll run all the way." responded Alberto.

. . . .

The little tune, normally on Filomena's lips as she returned from the fountain, carrying the heavy *conca* on her head was not there. She wore instead a worried frown. Three weeks had slipped by since she had watched the little party depart. Three weeks and no oak leaf to tell her Giorgio was safely back. A week since the murder of Ercolene and Anna and still no news.

Depositing her burden on a shelf beside the door, Filomena made for a place she liked to go when she wanted to be alone. Alone to think, alone at times to dream; to ponder over her secret thoughts. Lost in thought, she made her way up a narrow goat track, that led to a spot where an immense boulder loomed dark and grey. It had come to rest there in some distant age, before history began, dividing a clear mountain stream so that two new entities were born.

There was on one side the excited bubble of a miniature torrent, which cascaded down ledges and raced down steep slopes, before diving tumultuously into a stream lying far below. On the other side, there was its more placid brother, which found a way via a less precipitous route. Hugging the contours of the hill lovingly, it meandered, a silver rivulet, gently through the tree lined slopes round the edge of the hill; until it subsided gratefully, in peaceful union, with the river that watered the vast and fertile valley that spread out from the base of the mountain range.

In the streams first angry passage round the boulder, it had washed away the earth until only pebbles lay in the bottom of the pool it had made. A pool of such clarity that it seemed only inches deep.

Filomena liked it here, people seldom came. She felt private. She knelt beside the pool and her reflection stared back at her from the dark depths of a shadow cast by an overhanging tree. Because she was young, she liked what she saw reflected in the limpid water. She liked the smooth rounded cheeks and the full lips, which parted generously to reveal small evenly matched teeth. She also, secretly liked, the twin peaks which melted into the shape of her body.

Suddenly, a light breeze disturbed the surface of the pool, contorting the image of her reflection and breaking her reverie.

"Why doesn't Giorgio notice me?" she cried out involuntarily.

Now all Filomena could see were dancing points of light. She shivered momentarily; suddenly aware of the approach of winter. Pulling the coarse woollen jumper she wore closer round her shoulders, she secured the bottom button.

Seating herself with unconscious grace on one of the great smooth stones at the base of the boulder, Filomena began to comb her hair. She used long lazy strokes, enjoying to the full the only sensation of luxury she knew. Tossing back her head and revelling in the weight of the luxuriant growth which reached her waist.

Filomena was proud of her hair, it was her only vanity. She knew its rich chestnut colour attracted admiring glances and wished it would attract Giorgio. That he could see it wild and free like this and would want to make that casual caressing pat, that men, both young and old seemed unable to resist.

A light footstep behind her interrupted her thoughts and she heard a voice say,

"Hallo Filomena, Angelo said I might find you here."

Filomena looked round. Giorgio stood there with that rare smile of his softening his features.

"Oh! Giorgio, you're safe, I've been so worried," the words came out spontaneously. She couldn't stop herself. Neither could she stop the radiant smile that filled her face. Then, she flushed guiltily, thankful her thoughts couldn't be read. Somehow, she resisted the temptation to put her arms round Giorgio, contenting herself with allowing him to help her to her feet.

"Come, let's return to the house, I have much to tell you and there are plans to discuss with Angelo." Giorgio said, letting go of Filomena's hand and beckoning her to follow.

"Robin and Eric, are they safe?"

"They are probably on a boat by now, they don't lose much time repatriating returned prisoners of war."

"I'm so happy for them," Filomena's response was impulsive. "Their families will be so pleased to see them."

"With luck, they will have Christmas at home with their own folk."

"Oh how wonderful for them." Filomena said fervently and meekly followed Giorgio to the house, where she was surprised to see her father waiting in the doorway; it was the time of day when he would normally be at work in the valley.

"Babbo, I didn't expect to see you here." Then, a note of concern came into her voice as she followed with, "Is everything alright?"

"Nothing you need worry you head about." Angelo replied, but Filomena knew from the expression on his face that something had happened to disturb him.

In silence they entered the house. No one spoke, not even as the inevitable wine was being poured.

It was Giorgio who broke the silence, when in answer to Filomena's question, he said,

"One of Topo's guides is missing. . . ."

"Which guide?"

Filomena clutched Giorgio's arm; there was a note of anxiety in her voice as she followed with "Is Topo safe? I haven't seen his beech leaf lately."

"You wouldn't have done, he's been busy rounding up a party to take over the line." Giorgio frowned and cast his eyes in the direction of Angelo then back to Filomena before continuing,

"I hope so. He has left with a smaller party."

"Are you saying Topo left without his guide?" Angelo butted in. "What do you mean, a smaller party?"

"Sorry," Giorgio apologised, "I didn't tell you the missing guide was supposed to be meeting two of my English refugees and take them to an assembly point, but neither he, nor the two he was supposed to be escorting arrived."

Filomena wanted to repeat her question, 'which guide?' but was reluctant to intervene; since she was well aware the reply would probably be Guido, she decided the answer could wait.

While Giorgio was speaking, Angelo had risen from his seat, now he was pacing the floor as he said,

"Where were they supposed to meet him?"

"I am not sure, Topo has his own arrangements. They were seen walking along that path on the fringe of the woods. Topo's usual assembly point is the other side of the river, so that would be a logical place meet."

"Who saw them?" Angelo's voice was full of suspicion. "Not spies I hope," he added as the memory of Ercolene and Anna's fate swept through his mind.

"No need to worry on that score, the people who saw them are members of the family who had been looking after them."

"Do I know the family?" Angelo asked. Knowing, that even he would not get a direct answer, he was not surprised when Giorgio said,

"Probably." Then, noting the look of enquiry on Angelo's face Giorgio added, "Believe me, they can be trusted."

"I am not over happy about Topo making the trip without a guide," Angelo muttered quietly, more to himself than to Giorgio.

Giorgio didn't miss the comment and was quick to respond.

"Topo is well experienced and has made more crossings than Francesco and myself. I am sure he knows the route well enough."

"The old routes, maybe," Angelo said with a frown, "but they are risky. We have only just started using a few alternatives and he won't have been on any of them."

"Which is a good thing in its way, you know what the Tedeschi are like, if they have Gia-Guido and they make him talk." Quick as Giorgio was to correct himself, the slip was not missed by Filomena.

"Poor Giancarlo, I am sure he won't talk." There was a note of confidence tinged with sadness in Filomena's voice as the picture of a man with long sideboards and a saucy grin floated into her mind. She could almost hear him saying, as he so frequently did, *'never trust a man with sideboards if he is over thirty.'* Giancarlo was close to fifty and the comment usually made her laugh; now the memory brought her closer to tears.

Although Giancarlo was one of the few Guides whose real name was known, Giorgio had been reluctant to reveal it to Filomena, because he knew that he ranked among Filomena's best liked contacts. Cursing himself in rebuke for the mistake. He said,

"I am sure you are right. Hopefully, there is another reason for his absence."

Leaving Angelo and Giorgio to discuss the matters in hand, Filomena picked up the conca and thinking, 'I'll go to the fountain, there might be a beech leaf signal from Topo,' she adjusted her bandanna and slipped through the door.

Following the path that would take her to La Villa, Filomena cast an anxious glance at the sky which was beginning to cloud over. Although it had been a bright and sunny morning, she was not surprised, it was the time of the year for changeable weather.

By the time she reached the fountain, heavy clouds had formed and a wind had sprung into being. A quick glance was all that was needed to satisfy Filomena that no signal had been left.

Filomena was in two minds whether to call on Donnina while in the village, but the threatening clouds persuaded her to return home as soon as possible.

The first few heavy droplets came when Filomena was barely half way home. By the time she reached the door of her house, they had developed into a drenching downpour.

The sight of his dripping daughter in a dress so wet that it moulded itself to her shape brought a chuckle to Angelo's lips, taking the conca from her, he said.

"The sooner you get out of that wet dress the better. It's a good thing, Giorgio isn't in here."

"Where is he? Has he left already?" Filomena asked as she slipped through the door of her room.

"He is outside getting a couple of logs for the fire. Now hurry girl before he comes in."

The door had barely closed behind Filomena when Giorgio, laden with half a dozen logs, opened the door with his shoulder and dripped his way in. Dropping the logs by the fire he shook himself (much as a dog might do after a swim in the lake) and crossed the room to close the door. Then looked around the room and said,

"I wouldn't put a dog out on a night like this, is Filomena back yet?"

Angelo nodded and throwing a towel across the room to Giorgio, said,

"Yes, she just came in. I have never seen anyone so wet, like some half drowned creature of the wild.... She will be with us in a minute."

The words had scarcely left Angelo's lips, when Filomena appeared, she had changed into a dress that she normally only wore when attending Mass. Seeing her in it Angelo turned his head so that she wouldn't see the knowing smile that he knew he couldn't stop and said to Giorgio,

"If you don't have anything that can't wait until tomorrow, I suggest you stay here tonight, you can sleep on the *branda*[9]. Weather like this never lasts long. Mark my words, by the morning the sun will be shining."

Giorgio hesitated before replying, generally, he preferred not to accept offers of a bed for the night because of the added risks; not to himself, his concern was for the kindly person making the offer. However on reflection, he decided that there wasn't the slightest chance of a stray German knocking on the door of a house so remote as the one he was in, so accepted the invitation.

Angelo didn't have to tell Filomena to get the branda ready, she had already unfolded it and was busy spreading blankets. Finishing her task with consummate speed, she started to prepare the evening meal.

"La Cena[10] won't be long," Filomena said, with a radiant smile, "I know you will like what I am preparing. Gnocchi[11] alla Romana e vitello al forno[12] con pasta."

---

[9] Fold away bed.
[10] Main meal, usually in the evening.
[11] A type of pasta, made from potatoes. (Similar to dumplings).
[12] Roast calf.

CHAPTER SIX.

Alan frowned, held out his hand and said "I think we are in for a drenching Paul." Even as he spoke the sky clouded over and a few drops of rain splashed through the trees on to the path he and Paul were following. Within moments it had become a deluge, drenching their clothes and turning the earth into mud.

The two men stared at the empty path where they had expected to see a man who had promised to guide them into the hills and show them a track that would take them safely down to the river they would have to cross.

"What's happened to him?" Alan asked. "He hasn't waited for us."

"I'm not surprised, we are very late," Paul replied, "it must be well over half an hour since he was supposed to be here. Perhaps it's for the best, after all we don't know who that character was back there and for all we know he was following us."

"If he was following us, there's no sign of him now." Alan said, looking about him.

For the first time since leaving the prisoner of war camp he felt optimistic; he felt sure that this time they would be successful in reaching the Allies forward areas.

"Should we go back to Nazario?" Paul queried, "I'm sure he wouldn't mind. He didn't like us leaving anyway, he reckoned it would be more sensible to see the winter out with them and make an attempt in the spring."

"They have taken enough risks for us," Alan retorted, "You know what happened to their friend.... What was his name?"

"Ercolene."

"That's right; a bit too close for comfort. Emma was more than upset, and frightened too. It would not be fair to put them at risk any longer."

"You're right of course, I wasn't thinking straight." Paul paused a moment, as if collecting his thoughts before continuing with, "Then, there was that man they called Antonio. He looked like a soldier to me, if I'm right, it might not be safe with him around."

"Oh! I don't think we need worry about him," Alan responded. "I am sure he didn't see us. In any case, he was obviously their son. Why else would he call Emma Mama?"

Paul shook his head dubiously and said. "You can never be too sure. He might hand us over, if only to protect his family, or he could be a Fascist. It wouldn't be the first time one of those has betrayed his own family."

Alan laughed and said "Trust you to look on the glum side. Come on now, it's not so bad. I suggest we shelter under this rock tonight; it will get us out of the rain. We can decide on the best plan of action tomorrow."

"What's wrong with appealing to one of the other houses for help? They might let us sleep in the stable. We've done it before without much trouble."

"We would probably scare them out of their wits at this time of night, in any case, the Germans were thinner on the ground before and the reprisals hadn't started." Then noticing Paul's crestfallen face, Alan added, "Cheer up! The best is yet to come," and chuckled as he remembered the words, *'Cheer up! It may never happen,'* which were carved on the second of a pair of plaques that hung in his mother's kitchen.

Although the rain had only lasted a short time, it had been enough to swell the stream at the bottom of the gully and the cave like area beneath the rock was flooded.

"No good staying here." Robin commented, "We had better keep walking and try to cross the valley tonight."

"Hope it doesn't rain again." Paul said pessimistically.

Alan glanced at the sky before replying, there wasn't a cloud in sight and the night was as serene as it had been before the downpour. Then, deliberately failing to point out the lowering clouds obscuring the stars over the area they had left.

"I don't think it will," he said confidently, "at least not for a few hours, if at all."

Now that a decision had been made, Paul made no objection and quietly followed Alan as he clambered up the steep bank to the top of the small ravine, where the distant peak of Monte Corno could still be seen silhouetted against the sky. The dark outline of the Gran Sasso was barely visible overshadowing a silver ribbon of light, which was a river winding it's way through the centre of the moonlit valley. Ahead lay the high slopes of the Maiella.

"We still have a long way to go." Paul commented.

"All the more reason for making a move now," Alan replied cheerfully, "we must clear this area before daylight."

Paul surveyed the scene and said, "I can't see it makes much difference with so much light from the moon, it would make much more sense to hole up with someone for a couple of weeks; at least until the darker nights are with us."

Alan was beginning to wonder whether it had been wise to leave the protection of Nazario before Paul had completely recovered from the kick in the back. Whether they shouldn't have waited until Giorgio made another trip, instead of accepting the chance that had been offered to go with a different party arranged by his colleague, Topo. Perhaps, because he was tired, he felt irritated and his voice had a note of anger in it when he said,

"Do stop winging, you can't wait for dark nights all the time, in any case nobody will be moving around very much at this late hour."

For once Paul had no reply, as together they started the long descent down an ever widening rift in the hills, to a road which took them close to the entrance gateway of L'Aquila. The risk was unavoidable, there was no other way of reaching the protection of the olive groves that covered the valley.

"Providing we are careful crossing that main road, which from the size of it must be the link to Rome, it should be even easier than I expected," Alan remarked cheerfully. Then, as he led the way between closely planted trees, he added, "there seems to be plenty of cover here."

Plucking a handful of olives from one of the trees, Paul chuckled and replied in a happier tone than Alan had heard him use for some time.

"And it gives us something to chew."

"If it makes you happy," Alan laughed outright, "What a changeable joker you are, but it's good to see you back to yourself."

. . . .

The smile of triumph on Konrad's face slowly faded when he found that his attempt to hear what Alan and Paul were saying was being thwarted by the heavy rain which distorted their words. From the fragment of conversation, and particularly the words 'hasn't waited', he had overheard, he knew that, once again, his opportunity to see and possibly recognise their guide was gone. Gone also was the chance to follow and discover the local assembly place or 'Safe House' used by the people operating the evasion routes.

Disappointed, he shrank back in to some heavy undergrowth and, debating whether to follow or not, watched them pass within an arms length along the path that led to the river and open valley beyond.

The outline of Alan and Paul, just discernible through the pouring rain, was little more than a shadow against the lighter background of the opening at the end of the path when Konrad made up his mind.

Inwardly cursing the mud as his bare feet slipped on the slimy surface, he struggled to keep his balance on the steep slope that led down to the stream at the bottom of the ravine. For a while, he wondered whether his efforts were worthwhile. It seemed to him that he was merely going over old tracks. That nothing new would be learned that night. Then optimism returned as he watched his prey clamber up the steep bank on the other side of the stream and stand silhouetted against the now clear sky.

Thankful that the rain had stopped, Konrad washed the caked mud from his feet and eased the drenched clothes clinging to his skin. 'If nothing else,' he thought, 'they will lead me to the treacherous pig who is harbouring them.' A tight lipped, almost secretive smile twisted his features as splashing through the stream a further thought struck him. Scarcely aware he was talking to himself, he said,

"I'll show him what happens to traitors . . . I'll have such an example made that people will talk of it for years to come."

With renewed confidence Konrad swiftly climbed the steep bank to the top of a ravine, where he crouched for a moment searching the slopes below. At first he thought he had lost his quarry, then a movement caught his eye and he realised that he had been looking in the wrong place. Instead of being on the bullock track where he had expected them to be, they were rapidly descending a rift which ran parallel to it.

"Cunning swine!" he muttered and drew back from the edge.

For a moment he was nonplussed, the entrance to the rift was covered in loose stones. Furthermore, there was no cover on the steep, moonlit slope. There seemed no way of following without advertising his presence, then he remembered that the rift widened into a gully which ended a short distance above the point where the track joined a motor road.

With all the silence and grace of a cat, Konrad moved away, his shadow melting into the background as he made for the track. 'It won't be difficult to get ahead,' he thought, 'with any luck the safe house is close by.'

....

Morning found Alan and Paul trampling wearily up a wide, gently sloping path at the base of an escarpment which curved into the foothills of the Maiella. High above, precariously clinging to the edge, a castellated wall frowned down on them as if daring anyone to enter the town or village it protected.

"Looks like some medieval castle." Paul commented, pointing to the wall, "Reminds me of King Arthur and all that."

"Nothing very medieval about that," Alan replied, indicating a strange figure, waving an ancient lightweight machine gun, that had sprung out of a crevice in the rocks a short way ahead.

Dressed in loose cord breeches, a home spun jacket and strong knee high leather boots, the mauve silken beret with its unduly large pom-pom that the newcomer wore looked incongruously out of place. With amazing speed and agility he climbed an incredibly steep path to a point over their heads, pointed the gun menacingly at them and shouted something which they couldn't quite hear.

"I could make a good guess at what he wants us to do," Paul said in a calm voice, "perhaps we had better get our hands up."

"Not much else we can do. To run would be asking for trouble," Alan said as he raised his arms in the air and was relieved to note that Paul had regained his confidence, as if this was something he was used to and knew how to handle.

Pointing to another figure that had suddenly appeared, Paul added, in the same calm way,

"There's another, see him?"

"I think there's one behind us too," Alan replied.

Paul giggled; he couldn't help himself as he made the comment,

"Sporting the same weird hat I'll be bound."

"I don't know, I only caught a glimpse of him." Alan turned his head to look. "You're right you know. Hell! he can't be more than sixteen."

"*Hande hoche! Hande hoche! Hande hoche! Alza le mani! Hande hoche!*" The figure called in a shrill voice.

Alan swore and said "The bloody idiot thinks we are Germans," then catching sight of Paul's face, followed with "what's got into you?"

"Those hats, he does have one," Paul choked in reply, "who in hell thought them up?"

Hoping the laughter was not hysteria and trying hard not to succumb to the infectious giggles which Paul seemed unable to control, Alan replied, rather more sharply than usual.

"Never mind their hats, youngsters like those can be dangerous, particularly if they think you are laughing at them."

"*Americano!* . . . *Americano*, I talks *Americano*," one of them shouted excitedly, "you *Americani* No? . . . My name Carlo."

Then he said something in dialect that neither Alan nor Paul could understand and pointing to his colleague above, "Name *d'amico* Leopoldo."

"*Inglese*," Alan shouted.

The reaction was immediate. Within minutes, Alan and Paul were surrounded by a dozen wildly excited youths armed with a variety of weapons ranging from knives to ancient shot guns and rifles. Gone were the threatening gestures. Those who knew a few words of English wanted to say something, but their knowledge of the language was insufficient to make sense and they bombarded Alan and Paul with a series of nonsensical phrases.

"Well at least they seem less belligerent now," Paul remarked.

"Just as well." Alan replied and turning to Carlo said, "We were released from a prison of war camp near Ancona and are trying to get home."

Carlo looked at him blankly and repeated his previous statement,

"My name Carlo, name *d'amico* Leopoldo. Please to talk slow."

Replying in Italian, Alan explained what he had said and grinning now, followed with, "You must take the opportunity to practice your *Americano* with us while we are around."

Beckoning them to follow, Leopoldo, who seemed to be the leader, gave them a friendly smile and led the way, climbing a steep and narrow path, little better then a goat track, with such expert ease that Alan and Paul had difficulty in keeping up.

"Alright for him," Alan puffed, "He's not been walking all night. 'Struth can't he move?" Then, remembering Paul's injured back. "Are you O.K?"

"And some," Paul puffed back, ignoring the question.

The route took them through an ancient gate, unseen from below, and a maze of narrow back streets to a large house near the centre of the small hill town.

"The place is larger than it looks," Alan commented, "almost a town in fact"

As he spoke, Carlo's eyes brightened, "Town. Yes *Paese*, here us at Santa Stefano. This our house."

The only furniture in the room the gang used as headquarters was a large table, a lamp and a single rush bottom chair. Additionally there were mattresses and a few blankets spread on the floor by the walls, which were decorated with pictures of girl friends or other loved ones that their owners had pinned over the space allotted to them.

Almost with one accord, the young, would be, partisans flopped themselves down on their beds and occupied themselves cleaning their weapons.

"I don't believe that lot have a round of ammunition between them." Alan remarked.

"I'd noticed that, not even Leopoldo." Paul agreed, "I wonder where he got that machine gun from, I bet it's the only reason he is the leader."

"You are probably right," Alan shook his head dubiously and added, "God help them if they ever meet up with the Jerry, some of those rifles are minus their bolts and the shot guns don't look very efficient either."

As they talked some of the young men left their bed spaces and formed an interested circle round Alan and Paul, who had remained standing in the centre of the room. Meanwhile Leopoldo pulled the chair up to the table and making himself comfortable, called to Carlo to join him. Pleased with the opportunity to air his Americano in front of his friends Carlo beckoned to Alan and Paul and called out,

"You here."

"If we're going to get the third degree in English, it's going to take all day," Paul grumbled as he moved closer to the table.

"That's alright, once Leopoldo realises we can speak some Italian, he won't be interested in Carlo's interpretations." Alan remarked.

The questioning proved to be very perfunctory consisting mainly of a desire to find out where they had come from, what their plans were and what life was like in America.

Explaining that they were not Americans, Alan quickly outlined how they had left their prison camp when the guards disappeared and had been looked after by various friendly people as they made their way south. Eventually, apparently satisfied they were genuine, Leopold rose from the table and shook hands with both of them. Then saying,

"I have things to do," he wandered out of the room.

Seating himself on the edge of the table, Paul yawned and said,

"It must be nearly mid-day, I don't know about you, but I'm tired, where the hell are we supposed to doss down?"

"Not there, that's for sure . . . I'll be bound! Who wants sleep? . . . Look what's coming through the door. Hope they've got enough for us."

As Alan spoke, two women and a girl bustled through the door, carrying steaming pots of food.

Their guests forgotten, everyone made a dash for mess tins or mugs, crowding round the table where the pots had been deposited.

"*Pazienza*[13]*! Pazienza!*" the elder of the two women cried as she ladled a thick vegetable and pasta mixture into the eagerly poised receptacles, "There's plenty for all."

"Smells good." Paul commented.

Pausing for a moment in her work, she winked at Paul and speaking in English with scarcely any trace of accent, said,

"Good, yes, it is good, it ought to be. Are you American or English?"

"I'm English and so is he." Paul replied. "Where did you learn our lingo?"

Smiling, as she replied, she said,

---

[13] Patience.

"I'm English, I was born in Colchester." then, turning she pointed to the young girl, "This is my daughter Tina and the other lady is her Aunty Tania."

"And what do they call you?" Alan asked.

"Oh! I'm Pamella."

"I'm surprised they didn't intern you when Italy came in to the war."

"Well, it's been a long time, you know how it is," Pamella smiled and a distant look came into her eyes as she recalled a whirlwind romance, "I met Luigi while he was on holiday in England. I wasn't much more than a schoolgirl then. This is a remote place and apart from a few of our close friends, not many know I'm English by birth."

"How's that?"

"I lived in the Alps for twelve years before coming here six years ago. . . . By that time my Italian was not only fluent but had a northern accent. As the wife of an army officer there was no reason for anyone to suspect otherwise."

"What about the Fascists? I thought they suspected everyone who had not been inscribed?" Paul asked.

Smiling, Pamella replied in a rather roguish air,

"Everyone had to be inscribed, but not all were Fascists." Then commented more seriously, "Not all those who wear the black shirt would betray their friends like they do in the large towns . . . all the same, we have to be careful."

"And Tania, is she English too?"

"No, she's my sister in law. Here, you'd better have some of this before they come back for more. They're like a flock of gannets, don't even leave anything for the cat," then in Italian,

"Tina find two cans."

"Yes Mama."

Hearing the reply in English, Alan said,

"She can speak English then."

"More than her father realises, I have taught her, but her father insists she speaks Italian all the time, so she doesn't get much chance to practise."

Within moments the girl was back with two large metal basins. Smiling happily, she ladled a good helping into each and surprised Paul and Alan by saying, "Get stuck in." as she handed them over.

Pamella laughed and said,

"You see, she knows more than the odd word or two."

Taking the basins they looked around for spoons, but there were none to be seen.

Noting the look, Pamella said,

"You'll have to manage as best you can I'm afraid, spoons aren't used much here and this bunch have just about cleaned me out of eating irons."

"No matter." Alan replied, "We can manage."

"If you intend staying, I'll see what I can rustle up for you tomorrow."

Alan hesitated before replying, when he did, he said,

"I don't know about that. We are heading for the forward area and hope to make the Allied lines tonight."

"Not a good idea." Pamella's voice had a concerned note in it. "The Germans are very active in this sector. Without help you don't stand much chance," she ended emphatically.

"Perhaps we could sleep on it." Paul suggested hopefully.

Misinterpreting what Paul meant and noting the lines of tiredness in both their faces, Pamella felt guilty. After saying, "How thoughtless of me, of course you must be tired." she turned to Carlo and said,

"Tell a couple of your friends to give up their blankets for a few hours. These two need some sleep."

Quick to respond and anxious to please, Carlo strode over to his own bed space, patted the roll of blankets piled neatly on the mattress and said,

"My bed good, *materasso*[14]!"

Then, having pushed a youngster, reclining happily on a mattress alongside, from his, he turned to Alan and Paul and said,

"You, you, . . . two comfortable position, two *materassi*, you one, you one. . . . Good?"

---

[14] Mattress

Paul laughed, he couldn't help himself and said,

"Hope the poor kid doesn't mind."

As if the youngster had understood what Paul had said, he looked at him, smiled, pointed to the mattress and speaking in Italian, wished him a good sleep.

. . . .

When Alan woke the sun was streaming through the window. From its position, he knew it was late. Taking his watch from its place of concealment, he looked blankly at it.

"Has to be later than that." he grunted.

Puzzled that despite the shadows cast by the sun, which was now low in the sky, his watch indicated seventeen minutes to four, he put it to his ear. There was no reassuring tick, muttering,

"Must have forgot," he started to wind; looking round the room for a clock as he did so.

Paul, with a grin on his face and a mug of coffee like brew in his hand, was sitting up on his mattress watching him.

"Looks like coffee, don't smell like coffee, 'taint coffee." he said cheerfully. "You slept well! It's gone five."

"By how much?" Alan asked.

"About a quarter, I suppose, we'll ask Carlo."

Hearing his name spoken, Carlo came bustling over.

"You want me?" he beamed, "you ... *piaci?* ... like?" Paul nodded, like *caffé?*" and turning to Alan, "*caffé* - you"

"Please."

Carlo looked blank, a puzzled expression on his face.

"Yes," Alan amended and pointing to his watch said "Time, what is the time?"

"No *costa*, no pay *caffé*." Carlo shook his head vigorously and hurried to the table where Tina was serving the beverage from a large copper urn.

"He thinks you want to pay for the coffee with your watch." Paul giggled. "Believe me it isn't as good as that."

"My watch or the coffee?" Alan couldn't resist the question.

57

Paul looked at him and grinned but didn't deign to answer,

While Carlo was waiting to be served, one of the band, evidently on look out duty, rushed in to the room shouting in obvious excitement.

"Vincenzo comes, Vincenzo comes." The words were scarcely out of his mouth before the door of the room was blocked by the stocky figure of a man who's lack of height was more than compensated by the width of his shoulders.

"Who the devil is he?" Paul asked, nodding towards the doorway.

"Vincenzo, I suppose. If the way he is armed is anything to go by, he must be the real thing," Alan replied, taking in the loaded bandoleer slanting down from shoulder to the hip and a rifle slung baldric-wise across his back, "Whoever he is, they seem pleased to see him."

"Colourful character isn't he? What with that feather in his hat and the green rag round his neck, he could easily be mistaken for Robin Hood." Paul joked.

Ignoring Paul's comment, Alan went on to say, "Those stars on the shoulder boards probably indicate he is, or was, a captain in the army but I don't know what the bar indicates."

"Nor I, but I think the green patch with the star he is wearing on his shirt is called a flame and is normally worn as a collar patch," Paul observed, "I read somewhere that they have different colours for each regiment."

"Reminds me of the fellow we saw riding a horse near the escarpment. . . . He had a hat with a feather like that." Alan commented.

"That's right, he did have a feather, didn't he? would it be him I wonder."

"I don't think so." Alan paused and frowned thoughtfully before continuing. "I know it was a good two weeks or so ago, but if my memory isn't playing tricks, the man we saw was a lot taller and slim, to boot."

"That's true." Paul agreed, glancing again at the newcomer, who, surrounded by enthusiastic youngsters had entered the room and was striding towards them, his hand held out in friendly greeting.

Despite the fierce aspect created by heavy eyebrows above piercing eyes and an aquiline nose. Alan liked what he saw. The welcoming approach had a genuine quality about it that would have been difficult to fake. Rising to his feet, he took the outstretched hand and was not surprised by the firm feel of a grip which, notwithstanding obvious strength, didn't crush.

Saying, "My name's Alan and my friend is called Paul," he shook it warmly.

"So you speak Italian, that is good, my name's Vincenzo, Capitano Vincenzo, You have heard of me I expect."

Alan shook his head. "No can't say I have."

"I'm a professional soldier, my duty lies with my country, not the Tedeschi and the Fascisti, so I have become a partisan. . . . I don't like that word ribelli they all use, we are not rebels." Then he pointed to the bar on his shoulder board and said, "This bar is only awarded for many years service in the rank the stars denote."

"And the green patch?"

"That is the green flame of the Alpini," Capitano Vincenzo replied proudly, "it goes with the feather and this badge and shield on my hat." A sad look crossed his features. "One day I will put on my real uniform and walk the streets proudly as an Alpini officer should, but until then there is work to be done," then as the possibility of gaining two new recruits struck him, his voice strengthened and developed an enthusiastic ring, "Pamella tells me," he boomed. (The way he pronounced the name Pamella with the short A and a long E, sounded strange to Alan who was used to the English long A and short E of Pamela.) "you are soldiers that have been released from a prisoner of war camp. . . . We need men like you, experienced men, good fighting men."

Inspired by the man's fervour and mindful of an earlier temptation, Alan responded with almost equal enthusiasm.

"Glad to help in any way I can."

Vincenzo's response was immediate. It took Alan by surprise. He had not expected the enthusiastic embrace he received, nor the kiss on both his cheeks and felt embarrassed. Paul's amusement over Alan's discomfiture was short lived. Even as he giggled and muttered, "Serves you right you fool, but don't count me in," he received a similar embrace.

Alan chuckled, "You shouldn't have looked so happy, he thinks you want to stay as well."

"If you're staying, I might as well too. Fighting is something I am used to and it has to be better than hanging around in hiding," Paul replied in a more resolute tone than Alan had heard for a long time.

Happy in the knowledge that he had enlisted the help of two experienced soldiers, Vincenzo's stern features relaxed in a smile which brought into play the crows feet at the corners of his eyes and revealed a set of astonishingly small, even teeth.

"Tina," he almost bellowed, "Run, quickly now, tell your Mama to prepare a special meal this evening, I shall be bringing Alan and Paul to our house tonight."

Tina's smile was radiant as she replied,

"Yes Papa."

"You can see where she gets those tiny teeth from." Paul said in what he thought was an undertone.

"Yes she's a chip off the old block," Vincenzo surprised them by saying, "but she takes after her mother too, look at those blue eyes."

"You can speak English, yet made us talk in Italian," Paul said accusingly, "you must be Luigi. Pamela's husband."

"Of course, who else? but it is better you always speak in Italian. My wife's name is Pamella, you must remember to say it that way. I prefer it and it is safer for you." Then reverting to Italian. "The more you use our language the better you will get. If you are going to work with me, I don't want to hear you speaking in English ever again."

"How well trained are this lot? I hope they aren't the only troops you have, Luigi." Alan commented.

A fleeting frown crossed Capitano Vincenzo's brow as he said, "Don't address me as Luigi, it is better for discipline if you call me Capitano or Signore when talking to me." then as his smile returned, "At least while any of my men are about."

"Understood, *Signore*." Alan and Paul chorused in unison.

"Good! Now say it in Italian."

"*Capito. Signore.*"

Luigi smiled and said,

"You will soon get used to it. To answer your question, of course not. Most of my men served with me before we became partisans, these here are mere lads. They think they are, Matteotti." Then, noting their puzzled look, "The Anarchists." He grinned. "Socialists. We are a section of Giustizia e Liberta, associated with the Partito d'Azione. I suppose, I should really be with the Fiamma Verde, but they are in the North, as too are the Garibaldini." He paused for a moment and continued with, "I use these youngsters as look-outs or go-betweens. They are useful from time to time."

"Some of the older lads could be trained. I was an instructor at a training barracks before the war, so know something about the job. Suppose I pick out a team and train them?" Alan suggested.

Luigi gave him a shrewd look and said,

"So, you are a professional soldier, what is your rank?"

"Company Sgt Major," came the reply.

"We already have a sergeant major, you will meet him later. Your idea is good but as you can see, they are more or less unarmed, I am planning something to rectify that. What rank is your friend? Is he also a professional soldier?"

"No, he was conscripted at the beginning of the war and has reached the rank of sergeant."

"Then he should know enough to train them up. I have a more important role in mind for you."

. . . .

At first, looking round the small room where he had spent the night, Paul couldn't place where he was. Outside the window, seemingly only a foot away, a stone wall robbed the room of any sun. He stretched luxuriously, yawned and sat up. Alan was nowhere to be seen, only neatly folded blankets on the bed alongside. 'Always was an early bird,' he mused as he crossed to the window and looked out, 'I wonder where he is.'

The room he was in seemed to be on the third floor of a four storey building similar to one opposite. The narrow cobbled way, barely two metres wide, which separated the buildings was already busy with the comings and goings of the town's occupants. "Guess I'd better get going." Paul murmured to himself as he started to fold the covers.

The sound of a knock and the door opening made him turn.

Without waiting for his response, Pamella entered the room. She was carrying a tray laden with a teapot and a plate of toast.

"So you are up," she said brightly, "I have a rare treat for you, . . . tea and toast. Sorry there's no butter or marmalade, only olive oil and a pinch of salt. The tea has a peppermint flavour, but even in peacetime tea is a rarity. Now it is a positive luxury."

Smiling his thanks, Paul took the tray and said,

"No matter . . . toast! . . . tea! . . . What more could I want? I'd almost forgotten they existed."

"Milk?"

Paul nodded. "That too?"

"A bit strong I'm afraid, it's from a vacca." Pamella smiled. "You know, Ox's milk; what is the name for a female Ox? I have been away so long I've forgotten."

Paul thought for a moment, grinned and said,

"Cow, I suppose."

As they laughed in unison, Pamella picked up the teapot and tilting it over one of the two cups on the tray, said,

"I shall be Mother, at least for today."

"Where's Alan?" Paul asked.

"He's gone off with Luigi," Pamella answered. "to pick out the most likely lads for you to train, and perhaps a couple to take to his H.Q. when he takes you and Alan there tonight. . . . Did you enjoy last evening?"

"Just like being at home." Paul took a bite out of his toast and added, "This breakfast makes it even more so."

Sitting on the edge of the bed, they chatted about life in England and their home towns until the teapot was empty and all the toast had gone.

Brushing the crumbs that had fallen on to Paul's folded blankets, which they had used as a table, into her hand and saying, "I've enjoyed our chat." Pamella rose to her feet.

For a brief moment, as she lovingly handled the fine china, a melancholy look came over her face. Then, as her usual brisk nature asserted itself, she picked up the tray and made for the door, paused and said, wistfully,

"It's an age since I had news of England."

"You must let me have the name and address of your parents before I leave, I could take news of you and Luigi to them when I get home." Paul suggested.

"Oh if only you would!" Pamella exclaimed eagerly. "I don't even know whether they are still living," she added sadly.

CHAPTER SEVEN

High above the road Luigi Vincenzo pointed to a convoy of lorries, headed by an armoured car, winding their silent way along a road towards a gorge. Tapping his watch and turning to his companion, he said,

"You see Alan, it won't be too difficult, they come on alternate days, always at the same times, we need the arms and our stock of ammunition is getting low.... Are you with me?"

Alan looked down at the convoy and nodded in reply, then cast his eyes towards a small band of men crouching in the rocks above them. They were a motley looking bunch, dressed in a mixture of army and civilian clothing. The only common factor was the green bandanna at their necks and the feather some of them wore in their hat.

"Don't get me wrong," he said, "I'm game for anything that stands a chance of success, but I wouldn't think you can rely on much help from Leopoldo and his boys.... Surely you'll need more than this lot to tackle a convoy like that."

"Don't you believe it! All my men are veterans, experienced in hill fighting. The men who wear the black feather are the best shots, they are riflemen. Some of the others, those with the long Alpini feathers have been with me for a long time and have been specially trained for this type of terrain." Luigi gave a brief chuckle, "You won't know the song we partisans sing. *Il bersagliere ha cento penne e l'Alpino ne ha una solo, il Partigiano ne ha nessuna e sta sui monti a guerreggiar.*" Then, indicating a point where the road narrowed as it passed between two towering walls of rock, continued, "The Tedeschi may be foolish, but I am not.... If they expect us at all, it will be in a place like that over there.... You see?... Where the road is cut through the rock.... It's such an obvious place for an ambush they are bound to be on their guard.... Speed and surprise are the important factors... we will attack from a better place, a place where they will never expect us."

"I can understand why the Alpino has one feather and the partisan not even one, but why sing the rifleman has a hundred?" queried Alan.

"Your guess is as good as mine," was the reply.

They stood there side by side absorbed in thought, as if by mutual consent, while the convoy drew level and passed out of sight. Words seemed superfluous and none were spoken until Luigi broke the silence with,

"Come you should meet my men before we return."

Without more ado, he turned on his heel and led the way up a goat track to a narrow ledge just above an area where two men were crouching. With a perfunctory "Take care." he started to edge along it, pointing out the scant hand holds to Alan as he went. Privately thinking, 'the man's mad. . . . What am I doing here?' Alan followed.

Beyond the ledge, a comparatively easy path took them through a split in the face of the rock to a gently sloping area beneath an overhang, which formed the entrance to a cave.

When they stooped to enter, a barked command brought a number of men, who were sitting on empty ammunition boxes round a crudely constructed table, to their feet. One, who had been sitting apart cleaning his rifle, saluted and came forward. Luigi's salute in acknowledgement as he said, "carry on Sergeant major," was little more than a casual wave and a nod of the head.

The interior of the cave was considerably larger than Alan had anticipated. Although more than a dozen men were in there it didn't appear to be crowded; even the bunks placed against two of the walls didn't seem to take up any room. The subdued light which rendered lamps unnecessary had Alan puzzled for a while, until he saw a mirror, placed high in the roof, which collected light entering through a fissure in the rock and reflected it on to the floor.

Intimating that he had matters to discuss with the sergeant major outside, Luigi introduced him as Florio di Tirane. Then hinting that it would be a good opportunity to get acquainted, left Alan to his own devices.

By the time Luigi returned, Alan knew most of the men by name and had learned that the sergeant major was irreverently known as Il Tiranno. (The Tyrant.)

"How did you get on?" Luigi asked as they left the cave, "I expect they told you their name for the sergeant major."

Alan grinned, by way of reply.

"And their pet name for me, I'll be bound."

"No! What's that then?"

"You'll find out soon enough, it's not very complimentary, but these names never are. . . . Incidentally, I've discussed your suggestion of training the youngsters with Florio and we've decided to give it a trial . . . so I expect they'll find a name for Sgt Paul pretty soon."

"I hope so. it's usually a sign of affection."

"That's true, there's nothing those men there wouldn't do for me or their sergeant major."

"The feather some of them are wearing looks different to yours." Alan commented.

Thinking, what a strange remark, Luigi regarded him with a puzzled air before replying,

"It's a matter of rank," then as if suddenly realising that what was common knowledge in Italy was not common knowledge elsewhere, he went on to explain, "In the Alpini regiments, senior officers wear a white feather," he paused and his eyes twinkled, "Pamella says it is appropriate."

"I can't think why." Alan said and chuckled.

Luigi allowed himself a tight smile before continuing,

"Junior officers, such as I, wear a feather taken from an eagle, . . . the lower ranks one from a crow."

Half an hour later found them picking their way carefully down a shale covered slope towards a belt of conifers. By shielding his eyes against the bright morning sun, Alan could just make out the grey mass of the Gran Sasso, and the summit of Monte Corno; hanging as if suspended in the sky above the mist which shrouded the lower slopes of the Appenine range. Far below the path they were following, and some distance to their right; seemingly painted on the hillside, Alan could also see the roofs of Santa Stefano; clinging, it seemed, to the very edge of a precipitous descent into a gorge. In the bright morning light, the roofs stood out in stark relief against a background of shade, where the sun rising above the lower hills on the opposite side of the road had not yet reached. Returning his gaze to the distant mountain range, his thoughts centred on the friends who had sheltered Paul and himself. He found himself wondering how they had taken the news that the guide had not contacted them. Without realising he was speaking his thoughts out loud, he said,

"I wish there was some way of letting Nazario know we are safe."

"What did you say?"

"I didn't speak."

Luigi regarded him thoughtfully,

"You did you know, in English, but so softly I couldn't hear you properly, something about you wish you could let someone know. . . . It doesn't matter so much when we are alone, but if you must speak your thoughts aloud, you had better think in Italian."

Feeling slightly embarrassed and rather like a schoolboy caught in the act, Alan said,

"I was wishing it was possible to let the people who looked after us know that Paul and I are safe. They will have been, or will be told if they haven't already, that we didn't meet the guide and are sure to be wondering what happened to us."

"I expect something can be arranged, . . . we'll talk about it tonight."

. . . .

Making her unhurried way beneath a blazing sun, the heat of which, despite the lateness of the year could still be felt, Tina was thankful for the scant shade the olive trees provided as she passed between their serried ranks. Every now and then she would stop to look back at the great Maiella in the mountain range she had left that morning. Despite her attempts to banish her fears she couldn't stop thinking about her father. She felt sure he was planning something for that day. All the signs were there, his departure the previous evening with Alan and Paul; his preoccupation, her mother's tears, and the way he had held her before he left.

It was a long walk from Santa Stefano to Angelo's house, but she was used to walking great distances and didn't mind the loneliness of the route across the flat plain which separated the two mountain ranges. It made a pleasant change from the precipitous paths she generally had to use in her work as a courier for the leaf man they called Francesco.

By late afternoon, she could see the line of poplars that hid Casa dei Pioppi from view and on the opposite side of the small valley, the track that would lead her to Angelo's home.

Although Tina knew that Francesco, worked with a man called Angelo and had delivered messages for him to various contacts she had never been to his house and couldn't be sure that the Angelo she was going to see was the same person, neither did she know whether he would know the Michele that Alan and Paul had referred to. There was no doubt in her mind that this was the area described by Alan. In her mind, the house just a short way away, was, without a doubt the one that had given them shelter. For a moment she was tempted to deliver her news direct, but, her father's instructions not to go to the house that had been described had been emphatic. His words, *'Don't go to the house they've described. I know it would be nice, but you won't be sure you're right. . . . Angelo knows everyone in the area and can be trusted to be discreet. . . . A visit from him or his daughter, Filomena, will not cause any comment'* still rang in her mind.

Tina found Filomena in the stable, busy forking hay into a manger for Forli. As she entered, the horse raised his head, gazed briefly at her, decided there was nothing to be gained, and resumed eating. Absorbed in her task Filomena neither saw nor heard Tina enter, patting the horse fondly she laughed happily and said,

"I'm on this side of you, you fool."

"How are you Filomena?"

Startled by the unexpected voice but anticipating she would see someone she knew, Filomena replied,

"Not so bad." and turned to face the newcomer.

For what seemed an eternity of time, with alarm bells ringing in her head, Filomena stared at the bluest eyes she had ever seen. The barefooted girl wearing a faded blue skirt and home knitted cardigan that stood before her, was a complete stranger.

Tina smiled winningly, released her bandanna and said,

"Don't worry Filomena, I'm a friend and bring a message from Alan and Paul. My uncle is Domenico."

Although Filomena recognized the code, she still looked at Tina suspiciously; judging her to be about fifteen or sixteen. Speaking in a tone of voice that reflected the anger she felt with herself for allowing someone to creep up on her unawares, she said,

"Who are you? . . . You say you are a friend. . . . What are you doing here? . . . This is private property." Then she saw the sycamore leaf nestling in her thick, blonde hair and said,

"How is Charlie?"

"Francesco is with my uncle," Tina replied.

Sighing in relief Filomena forked a final load of hay into the manger and saying, "you've come a long way, you must be tired," she invited Tina to follow her in to the house.

"Is Angelo at home?"

Saying, "No, not yet, he usually comes in at dusk. Is it my father you have come to see?" Filomena placed a small metal basin on the seat of a chair. Then added rather dubiously, "I don't know if he knows, who was it you said? . . . Alan and Paul?"

"Yes and no," Tina replied. "I have a message for the good folk who were protecting Alan and Paul. They said that a man calling himself Giorgio brought someone named Michele to the house where they were staying. Michele is a common name, we can't wander around asking, which Michele? So we we're rather hoping Angelo might know. Giorgio would of course. Can you contact him?"

"No, he always contacts me, you know the rules."

"Will there be time to talk before Angelo arrives?" Tina asked.

Filomena shook her head. "Not really, he'll be here any moment now."

As she spoke she ladled water from a copper urn by the door into the basin and hung a towel across the back of the chair. Then, from seemingly nowhere, produced a bar of home made soap, placed it beside the basin and said,

"I expect you'll want to freshen up. . . . I think I know the Michele you want, he is a friend of ours. I'll take you to him later, we can talk there."

Smiling her thanks, Tina picked up the soap and made a mental resolve to bring Filomena some of the German supply her father had obtained during one of his raids. If she disliked the greasy slime Filomena's soap produced she made no comment, proper soap was almost impossible to get and the substitute was better than nothing. As she gratefully splashed her face with water the door opened and Angelo came in. He looked tired, but content.

With only the briefest glance at the girl washing in the corner, Angelo strode across the room to the table and helped himself to a plate of pasta from the steaming cauldron Filomena had placed there. Only then, did he speak. Without even asking Tina her name he said,

"Are you hungry girl?"

Tina nodded, words seemed superfluous. She hadn't eaten since leaving her house that morning and the smell of the food had made her realize how hungry she was.

"Come eat, . . . Daughter get a chair, make her comfortable." The words were spoken rapidly in the local dialect and were difficult for Tina to follow.

Saying, "Babbo, speak in correct Italian, . . . I don't think Tina knows our dialect, she's from another village," Filomena emptied the basin Tina had been using and placed the chair at the table.

"So that's her name." There was just a hint of humour in Angelo's voice as he spoke. Then turning to Tina, he said,

"I wondered how long it would take to find out your name. Welcome to our home Tina."

Although Angelo knew about Tina's work with the movement, he had never met her. He had however met her father, so made a guess and followed up with,

"So you are Tina," then, embraced her and added, "how is Luigi?"

"He keeps well."

"And your mother, Pamella?"

"They are both fine, Papa said to remember him to you."

When Tina had taken her seat at the table, Filomena filled two plates with the fragrant mixture and added a further scoop to her father's plate, then waited for him to make his usual thanks for the food they were about to eat before filling her own.

They ate in silence, each enjoying the quiet of the evening and the food before them, until noticing that Tina had emptied her plate, Angelo said,

"The girl's hungry, give her some more."

"No!" Tina protested, placing her hands over her plate and shaking her head, "I've had plenty, much more than usual."

"What's the matter, frightened of getting fat?" Angelo chuckled good humouredly.

Ignoring her pleas, Angelo ladled two further scoops on to Tina's plate and cut a massive slice of bread from the loaf Filomena had baked that afternoon. He wished he could think of something else to say but nothing suitable came to mind, so he contented himself by smiling happily at her as he watched her eat the second helping. When satisfied that his guest had eaten all she was going to eat, he said,

"What brings you here, Tina?"

"As I told Filomena, I come with a message for the people who protected Alan and Paul and we were hoping that you would know who they are."

"I know about them, but I'm afraid I don't know who their protectors were. Did they tell you their protectors name?"

"No, they said Michele would know who they are."

Surprised by her Father's apparent knowledge, Filomena gave him a straight look, and taking a gamble, she said,

"Tina, is looking for him. Would that be our friend Michele across the valley? I wonder."

Although he now knew that his daughter was also involved with the movement, Angelo hesitated before replying. Then, almost abruptly, he replied,

"Without a doubt, I will take Tina to him tomorrow."

Tina was never at a loss for words, they seemed to come to her naturally. She had taken an instant liking for this kindly, rather shy man. In no time she had him laughing over silly and sometimes exaggerated anecdotes involving her family and friends. Not even the local priest was spared. Uninhibited and a born prattler she chatted on until Filomena announced that she had promised Caterina she would visit that evening and suggested that Tina might like to come with her.

There was a worried frown on Angelo's face as he watched the two girls take the path that Filomena always used as a short cut when visiting Caterina. The appearance of Tina at his house was disqueting. There was an air of self assurance about the girl, that on reflection, was unusual in one so young. The idea had come into his mind that she might not be who she said she was. The notion frightened him. He wished he had been more vehement in his protests when Filomena announced that she was going to visit Caterina that evening, and Tina could go with her instead of waiting for the morning. 'I could have said it was too late,' he thought bitterly.

Unaware that a shadow had detached itself from the lee of the haystack on the edge of the clearing and melted into the darkness of the path the girls had taken, Angelo closed the door.

. . . .

"Have you seen Gianni?" Lucia asked as Mario was leaving the house.

"No. . . . Don't worry, no news is good news, if anything had happened to Gianni, we would have heard by now." Mario replied with a reassuring smile.

"He went with Donnola, they said they wouldn't be long," Lucia said in an anxious tone of voice. Making a brave attempt not to sound distressed, she added, "He wasn't supposed to be gone as long as this." then looked away to hide the tears she could feel forming. "I expected him back this afternoon."

"A bit silly, wasn't it? Going off with a complete stranger like that."

"He wasn't a stranger; Gianni said he was an old army friend. Donnola isn't his real name, He reckons it's better that way. All the ribelli have strange names, to protect the family from reprisals. If nobody knows who they are. Gianni said there wouldn't be any trouble."

"Then why are you worrying?"

"It's two days now," Lucia replied, trying not to let Mario see her tears.

Two years, Gianni's senior, Lucia had always, and still did, feel protective to towards her, (in her mind) 'Little Brother.'

Mario knew from the tone of her voice that she was crying and felt awkward, he was not used to women, especially when they were upset. Service in the Western desert, then the Russian front and latterly his special duties liaising with the evasion groups and the rebels had deprived him of their company for too long. His reply, when it came, was clumsy.

"You worry too much."

"Oh! You are unkind." she gasped and slammed the door.

Surprised by Lucia's reaction Mario lingered outside the house for several minutes before moving off. He wished now, he had said something else. 'Anything would have been better than that,' he mused, 'I didn't mean to be unkind.'

Slowly, he made his way down the dark cobbled street, across the valley and into the tree covered area below the escarpment, his mind trying to turn over the events of that day. But, the words, *'you are unkind,'* kept butting in to disturb his thought process.

The mood continued until something broke the natural rhythm of the night. Mario froze; less than fifty metres ahead, where the trees grew dense towards the top of the escarpment, he sensed, rather than saw a movement. Ears tuned to catch the faintest sound; not sure whether his imagination was playing tricks, he stood still, silently watching and waiting. Then, he saw it, a flash of light, so dim, he could not be certain, flitting across the path. It was as if the light of the moon filtering through the canopy of trees had struck something to reflect its rays. That was all. Treading softly, he moved swiftly forward. The track was empty. Muttering, "You're getting jumpy old son," he continued on his way.

The place where a steeply rising and little used path forked off the main path, was soon reached. Mario stopped a moment, debating in his mind which route to take. The partially overgrown path lay immediately below his house and was the shorter route. 'But,' he thought. 'if there is someone about, they will probably be on the main path, rather than the difficult to negotiate one.'

Originally it had been Mario's intention to call on Angelo while returning home from his visit to Lucia, to tell him that Gianni had decided to join the ribelli. However, the news that Gianni was missing, had delayed him. So he decided, it could wait.

"If someone is prowling about, it's just as well I didn't go to see Angelo," he told himself..

Suddenly the night air was split with a paroxysm of barking followed by the sound of someone or something crashing through the undergrowth. At the same time a girls voice crying out as if in pain or fear and the words (in a masculine voice) *"Was zum Teufel."* came distinctly to his ears. Then he heard Michele calling to his dog.

"What is it Leone? . . . Who is out there?"

"So that's what it was, some damn Tedesco out to steal whatever he can find," Mario muttered as he hurried along the path.

As if in confirmation that the right decision had been made, the commotion stopped as abruptly as it had begun. For a brief moment, the night returned to its normal serenity. Then, came the sound of someone running. Instinctively aware that the steps were coming closer, and thankful the trees were particularly thick where he was walking, Mario stepped behind one and waited. He didn't have long to wait. Although the shadow of the tree made it too dark to recognize the blurred figure that pounded past him, he could tell that the man was not in uniform; furthermore, he appeared to be barefooted. Only the exclamation, *"Gott! - Gott!"* that escaped from his lips, as he tried to kick away the dog snarling at his heels, betrayed the fact that he was a German. Thinking, 'That dog of ours will soon sort him out.' Mario stayed on the main path, which would take him through the woods to the line of poplars and Casa dei Pioppi.

Fearing Vincensina or Giuseppina may have been attacked, Mario sped along the path until the silhouette of Filomena and Tina, framed in the rectangle of subdued light at the end of the path, brought a sigh of relief to his lips. Because they were walking slowly, he thought at first that his mother and sister had stepped out of the house to take the air. Then, the notion that as it was a very chilly night, it was exceedingly unlikely that they would leave the warmth of the house and stray along the tree covered path after dark; especially when there had just been a disturbance, came in to his mind. Alarmed now, he wondered what had brought them out. It was only when he became aware that one was limping that he realized they may have been attacked after all.

"Have you been attacked Filomena?" Mario asked on recognizing her as he came abreast. "Why are you limping?"

Imperceptibly, Mario's eyes narrowed as he looked at Tina.

"Are you one of Domenico's daughters?" he asked.

Tina laughed; she couldn't help herself and answered,

"No I am not; I am one of Domenico's nieces." Then, with a twinkle in her eyes, added, "It's good to be cautious."

Satisfied with the reply, Mario relaxed and turning his attention back to Filomena said,

"That looks rather painful. Let me help you."

"No I'll be alright." Filomena replied, hastily stepping away as she tried to assert her sense of independence.

"Don't be silly, you need help," Mario insisted, adding, "You will only make matters worse."

Resisting an idiotic urge to repeat the phrase, *'Gosh! How could a paw be so little,'* he had once read in a wild west story, when studying the English language at Milan University, he took one of her hands in his and carried it over his shoulder; then, put his free hand round her waist.

Admitting that her ankle was giving her pain, Filomena couldn't help emitting a barely audible sigh of relief as she gratefully allowed him to take her weight.

As they reached the end of the path, Michele's dog Leone, proudly carrying a piece of clothing came bounding back; obviously happy with his prize. Pausing only to sniff suspiciously at the three on the path and wag his tail in recognition of Filomena and Mario, he trotted along beside them.

Unlike the night, when, glad to be home, Mario stood there, in the silver rays of a full moon, with Nove by his side, there was practically no light from the thin curve of a new moon, which now looked down from the sky. Even so, the yellow coat of Leone, wandering in and out of the lean-to, stood out clearly. Satisfied that if there was anyone about the dog would be acting differently, Mario gave Filomena an impulsive squeeze and said,

"I will just check, to make sure there is nobody about. Can you make it to the house alone?" Then, changed his mind and, with one eye on the stable door, in case Ernesto came out, escorted her to the door of the house.

The door opened, almost before they had time to lift the latch and Michele, with Giuseppina looking over his shoulder, stood there. If they were surprised to see a stranger with Filomena and Mario, they didn't show it as they waited patiently to be introduced.

"Are there any visitors? . . . Is it safe to talk?" Filomena queried. "I have brought a friend, her name is Tina, who has news of Alan and Paul, I think you know who they are and who was looking after them." she explained.

"Are they safe? . . . Yes! yes! Bring her in." Michele's voice, though low, rang with the relief he felt and his smile broadened with joy; only to fade as he noticed the awkward way Filomena moved.

"What ails you Girl? . . . Are you hurt?" he asked, his voice now full of concern.

"It's nothing, I had a fall and twisted my ankle."

As Filomena spoke, Vincensina joined Giuseppina and Michele at the door. Saying "Let me have a look." in a brusque tone that belied the sympathy she felt, she took charge.

"I want a quick word with Ernesto before he leaves, Mario announced as he turned to cross the cobbled courtyard to the stable.

"Don't stand there, chatting at the door," Vincensina said, in a tone that was more an order than a request. Then, as Filomena hobbled in, "What brings you here? Have you come to chat with my mother?"

"Yes and no." Filomena said, with a winning smile.

"What do you mean? . . . Yes and no."

"I have come for one of my usual chats with Caterina, but I also bring a message from Alan and Paul for Michele; or rather, Tina does." Filomena replied as she sat on the chair that had been offered.

"Alan and Paul, who are they? I don't think I know them." Vincensina gave an interrogative glance towards Michele as she spoke.

"Two unfortunates, like Eric and Robin, who would have been coming here, for an overnight stay," Michele said, in answer to her look.

While Filomena sipped alternatively the coffee Giuseppina had prepared and the sambuca Michele had poured, Tina explained the reason for her visit.

"Alan and Paul have joined my father's group of partisans," Tina began, "they have asked if we can contact the people who protected them; to let them know that they are safe, and also, to apologise for leaving without so much as a goodbye." Then, facing Michele, she continued, "They told us that a man called Michele had been brought to the house where they were staying, so if we could find him, he would know who to contact. I was hoping it would be you. When I heard you tell your wife who they were, it was a great relief. I knew then, that I had found the right contact."

"Yes, you've come to the right person, I know to whom you refer."

"Could you take me to see them tomorrow?"

"It will be safer if I go, the fewer who know who they are, the better." Michele replied. Then, noticing that Tina had finished her coffee, poured her a generous measure of sambuca and added,

"It's not that I don't trust you, but you know how it is."

Meanwhile, Filomena was looking in dismay at the bulge of leaves and bandage around her ankle and wondering how, even with Michele's or Mario's help, she was going to walk home, when, as if reading her mind, Vincensina, said,

"You'll have to use Mario's horse Nove, . . . Michele or Mario can go with you to bring it back."

"I hadn't thought of that, do you think, they will mind?" Filomena queried.

"Of course not. The exercise will do the animal good." Vincensina replied.

Although she knew it was the only practical solution, Filomena hated the thought that she would be a nuisance. She started to say "It won't be necessary, I'm fine now . . . " but Michele didn't allow her to finish, he cut in with,

"Don't be silly girl. I will enjoy the walk. Tina can ride behind you." Then the corners of his eyes crinkled and his lips creased in a mischievous grin as he said, "It's a long time since I had the opportunity to take two pretty young girls home. Don't deprive me of the pleasure."

Hearing his words, Vincensina laughed and turning to the girls said,

"Watch him. He always was a flirt."

It was warm in the stable, which bore the familiar acid odour of rotting straw, common to stables the world over, where Mario found Ernesto tending his beloved animals.

"Could you take a message to Lucia?" Mario began.

"Naturally, what is it?" Ernesto replied, before Mario could continue.

"Just say, . . . I didn't mean to be."

Ernesto looked at Mario shrewdly.

"She will know what I mean." Mario said.

"If you two have fallen out, don't involve me. Lucia is a sensitive girl, for all her seemingly tough exterior. Believe me, anything you have to say, will be better coming from you direct. I suggest you come back with me and put your mind at rest."

"Filomena has sprained her ankle and I was thinking of taking her home on Nove."

"It's barely eight o'clock, so I'm sure your father won't mind doing that for you. If not I will take her home. That will leave you free to go and see Lucia." Then, with a laugh, Ernesto added, "You don't need me with you to find your way to your girl friend. Do you?"

Relieved by the solution of his problem, Mario said,

"Sounds like a good idea. I suspect he would be disappointed if I didn't ask him to."

Inside the house, they found Filomena chatting with Caterina, while Tina was busily engaged in conversation, which from the smiles on the other two faces, must have included some of her more amusing anecdotes.

Before, Mario could pose the question, Michele, said,

"Filomena needs help getting home, so I have offered to take her on the back of Nove. I was sure you wouldn't mind."

"Of course not, Papa" Mario replied, smiling with relief, now that he had been spared the embarrassment of asking.

It was close on 9.30, rather later than they had expected it to be, when Ernesto and Mario finally stood on the threshold of Ernesto's home. The walk from Casa dei Pioppi to the house with a wolf for a knocker, normally took a little over an hour. However, they had been delayed. The sight of Nonna Ricci, chatting with the Sicilian and still spinning her yarn, in the open doorway of her home after dark, was unusual, particularly when there was a chill in the air.

"It's a cool night, Nonna, how are you keeping?" Ernesto called as they were passing.

"Not so bad." It was the response she always made, whether ill, well, or indifferent. Then, she added, "I have heard some terrible news."

Ernesto, half wished he hadn't called to her, but it was customary and in any case, he would not have been happy, had he passed her without acknowledging she was there.

"What's that then?" he asked, trying to sound interested.

Seeing Ernesto and Mario approach, the Sicilian bade Nonno Ricci goodnight and with a cursory wave of his hand, left.

"There has been a skirmish between the ribelli and the Tedeschi," Nonna Ricci began.

"And when wasn't there?" Ernesto whispered to Mario.

"They met a German patrol on the new road to Ascoli." she continued, "The entire group was wiped out and their weapons seized. The Tedeschi lost three of their men."

The thought that one of the rebels killed could be Gianni, struck both Mario and Ernesto immediately.

"Do you know who they were?" They chorused in unison.

Nonna Ricci shrugged her shoulders,

"Who knows? They all have those funny names." She paused a moment, and continued with, "And there was trouble in one of the villages, I don't know which one."

Anxious now, to get on their way both Ernesto and Mario reluctantly stayed to hear her story. As it happened, she didn't know much, merely that a group of drunken German soldiers had entered a village, played havoc with the inhabitants and hung a woman.

Dismissing the story as one of the rumours heard almost daily, they made their excuses to leave, and left a disappointed Nonna, with further bits of gossip to be told another time.

They found Lucia, apparently happy now, sitting beside a cosy fire, busy knitting a cardigan. Seeing Ernesto and Mario enter, she hastily hid the half finished garment away. Ernesto, who knew his daughter very well indeed, and never missed a thing, saw the almost guilty movement, and smiled inwardly.

"I'd wager a weeks pay, that is a Christmas present and not for me, nor Gianni." he told himself. "Whatever the quarrel was about, I reckon Mario's been forgiven."

Lucia rose so quickly that she knocked her chair over, then without waiting to pick it up, rushed over to Mario, who, still in the doorway, barely had time to enter.

"Oh Mario! . . . Oh Mario! I didn't mean to slam the door on you." she half sobbed and clung to him.

Mario could feel her trembling, as she pressed against him, he wanted to say,

"And I didn't mean to be unkind," but, there was a lump in his throat. The words locked in his heart, wouldn't come out of his mouth. They just wouldn't come.

Evidently, sensing his difficulty, Lucia smiled at him, and whispered,

"It's alright, I know - I know - It's alright now." and kissed him

All Mario could do, was look down at her and think, 'How could I hurt this lovely girl.' Somehow, he managed to say,

"Am I forgiven?"

Lucia looked up at him, and without asking for what, smiled and said,

"Of course."

Meanwhile, Ernesto took Donnina on one side, and told her of the gossip he had heard from Nonna Ricci.

"Don't say anything to Lucia," he counselled, "we don't want to worry her. Nonna's accounts are often exaggerated, merely unfounded rumours. Bits of gossip full of propaganda, that's all. Nevertheless we should brace ourselves for the worst."

Donnina remained silent for a while, then, without smiling said,

"I agree."

CHAPTER EIGHT

From his vantage point on the steep mountain path he was descending, Carlo saw Tina emerge from the serried rows of olive trees and start to cross the open cultivated ground that lay between her and the entrance to the gently sloping gully below Santa Stefano. Too far off to attract her attention, he left the path he was following and, hoping he would be in time to intercept her, took a shorter, but dangerously precipitous route. Leaping, with all the skill of his kind, over the many small fissures that barred his way and jumping down from precarious footholds to narrow ledges several feet below, he descended at incredible speed.

Carlo still had nearly two hundred feet to descend and the last dying rays of the sun had dipped out of sight when Tina reached the base of the escarpment. Unable to warn her not to enter the town, he could only stand by and watch her merge into the background as she climbed the narrow path leading to the ancient entrance gate. Distance and the ever deepening shadows thrown by the surrounding hills making her tiny figure more and more difficult to see.

The first thing Tina noticed as she approached the gateway was how quiet it seemed. There were no cheery calls of greeting from men returning to their home after a day's work on the fertile terraces below and the paths, which should have been populated with their weary shapes, were deserted.

"Where is everybody?" she asked herself, "It's not as if it's Sunday, or is it?" Then, counting off the days on her fingers and speaking out loud she said, "Let's see now - it was Tuesday when I left, . . . I stayed with Filomena Wednesday, . . . came back today. Must be Thursday."

Bewildered, her anxiety increasing with each step, she walked slowly through deserted streets bordered by closed doors and shuttered windows, towards her home. Then she saw the hated Tedeschi, they were standing in a knot at the corner of the street where she lived. Their helmeted figures silhouetted against the cracked and peeling paint of the houses, just outlines in the gathering dusk. Uncertain what to do, and trying not to panic, Tina turned. As she did so, a door opened.

"Quick! Get inside . . . don't you know there's a curfew at sunset?" The words came in a hoarse whisper, as strong hands grasped her arm, pulling her in to the house.

Startled by the suddenness of it, Tina only just succeeded in choking back the cry that rose to her lips. Recovering her composure she turned her head and found herself gazing into a pair of piercing eyes set in a gnarled and weather-beaten face.

Across the room, absorbed in her work on the pillow case she was decorating, an old lady sat on a rickety chair beside the fire, her grey hair seeming red as she bent low over her task and struggled to see the fine threads she was drawing in the scant light of its flickering flames. Without raising her head to speak, she said,

"Well Pasquale, is it Tina?"

"I am not sure Carlotina, I think so," her husband replied as he rekindled the lamp he had extinguished before opening the door, "come have a look."

Placing her work carefully aside, Carlotina hobbled across the tiny room and peered into Tina's face.

"You look tired my child," she said, her voice full of compassion, "come, take my chair by the fire, while I prepare a meal."

"Well is it?"

"Yes, I'm Tina. Don't you remember me Pasquale?" Tina replied for her.

"Of course she is, . . . don't you know Luigi's daughter when you see her? Who else would have those blue eyes?" Carlotina asked scornfully. Then, turning to Tina, "I expect you are hungry, a meal will soon be ready."

Saying, "Don't worry about me, I'm not so hungry that I can't wait until I get home," and trying to appear brighter than she felt, Tina gratefully took the chair that was offered.

"You can't go home tonight," Carlotina replied firmly, "you must stay here."

"Anyone about after sunset risks arrest. They say they will shoot anyone that runs." Pasquale explained.

"Then at least let me help," Tina pleaded, getting up from her chair.

"Sit down child, I don't need your help," Carlotina replied querulously as she threw a couple of handfuls of pasta in to a steaming pot that hung from a hook over the fire. Then, muttering, "I'm not a cripple yet," under her breath and ignoring the arthritis that filled every movement with pain, she bustled about preparing an extra place at the table.

As she watched Carlotina cut extra portions of bread from the huge home baked loaf and polished cherished glasses, normally only used for guests, the heat of the fire and the exertions of the day had their inevitable effect. Despite all her efforts to combat the growing drowsiness which beset her, Tina's eyelids drooped and her head nodded forward.

. . . .

Neither asleep, nor properly awake, Tina idly watched fine particles of dust dancing in the thin rays of sunlight which streamed through cracks in the wooden shutters at the window of her room and formed a criss cross pattern of light across the bed on which she lay.

At first she couldn't remember where she was, the matching jug and basin on a plain wooden table in the corner of the room, seemed out of place. She wondered if she was dreaming and pinched herself to see if she was. Tina had only seen one jug and basin set like that before, it was a wedding present, which stood on a marble topped wash-stand her mother had brought from England. Everything seemed strange. The plain rafters and bare roof tiles above her were unfamiliar, as also were the climbing boots hanging form their hook on the wall. As Tina looked at them, her gaze fell on a dust laden, worn feathered hat, lodged nonchalantly on the handle of a pick slung alongside the door and her memory flooded back. The Germans at the corner of her street. Pasquale's reference to a curfew. Carlo's grandmother, Carlotina, preparing a meal, which she couldn't recall eating.

"Of course! I'm in the home of Pasquale, . . . I remember now," she murmured, "he was a mountain guide when I was a little girl."

Thoroughly awake now, she swung herself out of bed and crossed to the table. There was water in the jug. 'What luxury,' she thought, splashing some sparingly into the basin.

Her face still wet and feeling wonderfully refreshed from her sleep, Tina descended the narrow stairs to the room below. Carlotina was busy making pasta. She stood in a shaft of sunlight which shone through the open door, casting her shadow over the table on which she worked and throwing into sharp relief the dark recesses in the corners of the room.

When Carlotina saw Tina, she stopped what she was doing and lifted a blackened pot from the embers of the smouldering fire.

"Do you like milk with your coffee?" she said, "your mother does," and cleared a space for two cups on the table.

Tina shook her head, she would have liked to say, plenty of sugar please, but knew how difficult it was to obtain.

As if reading her thoughts, Carlotina said,

"You like sugar - don't you?" Then, following up with, "I do and so does Carlo," she opened a wooden chest and produced a battered can, which she showed to Tina. Although almost empty she ladled two liberal spoons of sugar from it into each cup. "You must have sugar," she said with conviction, "it will make you strong."

Gratefully sipping the hot syrupy brew, Tina watched Carlotina hold a long knife by its ends and drag the sharp instrument towards her as she cut slices from the massive loaf balanced against her breast; but, it wasn't until she saw her pour olive oil over the bread and sprinkle it with rock salt that she realised how hungry she was.

"Where's Pasquale?" she asked glancing around the room, "I'd like to thank him before I go home."

A worried look flashed across Carlotina's face. Seating herself on the opposite side of the table; hesitating, before replying, she took hold of one of Tina's hands, gripping it tight with both of hers and said,

"You can't go home my dear, the Tedeschi are there."

Tina could feel Carlotina trembling and an icy chill clutched at her heart.

"What do you mean?" she replied, "Are the Tedeschi there?" and her voice quavered as some of Concertina's fear was transmitted to her. "What about Mama?"

"Your mother is safe, she is with your father . . . ."

"Where are they?" Tina cut in without waiting for Carlotina to finish what she was about to say.

"I don't know, Pasquale is meeting my grandson, . . . you know Carlo, don't you? . . . He will know where they are."

As Carlotina spoke, a shadow fell across the floor. Expecting to see Pasquale, Tina turned. In the doorway stood a German officer wearing lightweight battledress and a soft peaked hat. Behind him and to one side were two soldiers in similar dress. The officer, a tall, heavily built, man in his mid-thirties with stern eyes and a swarthy complexion had a pistol at his belt, but evidently didn't intend to use it because it remained in its holster. The two soldiers with him, who carried rifles slung from their shoulders, were little more than boys and Tina was relieved to note that they didn't appear to belong to one of the dreaded S.S. regiments. One of them smiled at her, rather shyly she thought, then, he blushed when she smiled back.

Speaking in impeccable Italian, the officer addressed himself to Carlotina, who had risen to her feet in alarm, knocking her chair over as she did so.

"Is this your house?" he asked, as he stooped to pick up the chair, then recognising the fear in her eyes, he added, "You have nothing to fear Mother, our war is not with women."

Something about the way he spoke, together with his unconscious courtesy, was reassuring and Carlotina's natural hospitality came to the fore. Despite her fear, she found herself saying, "Do come in. Stay a while and have some coffee," as she dragged chairs from under the table.

Motioning to the other two that they should stay outside the officer took a clip board from one of them and entered the tiny room. The door was so low he had to bend his knees and stoop to pass through. When he stood up inside, his head almost touched the rafters supporting the floor of the upper room. Tina didn't think she had ever seen such a tall man, not even her Uncle Charlie, from England, who had come on a visit to her home a short while before the war spoilt it all. Nodding his thanks, he said,

"I am the liaison officer for this garrison and am in charge of all billeting arrangements." Then, seated himself at the table and, introduced himself.

"My name is Schmidt. . . . Oberleutnant Schmidt. . . . I must ask you some questions. . . . Just your names and how many rooms you have to spare."

A suffocating silence followed his words as Carlotina stared unhappily at her unwanted guest. It lasted seconds only.

"Sit down Carlotina, I'll prepare fresh coffee for our guest." Tina's voice broke the silence which had seemed interminable.

"It is necessary for our records," the German added gently.

Carlotina nodded dumbly and tried to smile, but her fear was too great. She wished Pasquale was there to support and advise.

Having added coffee and water to the pot and blown the glowing embers into life with the aid of a long metal tube, Tina turned her attention to the newcomer. He looked uncomfortable, sitting as he was, askew at the table, one leg bent almost double with the foot tucked behind a leg of the chair; the other stretched before him, as he tried to accommodate his long legs.

Speaking in the local dialect she said to Carlotina, "It won't be long now, the water is almost boiling."

The oberleutnant eyed her suspiciously.

"What did you say?" he barked, jumping to his feet and bumping his head on the edge of a rafter that was lower than the rest.

"Nothing! . . . I only said the water is nearly boiling," Tina explained.

Hard pressed not to show her amusement she turned her back hoping that he would not see the laughter that was welling up inside her. Even so, she was unable to suppress the smothered giggle that came to the surface and it exploded in a snort.

"I suppose you think its funny." the oberleutnant grunted, trying to sound severe. Rubbing the spot ruefully he twisted the chair round and sat astride.

Somehow the incident cleared the air. Her eyes dancing with laughter Tina poured a cup of coffee and handed it to him.

"I shall have to watch these low ceilings," he said with a grin, as he took the cup from her, "are they all like this here?"

"Only in the older houses," Tina replied, "you speak very good Italian. Where did you learn it?"

Encouraged by her praise, he said,

"I learned your language a long time ago, when I studied art in Perugia," then, fumbled in his tunic pocket and brought out a small wallet containing a crumpled photograph of a woman with a little boy and a young girl at her side.

"I have two children a son and a *tochter*," he added, pointing proudly to his family and pausing as he sought for the correct word, "daughter, I mean, . . . she is about your age, - perhaps a bit younger, - fifteen, the boy is twelve."

Even before he put the cup to his lips, he knew he would not like the roasted acorn and grain substitute that served for coffee. Nevertheless, he drank it without comment. Politely refusing a second cup, he picked up the clip board and turned to Carlotina, who sat wide eyed opposite him,

"How many live here and what are their names?" he asked.

"No! - No!" she replied, "We are too confined here, there is no room for soldiers, we are old people and wouldn't be able to look after them."

There was the sound, almost of terror in her voice, which the oberleutnant was quick to recognise.

"Don't worry Mother," he said, "I can see that, just let me have your names." Turning his head, he clicked his fingers and called to the soldiers waiting outside, "*Kaffee, Zucker. - Schnell, schnell, bringen hier, - jetzt.*"

One of the soldiers, the one who had smiled at Tina, hurried in. Opening his haversack, he took out two packs and handed them to his officer.

The oberleutnant pushed them towards Carlotina and his eyes were smiling at her as he said,

"These are for you."

Suspicious of a motive behind the unexpected gift, the unhappy woman eyed the packages warily, gazed anxiously at Tina and pushed them aside."

"There are only two rooms here, this and the room upstairs," Tina volunteered.

"Where do you sleep then?"

Misinterpreting the intention of the question, Carlotina's anxiety for the safety of her young friend overcame her fear.

"She is too young," she protested indignantly, half rising to her feet.

"I don't live here, I come from another village across the valley," Tina replied, in answer to his question; wondering at the same time, 'who is the patron saint of fibbers?'

"Who lives here then?"

"Pasquale and Carlotina."

"What is the family name?"

"Bartolino."

The oberleutnant nodded and wrote something on his clip board, turned to the soldier who was still standing beside him (staring sheepishly at Tina) and waved him curtly outside.

Risking his officer's displeasure, the soldier dallied a moment while he gave Tina a last lingering look then hurriedly obeyed.

Watching him go, Tina couldn't help feeling sorry for him. He seemed so like the young and inexperienced lads she knew, it didn't seem possible that he was an enemy. 'He should have been a girl,' she thought, 'with those long blond eye-lashes.' Then, promptly forgot him as she turned to the oberleutnant, who had risen to his feet and was cautiuously avoiding the rafters as he made his way to the door.

. . . .

The mid morning sun barely penetrated the mist that lingered around the cave entrance as Pasquale approached it. In the town now far below he knew, that despite the chill in the light breeze signalling the approach of winter, humidity would make the heat oppressive, as the bleached walls of the houses reflected the sun's rays into the narrow streets. He took a deep breath of the crisp mountain air, filling his lungs to capacity and relishing the exhilarating sense of well-being it gave him, he murmured, "I'm lucky to be so fit at eighty that I can still do this; and enjoy it." A tinge of sadness crossed his features as he gazed at the tall peaks beyond the valley and reality came to him that he would never scale their lofty heights again.

Shrugging the mood off, Pasquale entered the cave. With the exception of a table, it was empty. He had expected to see Carlo there, but there was no sign of him. Thinking maybe he was too early, he pulled a huge turnip watch out of his pocket by the piece of string that kept it safe, then went to the entrance of the cave where he could see it better. The hands stood at a few minutes past ten. Satisfied that he was neither early nor late, Pasquale wandered along the path leading to the higher slopes.

Carlo was found sheltering from the wind, on a ledge above the belt of mist; he looked tired and was dozing in the warmth of the sun. Taking care not to startle him, Pasquale approached quietly.

"Carlo," he called softly, "why were you not in the cave as arranged?"

Carlo looked at him out of eyes, red from the lack of sleep.

"I must have dropped off," he said. "Is Tina safe?"

"You were supposed to be watching, where were you?"

Carlo flushed. "I was watching." there was a hint of resentment in his voice as he said it. "She came on a different path to the one I expected and I was too far off to intercept. . . . Even though I hurried down the short route I couldn't get down in time."

Pasquale gave him a long stern look, he knew the route Carlo' meant. While admiring the lad's courage, he didn't like the word hurried.

"That was very foolish. . . . If you still want to be a guide when this war is finished, you must learn not to take silly risks when people are depending on you."

Close to tears and smarting under the rebuke Carlo replied,

"I didn't know what to do, she was moving so quickly and I was such a long way up . . ." Carlo's eyes felt like dry balls of fire and there was a great lump in his throat which prevented him completing what he was about to say.

"That is a very dangerous route and should never be hurried, if you had fallen, you wouldn't have been much use," Pasquale explained, putting and arm round Carlo's shoulder and speaking gently, "come now, you know I'm right, let's not be silly,"

Carlo knew Pasquale could be harsh and very strict regarding safety in the mountains. He also knew he deserved the criticism. Seething with frustration and embarrassed by the show of affection, he was horribly conscious of his tender years and ashamed of his lack of manliness. It made him angry with himself; so angry that it showed in his tone of voice when he blurted,

"Leave me alone Nonno, you don't know what it was like." Instantly repentant yet stubbornly determined not to admit it, he glared at his grandfather.

Pasquale regarded him solemnly. Many years spent training would be climbers had made him wise in the ways of young men and boys approaching puberty; he ignored the outburst and waited for Carlo to speak.

Eventually the young lad dropped his eyes.

"I felt so helpless, watching Tina enter the town like that; knowing there was nothing I could do. . . . The thought of her falling into the hands of the Tedeschi kept me awake all night."

"Don't worry, she spent the night with us, . . . the poor child was so worn out I had to carry her upstairs, . . . Carlotina put her in our bed."

Carlo smiled momentarily in relief and managed to say,

"She is safe, you have seen her."

Then, the combination of relief and the strain of the night took affect. Carlo's legs turned to jelly and a fleeting wave of dizziness swept over him. He could hear Pasquale's voice in the distance and was vaguely aware that he had sat down and strong hands were pushing his head down between his legs.

"Are you alright Son?"

The robust climbing boots Pasquale was wearing seemed to swell in size as they swam before Carlo's eyes, then returned to normal as his vision cleared.

"I'm alright now," he gasped.

Pasquale brought Carlo to an upright position and offered him his flask.

Feeling something of a fool, nothing like this had ever happened to him before, Carlo took the flask. The cool water it contained refreshed him and he conjured up a weak smile.

Pasquale looked at him anxiously, placed the back of his hand on his forehead and nodded sagely.

"Better get some sleep Son, you will be safe in the cave. Have you eaten?"

Carlo shook his head, "Not since Wednesday.... I thought Tina would be coming back straight away, so only carried food for the one day."

Despite a mild flash of annoyance because Carlo had not prepared himself for any unexpected delay, Pasquale made no comment, he said instead,

"I must go now, your grandmother will be worrying if I'm away too long," then took a hard bread roll from his haversack and gave it to Carlo," I'll leave you this, ... have you water?"

Carlo pointed to the water flask swinging from his belt, shook it and said,

"Yes, plenty here."

"That's alright then, make sure you eat that bread and get some sleep, Tina will bring some food and prepare a proper meal for you when she comes."

"Did she say anything about going to her station? . . . Luigi was particularly worried about that," Carlo asked, instinctively lowering his voice as he spoke.

"No! But then she wouldn't know that I know about her work, would she?"

"I suppose not. Tell her Luigi's instructions are that she is to come to me at the cave, without deviation. . . . She will understand."

. . . .

It was turned two in the afternoon when Tina left the town and descended a narrow path down the cliff like face of the mountain. The load of neatly ironed washing in the round wicker basket, which she carried on her head, attracted little or no attention from the busy German soldiers as they bustled about their duties. On reaching a stone figure of the Madonna, staring over the valley from a recess hewn out of the rock, she curtsied as was her wont and spared a few moments to render her thanks that no one had detained her with awkward questions about what she was carrying and where she was going.

Nearby was an old abandoned house she remembered from childhood days as a place to meet her friends, it was their special place and they called it 'La Tana[15]'.

Driven by a nostalgic urge, Tina quickened her pace as the derelict building came into view. Although it was many years since she had been there, it was much as she recalled it. Uncared for walls, cracked by some long forgotten earthquake and weakened further by the rains which had soaked between sun bleached stones; now mellowed by the plant life growing from their crevices. The rest, little more than a pile of rubble beneath the sky.

Then, it was a place to hide and play. Now, creatures came through the open doors to search for delicacies in the rubbish people dumped there and the one time food and wine store had become a refuge for all manner of wild life. Plants, nourished by the rain which found its way from time to time through the disconnected tiles, sprouted in profusion from the floor, their flowers reminiscent of a florist's display in their variety. Tomatoes and pepperoni grew in abundance as their unharvested fruits fell each year, to rot and give life again with their seed, bursting asunder the paving of the floor with their

---

[15] The den.

vigour. Here and there, grain, without any hope of reaching maturity thrust their near white spikes towards the roof as they strove to find the sun; their knee high stems resembling a miniature forest.

Tina paused at the place that did for a doorway. The arch of the opening was still there, seemingly supported by an ancient vine which grew at its base. She looked in dismay at the mass of spines that barred her way. Beyond the thickly growing brambles she could just see the broken door of the store, standing ajar. Tina knew it would take more than two hours longer if she used the easy, winding route to the cave, she also knew that it was impossible to negotiate the difficult ledge leading to the rift which hid the cave's entrance with a basket balanced on her head. The intention had been to carry the food, which was hidden beneath the washing, in a back-pack, and hide the basket and its contents in the old food and wine store where it was unlikely to be spotted. Pasquale could then retrieve it without returning to the cave. The idea had seemed to be a good one, but they had not reckoned on the problem that now faced her.

Even though it was unlikely that anyone would steal it, Tina was reluctant to leave Carlotina's basket with its precious load outside the store, in a place, where, if Pasquale could see it others could too. Reasoning that if she could get into the upper room it would be safe until she could find a way of letting Pasquale know where it was, she made her way to the rear of the house. The balcony that she had thought of hung at a grotesque angle from brackets rusted with age and barely gripping the wall. As soon as Tina saw the balcony, she realised that it was hopeless. Even without the rampant growth of brambles pushing up between the rotting timbers of the collapsed stairway that had once hugged the wall, any attempt to mount the balcony would be courting disaster.

Disappointed she returned to the entrance and tried to force her way through the prickly growth to the store. Her efforts were in vain, legs and arms sorely scratched, her bare feet bleeding from the attempt, she was forced to retreat.

By the time Tina reached the gentle slope a kilometre above the entrance to the cave, it was dark. The overcast sky didn't permit even the smallest ray of the still thin moon to relieve the blackness of the night. Suddenly as she started the descent the sky cleared. Across the valley the sharp outline of distant hills, etched on a star studded sky, lent a velvet quality to the night that was almost magic.

Only when she paused to check that she was on the right path did Tina notice how much her feet were hurting her. The near freezing temperatures biting into the cuts she had sustained made every step an agony. Shivering in the chill mountain breeze which battered her face and penetrated her clothing, she drew her thin home knitted cardigan closer to her body. Eager now, to reach the warmth of the cave where she guessed Carlo would have built a fire, Tina hurried forward.

Carlo was waiting near the entrance to the cave and peering anxiously in the opposite direction when Tina rounded a bend and saw him. At first, because he was wearing a German trench coat he had found on a dump in the cave, she thought it was a German standing there and froze where she stood.

Despite her silent approach, Carlo heard her and spun round, his hand dropping nervously on the butt of a pistol Il Tiranno had given him.

"That is not a toy, keep it hidden and only use it if you have to," the sergeant major had warned him as, watched by the worried eyes of Luigi, he left the comparative safety of the house where the Alpini captain had taken Pamella.

When Carlo saw who it was approaching, he relaxed and his usual joyful grin spread across his features.

"Illo! Ow erre iu?" he greeted her, unable to resist the temptation to air his scant knowledge of English.

"OK." Tina replied and smiled in acknowledgement. Even to her, Carlo's pronunciation sounded strange.

Carlo moved forward to relieve her of her basket. As he embraced her the smile faded and a look of concern took its place. Reverting to Italian he removed the coat he was wearing and saying, "you are so cold, put this on," he draped it round her shoulders.

"It's only a few yards," she protested.

"Do it up properly," Carlo insisted, securing the top button for her, "here let me do it, keep your arms warm inside."

Inside the cave the heat of a fire set Tina's feet and fingers throbbing as they thawed out. Carlo looked at her and laughed, although taller than Tina, he was not a big lad, so it was not surprising that if the coat was too large for him, on her diminutive figure it was immense. She looked ridiculous, just standing there, as she was, in the flickering light of the flames; empty sleeves hanging down below her knees and a pistol protruding from one of the pockets of the coat.

"You should see yourself," Carlo spluttered.

Tina looked down the double row of robust buttons and giggled. The coat almost touched the floor and the tips of her toes, could only just be seen peeping out from beneath the hem.

Laughing together in unison, they felt close to each other, for a fleeting moment the brother and sister relationship that had always been there became something more intimate. The laughter died on their lips and Carlo looked away. Embarrassed by what he had felt and afraid she would laugh at him if she knew, he stirred the embers of the fire. Then, pretended to clear twigs away from the rocks, which he had put in position to support a cauldron, that had taken him most of the afternoon to fill with water. The place he had collected the water from was high up a crevice and he had painstakingly climbed there several times to fill his water bottle from a spring that was little more than a trickle.

"I feel warmer now," Tina said soberly, fumbling with fingers still numb with the cold as she struggled with buttons that seemed too large for their holes,

"Can you help me undo these?"

Carlo nodded, but, afraid now to speak, lest, by doing so he would reveal the unexplained surge of tenderness that had beset him, said nothing as he undid the buttons for her.

The coat, now neatly folded on Carlo's bed roll, Tina started to unpack her basket. Under the fascinated gaze of Carlo she produced olive oil, tomato purée, pasta, ready cut in the form known as tagliatelli, and dried bacon.

Overcoming his earlier reluctance to speak, Carlo said.

"No wonder that basket was so heavy. How much more do you have in there?"

Tina laughed happily, gaily waved a bottle of wine in the air, and said,

"Only this and some salad.

"Pasquale said you would prepare a proper meal, but I hadn't expected all this, Carlo said, his mouth watering from the thought of the meal he would soon be enjoying.

"Well he did hint that you hadn't eaten properly for several days and Carlotina reckons you have a good appetite."

"What are you going to do with her basket?"

"I shall leave it here for Pasquale to pick up." Tina replied, "When Pasquale sees the state of the place I was going to leave it, he will guess I will have brought it here."

"It's not far to the house where your mother is and the route is an easy one from here, paths all the way, so we could take it with us tomorrow. . . . If you like, I could easily take it back to my grandmother from there."

Tina just managed to smother a giggle, the idea of Carlo strolling into Santa Stefano, with a basket of laundry balanced on his head amused her.

"I could take it back to Carlotina myself. Once Mama knows I'm safe, she won't mind." she suggested.

"Then I'll come with you."

Tina looked at Carlo in surprise, he had spoken so emphatically.

"No you mustn't, it isn't necessary and is much too dangerous for you." Tina warned. "Anyway, if you come with me Mama will think it's too dangerous and start worrying again,"

"Don't look so worried, I'm not silly. I won't stay long." came the instant reply. "Pamella will be happier if you stay with her."

"But if the Tedeschi see you . . . ."

Carlo laughed, "Silly girl, they are not a problem, you forget, I'm not of military age, . . . it's only dangerous at night because of the curfew. . . . In any case I have to go, I promised Pasquale that when I had delivered you safely, I would let him know how we got on." Then, put a tentative hand on her arm and added, "There's no good reason for you to take the risk of coming with me."

Tina wanted to return to Santa Stefano, preferably alone. Francesco, the Leaf man, she acted as courier for, was also an escort for the evasion group and she was worried about a rumour Pasquale had passed on to her just before she left his house.

It seemed there was talk that the Germans had raided a house in the forward area and had taken away a party of prisoners of war. The guide escorting them was being held by the Gestapo and the people living in the house, which had been burned to the ground, had been shot and left hanging in a tree as a warning. Inevitably the thought came into her head, that it could be the party that Alan and Paul should have been with, but as far as she knew, they should have been with Topo and he had left without a guide. Beset by a nagging worry, that it could be one of the other contacts she worked with, she wanted an opportunity to visit her station to see if any of them had left their sign for her; but the subtle note of authority that had crept into Carlo's voice deterred her. Reasoning that once she had seen her mother, she would have no difficulty in finding a chance to slip away, she held her tongue.

"We'll have to do something about those feet before we leave tomorrow. What possessed you to come here bare-footed?" Carlo asked.

"I didn't have much option."

"Why was that?"

Tina smiled and shrugged her shoulders, she felt a little flattered by his obvious concern, but was careful not to reveal it when she said,

"It's an easy walk to La Villa and I move quicker without shoes, so didn't wear any, didn't Pasquale tell you? . . . He stopped me and dragged me into his house before I reached my home. So, I didn't have a chance to pick up a pair." Tina smiled again as she spoke; it sent Carlo's heart racing once more, but he managed to say,

"Well yes, he did say something about it, but as it's a long way to La Villa, I'm surprised you didn't take any shoes with you."

"I didn't think I would need them." Tina replied.

Carlo looked at her feet disapprovingly. He felt protective towards her. 'She could have found some before coming up here,' he thought, 'why didn't she ask my Nonna?'

"I asked Carlotina if she had anything I could borrow, but the only footwear she had were zoccolli[16]." It was as if she had read his thoughts, "Wooden sandals like that are worse than useless in the mountains."

An echo of Pasquale's oft repeated words, '*take no chances in the mountains, be prepared for any eventuality,*' sounded in Carlo's brain, but he hesitated to voice them. Instead, he said,

---

[16] Wooden type of sandal

"Never mind, it can't be helped, but you can't walk bare-foot with cut feet. There's an old haversack on the dump where I found the coat. After we've eaten, I will make some temporary shoes from it for you. They won't be strong, but they will be better than nothing."

Replete after their meal, the two sat side by side, sharing a blanket before the fire, just watching the flames and the showers of sparks that leaped from the embers when a log fell into them.

They must have sat like that, without speaking a word, for over an hour before Carlo broke the silence with,

"That was a good meal, but it's made me lazy, . . . I must start making those shoes now"

Gratified by the implied praise of her cooking, Tina smiled, stretched luxuriously and said,

"It wasn't much, I expect it tasted better because you were hungry."

Resisting a sudden urge to kiss her, Carlo rose to his feet and moved away from the fire. He was surprised how stiff he had become, just sitting still.

"While you are doing that I'll clean up the pots" Tina said.

"Before you start, come here." Carlo's tone of voice was almost an order.

Tina looked at him, he was rummaging in a pile of discarded equipment, that had been left in the cave, and breathed a sigh of relief. He had sounded so commanding. Remembering that electric moment earlier she had been hoping he wasn't going to become sentimental and spoil their friendship.

Totally unaware of what Tina had been thinking, Carlo grinned happily and beckoned her over,

"This should do the trick," he said, pulling out the haversack he was seeking.

Tina regarded both haversack and Carlo dubiously, but went to him as asked, she couldn't imagine how he could make shoes without tools.

"Put your foot on there," he said in the same commanding tone.

As he spoke, Carlo pointed to the flap of the haversack, which he was opening out on to the floor of the cave. Then, holding her foot firmly in place, he deftly scored round it with a piece of dead ember. As he did so, he remembered how ticklish she was and the fun they had had together when children because of it. With a mischievous grin, he tried to raise the foot, but Tina was too quick for him, she had seen his impish look and guessed what he was about to do.

"Oh no you don't!" she said with a laugh as she pulled her foot sharply away from him and retreated behind the table.

Carlo looked at her in mock amazement.

"What do you mean? . . . Oh no you don't! . . . What did you think I was going to do?" he asked innocently.

"You know very well," Tina replied with a giggle.

"Come back, I need to get some more measurements," Carlo urged.

Her eyes, now bright with laughter, she shook her head and started to tidy the table.

If he was disappointed, Carlo didn't show it. Settling down before the fire, he busied himself, patiently drawing the thick thread from the seams of the haversack with the point of his knife.

It didn't take Tina long to wash the few dishes there were and pack them away in the basket, ready for their departure in the morning. When she had finished, she filled both Carlo's and her own water bottle, and tipped the remainder of the water into the cauldron. Satisfied there was nothing more useful that she could do, she settled down beside Carlo and made herself comfortable while she watched him work. After a few moments, she could stand what she was seeing no longer.

"If you use that knife you'll cut the thread," she said with a laugh, "here give it to me, I'm used to that sort of work." As she spoke, she dived into one of the capacious pockets of her skirt, drew out a small khaki holdall and showed it to him, "Paul gave this to me, he said it was called a 'Hussiv' and that I would have more use for it than he would."

Inside the House-wife, or 'Hussiv,' as soldiers usually called it, were some darning needles, a pair of sharp pointed scissors and a bodkin, any wool or cotton thread that might have been there, was long since gone.

"I wish I'd known you had them," Carlo said, watching the expert way she was undoing the stitches and drawing out the thread, "I will need about two metres more."

"I doubt whether these needles will be strong enough to sew that heavy canvas," she said, eyeing the material Carlo had in his hand.

"No sewing will be necessary," he grunted in reply as he moved over to the table, "I need that thread to make laces."

Tina nodded her understanding and said, "OK! When I have enough, I'll twist it up for you."

Working in the dim light thrown by the fire, Carlo swiftly cut out the shapes he wanted.

"Try these for size," he called out triumphantly, placing the pieces he had prepared on the floor. "You had better make the holes for the laces, you'll know where you need them."

Tina looked at them with interest. Except that the bodies were fashioned in the shape and size of her foot, they looked more like two ginger bread men than footwear.

"I think I can see how to use them, but will they stay in place without a loop for the toe?" she asked with a puzzled frown.

Carlo placed his foot on one of the pieces of canvas. "They should do. . . . I'll show you. First, you have to cross these two straps behind your heel, then bring them up round your ankle," he said, demonstrating what he meant, "you can fasten them in front with a lace."

"That's what I thought, the other two straps come over the foot behind the toes, I suppose." Tina said, stretching out a hand to take one of the make-shift sandals.

"That's right, . . . I could make toe loops, but they wouldn't last long and you wouldn't be able to wrap your feet in this," Carlo replied, picking up a remnant of blanket, and adding, "you will need something to stop the straps rubbing on those cuts."

Even though the shepherd's couch made from young branches with their foliage still on them was comfortable to lie on, sleep wouldn't come to Tina. She spent most of the night staring at the slowly dying embers and listening to the soft rustle of Carlo's breathing behind the contrived screen he had erected. When, at last, she did manage to doze, the rumour, Pasquale had related to her, crept back into her mind and she found herself wide awake once more. Try as she might to dispel the recurring thoughts, she couldn't help wondering whether it was Topo's or Francesco's guide that was being held by the Gestapo and wished that she had checked her station before coming to the cave. The icy fear that clutched at her heart every time she thought of the possibility, and the terrible consequences if the Gestapo forced him to talk filled her with foreboding, making the hours of darkness seem much longer than usual.

'If only Carlo was awake,' she thought, 'he would talk to me and take my mind off things.'

. . . .

"That house jutting out below the overhang is where we are going," Carlo said, pointing to a house half-way up the opposite side of a narrow gorge. "it's an easy path to the bottom. The stream down there is not deep, but be careful as we cross this scree, there is nothing to stop you if you slip."

The house blended so well into the background that Tina had difficulty in seeing it from where they were standing; at the top of a pebble strewn slope that lay between them and the edge of the gorge.

Climbing the gently ascending path on the opposite side of the gorge, Tina realised, as she became closer, why the house had been almost invisible when viewed from the bottom of the gorge. The builder had used irregular shaped blocks of rock hewn from the area. From where she was now walking, the house was difficult to see. Were it not for the wisp of grey smoke issuing from a rusty iron pipe protruding from the narrow, steep roof, it would have seemed to be part of the cliff like face; against which it was built. Even the heavy wooden door, with its rusting hinges and the shutters at the windows were of a similar colour.

Some sixth sense must have told Pamella that her daughter was approaching. She was at the doorway, the ladle she had been using to serve the mid-day meal still in her hand, when Tina, a few steps ahead of Carlo in her eagerness to be re-united with her mother, came into view.

CHAPTER NINE

The deep cleft between Giorgio's eyes seemed more pronounced than usual as he waited on a damp woodland path below La Villa. He hadn't seen Filomena since the night Michele had taken her home on the back of Nove and he was beginning to wonder whether her damaged ankle was giving so much pain that she was unable to make her usual trip to the fountain.

'Perhaps Angelo has been fetching the water,' Giorgio mused, but immediately dismissed the thought as unlikely. 'If she couldn't get there,' he told himself, "now that Angelo knows that she is also involved with the movement, she would have either asked her father to check or asked him to leave her silver birch leaf in the usual place. Either way, she would have found a way of letting me know.'

Then he saw her. She looked lovely with her rich chestnut hair peeping from beneath the edge of a green bandanna; the high-lights scintillating in the bright morning sun. But he saw none of this. All he saw was his courier walking along the main track just below him.

Stepping from his place of concealment, he called softly to her,

"I'm here."

She turned sharply, as if taken by surprise, and peered in his general direction. Relieved, he hurried forward to meet her and said,

"I had almost given you up."

For a moment she appeared bewildered, then smiling charmingly at him, said,

"Were we supposed to meet? . . . There was no signal at the fountain."

Even then, when she smiled so charmingly at him, he didn't notice her beauty.

"I left it the night before last," he said in a matter of fact voice. "Originally I wanted to give you the news about Gianni. Then this other matter cropped up and it became important that I see you a.s.a.p. When you didn't come yesterday I began to worry and checked the fountain. The leaf had gone and I assumed you had taken it, so didn't come to your house."

"It must have got washed away with all that rain."

"It doesn't matter, you're here now. It goes to show though that one should never leave things to chance." Then, he added almost as an afterthought. "How's your ankle?"

"Oh, it's fine now." Filomena replied, "Vincensina came round, she really is a kind soul, wouldn't let me do anything about the house." Her eyes sparkled, "I had to get up extra early so that . . ."

Filomena never completed what she was about to say, Giorgio's finger on her lips stopped her in mid sentence. He had caught a glimpse, through a break in the trees, of someone approaching a bend in the track, a scant ten metres from where he and Filomena stood. So close, they could hear the footsteps. Hoping they had not been seen, he pulled Filomena away from the track and hid her behind a tree.

"Quick, put your arm round my neck," he whispered as he leant his body against the trunk and brought his face near to hers, to make it seem they were lovers. "Keep your face hidden. If it is that Sicilian, I don't want him to see you with me. I am sure he is a German spy and I believe he's been watching me." Then, added, "The unfortunate end of Francesco's last trip does seem to indicate that the Tedeschi are getting information of our movements."

As Giorgio drew Filomena to him and the warmth of his body permeated her clothing, a sensation akin to fear jolted her heart. It only lasted a moment, but it was enough to set her pulse racing. Remembering the last time they had met, how he had been at her home, when she returned from visiting Michele on the day she twisted her ankle. How he had lifted her down from Nove with his arm round her waist and the secret pleasure she had felt, she closed her eyes, less they betray her.

With bated breath, they waited until the distinctive sound of zoccolli faded into the distance. Only when the silence seemed complete did Giorgio speak.

"Whoever it was must have gone by now," he whispered in Filomena's ear, "do you think we were seen?"

Filomena shook her head and said,

"I don't know, I couldn't see, but I think, from the sound of those footsteps, there were two people. Whoever they were, they passed straight by." As she spoke a peal of boisterous laughter came loud and clear to their ears. Then there was only the faint rustle of leaves, disturbed by a light breeze, to break the silence of the forest.

"There's no mistaking that laugh. It has to be Donnina. I expect she's taking something down to Ernesto. It's about the right time."

"It certainly sounded like her," Giorgio agreed softly. "stay here a moment while I check."

"Safer if I go," Filomena replied, regarding him out of sombre eyes, "that laughter sounded like Donnina, but we can't be sure."

Giorgio was reluctant to let her go. He knew what she said made sense, yet, if the Sicilian was about and had seen him, it would be foolish to let her increase the risk of being seen and recognised.

Filomena must have read his thoughts. Resisting a sudden impulse to kiss him, she slipped gently out of his arms and said,

"Don't be silly. I live here, people are used to seeing me around." Then skipped smartly on to the path, before he could stop her,

"I can just see them, one is definitely Donnina, and I think the other is Concetta," she called back a few minutes later. Then, as he moved towards her, added, "They have always been friends, but since Gianni started courting Carina they have been seeing quite a lot of each other. You know how it is, a common interest and fond hopes of wedding bells with joint grandchildren to follow."

Giorgio moved silently towards her.

"Don't come any further," Filomena cautioned as he came in to view. "Someone has just come in sight, it looks like the Sicilian. but I can't be sure, he is half hidden by the trees. Stay hidden. I'll walk up the path towards him, as if I am on my way home, and wait for you where the path forks. You can join me there after he has passed on his way."

Suiting her action to her words, Filomena stooped and pretended to remove something from between her toes before starting to walk up the path. Coming abreast, she murmured a brief "Buon giorno" and resisting the temptation to look back, continued on her way.

"You said you hadn't seen my signal, so it's fortunate you came by," Giorgio said, handing her two envelopes, as he rejoined her. "There is no time to lose. We had planned a crossing for tomorrow night, but have decided in the light of recent events to cancel the planned trip. It has also been decided that there will be no more trips until the spring. The new route could be blocked by snow any day now. The usual information about the men who were to form the party are in Tina's envelope. . . . We don't want them assembled unnecessarily, so make sure you deliver the one marked with a cross tomorrow, Tina will know who to give it to. The other envelope must be with Favilla today."

Filomena took the envelopes and turned modestly while she hid them in a special pocket inside her skirt. "Were you going?" she asked, her eyes clouding with anxiety as she turned again to face him and without waiting for an answer, added, "Did the Sicilian, see you?"

Giorgio shook his head and ignoring the first question replied,

"No! I don't think so."

"You said you had news of Gianni."

"That's right. He is safe; he was involved in a skirmish with a German patrol and the group he was with had to retreat deep into the mountains. His wound is very nearly healed..." Giorgio started to tell Filomena but she cut in with,

"What wound? We haven't heard anything of him since he went off with Donnola."

"I haven't seen him myself, but according to Luigi, he is with the same sisters of mercy that are taking care of Francesco.... The wound Francesco sustained when the Tedeschi captured his party, was not as serious as we first thought, but it was bad enough to stop him from walking for a while. It is very nearly healed and he is improving every day. Guido, might be small, but he is surprisingly strong. He carried Francesco, who is by no means slim to a safe place of hiding, then, all the way to the convent."

"Which Guido was being used? All the guides use that name. Was it Gino?"

"No! I don't know if you have met him. So, it's best if you don't know his real name."

Filomena was not disappointed by the apparent lack of trust; she knew it was normal so made no comment. Nothing was said for a few minutes, as they made their way along the path, then, she broke the silence with,

"I must let Donnina know Gianni is safe. I would like to let her know now, but we know she isn't at home and I have Favilla's letter to deliver, so I'll go tomorrow morning."

Giorgio suppressed a smile. She looked so concerned.

"I doubt whether you will have time," he said in a tone that was unusually gentle.

"But the sooner Doninna knows, the better," Filomena protested. "It's not far out of the way and I can pop in tomorrow morning before going to Santa Stefano."

Giorgio allowed himself one of his rare smiles and said,

"Don't worry, Gianni will be home tomorrow or the next day at the latest. I want to see you early tomorrow. Can you be here by six?" Then, without waiting for a reply continued with, "I have to make contact with one of our agents at nine o'clock tomorrow morning. As you will have to leave in the dark, if you are going to get to Tina before it gets dark again, it makes sense if someone is with you. No matter what occurs, you must not enter Santa Stefano after sundown, it is virtually a German garrison now, and there is a curfew at night. While we are walking, I can tell you how to locate the house where Tina is staying." He paused a moment, gazed at the sky, and said, "By the look of the sky, we'll have snow tomorrow or the next day. The sooner you get back here the better. Make sure you have decent footwear."

Filomena hadn't expected to see him again so soon and her heart was playing tricks. She wished she could tell him she would be counting the minutes. Eyes sparkling with the new found happiness bubbling inside her and barely trusting herself to speak, she replied,

"Of course I can."

. . . .

It hadn't been an easy life for Concetta. Having lost her husband, Giuseppe, in Abyssinia, while her child was still at school, she was left to bring up Carina on her own. Somehow, she eked out a living, baking traditional cakes for sale in the market on Sunday and helping with the washing of her more fortunate friends, who, despite their own poverty, were happy to be of assistance. If selling her cakes on a Sunday meant she had to miss Mass, then, so be it. She felt in her heart and truly believed that God would forgive her, providing she never forgot to say her prayers in the evening.

Concetta was a stern looking woman, whose expression hid a kindly nature. Despite the passage of years, she still grieved over her lost love, a grief that manifested itself by the frequency that his name came up in conversation.

Carina's lack of her usual bounce didn't go without notice by Concetta, who wisely said nothing, guessing that the reason for her daughter's lack lustre was the missing Gianni. She prayed that history would not repeat itself; that Gianni would re-appear safe and well. No matter how she tried, she couldn't get Nonna Ricci's rumour of a battle between a German Patrol and a group of rebels out of her mind. The words, *"All the rebels were killed,"* haunted her and wouldn't go away

Thinking back to Carina's childhood days, how upset she could be when one of her precious turkeys was killed or sold; how it was always her favourite bird, only reminded Concetta how sensitive her daughter was; she knew, only too well how hard Carina would suffer if the unthinkable had happened.

The sun had only just risen, painting the sky red, when Concetta looked out of the door on a crisp December morning. 'Could be rain or even snow,' she thought as she looked about her. There was no sign of Carina. Then, she noticed the basket of washing was missing.

"Dear child," she murmured to herself, "she is good to me. She will be down at the stream, making sure she gets there before I do." Then smiled and thought, 'Doing the wash, which will include her hair. I never knew a girl wash her hair as often as she does. I wonder how she would manage if that little waterfall wasn't there. I must go down and give her a hand.'

Dipping the contents of her basket into the water, Carina bent resolutely to the task, beating the clothing on one of several large flat stones, worn smooth by countless previous washes.

Absorbed in her task, Carina wouldn't have been aware that her mother was approaching, were it not for a small noise. A crisp sound, faint, but distinct which came from the path above her, as if to warn her somebody was coming and would see her hair wet and in disarray. Reluctantly she set about braiding two thick plaits, her nimble fingers dexterously forming the silken tresses into a bun. By the time the newcomer arrived the corners of her bandanna were firmly knotted under her chin, imprisoning the natural beauty of her hair within its ample folds.

Still slight of build, except for the stern expression, Concetta was not unlike an older edition of her daughter. There was no mistaking who Carina's mother was, the resemblance was so strong. Were it not for the age difference, they could have been mistaken for twin sisters. So strong, that even in this place of intermingling families, it was remarked on by all that knew them. But, the similarity didn't end there, Carina had also inherited her mother's determination.

Seeing the young girl, bent and engrossed in her task, the damp patch in her bandanna betraying the still wet hair beneath, Concetta smiled indulgently.

"How the years have passed," she murmured to herself.

Memories of long ago, of a young Giuseppe Tocco who had courted her at this very spot; by the waterfall, flashed through her mind, and her eyes softened tenderly as she recalled those happy days.

Hearing the approach of her mother, Carina turned and managed a woeful smile,

"Hallo Mama, I beat you to it, there is only this blouse to do now and I will be finished."

Carina's damp eyes didn't go without notice, but Concetta made no comment, she knew a display of sympathy could have the wrong affect. She said instead,

"Hallo darling, you are good to me. I am going to the church presently and I thought you might like to come with me."

Carina looked at her in surprise. Her mother never went to the church during the day. On the rare occasions that she felt the need, it was always in the evening.

"We could light a couple of candles and ask Don Umberto to pray with us for the safe return of Gianni," Concetta said.

"Oh Mama! What a lovely idea, of course I want to come. The turkeys won't mind going out a bit late. They will be happy enough if I throw them a few scraps before we leave."

Concetta couldn't repress a little smile as she thought, 'how typical of her to think of her turkeys.'

Dipping the remaining garment hurriedly into the water, Carina wrung it out and with almost indecent haste scrambled up the bank to her mother.

On reaching the house, Carina, helped by Concetta, soon had the washing hung along a line. Then, it took just a minute to change her dress for the one she used on special occasions.

"Are you ready then?" Concetta said, as Carina appeared in the doorway.

Carina was pleased to see that her Mother had also changed out of her everyday work clothes and with a now radiant smile, said,

"Let's go."

When they arrived at the little church above the village, Don Umberto's perpetua[17] was busy cleaning between the aisles.

"Is Don Umberto here?" Concetta asked

"Yes," came the reply. "God bless you, I will fetch him."

They only had a few minutes to wait before Don Umberto appeared in the doorway. Adjusting his surplice as he came forward to greet them, he said,

"God bless you my children, what brings you here?" Then, turning to Concetta. "We don't see you very often. Have you come to confess?"

Concetta was used to the comment from Don Umberto, she felt she had nothing that needed confessing, so ignored the question and said instead,

"We want to light some candles and ask you to pray with us for the safe..."

"Return of Gianni," Don Umberto finished for her. There was very little in his parish that escaped his notice. "Be assured, God will listen to your plea."

Taking two tapers from a container, Don Umberto gave Concetta and Carina one each and waving aside Concetta's offer of payment, led the way to a pew and said,

"Light your candles and let us pray."

The sun, which now had an angry look about it, was high in the sky, when, feeling refreshed and uplifted by their prayers and the counselling given by Don Umberto, Concetta and Carina left the church.

Looking at the sky, Concetta said,

"Mark my words, we will have snow before the day is out." As Concetta spoke, a cold blast of wind stirred the leaves of the trees, penetrating their thin clothing. "Better get a move on," she added, "we have work to do and you will have to get in to something a bit warmer, than that pretty dress."

Carina gave her mother a quick hug, and said,

---

[17] Housekeeper for the clergy.

"I know Mama, thank you for taking me to the church. Umba, (it was her name, from childhood days, for Don Umberto) was so kind and understanding."

"He's a good man." was Concetta's only comment.

As they entered the top end of the village, unseen by them, a figure, with one arm in a sling, emerged from the heavily wooded area above the church.

Hurrying down the steep path that led to the village, Gianni was just in time to see Concetta and Carina disappear into the cluster of houses below.

Eager to catch them up, he lengthened his stride and nearly came to grief on the wet grass, when he tried to take a short cut which avoided the curve of the path he was following.

Perhaps it was some sixth sense, or maybe, just good fortune, that although Concetta had changed into her every day clothes when Gianni knocked on their door, Carina still wore her pretty frock when she opened it. Her first words were,

"Oh Gianni! What have you done to your arm?"

Uncaring, that Gianni's clothes were mud spattered, Carina returned his close embrace, burying her face in his neck as she tried to convince herself that he really was there, that he was in her arms; that he was safe. Unable to control herself, she cried out,

"Thank you God, thank you Umba. Thank you . . . thank you."

Carina was so engrossed, she didn't hear her mother say,

"You look tired Gianni, Have you been hurt? When did you get home?"

Looking over Carina's shoulder, Gianni smiled and said,

"I've only just got here, haven't been home yet."

"Then you had better get along, Donnina will never forgive me if we keep you dallying here while she is still fretting over your whereabouts . . . because she doesn't know you are only a few doors away."

Gianni knew that what Concetta said was true, and was reluctant to draw away from the girl he had his good arm round. Nevertheless he did so.

109

"I'll see you again before the day is out," he said to Carina as he stole a quick kiss before turning to go.

"If Donnina and Lucia will let you come back for a meal with us this evening," Concetta called after him.

"Why don't you come to us," he called back.

There was a thin covering of snow on the ground when Carina and Concetta arrived at the house that had a wolf for a knocker. Somehow, between caring for her turkeys and attending to her other daily tasks, Carina had found time to iron out the creases in her frock. If Gianni had made any muddy patches, they had also been removed. Donnina was quick to notice the special effort and smiled inwardly as the thought occurred to her that Gianni, being a man would probably only see the girl and not the frock. She also noticed the thin patches of wear and remembered some material she had bought, long ago, when on honeymoon, to make a frock, that never did get made. Thinking, 'I'm much too big now to make a frock out of that for myself, Lucia has plenty of dresses, why not use it to make a nice frock for Carina,' Donnina welcomed her two visitors in and said,

"Ernesto won't be long, the meal is ready to serve as soon as he arrives. Do have some wine, while we are waiting."

The meal Donnina had prepared was tagliatella and black horse beans, with a richly seasoned, with aromatic herbs and shredded onions, tomato purée, dressed with a sprinkling of small chips of pork, fried until crisp, and grated cheese. A large dish of mixed salad, collected from the surrounding countryside and a platter of grapes occupied the centre of the table.

As soon as they had finished eating, the family, with their guests gathered round the fire. True to character, Dora was quick to steal the best seat. She knew that she would be told to give it up for one of the guests and did so, without protest, when her mother rebuked her.

Only after Ernesto had led them in a prayer of thanksgiving and a couple of hymns had been sung, did they settle down to talk. Not surprisingly, the main topic was, where had Gianni been, and why was his arm in a sling.

Lucia, having at last managed to prise Gianni away from Carina was about to ask him to tell his story, when there was a knock on the door and Mario walked in.

"So you're back." he boomed, "they told me you would be."

Reluctant at first to tell what had happened, Gianni was at last persuaded to speak.

"I only intended to visit the group. Donnola was going to introduce me to some of his men," Gianni began, "the idea was to have a look at the set-up and come to a decision later." Pausing a moment, to gather his thoughts, Gianni continued with, "We didn't even get as far as his H.Q. We came face to face with one of those rastrellamento patrols doing their usual combing out. As soon as they saw us, even though we were both unarmed, they raised their guns and shouted for us to lay down ours. We had barely put our hands in the air, when a party of Matteoti appeared on a ledge above and opened fire. Which drew their attention away from us. Someone threw me an old Tommy gun." Gianni grinned ruefully, "It jammed after only a few rounds. It was then that I was hit, fortunately the bullet went between my arm and chest. Apart from a burn mark on the rib cage and a nasty gash on the upper arm, no real damage was done. When some of Donnola's group arrived, the Tedeschi realised they were outnumbered, leaving their dead on the ground, they made a rapid retreat. Sadly, two of the Matteoti also fell."

"Why didn't you return here as soon as the fighting was over?" Lucia asked, "We've been worried sick about you."

"I didn't have much option, by the time we reached the encampment, I had lost quite a bit of blood and was feeling pretty sick."

"Why didn't you bind it with something as soon as it happened?" Donnina asked, "You know how important it is with gunshot wounds."

Gianni looked at his mother, scarce able to believe his ears. "We were rather busy," he replied.

A brief chuckle from Ernesto broke the short spell of silence which fell after Gianni had spoken. Evidently, the chuckle reminded Donnina of Gianni's answer. She burst out laughing and between chuckles, managed to say,

"Yes! I suppose you were."

"Donnola wasn't very happy about things and insisted I get help. There's a friendly doctor, who can be trusted in a village overlooking Ascoli. He sent one of his group to fetch him, and the doctor arranged for me to be seen by the sisters at the convent. They kept me there for a short while, until they were satisfied not only that there was no infection, but also that I had recovered my strength."

It was approaching ten o'clock when Donnina's guests left. Looking out of the door, she said,

"That snow is lying quite thick now, it'll be deep come morning.... I'm glad you only have a few steps to go." Then, drawing Concetta to one side and speaking very quietly, "Can I borrow an old dress of Carina's? I want to take some measurements."

If Concetta guessed what was in Donnina's mind, she made no comment other than to say,

"I'll see what I can find."

CHAPTER TEN

When the snow came, Filomena was still a two hour walk from home. It started as a fine mist which quickly developed into sleet, then snow flakes which rapidly grew in size. With the snow came a stiff breeze of icy content.

Glad now that her father had insisted on her taking a storm proof coat with her, Filomena tightened the waist cord, secured the hood and fastened the top buttons tightly round her neck. As she did so, Angelo's words flashed through her mind. *"The weather could change any time now. I know that coat is heavy, but be sensible. The stars may be bright in the sky now; it's still early in the day and you won't be back here until tomorrow evening. You don't know what it will be like by then."* Filomena also remembered that Giorgio said, *"If you don't wear decent footwear, you might regret it."* Reluctantly she had taken their advice.

By the time Filomena reached the fork in the track which would take her to the woodland path climbing to her house a blizzard was raging. Snow, now lay thick on the ground. Defying a near gale force wind which, relentlessly thrashed her face and legs in it's fury, she plodded resolutely forward.

It was a little after seven o'clock when Filomena reached the clearing outside her home. Angelo was at the door, anxiously watching for sign of her return.

"Thank God you're home," he said and dragged her through the door.

The blizzard lasted through the night, bringing down trees and forming deep drifts in all the more sheltered places. By morning, the drifts were so deep that, not only Angelo and Filomena, but also the farmers in outlying areas, were snow bound in their homesteads. Although, by mid-day, the wind had subsided, the snow continued to fall, and did so without cease, for a further seven days.

These conditions were not new to the people living on the slopes surrounding La Villa and nearby regions. It happened every winter, so all were prepared for a period of isolation. Throughout the year, logs had been cut and ginestra piled in a location as close to the house as possible. The almost daily clearing of a narrow track to the store of fuel and other places that needed frequent access was not a problem. However, it was not practical to travel the considerable distance, to La fonte, (the fountain) that some had to make, to get a supply of water. Wearing snow-shoes, with a conca balanced on their heads, over undulating ground and, at times, steep gradients made their route, not only difficult, but also dangerous. Those who were not fortunate enough to have acqua sorgente[18] or a well, close to their home, were forced to rely on melted snow for water.

This year, it was different; it actually created a feeling of relief, a sense of freedom. The thinking was that if they couldn't get far without their snow-shoes, the Tedeschi were unlikely to come visiting. Some, would chuckle and say, "If they come, I hope they walk over a well." Without exception they took their lot philosophically and were content.

In La Villa, many hands made light work of clearing the streets and the route down to La fonte and the stream, which had never been known to freeze, was rigorously maintained. Because the men folk, mainly farm labourers, were unable to work the soil, they had time on their hands and gathered daily at La Locale or Renzo's bar, as some preferred to call it.

It was pleasantly snug in the bar, the regulars had tables, which were universally acknowledged as being theirs. Talk invariably centred round the harvest and in particular the vendemmia, accompanied by knowing winks, relating to how much grappa was being distilled.

Gianni, sitting with Ernesto, listened silently to the arguments and different opinions of the friends sharing Ernesto's table. He hadn't joined in, somehow he felt out of touch, as if the years he had been away had made him a stranger. Perhaps he had grown used to a different life, remote from farming.

Inevitably, the talk turned to the state of the country and voices lowered as they expressed forbidden opinions, on political issues. Suddenly, Ernesto's voice boomed out,

"It would be better if men were free to make sensible laws and govern themselves." As always, he had become embroiled in one of the eternal discussions. "I don't trust this new government, the Replublichini," he added in the same loud tone.

The reference to the new republic in the North (*Repubblica Sociale Italiana*) and the scathing inference in the term Republichini[19], scared nearly everybody there. They still feared their erstwhile Fascist masters, and preferred that such remarks were left unsaid.

---

[18] Water source. (Usually a spring.)
[19] A derogatory term referring to Republica Sociale Italiana created by the fascists during the Nazi occupation of central and North Italy. (December 1943-Apr)

The hum of conversation dropped, leaving a silence that could almost be felt. Those at nearby tables, hearing the remark, glanced nervously at each other. Others, further away from Ernesto's table in the corner, while secretly agreeing with the comment, felt a vaguely disturbed relief that they could not be accused of being a part of the discussion and, edged surreptitiously towards the door.

Ernesto grinned sheepishly and shifted his feet under the table, although he hated the Fascisti almost as much as he did the Tedeschi, it was not his habit to advertise the fact.

Michele, whose limp did not affect his ability to ski, accompanied by Mario, relished the opportunity to practise a sport they both loved, made a daily visit to La Villa. Michele, to go to the bar; at times to meet Angelo, others for the company and as an excuse to ski. Mario's only reason was to visit Lucia.

As Michele entered La Locale he heard the remark and had difficulty in suppressing a grin. Thinking, 'typical of Ernesto,' he broke the embarrassed silence with a joke about '*Foro di Mussolini*'. It was a safe joke, that lost none of its bite for the repetition. An appreciative chuckle rippled through occupants of the bar as all and sundry remembered the meeting called by Il Duce. An association of words, which, together with a peculiar twist of fate, had linked, forever in their minds, *Foro di Mussolini* with *Quinto foro della cinghia*, (fifth hole in the belt). An allusion to the lack of food.

Grinning sheepishly, Ernesto took a huge, multicoloured handkerchief from his pocket, mopped his forehead, and looked anxiously at the faces of his friends. Being the friends that they were, they delighted in grinning back, with mischievous glee. One even dared to say, quite loudly,

"Bravo! And so say all of us."

The words were loud enough for all to hear. Someone chuckled and others joined in, this time over the discomfiture of Ernesto.

Seizing the moment to digress, Ernesto said,

"All this snow, might not be for us, Bruto and Bella certainly like being tucked up in the stable...."

"Surely you don't still have those oldies. They must have white beards by now. How can you expect them to work?"

The comment came from Pasquale, the son of one of Ernesto's friends. Still in his early thirties, he was one of the many, who had made their way home after the armistice. With a gleeful chuckle he added,

"I can well understand those feeble Maremmano milk cows are glad of a rest, but what else can you expect with those long and heavy horns?"

Ernesto snorted indignantly. Quick to defend his beloved Bruto and Bella, he said,

"What other beasts could pull a cart up these steep tracks the way those two pull that heavy cart of Michele's father, Domenico. Or for that matter, plough the steep ground where it enters the hills; as they do?" Ernesto snorted again, "They are strong I tell you. Stronger than those fat and lazy Svizzeri of your father's that you take a pride in."

Enrico, Pasquale's father hid a smile behind his hand, he and Ernesto were friends of long standing and he knew, from past experience what was coming.

"They may be old as working beasts go." Ernesto continued. "Age makes no difference. Give me your hand and I will show you the proof."

Grinning now, in anticipation, Ernesto assiduously wiped his hands on the rough cloth of his breeches and placed an elbow on the table in unmistakable invitation.

Pasquale was quick to take up the challenge. It was a long time since he had pitted his, not inconsiderable strength, against a worthy opponent. As he positioned himself for the tussle, he had no doubt in his mind who would win.

Feeling the supple strength in the wrist of the younger man, Ernesto took a firm hold. 'Here,' he thought, 'is a worthy challenger.' and his brown eyes, so dark as to be almost black twinkled in quick and impish humour as he gauged the strength of the other and pretended to yield.

Ernesto was not a big man, but he was strong, he had broad shoulders and the tough resilience of a man who had spent a life-time tilling the soil. He knew, there were not many who could beat him at this form of arm wrestling, known as 'Braccio duro,' that he could afford to take risks to wear his opponent down.

As the minutes sped by, delighted winks were exchanged between the watchers, now grouped around the table; their earlier embarrassment forgotten. Like most men in convivial company, they enjoyed the chance to wager and avidly seized the opportunity offered by the bout. Now they eagerly awaited the outcome as Ernesto played a cat and mouse game of, now yielding, now not.

Soon, both men were bathed in perspiration and now there was no pretence on Ernesto's part as first one gained the advantage, and then, the other.

Slowly, the grins faded from the faces of those who had placed their bets on the older man. The atmosphere became tense as all wondered if, at last, Ernesto was to be eclipsed.

Five minutes became ten, elbows pressed even more firmly on the table. With hands locked strongly in a vice like grasp; feet spread and legs straddling the chairs, each strove grimly to ignore their now aching muscles.

Suddenly, it was all over, with Pasquale ruefully rubbing rapped knuckles as he laughingly refused a return bout.

"You're too strong for me," he gasped.

Ernesto's almost apple round face creased in happiness. His eyes brimming with emotion, he chuckled huskily and said,

"I am strong, stronger than you. Didn't I tell you that age doesn't matter?"

Ernesto boasted, without knowing it. To him the statement was one of fact; proved by the outcome of the contest and he was very proud of his immense strength. He looked at Pasquale slyly,

"What class are you?"

It was his way of asking, what year were you born?

Pasquale had expected it, and responded quickly,

"1911. And you?" came the reply.

Ernesto laughed exultantly.

"1886, I have seen," he paused to calculate, "twenty five years more than you."

"No wonder you won, Pasquale retorted, "You've had so much more practise than me."

Pasquale's quick answer, brought a ripple of laughter from all who heard it.

Reluctantly, as the afternoon drew to a close, goodbyes were said, as one by one the occupants made their way home. The light was beginning to fade, and Renzo's bar was nearly empty, when Michele decided it was safe to discuss a subject on his mind with Angelo.

"I have been told," he began, "that there is one those unfortunate English living in a shepherd's, refuge. That's no place to be in this weather. If he doesn't die of the cold, he will of starvation."

"Where is the refuge?" Angelo asked.

"On the slopes of the Gran Sasso, a little above Villa Celiera. I have discussed it with Vincensina, and we are prepared to give him refuge in our stable, until the weather improves."

"Have you seen him?" Angelo asked.

"No I only heard about him yesterday, it's quite a way from here and I wanted to discuss the matter with you before doing anything."

"Quite right too, we must be careful. Without Giorgio there's no way of checking his credentials. Anything he tells us about himself will have to be taken on trust. Are you prepared to take that risk?"

Michele thought a moment before replying.

"That hadn't occurred to me," he replied, "but it can't be right to leave him up there."

"Who told you about him?"

"Young Alberto," Michele replied, "that kid gets around and can be trusted not to talk."

Angelo sat in silence for a while, while he turned the matter over in his mind. Finally, he said,

"Leave it to me, I'll have a word with Alberto and check it out. If we move him, it will have to be in daylight and that could be a problem."

Having agreed to meet again on the following day, they walked together to the end of the village before parting and making their way home.

. . . .

Filomena stretched luxuriously in her bed on a bright February morning, and gazed, half dreaming at the frosted window of her room. Reluctantly rising, she gazed out on a scene of glistening white beauty, etched against a vividly blue sky, which was decorated by the sharp outline of mountain summits. The only trace of other colour was the dark green of conifers that had shaken off the snow covering their leaves, to reveal the full splendour of their being.

"How lucky we are," she told herself, "to have that sorgente[20] so close to the house."

The realisation that she didn't have to make the journey to the fountain pleased her. Giorgio had told her that he would be away for a while. There were matters to attend and, as the last signal he left had disappeared, he might decide to change her station. Until then, she was to wait until he contacted her.

Moving quickly now, she washed in the bowl of water in her room and dressed. It did not surprise her, when she entered the living room, that Angelo had already stirred up the fire and had a good blaze burning. Smiling, she said,

"Buon giorno Babbo, una bella giornata" and kissed him on the cheek.

The daily morning kiss on the cheek was something new, that Angelo, secretly looked forward to. It had started the day after he and Filomena had watched the departure of Eric and Robin, when a new and very special bond had surfaced between father and daughter. Time seemed to have passed with the speed of light since that day. So much had happened; Angelo's mind wandered back over the events.

The return of Filomena on the first day of the snow, frozen, but seemingly uncaring. The arrival of a young man named Peter at Casa dei Pioppi, in a toboggan dragged by Alberto and a young girl, Francesca, who invariably accompanied him as a fellow Staffetini. Hiding Peter in the bottom of a toboggan pulled by two children had been Alberto's idea; the recollection of him saying, "*Nobody will suspect two children at play with a toboggan and I know where I can get one.*" brought a smile to Angelo's face.

Then there had been Christmas, when Ernesto's family accompanied by Concetta and Carina, proudly wearing the new frock that Donnina had made, braved the conditions and made their way across the snow covered valley to the house on top of the escarpment.

Unlike many others in the area, who vowed they would not celebrate until the war was over, Michele and his friends grabbed every opportunity. Ernesto, brought his fisarmonica with him, which gave them music for dancing. Peter, despite his very scant smattering of

---

[20] Spring

Italian, not only knew the words of many of the favourites, such as *Santa Lucia* and *Non te scordare di me*, but also, to their amazement, some of the popular modern songs, had a fine tenor voice, which delighted them. With Mario acting as interpreter, he was able to tell them about his voice studies in England and the church choir that he enjoyed singing in.

Time, since then had slipped by with the amazing speed that time does.

"Only three or four weeks, at the most and all this snow will be gone," Angelo said, to Filomena, who was busy preparing the morning meal. "In a way, I won't be sorry."

"Now Babbo, you know you've enjoyed the skiing, you can't do it on grass," Filomena said with a laugh as she pulled a chair out from under the table and put a plate with two massive slices of bread, smeared with olive oil in front of him. Then, saying, "I haven't salted it, you know how much you like," she sat opposite him and poured herself a cup of coffee.

CHAPTER ELEVEN

The thaw came during the last week of February, slowly at first, as the mid-day sun cast its warming rays over the snow bound slopes. When the rain came at the beginning of March, it washed away the remaining patches of snow which still lingered in the streets of La Villa and turned into slush any snow remaining on the steep mountain tracks. Before the thaw, passage over the snow, wearing snow shoes or skis was comparatively easy. Now however, it was unable to support any weight. To add to the difficulties, the slopes harboured glacier like areas, which were too steep and too cluttered with small rocks to permit the use of either snow shoes or skis. However, this didn't deter the 'softies', as the partisans who had spent the winter in the mountains, called the few who had returned home when the snow came, from returning to their comrades. It didn't stop Gianni either, from keeping his promise to join Donnola's company of partisans. Bidding a fond farewell to a tearful Carina, he said,

"I won't be far away, and will be able to come and see you quite often."

"Do be careful. Promise you won't take any silly risks," she urged, clinging to him and trying to put on a brave face.

The rain was falling steadily when, a few days after Gianni had left, Lucia glanced out of the window of her room. She had spent a sleepless night, with repeated visions of Enrico, the man her grandfather was determined she should marry. The vista of dripping buildings and a street that resembled a miniature stream only depressed her further.

"Why does he have to come here with his whims and fancies?" she asked herself. "I wouldn't marry that unctuous son of a friend of his, if he was the last man on earth," she muttered. "Why should I marry someone he arranges? He is not my father Just because he is Mama's father and she is the youngest child of a large family, he has no right to lord it over us. Who does he . . ."

Donnina's voice cut in to her thoughts.

"I think we are out of water, could you get some?"

Glad of something to occupy her mind, Lucia draped a small jacket round her shoulders, came out of the bedroom and cast her eyes towards the conca standing its ledge. Then, through the open door, at the falling rain and said,

"It's raining quite heavily now, but I don't mind going."

"You are a good girl. Be careful not to slip, there might be some ice around the more shaded areas," Doninna warned.

Tucking the conca under her arm, she picked up her cercine and went through the open door into the street. The temperature of the rain was milder than she had expected.

Rivulets of water, carrying all manner of debris coursed between the cobbled stones as she made her way towards the steeply descending track which led down to the fountain, several metres below. Like the miniature tributaries they resembled, they made their way down furrows forged by centuries of iron clad wheels trundling over the surface. Eager, it seemed to get to the swollen stream hugging the foot of the hill.

Lucia didn't mind the rain and rather enjoyed the feel of water washing over her feet. The deserted square was awash when she crossed it and she felt thankful she didn't have to use the rain drenched and mud laden paths of the woodland tracks. Lucia knew from experience they would be slippery and difficult to negotiate with the weight of a water laden conca on her head.

Descending the steep path to the fountain a holly leaf floating on the surface of a fast moving rivulet caught her eye. The way it dodged round obstacles in its passage intrigued her. Lucia imagined it to be a ship, with Mario at the helm steering her dream ship home. In her mind, the stalk became the bowsprit of a sailing vessel from a bygone age and the jagged edges, the oars.

Dimly recollected tales of her childhood drifted through her mind and she romantically likened herself to Helen of Troy with Mario as Paris, fighting the turbulent waters. With infinite care, she plucked the leaf from the heaving surface and set it gently down on the calmer waters in the trough, Then, dreamily watched it until it came to rest in a quiet corner.

Breaking from her reverie, she picked up her conca and offered it to one of the three pipes protruding from the rock. The combination of the thaw and the rain, had increased the normal strength of the flow, to such an extent, that it knocked the conca from her hand. She tried resting the vessel on the edge of the trough, but the water shot over the top and gushed in gay abandon on to the flooded surface below. Resisting the temptation to risk pollution by dipping the conca in to the trough, she tried again and after two or three abortive attempts, she found herself splashing triumphantly towards her home.

The rain stopped as suddenly as it had begun. Lucia had not expected such a blue sky and the warmth of the sun which promised to dry her clothes did much to restore her spirits.

"You worry too much," she told herself, "You don't have to marry him, and I know Papa won't allow Nonno to have his way." Then, smothered a giggle as she remembered Mario had said those same words when Gianni was missing. "Perhaps I do," she said out loud.

Singing '*Il Capo da Banda*', a popular song of the day, Lucia pushed open the door with a wolf for a knocker and stepped inside. The song died on her lips.

"Hallo Nonno," she said, and hoping her voice wouldn't betray her feelings, added, "how nice to see you."

Anticipating his next move, Lucia placed the conca on its ledge and skipped lightly round the advancing grandfather into her bedroom, before he could embrace her.

Il Maresciallo as her grandfather preferred to be called, resented any real, or imagined, flaunt of his authority and was quick to rise to the occasion.

"Come back here, you wilful girl," he shouted, his face going red with anger. Hoping to cool the situation, Lucia came out of her bedroom, carrying a towel. Somehow, she managed a bright smile, as she said,

"Sorry Nonno, I didn't mean to be disrespectful, I needed to dry my hair, which is soaking wet from the rain."

Her grandfather scowled at her, as if he was going to rebuke her again, instead, he said,

"Your future husband, Enrico, is coming to see you tomorrow. So look your best for him."

Lucia could feel her blood rising and started to say. "I would rather die than..."

"If your mother had not run off and married your father in secret, you wouldn't be living in a poor home like this, with a farm labourer for a father," he cut in.

"And I wouldn't have the kind and wonderful father that I have," Lucia retorted hotly.

123

Her grandfather's face went almost purple as he shouted,

"Don't be impudent girl I'm head of the family and you'll marry who I say, or live to regr . . ."

Lucia didn't hear the rest of what he had to say. Resisting the temptation to slap his face she turned on her heel and dashed back into her bedroom; the irate grandfather tried to follow her.

"How dare you try to come into my bedroom," Lucia, now thoroughly roused, almost shrieked.

"This room is private. It's mine and you have no right of entry."

It was at that moment, that Donnina walked in and said, in a joyful tone,

"It's quite bright now, but there's still a chill in the air," then, broke off, looked at her father, with his hand on the door, trying to push it open, and demanded, sharply, "What's going on? You two quarrelling already?"

"Lucia is being insolent, I won't have it. I forbid her to marry anybody except Enrico."

Donnina could feel herself getting cross. Fearing she would lose her calm, she laughed scornfully and using his baptised name, said,

"Antonio, who do you think you are? Lucia is the daughter of Ernesto and me. You should know that neither of us believe in arranged marriages. She can marry whomsoever she wishes," then, looking her father straight in the eye, added, "with our blessing."

Having, on more than one occasion experienced Donnina's wrath when roused, Antonio turned on his heel and stalked out into the street.

Despite the comparatively early hour, there was the usual cluster off regulars in Renzo's bar when Antonio entered. Still seething with hurt pride, he cast his eyes over the occupants, hoping to see someone he knew well enough to buy a drink and engage in conversation.

"If it's that Mario I've heard talk of," he murmured to himself, "I know how I can put a stop to his little game."

Still grumbling to himself, Antonio bought a drink and sat at a table, he knew to be Angelo's. 'Maybe Michele or Angelo will come in,' he thought.

. . . .

Notwithstanding the difficulties and his time absorbing involvement with the Partito d' Azione, Mario contrived to visit Lucia every day. It was something she looked forward to; something to take her mind off the annual visit of her grandfather. His heart skipped a beat as he hurried towards the corner of the square where Lucia, her bandanna draped round her shoulders, was waiting in the late afternoon sun, which brought out the full beauty of the deep copper tints in her hair and somehow enhanced the dimples that always appeared in her cheeks when she smiled.

Just being there was all that Mario needed from Lucia. Hand in hand, the two walked in silence. Words were not necessary, they were content to be together as they made their way towards a secluded woodland path and the privacy it offered. It was the moment they had dreamed about for so long; forever, it seemed, a chance to talk, to say those intimate things young lovers say when nobody else is there to hear. A sudden shower, sent them scurrying into a nearby barn. Laughing now, they looked at each other's dripping faces and shook the droplets of water from their clothing.

Now that they were alone, Mario took Lucia in his arms. He kissed her, tenderly at first, then more passionately as his ardour increased. Unexpectedly, for no apparent reason, he felt her stiffen in his arms.

"No! No! We mustn't" Lucia whispered, as she interposed a finger between their lips and gently tried to push him away.

Dimly aware that something was wrong, Mario yielded. Holding her at arm's length, he looked at her, there were tears in her eyes.

"Why the forlorn face," he asked in the most cheerful tone he could muster. Then, unable to understand the sudden change, added. "Don't you still love me?"

Lucia blushed and regarded him dolefully. For once, she appeared to have nothing to say, as struggling to find the words that wouldn't come, she resisted Mario's attempts to take her back in his arms.

"Are you sure you are alright?" Mario asked as he tried to persuade Lucia to look at him. "You do still love me don't you?"

Lucia nodded dumbly, but kept her head averted. Somehow, her silence intensified the sound of the rain on the thatched roof of the barn.

Mario looked fondly at the blurred outline of Lucia's head, gently touched the wet bandanna which covered it, and said,

"It's very wet, why don't you take it off?" Then, with the words, "Here, let me help you," felt for the knot beneath her chin.

"I-It's not that," Lucia stammered at last, "I do love you. . . . I do," then blurting, "It's Nonno! . . . Oh Mario, it's Antonio, my grandfather. He arrived this morning and still thinks he is a maresciallo in the Carabinieri," she melted back into Mario's arms.

"Come now, it can't be that bad," Mario said, stroking her hair with one hand while the other fumbled for the clean handkerchief he always carried in his hip pocket. "Nothing is worth all these tears."

"He says I must stop seeing you and marry Enrico, or I will bring disgrace on the family"

"The idiot talks nonsense, don't take any notice of him." Mario said, scornfully. Then led the way to a broken down bench, cleared away the debris and draped his coat over the rough wood so that Lucia could sit in comfort and murmured, "I would do anything for you."

Under Mario's soothing influence, Lucia gradually calmed down, but try as she might, she couldn't bring herself to say what was on her mind. Finally, with some of her usual vivacity, she peeped up at him, conjured up a weak little smile and said,

"Sorry, I was just being silly."

"What's really troubling you?"

"Nothing," Lucia mumbled into his neck

"Are you happy?"

"Yes," Lucia whispered, "now that I am with you."

Unconvinced, Mario held Lucia close, he was acutely aware that the girl he loved was far from happy.

When the words Lucia couldn't say finally came to the surface, she rested her head on his shoulder and clung to him. Then, at last, she spoke. Her throat felt dry and the words came out in a flood; tumbling over each other, as if impatient to get out.

"It's Nonno. When he forbade me to see you, he told Mama that if you don't stop calling he will report you as a deserter to the Podesta in Paese; Michele too, for harbouring you. If you go with him to report back to the army, there will be no trouble."

Scarce able to believe what he was hearing, Mario could feel himself growing cold. Memories of what he had suffered were still too fresh in his mind. Pictures of the atrocities perpetrated by the Fascists and their German masters swam before his eyes.

Slowly the sound of Lucia's sobbing penetrated the tortured recesses of Mario's numbed mind. He felt himself move forward, it was an eerie sensation, a strange ethereal feeling, where he seemed to have no control over his actions. As in a dream, he gathered Lucia in his arms. From somewhere far away, he heard himself say,

"I'm sorry darling, I love you; too much to stop seeing you. Believe me, he might bark, but I won't let him bite."

Mario had no idea how long he had been sitting there; just staring into space, with the slight figure of Lucia curled up against him. He only knew it was almost dark and his limbs were stiff, when, with a contented sigh she lifted her head, smiled, then, dropped her head back on to his shoulder and drifted into a state that was neither asleep nor awake.

Impulsively, Mario turned his head to kiss the soft tresses laying against his cheek. Disturbed by the movement, Lucia stirred and he found himself gazing into her eyes. Their lips met and time stood still.

. . . .

It was late when Mario and Lucia approached the outskirts of La Villa. When they reached the exit of the square, they could see, silhouetted against the dim light of an oil lamp which lit the living room of Lucia's home, Ernesto standing in the open doorway.

"Don't come any further," Lucia whispered as they came to a halt. Antonio will be there, he will be angry if he sees you with me, . . . if he doesn't see me, I can say I've been visiting a friend."

"There shouldn't be any need for subterfuge," Mario retorted.

"You don't understand, Antonio gets furious if he sees me talking to any man. Not just you." Lucia said, as she gave Mario an appealing look. "You don't know what he is like, he doesn't just get angry, he goes berserk. Then takes it out on Mama. He claims to be the head of the family, as such, he must be obeyed. He says he has no time for deserters, and you know from what I told you, he means you, and will take disciplinary action if you persist on calling."

Mario wanted to laugh, but remembering how upset Lucia had been, managed to hide the absurdity he found in il Maresciallo's arrogance. Instead, he said.

"The man's a conceited fool, I know he holds on to his army rank, he forgets he is a civilian now and has no authority, whereas I am still a serving officer - on release - of an Alpini regiment. Not a deserter. I knew, that in his opinion, you should marry someone of his choice and that your mother has told him arranged marriages are old fashioned. But, I didn't know he was trying to pull army rank. Leave that to me, I'll soon sort him out."

Lucia didn't reply immediately, she just stood there, looking at Mario. Then, as if she had suddenly made up her mind what to say, she said,

"It's better this way, please trust me." gave Mario a hurried kiss and was gone.

Hoping Lucia would turn and wave when she reached the doorway, Mario watched her run down the street. He saw her hesitate on the threshold as she exchanged a few words with her father, then the door closed behind them. Disappointed that she had not blown a kiss, Mario trod the lonely path home.

"You've been out with Mario" Antonio shouted as Lucia entered the house.

Lucia knew her grandfather's wrath could be fierce and uncontrollable, but something in her mother's determination that she had inherited, made her answer quickly and firmly.

"Of course not. . . . In the rain we've had this afternoon?"

Annoyed by the tone of Lucia's response, Antonio stormed across the room and said,

"Don't lie, Dora saw you with him."

Lucia could feel her face and neck going red and she looked unhappily at Dora who was edging towards the door of the bedroom that she shared with her sister. Shaking her head, she mimed,

"No I didn't," and took refuge in the bedroom,

"What's the matter with you?" Donnina interjected, springing to the defence of her daughter.

"I know the girl has been seeing that renegade officer," Antonio snapped back.

"I love him and he loves me. I don't care what you think," Lucia, now defiant, said, staring her grandfather in the face.

For a moment, it looked as though Antonio was about to strike Lucia.

Returning from the back of the house, where he had gone to fetch some extra fuel for the fire. Ernesto heard Antonio's last comment. Without showing the anger he felt, he cut in with the quiet authoritative tone he knew how to muster,

"Behave yourself Antonio, while you are in my home, you keep the peace. I don't want to hear any more nonsense from you regarding my daughters friends."

. . . .

All the elation Mario had enjoyed that afternoon and evening seemed to have deserted him. Tormented with jealousy because Lucia was promised to another man, Rage, when he thought of how Antonio had accused him of treachery. Disappointment, over the way the day had ended. The three formed a trilogy of conflicting thoughts that gave him a sleepless night.

When Mario opened the shutters the next morning, it was still dark, more so than usual because the sky was clouded over and there was drizzle in the air. For the first time in his life, Mario knew the meaning of real and unreasoning anger. Thinking that perhaps an hour or two in the saddle would drive away his morbid mood, he wandered out into the stable. The drizzle had turned into steady rain. "Even the elements are against me," he muttered bitterly to Nove as he placed a small oil lamp in its niche and picked up curry comb and brush instead of the saddle. Whinnying softly, the horse moved towards him and nestled its great head on his shoulder. Changing his mind again, Mario put down the grooming aids and with the words,

"You don't mind getting wet do you old friend?" he took the saddle from its hook on the wall.

Excited by the prospects of exercise, Nove tossed his head and pranced around the stable like a young colt. Cheered by the antics of his horse, Mario said,

"They say, first you must catch your horse, but no one has ever said what to do if the devil won't stand still."

By the time the two left the stable, the rain had become a heavy downpour. Mario glanced at the sky, there was no hint of a break. Just solid blackness, without so much as a solitary star or the first grey streaks of dawn to soften it.

"Sorry, we can't gallop over this terrain in the dark," Mario said as, patting Nove's neck he turned into the avenue of poplars, "Better times will come my friend."

The black sky had turned into a vast smudge of monotonous grey, which stretched as far as the eye could see, when Michele entered the stable and found Mario drying off the horse.

"Go inside and get yourself changed. I don't know what your mother would say if she saw you," Michele said, with fatherly concern as he placed his hand on Mario's drenched clothing, "I'll look after Nove for you."

Turning his head to answer, Mario was relieved to find that although he still felt tense, his anger had evaporated.

"I'm used to getting wet Papa and enjoy tending to Nove," he said. Then, looked at his horse and added, "Don't I my dear friend."

"Then at least let me help," said Michele, picking up a spare rubbing cloth and busying himself with the task.

Somehow working with his father, sharing a task they both loved doing, helped, even more than the ride on Nove, to restore Mario's normal good humour. Now, there was an urge to unburden himself, to share his thoughts with someone who would understand. However, he couldn't bring himself to say anything, not even to his own father; the whole sorry matter seemed too private. Whatever the reason, Mario felt incapable of breaking the silence that persisted between them.

Sensing something was worrying Mario, Michele worked without making his usual quips, as he watched his son for any sign that would indicate he had a problem and would like to talk. The two had barely finished, when Vincensina called from the open doorway of the house,

"Aren't you two finished yet? I've prepared some hot broth for you. Come eat."

To Michele's great relief, Mario gave Nove a slap on the neck. Then, turned to him, grinned in his usual jovial manner and said,

"Thanks Papa, you've helped me more than you know Lets get it before it goes cold."

CHAPTER TWELVE

The grey roofs of the houses perched on the edge of a precipitous drop overlooking a canyon were just a smudge below the heavily wooded slopes when Lieutenant Philip Cargil leaned out of the small plane. Far below, stretched a grey mass, which Philip guessed to be the olive groves that stretched across the low lying valley. Cursing the fitful light he searched among the deceptive shadows for a glimpse of a dilapidated building, where he was to meet his contact.

"It's no good Jack, I can't see a bloody thing. If I could see the track I would know where to look. Can you take me a bit lower?"

Acknowledging the request with a wave of his hand, the Pilot eased the plane into a gentle glide.

The plane lost height rapidly and the motor road, a black pencil line, crossing the valley soon came into view, but, even when they had dropped several hundred feet, sight of the building Philip was looking for remained elusive.

. . . .

Although only minutes behind schedule, it seemed much longer before Tina heard the throbbing note of the Lysander and saw the shape of its up-swept wings etched against the sky. Breathing a sigh of relief, she watched the plane come closer to where she waited, only to gasp in despair when it circled above her, turned away and flew off over the hills.

It was five minutes before she caught a glimpse of it again, far over to the right and on the wrong side of the valley. Straining her eyes, she managed to keep the plane in view until it disappeared in low lying clouds.

"If this goes on much longer," Tina told herself, "the place will be alive with the Tedeschi."

. . . .

Philip Cargil landed awkwardly on uneven rocks scattered over a narrow strip of rough ground separating the rising slopes of the mountain from an olive grove. To his left, he could just make out, mere shapes in the grey light of dawn, a group of people congregating at the entrance to the small town.

Unbuckling his harness, he gathered the bulky silk together with a speed born of practise and stuffed it hurriedly beneath one of the rocks. Then, dropped on hands and knees to crawl through tall growing grass into the olive grove. Satisfied he had gone far enough, he lay still, listening to the sound of the receding plane and prayed that despite the ever increasing light no one had seen him drop.

With the departure of the plane, the commotion outside the entrance to the town died down and the group of people dispersed. Confident now, that he had dropped unseen, Philip stood up.

"That was a stupid place to land."

The voice, seeming to come from nowhere, startled Philip; he thought he detected an almost imperceptible trace of a foreign accent. His hand dropped to his gun.

As the owner of the voice came into view, he stooped to run the thumb and finger of his right hand down what should have been a crease in his baggy trousers and said,

"Put that thing away Philip, I'm as British as you are."

Philip relaxed. 'Dammit! Must be getting nervous,' he thought. Then, putting his gun away, he said,

"I thought you were the Hun. Where have all the others gone?"

"I didn't see anybody else come down. How many were there?" came the reply.

From the answer, which should have been, '*Long time passing*' Philip knew the stranger was not a replacement for the girl, who, he had been told, would take him to the men he had to meet. Wondering how, if the man was the enemy, he knew his name, he said,

"I thought you were someone else. . . . Who are you? What are you doing here?"

"They call me Marco, but actually, my name is Jim. I am a released prisoner of war working with the people you have to meet." Konrad said with a disarming smile.

Still on the alert, and wondering how he could get Konrad away from the area, Philip stepped out of the grove on to the strip of rough ground. As he did so, he caught a glimpse of the building he had been looking for; scarcely fifty metres away. Although partially hidden by trees, he wondered why it had been so difficult to find. As he looked, he saw the slight figure of a girl step into the open. Guessing it to be his genuine contact, he gave the figure a quick wave to confirm he had seen her, then, dropped his hand, pretended to scratch his head and said,

"Have you been waiting long Jim? Do you know a shrine near the Comunanza to Santa Stefano road?"

Konrad nodded and said,

"That would be Santo Francesco, it's only about one mile from here, I'll take you there, but be careful when we cross the road near the entrance to the canyon."

Tina had seen the vague shape of Philip drop out of the sky, she had also seen him crawl through the grass in to the olive grove and couldn't resist a grin, as the thought, 'I bet he thinks he can't be seen,' crossed her mind. Seeing him reappear with another person, set alarm bells ringing in her head. However, when she saw Philip wave and set off in the opposite direction, she knew he had seen her and guessed he would join her as soon as he could. So, decided to wait.

Konrad, who knew from intelligence, that the shrine was not the meeting place, decided that Philip was no fool and no useful purpose would be served by staying with him. There was little time to spare and it was imperative that a message confirming Philip's arrival be sent that night. Having pointed out the direction of the shrine and made an excuse for not going the whole way, he set off across the valley.

It was only a few minutes short of mid-day when Philip arrived at the meeting place and found Tina almost on the point of leaving,

"What took you so long?" Tina asked, "I had almost given you up."

"I guessed you had seen me, so waved to re-assure you that I knew you were there and would join you when it was safe." Philip replied, then, grinned boyishly and added. "It didn't occur to me that you might not know what I intended to do."

Tina laughed and said,

"You men are all alike, you seem to think we can read your thoughts."

"Well can't you?" Philip quipped. "We had better get moving."

They found a worried Pamella waiting on the narrow track leading to the house. She had seen them cross the river at the bottom of the canyon and could scarcely wait for the safe return of her daughter.

"I was so worried," Pamella said, "imagining all sorts of things. We heard the sound of the plane, it went on for so long, we began to wonder why."

"We had some problems," Philip said, as they approached the door of the house, where Tina's aunt, Tania, with a worried frown creasing her forehead was waiting.

"I wondered where you had gone," she said to Pamella as they entered the house, "It's silly, I know, but you had me worried for a moment." Then, turning to Tina and Philip, "Would you like some coffee?"

Inside the main room, chairs had been set round a table, which was furnished with pencil and paper. Mugs and a carafe of water were also provided. Already seated at the table were Luigi Vincenzo, at the head, with Donnola on one side and the sergeant major on the other. Francesco and Alan sat opposite each other, and a further seat was provided for Philip. As they entered, Luigi rose, proffered an outstretched hand to Philip, then, introduced him to the other occupants of the room and said,

"Glad you made it, what took you so long? Come be seated. . . . We must get started," Then, to Tina, "Well done Precious."

"There were unexpected delays." Philip said, in answer to Luigi's question, "We wasted a lot of time trying to locate the right place for me to come down. The light was not good, despite a near full moon. Too many clouds which threw shadows, making things on the ground more difficult to see." He looked at Tina, who was leaving the room, as if seeking her corroboration, then, continued with, "We were already late when I jumped. At first, I thought I had hit the deck way off target . . . I seemed to be too close to the town and didn't know whether the characters congregating at the entrance had seen me drop, so lay low for a while. Then some cove claiming to be a released POW called Jim, but known as Marco accosted me, pretending to be my contact." He frowned and added, "What worries me, is that he knew my name. Something we will have to discuss."

Opening the conference, Luigi started with,

"You have all heard what Philip said." His words were interrupted by Tania, who came bustling in with a cup of steaming coffee for Philip, who smiled his thanks and would have said something, if Luigi's disapproving look hadn't sent her scurrying out of the room. "It explains his delay, and the reason is disturbing news, but enough time has been lost, we must now get down to the business in hand. Have you any comments?"

The first to speak was Francesco,

"It seems to me," he said, "that there is a mole in Allied H.Q. Ever since the disastrous end of my last trip through the forward area, I've had my suspicions. There were several thwarted efforts during October and November last year. Giorgio cancelled his last trip because so much was going wrong. We've known for a long time that the Sicilian is not what he pretends to be, but, if he is the agent in the field, it's a mystery how he gets hold of information that is only known to a few of us and the Allies H.Q."

Francesco paused a moment and would have added to his theme, had Luigi not cut him short by saying,

"That is something you Leaf men will have to sort out. It is not what we are here to discuss." Then, followed on from his opening sentence with, "Our main purpose is to finalise arrangements, for the reception of the arms and ammunition which will be dropped in two days time."

"I wouldn't agree," Francesco interrupted Luigi, and continued with, "with all due respect; the Germans obviously know a great deal more about this operation than they should. I think it imperative that the location and date be changed. While agreeing that 'Operation Guntac' should be discussed first, I think It is important we pay some attention to this other problem."

"Which in view of what we have learned today, has to be different to the original arrangements" Donnola said, without waiting for Luigi's comments. Then, posed the question,

"What are the possibilities of two drops, Philip?"

"What do you mean, two drops?" Philip replied and added, "I don't know whether the powers that be would take kindly to doing that."

Il Tiranno, who had been listening in silence to what was being said, suddenly grinned, in a powerful voice, he seemed incapable of talking quietly, boomed,

"If you are suggesting what I think you are, the idea has possibilities." Then, cast his eyes towards Luigi, who responded immediately with,

"And that is?"

"As if in one combined thought, Donnola and Il Tiranno started to speak together. Using identical words they both said,

"A dummy run and . . ."

The short silence that followed was broken by Luigi, who chuckled briefly and said,

"Carry on Donnola, I think both the sergeant major and myself know what you are about to suggest."

Clearing his throat, Donnola took a sip of water from the mug by his side and started with,

"I can't see any reason why a dummy drop of sacks of earth or other rubbish," he grinned and continued with, "couldn't be dropped at a location well away from the one where the real consignment will be dropped."

"Just what I was thinking," boomed Il Tiranno. "I could put a small force of men in the hills round the original site of the drop. Which is where the Tedeschi will be expecting us to be. Their task will be one of distraction, to give the impression that the supplies are being dropped where their intelligence has informed them they would be. Leopoldo's youngsters can collect the real hardware, protected by a few experienced fighters.

"That's all very well, and has every possibility of success, I am sure that H.Q would agree to something like that," Philip said, "but," he added, "if there is a mole at H.Q. how can we be sure that our plans will not be intercepted?"

"I've been thinking about that," Francesco cut in. "The main problem as I see it, is that we only have two days to make all the arrangements. Getting a message to a trusted officer can be arranged. Time is the problem."

There followed a short period of silence, which was eventually broken by Donnola, who said,

"With all this talk of moles, how do you propose to do that?"

"Angelo has a special, password protected, route for emergency use only. Problem is, getting a message to him in time." Francesco said in reply, "He is the only one among us that can use it. Time is tight, I know. But, if we can get to him by tomorrow night, there will still be a day for arrangements to be made." Then, turning to Luigi, he added, "Tina could be with him by then. That is assuming you will allow her to go"

"I couldn't stop her, she would deem it her duty," Luigi replied, there was a hint of pride in his voice. "Do we all agree this is a workable idea and should be adopted?"

"Providing, the real drop is made well away from the dummy, "Donnola said, "I think it should work. After all, we don't want the Tedeschi to hear any action, should it become necessary."

"You are quite right." Il Tiranno said, "Have you a location in mind?"

"Somewhere near Ascoli, which is the other side of the valley from here." came the reply.

Luigi, chuckled, and said,

"And in your territory... but it makes sense. Are you all agreed?"

This time, the assent was universal.

"My men know the area and will be able to help position your task force," Donnola pointed out, "we haven't any time to lose, so I suggest I take you there tonight to see if you approve."

"No need for that." Luigi said in answer, "It would be a waste of time, I am sure the place you have in mind will be fine. Do you know the map reference?"

For a moment Donnola looked lost, then, his face brightened as he said,

"No, but if you have a map, I can show you the exact spot."

Philip, who had been listening to the comments following Donnola's suggestion, turned to Francesco and said,

"You mentioned someone called Angelo. Would he be the agent I have been told will get me back across the forward area?"

"Without doubt. He is in control of the agents. I'm surprised though that they didn't tell you to contact me direct as you are in my area of operations. You're in luck, he is planning a trip within the next few days." Francesco replied.

"Perhaps that's why," Philip remarked.

Francesco shook his, and said,

"No! Allied H.Q. Never knows about these trips until late in the day preceding."

"How do I make contact? Or will you do that?" Philip asked.

"You could go part way with Donnola, but it would take you a good distance out of your way." Francesco paused and looked at Luigi, who interpreted his thoughts and said,

137

"Tina could take you to Angelo tomorrow." Then, looked at Philip's slight figure and added, "How are you for walking?"

Philip shrugged his shoulders and said I'm used to hiking and the army makes sure we keep fit. I'm sure I will be OK."

"It's quite a long trek. Even walking briskly, it will take you all day. Tina is an early riser and will leave at first light so make sure you are up and about early," Luigi said, in a jovial manner. Then, more seriously, added, "Make sure you look after her."

. . . .

The day's exertion and a heavy meal at Angelo's table had a soporific effect on Philip, who, seated beside a blazing fire fought to keep awake.

"No good dozing, my son," Angelo said, with a twinkle in his eye. "You still have a little walking to do. Filomena will take you to Michele, who will look after you until Giorgio, who will arrange your escort, comes."

At that moment, Filomena appeared carrying a mug of steaming black coffee, offering it to Philip, she said,

"I know you English prefer your coffee this way. Come, drink it, it'll wake you up."

Philip gratefully took the coffee, swallowed a mouthful, gasped and said,

"Gosh! It's hot. . . . Thanks, it's the way I like it"

Trying hard not to laugh, Angelo watched Philip fan his mouth, and said,

"It is beginning to get dark, so it is safe for you to go now, Filomena will take you, . . . and you had better go with them, Tina. I have work to do so won't be much company if you stay."

When Filomena knocked on the door of Casa dei Pioppi, Michele opened the door before she had time to do so and said,

"What brings you here Filomena? Come to see Caterina?" Then, to Tina, "Hallo Tina, we haven't seen you since before the snow. How are you?"

"Fine," Tina replied, "I have brought a friend, who was instructed to contact Angelo. His name is Philip."

Michele frowned. Hitherto, with the exception of Peter, he had only accepted guests introduced by Giorgio, who would have vetted them first.

Tina was quick to notice the hesitation and said,

"He has come to us on a special mission involving Papa and now has to get back across the line. I can't say more."

Somewhat relieved, Michele shook Philip's hand, stood to one side and said,

"Then you are welcome, come in. Would you like some wine?"

Philip followed the two girls in, smiled and said,

"That's a civil idea. Thank you."

Caterina didn't have to see Filomena and Tina to know who was entering. She had not only heard Michele's words of greeting, she had also recognised their voices. The name Philip was new to her and she peered, unsuccessfully, across the room in an effort to see who it was. Filomena embraced her and said,

"You remember Tina, don't you. She has been looking forward to seeing you again."

"Of course I do, She was here in the Autumn." Caterina replied, paused, then, added,

"I don't think I've met your friend."

Filomena smiled, gave the old lady another hug, beckoned Philip over and said,

"Come over here Philip, Caterina would like to meet you," Then, turning to Caterina said, "His name is Philip."

"I know that, I heard you say it," Caterina retorted almost querulously, then, smiled and said "Come closer young man so that I can see you."

As the evening progressed, Filomena was surprised, and not a little worried to notice that Tina seemed to be obsessed by Peter; engaging him in conversation at every opportunity that presented itself. Speaking in English, with the pretence that she wanted to practise the language, she monopolised him to the extent that Giuseppina was beginning to look annoyed. Filomena knew her well, and knew how volatile she could be, so was relieved to notice that she was suffering in silence.

Returning home, later that evening, Filomena couldn't help noticing, that Tina was unusually quiet. Seeking to break the silence, she said,

"You're not saying much, are you tired?"

Tina shook her head, but didn't reply immediately. When she did, she said, rather haltingly,

"I am tired. . . . It's not that, . . . I am sure I've seen Peter before, I can't think where. . . . At first I thought he was Gordon."

"Gordon, who's that?" Filomena asked.

"Not anybody you would know," Tina smiled as she spoke, and continued with, "I only saw him briefly, he was in a party led by Francesco. But . . . it can't be him, they were all captured. That was when Francesco got hurt. Remember, Guido carried him to safety. In any case, Gordon had a small beard, and could speak our language, whereas, Peter only knows enough to get by. I tested him several times while pretending to practise my English."

"You seem to be quite good at that language," Filomena commented.

Tina giggled and there was her usual merriment in her eyes as she responded with,

"Mama taught me. I have to pretend I don't know more than a few words, Papa's funny that way. He speaks English very well and, as you know, Mama is English, but, he wants his little girl to remain Italian." Tina giggled again and added. "He even had Mama change her name from Pamela to Pamella."

"If you have seen him before, it couldn't have been here," Filomena remarked, "Alberto and Francesca, they are Staffetini, rescued him from a shepherd's shelter on the slopes of the Gran Sasso. He is a nice lad, and very polite." Filomena paused and smiled, "Guiseppina is a little smitten by him."

"I had noticed that," Tina commented.

"She is always commenting on what beautiful hands he has," Filomena couldn't repress a chuckle, as she added, "but they do have something in common. Peter has a nice tenor voice voice, which blends beautifully with Giuseppina's. They spent a lot of time during the winter trying out various Operatic pieces."

"Alan and Paul have lovely hands too," Tina commented.

. . . .

There was a full moon, in a clear sky on the night of the drop, revealing in sheer relief the shape of the Caproni circling overhead. There was no mistaking the 'Wow-wow' sound of its engines. Il Tiranno glanced at his watch. Two-thirty in the morning, the drop was scheduled for Two - forty. A feeling of elation swept over him as the realisation came that the enemy had been fooled and were watching the area. The unmistakable shape and drone of two Messerschmitts circling high overhead seemed to confirm it and he uttered a silent prayer for the safety of the carrier plane, which was about to arrive.

As Il Tiranno gazed, the outline of a heavier aircraft appeared as a small dot to the south-east of where he stood. Even as he watched, a Spitfire appeared, as if by magic, climbing rapidly toward the two fighter planes circling above. Engagement was swift and dramatic.

Flying between the two enemy planes, the Spitfire looped over in an incredibly tight curve arriving on their tails in one graceful movement. Fascinated, Il Tiranno watched the two Messerschmitts separate as the tracers from the Spitfire tore harmlessly into space. With superb precision, the enemy planes flew together again until over the Spitfire, then split apart, to attack from either side. With equal precision and speed, the Spitfire dived towards the spot where Il Tiranno was standing.

"Santa Porca Diavalo!"

The oath burst from Il Tiranno's lips as he leaped for the safety of an overhang and watched the spurts of dust made by the bullets of the enemy planes, (which had been quick to follow) as they hit the track; inches from where he was standing. From the corner of his eye, he saw the Spitfire fly in to the narrow confines of the canyon before climbing again high into the sky and watched in amazement as one of the Messerschmitts followed. The sound of an explosion, followed by a glow, which threw into sharp relief the shape of the houses on the cliff like edge, told its own story.

Now, so high, they were almost invisible, the two remaining planes, seemingly bent on suicide, converged on each other. Had their tracers not lit the sky, it is doubtful whether Il Tiranno and Luigi, who now stood beside him, would have been able to locate them. Fascinated, they watched the two rapidly draw closer to each other. It seemed they had to collide when, as suddenly as it had begun, the German plane lost height and dived, apparently out of control, towards the ground. Although, seasoned in battle, Il Tiranno heard himself say to Luigi,

"Brave men!"

The Spitfire followed the plane on its downward flight, then levelled off and dipped in salute, before performing an almost obligatory Victory roll.

The battle in the air was barely over, when the plane carrying the cargo to be dropped over the site arrived. No time was lost, before the waited for bundles could be seen parachuting down. One of the bundles drifted towards Luigi and his sergeant major before it headed for the tree lined slopes of the hills above the valley

"I'm glad we won't have to look for that," Il Tiranno said.

Luigi didn't comment immediately, he was staring, almost in disbelief, at the bundle that had just floated by. Finally, he said,

"Don't be too sure. I think I saw rifles in that load and have a nasty feeling that our suggested alterations for 'Operation Guntac' have been ignored. If I'm right, that little load is the only one we are likely to get."

As if to confirm Luigi's comment, an armoured vehicle appeared at each end of the narrow valley. Both were followed by lorry loads of troops. Regretting his decision to mount only a few men, Il Tiranno said,

"I wish we had brought more men. Those down there are very exposed. If you are right about what has been dropped, we would have collected our supplies."

"It wouldn't have made any difference if we had a hundred men; which we haven't. It's obvious the Tedeschi knew all about this operation. Without the element of surprise, any attempt to attack such a large formation would be little short of suicide." Luigi pointed out.

. . . .

On the slopes above Ascoli, Donnola looked anxiously at his watch; a huge turnip like affair handed down from his grandfather, stared into the sky and said to Gianni standing beside him and addressing him by his adopted name said,

"I hope, Lepre, that they are coming. It was supposed to be two-forty and it's nearly three o'clock. Can you see anything?"

The other stared into the distance. It was a clear night, with a full moon that turned the lower ground into a panorama of silver that stretched as far as the eye could see. There was no shadow of a low flying aircraft on the ground, or shape in the sky. He shook his head and said,

"I hope this doesn't mean they are not coming. Are you sure you have the time right?"

"Date and time are both right, there's no mistake abut that," Donnola replied. "I was hoping that the Allies had adopted our suggestions. But, it is beginning to look as if they have gone ahead with the original plan."

"If you are right about the Tedeschi knowing about 'Guntac' Luigi and his sergeant major won't be able to do much, with so few men."

Donnola nodded in agreement, looked at the sky again and said,

"That is true, but the Tedeschi doesn't take chances. Believe me, even with all the men we have, the force they would put there would be too big for us to tackle. I suggest we wait a few more minutes. If there is still no sign of the plane, we will go."

"Why not make it a quarter of an hour? We've lost half the night, a little longer won't make much difference." Gianni said, then, looked at Donnola and added, "At least that way, we'll have a clear conscience."

Donnola shrugged his shoulders and said,

"If you don't mind I don't. Unfortunately, I don't think they are coming."

Fifteen minutes stretched to twenty. In exasperation, Donnola picked up a back pack he had laid on the ground and said.

"Enough! Let's go."

Donnola had barely uttered the words when Carlo came running to them, there was no mistaking the air of excitement that he bore.

"They are coming, I can hear the plane," he gasped out.

Both Donnola and Gianni stopped what they were doing and strained their ears to listen. Being unable to hear anything, Donnola turned to Gianni and said,

"I can't hear anything, can you Lepre?"

Gianni shook his head.

"I can." Leopoldo said, as he joined them at a more leisurely pace.

"If you can, you must have very good hearing," Gianni said. Then, added, "Just a moment, I think I heard something too."

Scarcely daring to speak, the four stood in silence, listening to the drone of an aircraft as it came nearer.

Leopoldo's enthusiastic band of would be partisans, could barely contain themselves as they waited for the plane, now clearly visible, to drop its cargo.

From where they stood, on the slope overlooking the area, Donnola and Gianni watched the lads tumbling over each other, as they each strove to be the first to pick up a bundle.

"I'd wager a fortune they don't realise how heavy those loads will be. It will probably take two of them to lift some of them. Where are the donkeys and that cart Gregorio promised us? I hope they didn't get tired of waiting and leave." Donnola said, looking towards a gap in the surrounding hills.

"One of the donkeys has just come in and I can see the cart behind it," Gianni said, then added, "Where are those two English recruits? I thought they were supposed to be helping."

"Alan and Paul? They've already gone down and are helping. It's time we went as well."

As they reached the cart, one of the packages broke open to reveal a good supply of 'Camel' cigarettes.

"A present from the Yanks!" Paul exclaimed and pocketed a packet.

"Put it back." Alan's voice was sharp, "Those will be distributed properly. I don't know what Captain Vincenzo would say if he saw you."

Paul went red in the face, he felt annoyed at the rebuke. Realising that it was merited, he put the packet back and said,

"Sorry, I wasn't thinking."

"Then you should." Alan retorted. "It's not much I know, but you are a sergeant in charge of training so should know better."

Paul could feel his blood rising, but controlled his temper; he wanted to say alright, don't go on, but years of discipline came to the fore; he thought better of it and remained silent.

Donnola, who hadn't seen the incident with the cigarettes, knew from the tone of their voices that some form of dispute was going on, intervened curtly,

"Speak in Italian, so that we can understand you"

As Donnola spoke, Gianni, who was helping to carry a heavy metal bound case arrived beside the cart. Whatever Donnola was about to say was left unsaid. Turning his attention to the two, now lifting the heavy weight on to the cart, he said instead,

"I wondered where you were Lepre. That box isn't very big, but by the look of you two, it's very heavy."

"It is," Gianni gasped, "It's ammunition, that's why."

Picking up a Sten gun in one hand and a Bren in the other, Donnola said,

"Capitano Vincenzo said you need a decent weapon and may choose something straight away."

Gianni couldn't believe his luck. Without even bothering to examine the two weapons, he took the one nearest, which was the Bren and said,

"This is marvellous. I won't be sorry to say goodbye to that old Tommy gun, it was always jamming."

Donnola watched, with an amused expression on his face, as Gianni balanced the weapon in his hands and pointed it towards the ground. Then, grinning broadly, he said,

"So long as you're happy, put it down for now, we have work to do. I'll give you some ammunition before we leave."

. . . .

Oberst[21] Ludwig Von Hoffmann, in command of the German garrison at Santa Stefano gazed incredulously at the broken, useless weapons piled on the warehouse floor.

"That group has fooled us again." he said to the man standing beside him, Did you see any of them Karl?"

Hauptmann[22] Karl Schmitt, who had been in command of the task force sent to intercept the drop, shook his head and said in reply,

---

[21] Colonel
[22] Captain

"I don't think any of the rebels were there. If they had been, surely they would have mounted some sort of attack."

"They were there, you can bet your boots on that," the oberst replied, and grinned as he added," no doubt up there in the forest, laughing their heads off. You have to admire them for their gall."

"Surely, if they had been hiding in the trees, we would have been sitting ducks." Karl remarked, hesitantly.

"That leader of theirs is no fool. Think about it Karl. Why do you think that place was chosen?"

The hauptmann thought for a moment, shook his head, looked hesitantly at his commanding officer and said,

"I assume it was because it was an ideal spot for an ambush."

"If you think that, I shall have to give some thought to your future promotion."

Karl looked crestfallen for a moment, then said in an almost timid tone,

"I suppose, because the forest is so high up the mountain and the area below so wide, it would be impossible to make a surprise attack."

Ludwig and Karl had been comrades in arms for many years but because of promotion they couldn't be as close as they once were. Feeling a little sorry for his old friend, Ludwig said,

"Precisely, they might have that verse at the end of their song, 'The Rifleman', that more or less says, 'Don't cry if wounded they fall and die, what does it matter if by dying they are liberated.' But that doesn't mean they want to commit suicide. Well done!"

CHAPTER THIRTEEN

Every detail of the tiny store they called il Sale Tabac was visible in the clear light of the rising half moon, which shone from a star lit sky as Philip and Peter passed on their way to the rendezvous indicated by Michele earlier that day. Barely visible in the heavy shadows, the man, talking to Nonna Ricci would have passed unnoticed, had he not stepped into the light from her doorway. Dressed as he was, in a faded blue shirt, that had seen better days and a pair of light coloured baggy trousers, the shape of him became clearly visible. He looked in their direction and waved.

When Peter waved back, Philip became instantly alert, he was aware that his heart was beating quicker as he said,

"Who was that?"

"A friend. His name is Marco."

"How do you know him?"

"Since the decent weather started, I've spent a lot of the day just wandering around. You know how it is, you meet people and talk a bit. His English is pretty good and he has helped me out with the odd word here and there that I didn't know." Peter paused, then added, almost as an after-thought, "He was an Italian soldier, but since the armistice he has been wandering round waiting for a chance to get to his home, which he told me is in Basilicata. Where is that by the way?"

"Way South of here. It's one of the Provinces."

Philip relaxed a little as he replied, but still felt cautious. He looked sternly at Peter and said,

"You shouldn't have waved back, it was tantamount to inviting him over. Now we must make a detour, by circling round and hope we don't lose our way. Fortunately, the village isn't very big, so that shouldn't be a problem. Timekeeping is though. We must hope our guide will wait."

If Peter was annoyed or embarrassed by the rebuke, he didn't show it when he said,

"I can't see why that should be necessary."

"Nevertheless, we shall do it." Philip replied curtly.

Together, they turned down a narrow alley between the houses and circled part way round the outer perimeter of the village. When satisfied that they weren't being followed, Philip led the way along a winding track which he calculated would be one that Michele had pointed out on a map as an alternative route should they lose their way.

The hands of Philip's watch stood at eight-forty five when Peter asked,

"Do you think he's left?"

"I wouldn't have thought so." Philip replied in a tone more confident than he felt, "We are only about twenty minutes late and in this game, they must be used to delays."

They found Gino, who introduced himself as Guido, waiting on a path that wound through the wooded slopes high above La Villa. Here in the darkness beneath the trees, the sharp tang of living pine mingled, harmoniously, with the odour of the rotting leaves and pine needles that covered the path, filling the air with their fragrance.

Suddenly, the darkness became more intense as a cloud, which seemed to come from nowhere, obscured the moon. A light breeze rustled the leaves of the trees as if to warn them that rain was on the way. When it came, only a few minutes later, it was as furious as it was unexpected. Quickly soaking through the canopy of leaves above, it added a chill to the air that had not been there before. Philip shivered as he felt the rain seeping through his clothing and found himself hoping that the following day would bring better weather.

When the rain stopped, as suddenly as it had begun, a ghost like blur, barely visible in the gloom, came into view. No glimmer of light could be seen filtering through the cracked and splintered shutters. It was obvious the place had not been lived in for many years.

Guessing it to be their destination, Philip said, almost jocularly,

"The rain could have waited a few minutes."

Gino put his fingers to his lips and said in a low tone,

"Keep your voice down. I don't expect trouble, but we must always be attentive. Wait a moment I'll check."

Gino approached the house cautiously. Even so, the door opened before he arrived and Angelo's head appeared round a curtain that obscured the entrance.

Gino turned and beckoned to Philip and Peter, then taking care not to part the curtain obscuring the room behind it until the other two were safely behind the closed door, stepped inside.

The only light came from a tiny Aladin's lantern type of oil lamp, which gave no more light than a small candle would, and because there wasn't a fire in the hearth to relieve the gloom, the faces that turned towards them as they stepped through the curtain, were difficult to discern. However, Philip was able to recognise Angelo, seated at a table. Angelo immediately rose to greet the new arrivals, then, as he returned to the table, he said to Peter,

"So you decided to come after all," and followed with, "I have to have the customary details of both of you. Ranks, names and numbers only."

Having recorded the necessary information on a list, he rose again from the table, handed a copy to Philip and said,

"With you in the party, it isn't necessary for one of the escorts to go with you. Take note of everything Guido says and follow his instructions implicitly. . . .We are all here now, I will introduce you to the others."

The group Philip was to escort was not large,

"We don't like more than six in these expeditions," Angelo explained.

Having introduced Philip and Peter to an S.A.S. man, who was returning from a mission, as Geof and a prisoner of war who not only had a broad Scotch accent, but also proudly displayed, a tattoo on his brawny arm, depicting a pair of bagpipes surmounted by a thistle.

"He likes to be called Jock." Angelo said as he led the way across the room to a corner where a flight lieutenant was changing out of his service clothing into less conspicuous attire.

"I pranged the kite. You can call me Archie, they all do," the flight lieutenant said, with a disarming grin, as he struggled into a well worn jacket that was too small.

Turning to the remaining character, who had just joined them, Angelo said,

"John, meet Philip and . . ."

Before he could finish, John grasped Peter's hand and said,

"Fancy seeing you here Charlie. Haven't seen you since that party at Maud's place. What a night that was."

Peter looked at him blankly and seemed to hesitate for a moment, before he said,

"I think you must be mistaken, I don't think we have ever met. I don't know anyone named Maud."

"He ran that place in Shoreditch, you know, where we used to get the used bits and pieces for our home built short wave wirelesses. Surely you must remember Giorgie hanging by his toes from that rafter and his surprise when he fell off." John chuckled as he recalled the event. "It was just before the Munich crisis. That fellow Mosley was there, trying to get some of us to join his Blackshirts." John chuckled again. "He was quite annoyed when I said I only wear white shirts."

"A long time ago then," Peter replied, I expect your memory is playing tricks. I've never been to Shoreditch in my life and certainly never met Oswald Mosley."

"Maybe. Sorry! I could have sworn it was you I met there." John said as shaking his head, he returned to a chair he had vacated.

As he sat down, Filomena left the room. When she returned, she was carrying a cauldron of steaming spaghetti, which she dumped on the table. Then, as she turned to fetch plates, forks and sugo she saw Philip, crossing the room to say hallo. There was no mistaking the warmth of her greeting as she said,

"It's a pleasure Philip, to see you again." Then, as he embraced her, she added, "How wet you are. Did you get caught in that rain?"

As Philip gazed down at the small figure not much higher than his chest, something of her exuberance was transmitted to him. Momentarily, his gloomy thoughts relating to the reason for a detour were dissipated.

A quiet, almost shy smile hovered on the lips of Angelo. In a way that was peculiar to him, as from a corner in the room, he watched his young daughter slip out of Philip's arms and bustle around the table preparing it for a meal, before disappearing again through the door.

Typical of her kind, Filomena felt hospitality was lacking if a meal was not offered, so, even though she was not in her home, she had made sure they would not be hungry. Besides, she enjoyed watching her guests eating.

"Come eat," she said happily.

Then noting that Philip had not joined the others, either seated or seating themselves, at the table, she took his hand and led him to a vacant chair.

Laughing, Philip shook his head.

"I've eaten already," he protested. Then, as the smile faded from Filomena's face, "perhaps some wine?"

Deftly pulling the stopper from a bottle of wine, Filomena poured two glasses and in one swift movement that was poetry to watch, handed a glass, first to Philip, then to her father.

"Won't you join us?" Philip asked as he took his glass.

Filomena hesitated a moment, looked at her father, then as he nodded, she said,

"Well just a small one."

Angelo laughed, and said,

"She likes sambuca, when we can get it." Then, raising his glass in the traditional toast,

"Da salute!"

"A Milano!" Philip responded.

Angelo chuckled and made his often repeated pun in response, "Bel' Brindisi!" A pun relating to the two towns, Milan and Brindisi (A thousand years and a lovely toast),

Becoming serious again, Angelo said,

"What did you make of that business between Peter and John?"

Something in the manner of this, seemingly, shy man, could be detected in the low, yet crisp tone of his voice. It was as if he was he was a different person.

"I wondered about that too," said Philip in an equally low voice.

Hearing the remarks, Filomena recalled Tina's words, made while returning from Michele's a few evenings before. '*I am sure I've seen Peter before, . . . I can't think where. . . . At first I thought it was Gordon. But, it couldn't be him . . . Gordon was in the party that was captured when Francesco was hurt.*' Her voice barely above a whisper, she told them about it.

"It does seem a bit odd." Philip commented, "Perhaps he has one of those faces that always looks familiar."

"I don't suppose it means anything." Angelo said, rather dubiously. "Peter seems to be a nice lad and has been with Michele ever since the snow came. Had there been anything untoward, Michele would have had unwanted visitors by now. Nevertheless, it would be prudent to keep him in sight tomorrow."

A stunned silence followed Angelo's words and for a pregnant moment neither of them spoke, as awareness of a possible added risk filled both their thoughts."

Finally, Angelo broke the spell by saying,

"Nobody, including Peter, knew we would be gathering tonight, ready to leave tomorrow morning; except Giorgio and myself. Not even Filomena, until it was almost time to come here." A frown creased Angelo's forehead as he paused, before adding, "No one would have had the opportunity to pass on useful information."

Having briefed Philip thoroughly and warned him once again to keep an eye on Peter, Angelo said,

"We must get back home now, there are things that have to be done tonight." Then, addressing Filomena, who was busy clearing the table, "Leave that to them. We are going now."

As the door closed behind them, Angelo was heard to say,

"It's a serene night, bids well for tomorrow."

Having left the house, Angelo and Filomena followed a little used path, which circled high above La Villa before hugging the bank of the rivulet which emptied into the pool that Filomena liked to sit beside when she wanted to be alone. As they passed the pool, Filomena recalled the day that Giorgio had found her there, and a whimsical smile hovered on her lips.

Pushing open the door, which had been left unlocked, of their home, Angelo said,

"I am not happy with what we heard tonight. I wish there was some way of letting Luigi and his partisans know. It's a pity we don't have radio link with them."

"What could they do about it that might help?" Filomena asked in a dubious tone.

"Francesco would know the stopping houses," Angelo replied, there's only two of them. If the Tedeschi knows about them and has information about tomorrow, they are likely to follow previous patterns. From what Francesco told me, it was quite a small patrol that surrounded them, about twelve in number, travelling in a single truck, A staff car carrying an S.S. officer arrived some five minutes later. There are only two roads capable of being used by motors, One to each house. Luigi is more than capable of dealing with units as small as that."

. . . .

Watched by Angelo and Filomena from the high point above their house, the small party, led by Gino, wearing a white pull-over, with Philip walking beside him. made their way across the valley towards the distant shape that was the Maiella. Although only just past first light, their shapes were clearly visible.

By the time the sun was a fiery ball in the East, Philip's group had spread out and the last man had left the shelter of the olive groves. Now, it was riding high and the heat of the day was beginning to make itself felt. Gino's white pull-over made an easy marker for Archie, who, wearing the ill fitting jacket that had seen better days, followed some fifty metres behind. Nevertheless, every now and then, Gino would look back to ensure that Archie, and John who was walking with him, were still in sight.

Far beyond Gino's view, behind Peter and Jock, Geof acted as the back marker for the spread out group.

The cool shade shed by the olive trees lay far behind and Philip could feel the veins in his hands swelling as his system coped with the continuous exercise; which he found exhilarating. Sight of the entrance to the canyon, with the small town perched on the edge, reminded him of the letter Pamella had asked him to deliver if at all possible. He felt in his pocket to make sure it was sill there, then, withdrew it to memorise the address as a precaution against losing it. Thinking,'You don't see writing like that very often.' Philip read the incredibly neat copperplate writing which formed the address. As he did so, he stumbled against a loose rock, making him drop the envelope. Caught by the breeze the envelope danced ahead. Recovering his balance, Philip gave chase and succeeded in trapping it with his foot. As he stooped to pick it up, a tiny St Christopher medallion fell from the neck of his shirt and dangled on the end of a piece of string, which served as a lanyard to keep it safe. Memory of a pair of piercing blue eyes as he returned the memento to its place, brought a smile to his lips as he heard again the words, '*It will protect you on your journey. Santa Cristoforo is the patron saint of travellers.*' The

153

words had been said with such conviction that he found himself almost believing them. The smile broadened into a grin as he recalled the torrid look of jealousy in Carlo's eyes, when Tina insisted he should accept her gift.

Alone with his thoughts, which were less pleasant, Geof tried to expel the memory of Storm troopers which had surrounded the small band of Garabaldini he had been sent to liaise with. He heard again the sounds he would never forget. The fading voice of Graham, his partner in the venture. He wished he had been able to hear what his friend wanted to say, but the noise of battle drowned out his voice. All he had managed to hear, was, the name Jeanie, and, '*tell her*,' before blood spurted from between the pale lips, preventing further speech. In all the background noise, he heard someone shout. '*Now we die*,' Had it not been for the Matteotti group arriving on the scene, they would have been massacred. Instead, it was the Germans that suffered that fate. Sadly, Geof took a crumpled photograph from a pocket and studied the face of a dark haired girl sitting on a tree stump, that smiled at him from a once glossy surface. The faded signature, with it's message, '*Come back my darling. Love, Jeanie X X X.*' was difficult to read against the dark background. Slowly, Geof turned the photograph over, to look again for the address that he knew was not there, and read, once more, the words scrawled, as if in haste, on the back. Words, not intended for others to read, which brought a lump to his throat, '*Grampound is not the same without you.*' "Come what may," he vowed, his thoughts loud on his lips, "If I get out of this alive, I'll find her. I expect she would like this picture back.... If she wants to, I shall bring her here to visit Graham's final resting place."

The group reached their stopping place shortly after mid-day.

"Wait in there Philip," Gino said, indicating a barn, which had somehow escaped the flames which had destroyed the farmhouse, "I'll check that everything is OK."

Watchful for any suspicious sign, Philip patiently waited for his charges to join him. A short distance away, barely visible against the heavily wooded slopes behind it, a thin wisp of smoke issued from the chimney of another farmhouse, which was the 'Safe house', where Gino had said they would get a meal. The thought of friendly hands busy preparing for the arrival of their guests brought a smile of anticipation to his face; as did also, the awareness that if all went to plan, this would be the last meal in German occupied territory. Switching his gaze, Philip thoughtfully contemplated a pellucid ribbon of silver that split the distant valley. Beyond the river a lone truck would be waiting to carry them on the final stage of their journey. He hoped the recent rain would not make the crossing too difficult.

"Almost there," he said to Geof as he entered the barn, then closed the door.

With the door closed, it was dark, the only light being that which filtered through cracks in the ancient woodwork. Philip wrinkled his nose as he tried to abort a sneeze, provoked by a pungent smell that pervaded the air, and waited for his eyes to adjust.

"Och! What a pong!" Jock's voice came out of the darkness.

"I've smelt worse," Geof said, with a chuckle, and added, "Lived next door to a pig farm once."

"It's bluidy dark. Can'na see a thing. Should have a wee bit of candle somewhere." Jock said. Then, while fumbling in his pocket, followed up with, "Are we all here?"

"Philip wouldn't have closed the door, if we weren't," John remarked. Nevertheless, he strained his eyes in an effort to count the vague shapes.

The sudden brightness of the sun sending its rays through the door, when Gino opened it on his return, made everyone blink. Philip looked at his watch as he rose stiffly to his feet. Nearly two hours had passed since the guide had told him to wait.

"Everything O.K?" He queried.

Gino nodded and said,

"I've had a good reconnoitre. Everything seems normal. No sign of the Tedeschi, which is good." he then pointed towards the house, and addressing the party in general, added, "All the same, it will be safer to wait until its dark before going to the house. When we do, leave one at a time and keep out of sight as much as possible. Donna knows you are here and will be waiting for you."

. . . .

From his look-out point on a ledge above the motor road, barely fifty metres from where he stood, Gino watched the dark, unlit shapes of three trucks and two staff cars travelling, at high speed. Filled with foreboding, he saw the convoy split. Without slackening their pace, one truck and a car continued on the motor road, while the remainder of the convoy, unexpectedly took the narrow and winding track that would take them to the 'Safe house'.

Desperately, Gino broke into a run, but it was hopeless. Without abating speed, the vehicles bumped and jumped over the rough track, coming to rest by the barn that had protected his charges during the afternoon.

There was nothing Gino could do, he was still a hundred metres away, when a score of German soldiers, leaped from the two trucks and ran toward the house. When the sound of rifle fire came to his ears, he was still too far away to give warning. Realising that there was absolutely nothing he could do, Gino pulled off his white sweater and made for the forest above him.

. . . .

"That was good!" John remarked, leaning back in his chair.

On hearing the word good, the hostess who had been introduced as Donna, smiled briefly and stepped forward with a huge ladle, ready to serve.

"You like? Eat, eat." she said, her face wreathed in a happy smile.

Covering his plate with his hand, John shook his head and said,

"Grazie No. I've eaten more than I need."

Undaunted by his protest, Donna pushed aside his hand and emptied the ladle on to his plate.

"Eat, eat, you like," she insisted.

John regarded his overflowing plate with a mixture of amusement and dismay. He never ceased to be amazed by the amount of food, the average lady of the house expected him to eat.

Philip looked at the mound of pasta on John's plate, switched his gaze to his face, and, eyes dancing with amusement, said,

"I haven't been here as long as you John, but already, I've learned not to praise the food on my plate. It's asking for trouble. They always think it means you would like some more."

"They always think that anyway. Now, if you don't polish it off, she'll be upset." Peter put in.

All at the table, laughed at the comment, including, (in spite of being the butt of the joke,) John.

Under the eagle eyes of Donna, John sopped up the remains of sugo with a piece of bread, and surreptitiously offered it to a large, yellow dog. Sensing sympathy, the dog regarded him from sombre brown eyes, wagged his tail, and drooled hopefully.

Noticing that Donna had seen the sly movement, John said,

"What do you call him, Donna?" Then, realising that she hadn't understood him, "Name, you Donna," and pointing to himself, "Me John," then, indicating the dog, "him?"

Donna shrugged her shoulders and said,

"He Cane."

John was unsure whether Donna meant the name of the dog was Cane, or was telling him the Italian word for dog, until, apparently recognising his name, the dog looked hopefully at Donna, wagged his tail, lazily this time, and sneaked under the table; coming to rest at John's feet.

It was a long time since John had enjoyed the companionship of a dog and the weight of Cane across his feet filled him with a sense of well-being. Stretching down, he casually fondled one of the clipped ears.

"Do you like that Max?" he murmured, absent mindedly using the name of his dog at home.

As if in reply, the dog grunted contentedly and put his head on John's lap.

"You could do with a good grooming," John said as he fiddled with a clump of knotted hair in the dog's mane.

Suddenly Cane stiffened and growled.

"Sorry, did I hurt you?" John asked, moving his hand to one of the ears.

Cane growled again and leaped for the door, overturning one of the vacated chairs in his hurry to get there.

"What's upset him?" John asked, addressing Donna, who's face had paled.

In one smooth movement, Donna put a finger of one hand on her lips and with the forefinger and thumb of the other, dowsed the small oil lamp that lit the room.

It seemed an age, sitting in the darkness, with pounding hearts; listening to the dog growling, before a slit of silvery light told Philip and his charges that Donna had opened the door to peer out.

"Scappa scappa, vengono i tedeschi." Donna called out, her voice shrill with urgency.

Throwing the door open she made a desperate dash for the rear of the house. Ahead, the forest loomed black and inviting, a sanctuary beneath a canopy of silver. Somehow, it had never seemed so far away, as unconscious of anything except a desperate need to evade the rapidly approaching shadows, Donna fled.

Ignoring the deep ruts in the once ploughed slope, and thankful that the Germans could not shoot without the risk of bringing their comrades under fire, Donna sprinted through a narrowing gap between the two lines of helmeted figures converging on her.

Weaving and dodging, with an agility surprising in a woman of her bulk, Donna succeeded in reaching the comparative safety of the grass covered slope that bordered the forest.

Suddenly, when about to enter the forest, it didn't matter any more. A deep burning pain in her side, robbed Donna of the will to go on. A wave of nausea swept over her and all the strength seemed to drain from her legs. There was a roaring in her ears that drowned out the distant shouts below. Slowly, almost gracefully, Donna sank to the ground.

Oblivious to the drifting sensation that assailed her, Donna lay on her back, watching, without interest, a small cloud pass across the face of the moon. 'Just a few minutes rest, that's all I need,' she mused, then, as darkness closed around her she murmured,

"I'm coming Osvaldo, I'm coming."

Meanwhile, outlined against the sky, their bayonets reflecting the light of the moon half a dozen figures were running toward the house.

Vaguely aware that Cane was bounding silently towards them, John leaped from his chair and dashed through the open door, but it was already too late. Help was impossible and there was no place to hide. The hollow crack of a rifle being fired came simultaneously with a flash of orange light and a howl of pain as a bullet found its mark, bringing Cane to a halt. With a growing sense of helplessness, John watched the dog stumble, then hurl itself forward, a yellow bundle of fury, as he charged his nearest enemy. With tears of frustration, John saw the German catch Cane on the point of his bayonet and stamp heavily on the dog's broken body to withdraw the weapon. The high pitched, almost boyish laughter which followed, as the soldier kicked the animal out of his path filled John with rage.

"Bastards!" He shouted, reaching for the gun he no longer carried.

The Germans fanned out round the house and were now coming from every direction. Flight was impossible and there was no place to hide.

"Steady on young man,... put your hands in the air, before you get all of us shot."

The cool authoritative voice of Philip sobered him. Angrily brushing the tears away, John reluctantly raised his hands and said,

"Did Donna get away?"

As if in answer to his question, the sound of three shots in rapid succession, coming from behind the house, cut him short.

"Who is in charge?"

The words in clipped but precise English, came from a German officer wearing the insignia of an oberleutnant, that had entered the door.

Philip stepped forward, saluted and introducing himself, said,

"Lieutenant Cargil. I expect you to treat these men correctly as prisoners of war."

The German smiled, a thin, tight lipped movement of the lips, which did nothing to detract from the coldness of his manner as he returned the salute and said,

"Oberleutnant Wolfgang. Tell your men to line up and wait. Are they all here?"

Philip looked round, as if he was checking, and said,

"Yes, all present and correct."

The oberleutnant regarded Philip suspiciously and in a curt tone, said,

"I was told there were six of you, and a guide. Where is your guide?"

"I am the guide," Philip lied

"The man in the white top. Where is he?"

Hoping Gino would have seen the Germans when returning from his reconnoitre and, being unable to do get to them in time to give warning, had taken evasive action. Philip thought a moment before answering,

"Whoever told you that, was mistaken," Philip retorted. Then, remembering a tiny speck in the sky which he had seen shortly after they had left the fork that would bring them on the higher route, he took a chance and said, "I expect your spy saw that fellow who walked with us for a few kilometres earlier on today. He left us when we reached the fork that goes towards Atessa."

The oberleutnant grunted in response and in unconcealed triumph, strode over to the men lined up against the wall and surveyed his captives. Stopping in front of Peter, he tapped him on the shoulder, beckoned to one of the soldiers and said,

"You know what to do."

Almost immediately after Peter had been led away. There came the sound of a shot.

"I hope that doesn't mean what I think it does," Archie said to Philip.

"If it does, I have a long memory and know that officers name," Philip replied.

. . . .

From his position high in a tree, obscured by leaves, Gino watched two figures (too far away to recognise in the scant light) come round the end of the house. They stood there for a few minutes; apparently talking. Distracted by a vague shape on the ground, he concentrated his gaze on it; but it was too indistinct to see properly. When after the sound of a shot drew his attention away, he looked again, the figures had gone.

CHAPTER FOURTEEN

Making their way back to the house after watching Gino and the group he was guiding, recede into the distance, the words of Tina, '*I thought it was Gordon.*' intermingled with those of John, '*Charlie. Fancy seeing you here. Haven't seen you since that party at Maud's place.*' kept running through Filomena's mind. Eventually, unable to contain herself any longer, she blurted out,

"I'm not happy Babbo."

"What's troubling you?" Angelo asked. Then, added, impishly, "Giorgio not with them last night?"

Filomena blushed and remained silent for a moment, before answering.

"That exchange between Peter and John. I told you about Tina saying she thought when she first saw Peter at Michele's, that he was someone called Gordon."

"I don't think there's a great deal to worry about. Gordon and Peter might be twins. Surely, if Peter is a spy. . . .That is what you are thinking, isn't it? Michele would have had unwelcome visitors by now. Anyway, for better or worse, they have already left, so there's little we can do about it." Angelo said, in a not very convincing tone.

"Well, yes. That's what is worrying me. I would have thought that if Charlie and Peter are twins, Peter would have said something like, you must be confusing me with my brother. His name is Charlie; it doesn't explain why Tina thought Peter was Gordon. It's all too much of a coincidence."

"And you want to try and do something about it," Angelo said, giving her a quizzical look.

"Well, yes." Filomena said, her eyes brightening as she spoke. "I expect Tina will have told Luigi about her fears, but she doesn't know about last night's episode, nor that a party is leaving today, and that Peter is in it. They are not much above half an hour ahead of us and if I leave now, I could be with Luigi by mid-afternoon."

"You are not leaving here, on what could be a wild goose chase, without having a proper meal first." Angelo said in a firm voice.

"But, there's . . ."

Angelo cut Filomena short and butted in with,

"There is plenty of time, the crossing isn't usually made until it's dark. They will hole up somewhere, even I don't know where. That information is only known to the guide and the leaf man organising the trip. Even he doesn't always know which 'safe house' is to be used. An extra half hour won't make much difference."

Late afternoon towards four, found Filomena walking up the narrow path on the side of the canyon. Her clothes were drenched. Melting snow, high up the mountain, coupled with recent heavy rainfalls, had swollen the river to such an extent that it now not only reached her waist, but also resembled a torrent, instead of the gently flowing stretch of water, that it normally was.

"Look at the state of you." Pamella's voice was full of concern, "Why didn't you cross on the plank? It's only a short way up stream,"

"I didn't want to waste time," Filomena replied. "Is Luigi here?"

"No, he left half an hour ago, so won't be back for a while." Quick to note the obvious disappointment manifested by her reply, Pamella added, "We are not likely to see him until tomorrow. Is it important?"

Filomena felt like saying, I wouldn't have walked all this way if it wasn't, but held her tongue and said instead,

"Yes it is rather."

Before she could say anything further, Tania came bustling in with a towel and clothing. Grabbing Filomena by the hand, she led her to another room and said,

"It can wait. Let's get you out of that wet clothing, immediately."

With Tania wearing a don't argue, I know best look, Filomena shrugged her shoulders, decided, best to obey and went meekly.

Dressed in borrowed clothing and wrapped in a blanket, Filomena gratefully hugged a steaming cup of coffee, made by Pamella, in the English way.

"No wonder, they like it this way," she murmured to herself.

"What did you say? I didn't catch it." Pamella asked.

Filomena smiled and said,

"I was talking to myself while thinking, no wonder you like your coffee made this way. It's really warming."

Pamella laughed. and said,

"I'm glad you like it. You'll have to make some for Angelo."

The thought of Angelo, who liked his coffee, nearly cold, in a tiny cup half full of sugar, when it was available, made Filomena giggle. But, she kept her thoughts to herself.

"You seem anxious. I realise you wouldn't have come all this way unless you thought it was necessary. What is it that Luigi must know?"

Filomena hesitated a moment before replying. Revelation of any movement of the evasion groups was strictly prohibited. However, she felt it would be silly not to pass on the information she had specifically made the journey for. She started by saying,

"Guido is leading a group today and we think there might be a spy with them."

"I thought that might be it," Pamella cut in, and followed up with, "Tina had the same suspicion and told her father. We knew, from what was said at the conference, that one of Giorgio's crossings was imminent, but we didn't know when. Young Carlo has been keeping watch daily. There are not many logical routes and young eyes can see a long way. He spotted the group around mid-day today and rushed back here to tell us."

Filomena gave a sigh of relief and said,

"Then he already knows."

"We don't know what routes they use, or where the safe houses are," Pamella began, "But Luigi reckons that they have to cross the Sangro; so there are only two or three, at most, logical routes that can be used. From what Carlo told us, he thinks they intend to use the route above the motor road, rather than the one below. They both go in roughly the same direction, skirting Guardiagrele, but, with the forest belt, there is more cover in the higher road. There are one or two derelict or deserted houses along that track, any one of which could be used as a stopping place to get a meal and hide in until dark."

"Your friend, Donna used to live along there," Tania cut in.

"That's right," Pamella affirmed, "I don't know if she still does, we haven't seen much of her since she lost Osvaldo. It must be very lonely without him."

"Papa doesn't think they will use the lower route, because, although it is nearer the river, it passes much closer to Guardiagrele, which is practically a fortress," Tina said as she entered the room,

"I didn't see you. When did you come in? What's happening? Is Luigi safe?" The words came tumbling out of Pamella's mouth.

"Everything is fine, Carlo has gone scouting ahead. I hope he doesn't get himself into trouble. You know what he is like, so impetuous. Even Papa couldn't stop him. I heard him say to Micio[23] that the path Giudo would probably use branches off from a track, that curves in a crescent through an area of scrub before rejoining the motor road half a kilometre ahead. The lower track which could be used, is within sight of one of the junctions, either of which, would have to be passed if the Tedeschi decide to go down that route; so, he suggested, that since the lower track leaves the motor road between the other two junctions, there is no point in mounting a check point there.

Pamella at this stage broke into laughter, stopping Tina's dialogue, and using the sergeant major's Christian name, said.

"Don't let Ricardo hear you call him that."

Tina grinned happily and said,

"Well, he is a great big pussy cat, isn't he?"

. . . .

It was already dark, when Luigi and his partisans reached the first of the two junctions. Luigi had hoped to get there during daylight and wished he had received the information earlier. The distant sound of rifle fire, less than fifteen minutes after his sergeant major had left with a squad of twelve men worried him. He knew Il Tiranno hadn't had time to reach the other end of the track and the noise coming from a higher level told him that something was happening along the higher track. He also knew, by the absence of rapid fire, that his detachment was not involved.

"I'll find out what's happening," Carlo said.

"No, Wait here," Luigi commanded. Then, realising his order had come too late, he shouted after the rapidly receding figure, "Don't take stupid risks."

Beckoning to one of the partisans, Luigi said,

"Come here Lombo, Run after the Sgt Major, tell him he is to take half his squad up the track, leaving Alan in charge of the rest. Tell him also, that I believe the Tedeschi are up there and Guido and his party

---

[23] Pussy cat.

are in trouble. If I am right and he gets to them first, he is to stay out of sight and wait till I arrive."

"Am I to return here?" Lombo asked.

"No, that won't be necessary."

The words were scarcely out of Luigi's mouth when a staff car travelling at high speed down the track toward them appeared. As the car drew closer, one of Luigi's partisans steadied his Sten, ready to fire.

"Let it pass Proco. Now, is no time to advertise our presence." Luigi said. Then, addressing his crew, followed on with, "Stay prepared for action. I don't need to tell you to keep under cover as much as possible."

They had been making their way up the track for half an hour, and Luigi was beginning to worry about the whereabouts of Carlo, when he suddenly appeared.

There was no mistaking Carlo's excitement as he said, in a hoarse whisper, which was difficult to interpret,

"The Tedeschi are in Osvaldo's new house, the one he built when the other burnt down. I don't know how many, but there's quite a lot. I saw them bring Filippo and four others out and put them in a barn next to the old house.

Luigi looked a little concerned and said,

"You say Philip and four others, there should be seven all told. Was one wearing a white sweater?"

"No," Carlo replied, "there were only five. The only one I knew was Filippo ."

"If two of them are in the house," Luigi said, more to himself than to Carlo. "It's going to complicate things, we shall have to be careful how we attack."

"Sorry Capitano . . . what did you say?"

"No matter Carlo," Luigi replied and posed the question, "Did you see what sort of guard they mounted on the barn.

Feeling he had done well, and more than a little proud of himself, Carlo smiled happily and said,

"I specially waited to see that Capitano. There is one man standing outside the door and another walking round the barn."

If Carlo had expected praise for his prowess, he was disappointed.

"What arms were they carrying?" Luigi asked.

"Rifles with fixed bayonets."

"I don't think we will have much trouble there. Is the barn within sight of the house?" Luigi then asked, and received the reply,

"Yes Capitano."

When Luigi and his section reached the barn, where Philip and the others were being held, the sentry by the door was only just visible. A large cloud obscured the moon, bringing with it a velvety blackness; from where they stood, even the derelict house was little more than an outline.

Motioning to the others to wait, Luigi crept forward to a point, where under the welcoming cover of a clump of trees, he could view the house where Carlo had said the Germans were. An almost secret smile of satisfaction creased his lips as he noted that the trucks they had come in were parked in the cleared area in front of the house.

"There will be about twenty four, twenty six with the drivers. Apart from the two on guard, they will all be inside the house," he told himself.

As if to prove him wrong, the silence of the night was split by the distant sound of three rapid bursts of gunfire. There followed a short moment of silence. Then the noise resumed, but now, the sharp crack of rifle shots were mingled with the rapid chatter of Sten guns. Full of foreboding, Luigi saw the door of the house open and an oberleutnant look out. He was joined a moment later, by two others each holding a bottle of wine. They stood framed in the doorway for several minutes; seemingly, from the movement of their heads, talking. Suddenly, as suddenly as it had begun the noise from below stopped and silence reigned once more.

Breathing a sigh of relief that Il Tiranno had not appeared during those crucial moments, Luigi returned to his men.

A faint rustle, which seemed to come from behind the barn caused all heads to turn in that direction. Ready for instant action, they silently spread apart.

. . . .

The appearance of a staff car, followed by a transport truck carrying the usual six a side helmeted figures, almost took Alan by surprise, coming as it did from the lower track. Because, of the speed and direction they were travelling, he thought they were on their way to the forward area. Nevertheless, he took no chances and gave the order to stand by.

When the staff car reduced speed and swerved on to the track some fifty metres below an area of scrub, where he and his men were hidden, Alan knew he was right to be cautious.

An order from Alan, to open fire was unnecessary, the men were experienced fighters, more experienced than he was with Guerilla warfare. The short burst of fire, which tore into the windscreen of the car, did it for him.

Alan saw, without emotion, the windscreen of the car shatter and the driver slump across the steering wheel. Minus a driver, the car slowed abruptly and curved off the track, where it collided with a tree and burst into flames.

Even before the car hit the tree, the men in the following truck, with an agility that must have been drilled into them, slipped over the side and took up positions in the shelter of the vehicle. Only the driver was slow in getting out, nevertheless he escaped the bursts of fire which came from the partisans, who were already fanning out and advancing round the two ends of the truck.

The exchange of fire was immediate and, at such short range, deadly. However the rifles of the Germans were no match against the rapid bursts of fire from the Sten guns which had been collected not very many days before. One German in a gallant show of valour, leaped from behind the truck, arm raised; ready to hurl a stick bomb into the cluster of partisans closest to him. The single bullet hole in the centre of his forehead, not only dropped him in his tracks, the stick bomb still firmly clasped in his hand, but also paid tribute to the expertise of the man, wearing a black feather in his hat, who had fired the shot.

With one of those strange flashes of memory, which come at times in the heat of battle, Alan recalled the words of Capitano Vincenzo, 'The ones with the feathers are the best.'

The skirmish didn't last long; it ended as quickly as it had begun, with the loss of two partisans. Neither side gave, or expected, mercy and fought with equal ferocity. The twelve German soldiers and their driver, were massacred. Armed with rifles only, they stood little chance against the six Sten guns and one rifle of a group of men, who cared not whether they lived or died.

When Il Tiranno appeared, very shortly after the cessation of the firing, he was carrying in addition to his Sten gun, a rifle, with fixed bayonet, slung baldric-wise across his back. Following close behind were the six men who were accompanying him. Fearing his sergeant major would step out in to an area where he could be seen, not only by the sentry, but also anyone who chanced to look out of the house, Luigi motioned to him to stay where he was and slipped across the intervening space to meet him. Keeping his voice low, he said,

"We know, from Carlo's reconnoitre that five of the group are held in the barn and assume the other two are in the house. One would be the guide but we don't know who the other is. There is a sentry at the door of the barn and another circling the area."

There was a tight lipped smile on Il Tiranno's face as he cut in and said,

"That one's been dealt with, Lama saw to that," and indicating the rifle on his back, added, "this rifle was his."

Luigi nodded his appreciation, but didn't comment. Instead, he continued with,

"We can only assume that the other two are in the house; possibly being interrogated. There is the possibility, of course, that they were put in the barn with the others after Carlo left the scene."

"We'll know the position better when we release the men in the barn," Il Tiranno commented, adding, "The first priority is going to be to deal with the sentry who you say is at the door of the barn, as silently as possible." He paused momentarily, smiled and said, "That shouldn't be a problem, Lama's accuracy with a knife is phenomenal, he did a Circus act with knives before the war."

Luigi nodded his head in approval and said,

"That has a reasonable chance of success. It's not often a Circus act comes in useful during a war; but, we will have to be careful. The sentry is in full view of the house. If that cloud clears the moon, anyone in the clearing will be visible. Once dealt with, we will have to be quick; the absence of a sentry is bound to be noted . . ."

"Capitano . . . Capitano. I have an idea." Carlo, who had sneaked across the clearing to join Luigi and the sergeant major, interrupted.

Although irritated by the interruption and tempted to say, 'don't interrupt. What are you doing here?' Luigi asked instead,

"What do you find so important, that you dare to butt into my conversation?"

Carlo stiffened. He hated being rebuked and felt affronted. He stood his ground and instead of answering the question, said,

"If I was to stand at the barn door, wearing the sentry's helmet and coat and holding his rifle, it would look, in this poor light, as if he was still there."

Luigi chuckled, he couldn't help himself. The whole idea seemed absurd, but on reflection, thought it might work.

. . . .

Schütze[24] Maxmilian Braur, Max to his friends, could hear the revelry coming from the house, and had seen, when the door opened, the bottles in the hands of two of his comrades.

"Why should I have to guard this door and miss all the fun?" he asked himself.

Max felt resentful, he hated the weight of the rifle, which seemed to burn into his shoulder. "That gefreiter hates me, and I hate him. He is always coming down on me. It's his fault I'm here," he grumbled out loud.

Despite strict instructions not to stray away from the door of the barn, and, be ready for any attempt by the prisoners to break it open, Max moved out to the centre of the clearing. It would have been the ideal opportunity for Lama, had the door of the house not been opened by the gefreiter. Seeing his sentry so far away from the barn, he strode across to him. Lama, who was ready, knife in hand, found himself forced to shrink back and wait for the next opportunity.

With the sentry standing correctly, close to the door and looking forward it was impossible to get a suitable angle, without being seen, for Lama to throw his knife.

Luigi was reluctant to put at risk, the safety of the men in the barn, by gambling that the sentry would not either shout, or fire a shot, if one of his men was sighted. Turning to Il Tiranno, he said,

"The sides of the barn are so flimsy, we mustn't risk any crossfire until the men are out of that death trap. Any suggestions, Florio?"

---

[24] German private.

"I agree," the sergeant major replied, "bullets will go through those wooden walls like a knife goes through soft ice cream. Don't worry, I don't think we will have to wait long. That sentry is an undisciplined oaf. I'd be willing to wager that before long, he will move away from the door. If he does, Lama never misses."

Il Tiranno, proved to be right, they didn't have to wait long. When Max fulfilled his prediction and stepped away from the door, fortune favoured. The cloud that had hidden the moon, cleared away. There was a flash of light on steel, as a knife found its target and an almost inaudible scurry of feet as Carlo and Lama glided swiftly over the open area, to hide the body and remove the coat. The whole performance was over in less than two minutes. Simultaneously Luigi opened the door of the barn. The occupants needed no invitation, almost wraith like, they slid through the door and melted in to the forest.

Safely out of sight, and a reasonable distance away, Luigi beckoned Carlo over and said,

"Do you know these paths and the old mill?"

"Yes Capitano. Yes." Pleased to be asked, Carlo beamed back.

"Then, take these men to the mill and wait until I arrive. Be careful not to make a noise, and keep a watchful eye for any of the Tedeschi. There might be others about." Then, Luigi conjured up a serious expression, and added, as if it were an afterthought. "Can I trust you?"

"Yes Capitano yes . . . yes . . . You can trust Carlo."

Luigi tried hard to suppress a grin, but was not successful, as he said,

"Good man. Take care."

Having given Carlo his orders, Luigi turned to Geof and Philip, handed the rifles taken from the sentries to them, and said,

"I hope you don't have to use them."

Luigi had scarcely finished speaking, when a rumpus, followed by the sound of Sten guns in action broke the silence of the night.

"I must go," Luigi said as he moved away.

"I'll come with you," Geof offered.

"Stay with the others, you might be needed," Luigi's words were rapped out in a peremptory order.

"Filippo! Filippo! . . . So glad to see you safe."

Carlo's voice, in an excited whisper, as he proudly led his party away, cut into Philip's thoughts. The unexpected appearance of the little Italian, who he hadn't seen since he left the house on the side of the canyon, brought a smile of pleasure to his lips. Although, he had only met him briefly, the youngster, so eager and keen, had left a lasting impression.

"Where the devil did you spring from?" Philip asked, more as something to say, than an enquiry.

Carlo's face went blank, as he said,

"Devil . . , Spring . . . *Che significa*[25]?"

Philip laughed, he couldn't help it, Carlo sounded so perplexed.

"Where did you come from?" Philip explained.

"Me with il Capitano," Carlo clicked his finger impatiently, as he struggled to find English words, Then, blurted hurriedly, "Come this . . . this . . . *sentiero*[26]"

"Path." Philip supplied.

"I walk you a piece . . . this path." Carlo said, proudly using his new word and totally unaware that he was mixing Italian in his speech, added, "Walk *altro*[27] path soon."

The old disused mill, a gaunt structure rising out of a confusion of leaves, flowers and thorns, was soon reached. Only the entrance, devoid of hinges for the still existing door, which leaned, as if drunk, against an inner wall was clear of the wildly growing plant life. The interior was surprisingly clean; a tin can on a plain wood table, surrounded by cut logs, stood on end, which served as seats, could be seen in the far corner and a mixture of brushwood and straw spread, on a section of the floor, gave evidence of people having slept there .

"Someone seems to have been living here," John remarked as they entered.

"Probably partisans, during the winter months," suggested Geof, as he looked around the room. "Whoever it was, they seem to have left."

---

[25] What does it mean?
[26] Path
[27] Other

As if to give a lie to his words, the sound of someone approaching seeming louder than it really was, came to their ears.

Motioning to the others to keep silent, Philip joined Geof at the doorway.

A blurred figure, little more than a flicker of movement, could be seen under the canopy of trees over the path they had recently used. Had it not been for the distant sound of gunfire, they might have thought it was one of Luigi's men. Whoever it was, he or she, seemed to be on their own.

As the figure, little more than a shadow, approached, Geof whispered,

"I think I know that shape, but taking no chances, he called out,

"We are armed, put your hands up and make no sudden moves. Approach slowly, and we won't harm you."

Gino, not only recognised the voice, but also, because, what moonlight there was shone directly on the entrance to the mill, he was able to see who had challenged him.

"Stay calm Geof. I'm Guido." The figure replied.

"Thank God you are safe, where were you when the Tedeschi arrived?" Philip asked as he stepped out, albeit rifle ready, to welcome their guide.

"I saw them arriving, but they were moving so fast, I couldn't outrun them." Gino said as he passed through the doorway, "By the time I arrived, they had entered the house. Also, close on a dozen had surrounded the place. There was nothing I could do except save my own skin. I hid up a tree, and lay quiet." He finished, almost shamefacedly.

Geof emitted an almost silent chuckle, as he said,

"Who could blame you, I would have done the same thing."

Between, at times, long period of silence, the distant crack of rifles, mingling with the short bursts of fire from Sten guns could be heard intermittently until the early hours of the morning.

"They are having a right ding-dong there," Archie commented, to no one in particular.

"That house is a pretty solid building of stone. The Hun will be watching the windows, that's for sure and you can bet your bottom dollar they won't be offering any easy targets," Geof paused, and his voice took on a more serious tone as he continued with, "From what I saw, they only had rifles. In all propbability, the only ammunition they have, is what is loaded in them."

"Och! We could na' see a thing in that barn, so dinna' ken what reenforcements, if any, were in those wee trucks we heard come up." Jock pointed out.

"Or how they were armed." John entered the discussion, adding, "They had plenty of time to prepare for action, before those partisans turned up."

"True . . . True," Geof conceded, "let's not be pessimistic. I suspect those Jerries were as surprised by the arrival of that bunch of partisans as we were . . . bit of luck, them turning up. Why else would they have left only one bod on the door of the barn, while the rest went in to the house to enjoy themselves. You all heard the noise they were making, it sounded like a right old party.

Philip, who had been listening to the discussion, with some amusement, pointed out,

"Any new arrivals, would have joined the party; if they had heavier equipment, it's unlikely they would have taken it in with them. If Geof's surmise is right, the only ammunition they have with them is loaded in their rifles. You all saw where the trucks were standing. It would be a brave man, or rather, foolhardy man, who would venture across that yard to get supplies."

"I don't reckon there was anybody except the drivers in them trucks, surely, we would have heard their footsteps on those cobbles." John commented, adding, "I would be surprised if a bunch of men getting out of a truck weren't talking. Even if they weren't, someone in command would have been telling them what to do. What I am saying is, I can't imagine a load of squadies getting out of a truck in total silence."

It was a long discourse for John, who rarely voiced an opinion, and he smiled, rather self consciously as he finished.

"That makes sense." Geof 's remark was followed by, "The Boss man, seemed to know you Philip."

"He does, we have met before." Philip replied in a matter of fact voice.

The first grey streaks of dawn were in the sky when Luigi, accompanied by three others emerged from the surrounding woodland. Geof and Philip, who had remained on guard all night, rose stiffly from the log seats, that had been placed by the door. There was no mistaking the feather in the hat Luigi always wore with pride, when in action, so they made no challenge as they stepped outside to greet him. Though jubilant, he looked tired and gratefully accepted, the offer of coffee made by Carlo, who had suddenly appeared at his side. Without thinking, he said,

"That would be nice." Then, as he realized what he was saying, he added, "Coffee? What do you mean, coffee?"

By way of reply, Carlo slipped the little back pack, he never seemed to be without, from his back and produced a small round tin, bearing the legend 'Bulwark', a small mug and a tin water bottle. Putting the water bottle back in his pack, he said, in triumphant tone,

"We won't need this, there's a well outside."

"That lad will never cease to amaze me," Luigi said. "I've often wondered what's in that pack he seems to be reluctant to be without."

Carlo, who had overheard the remark, said,

"Nonno says that if I am to be a mountain guide, like him, I must always be prepared. He gave me this pack and the tobacco tin to put the coffee in and said, I should always have it with me."

"Quite right too. You never know, what might happen in the mountains." Gino said, as he joined the group at the door.

Within minutes, a small fire was burning on the empty hearth. Small logs collected from outside, served as supports for the tin can they had found on the table. The water soon boiled and the coffee prepared. Deftly, Carlo poured some into his little mug and handed it to his Capitano. Turning to the others, he apologised by saying,

"I'm sorry, I only have the one mug."

"We were wondering what was happening," Philip said later, as he sipped his coffee, "There was such a long silence after that last prolonged burst of firing."

"When they tried to break out," Luigi began, "we were lucky that none of our lot were killed. They came out in force, jumping from the windows and bursting through the door. We got away with three wounded, one serious. Cedro has taken them in one of the trucks, we burned the other, to a friend, who will get them seen to. Florio, . . . our sergeant major . . . and two others have gone with them in case they meet trouble."

Philip shook his head, almost in disbelief and said,

"What possessed them to do that? I wonder, that lieutenant was young, but I didn't think he was a fool. Had it been me, I would have been inclined to weather the storm in the hope that reinforcements would come, when we failed to arrive back at H.Q. in the morning." Philip reflected a moment, then added in a slightly perplexed tone,"Florio! I thought I heard Pamella call him Ricardo."

Luigi smiled and said,

Ricardo is his real name, you know how it is, Florio di Tirane is his adopted name and the men have their own name for him, which is a play on Tirane." He paused, ruminating on Philip's observation, then continued with, "The Tedeschi probably saw us gathering brushwood and thought we might try and set light to the building. Also, there were stick bombs in the trucks. One of those lobbed through a window would have done a lot of damage. After the fracas, we had a lot of clearing up to do. We put the dead in the house and spread earth over the blood. Then, we checked around the area, found Donna and buried her where she fell. I'll leave it a few days, then bring a priest to do the rites. It's the least I can do for her."

"What about Peter? Did you find him? . . . We thought he had been shot." Philip asked.

"No, there was only Donna," came the reply.

There followed one of those strange periods of silence, which often happen where people are gathered together, it was broken by Luigi saying.

"My men and I must get back to our haunts without delay. Now that Gino is here, you won't need my presence." Then, turning to Gino, he added, "My advice to you is to get away from this area as soon as possible. When the Tedeschi find what is in the house, all hell will break out. The place will be swarming with them."

"I've been thinking exactly the same way and know a safe place for today." Gino replied.

Luigi, then shook hands with Gino, gave a perfunctory wave, which was practically a salute, to the others, who returned the gesture in an equally laconic way. Then, as he turned to go, he said,

"Stay alert . . . the forest has eyes. . . . Come Guerriero, we have work to do"

Carlo, almost visibly swelled with pride over being addressed in such a way, thinking, 'he called me Guerriero. I'll make that my adopted name,' he said,

"Coming Capitano, I'm ready."

Philip watched the departure of Carlo with an almost nostalgic regret, he had grown to like the young lad and could remember the days, when at University, he had been filled with the same enthusiastic zeal, but it was rowing then, and the desire to beat that other lot on the river. He emitted an only just audible chuckle and smiled as he remembered a trivial incident during practise.

"What amused you?" Geof asked,

"Nothing really, but it made quite a splash." Philip replied.

If Geof was dissatisfied with such a non committal answer, he didn't say so. After a moments silence, he said,

"What's the possibility of making a crossing tonight? The sooner I get back and make my report the better.

"If you all want to," Gino replied for Philip, "I can take you tonight, but the usual routes will be far from safe. The paths I have in mind are high in the mountains and although no climbing skills, or experience, for that matter are necessary, it is essential that everyone has a steady head for heights. At least two of them are little wider than a windowsill, passable but, with care."

"Canna' be worse than some of those wee ways up Ben Nevis." Jock responded, his eyes twinkling as he spoke.

"If any of you are unsure, now is the time to say. Once we start, there is no turning back." Gino looked hard at every face as he spoke, before posing the questing, "What's the verdict?"

The response was a chorus of "I'm game ... OK by me ... When do we start? . . . Let' get going." said in unison, without hesitation and almost drowning each other out.

CHAPTER FIFTEEN

So much had happened, since Filomena watched the German boy descend the track, where she now waited, that she found it difficult to believe it was only a matter of eight months. With the passage of time, her early fears, that he would return with others and steal her beloved Forli, had long since faded into the background of her mind; giving way to the problems of more recent events.

There had always been the occasional reprisal, but now, scarcely a day seem to pass by, without the disturbing news, that someone had been denounced as a traitor for harbouring enemies or helping the ribelli. The betrayal of the safe house above La Villa, used by her father as an assembly point for those attempting to cross the line, was too close to home. Happening so soon after the raid at Donna's house, was disturbing. There were too many unexplained instances, where the Tedeschi had foreknowledge of their plans and laid a trap.

'Are they already suspicious of me? . . . Do they know about me? . . . Do they know about Giorgio? . . . Is someone working within the group?' The questions flashed through Filomena's brain, tormenting her with their insistence. She shook herself angrily, and the mood passed. Nevertheless, she was relieved when she saw Giorgio smiling at her as he ascended the track and approached.

"Salve!"

Filomena's heart gave a great leap; Giorgio didn't usually adopt the more intimate form of greeting and he rarely smiled as he did now. She had never seen him smile like that, as if he was smiling at a special friend. Robbed of speech, she could only stare at him.

Filomena was glad she was wearing the new blouse, made from some parachute silk, retrieved from the arms drop. She had never worn silk before and it felt good against her skin and was even more glad she had dyed it green; she knew she looked nice in that colour. As usual, her heart was playing tricks and she hoped, that Giorgio couldn't see how wildly it was beating.

"There has been another betrayal." Giorgio's smile faded as he spoke. Another of our agents has been arrested, and some fool in his group had kept a record of the names of everybody who had helped him." Then, speaking rapidly, his voice barely audible, yet each word clear and distinct he handed Filomena an envelope and said, "Tell Favilla it's written in code 'F'. She is to destroy the radio as soon as the message has been sent and get away immediately afterwards. She will already know where to go, Tina will meet her there. Incidentally tell your father to make sure his radio is well hidden."

With a feeling of foreboding, Filomena took the envelope and placed it in the secret pocket in her skirt. Words were pointless, she knew what she had to do; in her mind she had a duty to fulfil, so said nothing,

Placing an arm round Filomena's shoulder in a half embrace, a gesture so unusual for Giorgio, it seemed almost out of character, he continued in a tender tone,

"Take care, the 'Death Head' Platoon is in Paese and a squad of the Black brigade is foraging around the countryside. They have shot Cesira, Filippo's mother, and left her hanging from a tree as a warning for him to find when he returns home.

Filomena nodded her understanding and tried to smile, She didn't know Cesira, who lived on the other side of Paese, but knew her son, Filippo. Some of her anxiety had returned and she asked anxiously,

"What about Gino, is he safe?"

"I don't know, we haven't had any news."

Surprised by the strangely protective emotion that came over him when Filomena posed the question, Giorgio gave her a gentle squeeze. Seeking to allay her fears, he released her and said,

"Don't worry, it's only just a week since they left; we know about the delay and no news is normally good news." The cheerful tone Giorgio used, masked his concern and brought a smile to Filomena's face.

Quick to note any change in expression, Giorgio smiled at her in encouragement.

'How different he looks when he smiles like that,' Filomena thought. Suddenly happy, she smiled radiantly back at him.

Giorgio had great faith in the ability of this girl he had known for such a short time and was relieved to note the change in her demeanour. He also knew, from experience, that his original judgement of Filomena's character was well founded; that she had the courage to carry out any mission, no matter how perilous, that was entrusted to her.

Placing his hands on her waist, Giorgio turned Filomena towards him; for a fleeting moment their eyes met. Repeating his words of caution, he said.

"Take care! Don't take any silly risks."

The words came out abruptly, almost brusquely; then, he was gone. His strangely graceful stride carrying him rapidly out of sight. Filomena felt an almost irresistible urge to run after him, to tell him he too must take care.

. . . .

With sinking heart, Filomena entered Paese, she had seen a dear friend swinging from a tree just outside the town, his body was stripped of clothing and it saddened her. A familiar sight, with his donkey, seemingly always overloaded with bundles of charcoal. Filippo was known and loved by all In the area, whether they lived in town, village, countryside or high on the mountain slopes. Now even the donkey was dead, its body pulled to the side of the road and left as carrion for the crows, which were already pecking at the carcase; others were investigating the corpse of its master.

"Why the donkey?" Filomena asked herself, "What harm has it done?"

It was late afternoon and the residents of Paese had shut themselves in their houses. The few that were still outside, scurried along the narrow streets, averting their eyes in a vain attempt not to see the many dead; as if by doing so, they would escape their fate. Entering the square, Filomena was forced to step off the pavement into the road to avoid walking on four dead bodies grotesquely strewn across the path. There were other corpses dotted about the square, so many, it might have been a battle field; but, it was the group by the door of the church that sickened her. There were three boys, barely into their teens, slumped against the wall where they had been shot and a woman she recognised as Emma, their mother, hanging from the balcony of a house. On a card, hanging from her neck, crudely scrawled in large letters, were the words, HA PROCREATO DEI TRADITORI[28]. The two girls, mere children, who lay beside her, were her daughters, Ida and Irma. The elderly man, propped up against the doorway of the church, his stick raised, supported by the brass knocker where it had caught when he fell, was Emma's grand-father, Salvatoro, who lived in the small town.

"They must have been visiting him," Filomena almost shouted in her anger, "Why the two girls? Why a white haired old man? . . . Why the donkey? What harm has it done?

---

[28] She procreated traitors.

In her heart, Filomena knew the answer. The skull and cross-bones emblem on the helmets of the soldiers. The Swastika chalked on the church door. The group of German soldiers, standing around two armoured cars, chatting and laughing, as if it were normal, with a group wearing the hated uniform of the Decima Flottiliglia, told it all. For men such as these, there didn't have to be a reason.

When Filomena saw Mario, he had Lucia with him. They were on the other side of the square, hiding in a narrow alley-way, close by a group of soldiers. It seemed to Filomena that every eye was watching; making her acutely concious of the package secreted in her clothing. She hoped that Mario and Lucia had not seen her and wished the message she carried was one that could be committed to memory.

Raising a hand in greeting, Mario grinned and to Filomena's dismay, started across the square toward her.

"Salve!" The greeting sounded natural, as if he were pleased to see her, as if the Germans were not in the corner of the square.

Filomena looked at Lucia, crossing the square with Mario; the girl seemed as unconcerned as he was. Fighting a moment of panic, Filomena waited.

"What are you doing here?" Mario barked, in a hoarse whisper. Then, without waiting for a reply he grabbed Filomena by the arm and whisked her into a narrow way bordered on either side by tall houses, which blocked out the sky and tainted the air with the smell of their musty interiors.

Filomena wrinkled her nose in disgust and murmured, more for something to say, than anything else,

"I wouldn't like to live here."

Mario looked at her, surprised by the remark and shrugged his shoulders. His mind was on other things and his voice sounded flat as he said,

"It's what they are used to."

"What brings you here?" Lucia asked. Despite the gleam of happiness in her eyes, there was a tinge of anxiety in her voice.

"Visiting a sick friend." Filomena lied.

Lucia looked intrigued, "Who is that? . . . Someone I know?" she asked.

Filomena didn't answer the question. Her mind was in a turmoil as she tried to equate Mario's nonchalant deportment and Lucia's obvious happiness, in the midst of the terrifying surroundings. 'Lucia's grandfather, Antonio, had they been to see him?' she wondered. But, knowing his attitude, and Lucia's aversion to him, she thought it unlikely.

Lucia looked at Filomena quizzically, as if weighing her up, then, her cheeks dimpled and her eyes sparkled. With an almost secretive move of the hand, she brought Filomena's attention to a beautiful diamond ring on her finger, and said.

"Aren't you going to congratulate me?"

"Of course," Filomena replied. Then, turning to Mario, "How on earth, did you manage to buy that?"

"It's not new, old Gargiulio, you remember he was a pawn-broker before he had to shut down. He still has a few bits and pieces and I rather liked this one." Lucia smiled happily as she spoke.

Filomena looked again at the ring and said,

"Isn't it lovely, you must tell me all about your plans next time we meet." Then, turned to leave and added, in a voice firm with her determination to complete her mission, "I must leave."

"Wait!" Mario placed a restraining hand on Filomena's arm, "Let me come with you. It's too dangerous for you to be on your own, my Lasciapassare[29] will protect you and if necessary, we can call on the Podesta for help."

With a lithe, almost imperceptible movement, Filomena moved away and said,

"I'll be safe enough, it isn't far to go."

For a brief moment, Filomena stood there, regarding Mario solemnly, her dark brown eyes seeming almost black in comparison with the lighter coloured eyes of Lucia. Her mind was racing with questions, 'How did he get a Lasciapassare? Is Mario the source of the leaks?' Looking him straight in the eye, she said,

"How did you get that?"

Mario smiled, disarmingly, he could almost read the suspicion in Filomena's eyes and paused before. answering, then, said,

---

[29] Italian pass, giving freedom of entry anywhere.

"A bit of nastiness went wrong, Lucia's grandfather, il Maresciallo" the word Maresciallo was said in a tone of scorn, "had me taken to the Podesta, to denounce me a traitor. Recognition was instant, the Podesta is an old friend from University days; we shared digs for three years. He couldn't have been more pleased to see me. Nor, I him. He always was a crafty one; seemed to get away with everything. I wouldn't be surprised if he isn't playing with both ends of the cord. Ready to jump whichever way is best."

While Mario had been talking, a lorry had arrived and the Germans, helped by their Fascist friends, were now busy shepherding a bunch of unhappy looking men into it. Even as they watched, the two armoured cars drove off and the remaining soldiers clambered into another lorry that had entered the square.

The going of the death squad was followed by a silence that seemed interminable in its intensity. It ended abruptly when the clamour started as people dashed from their homes. Some gathering in small groups; all talking at once, striving to be heard, as they tried to tell their version of what had happened. Others, searched among the dead, dreading they might find the missing loved one.

Filomena pointed towards the square, and without changing expression, said,

"There won't be any danger now, look, the Tedeschi have already left."

. . . .

Filomena knew something was wrong when the door of Favilla's house swung open to her touch. The remains of a meal, barely started, on the table and the smashed radio on the floor in the corner, told their own story. Quickly, she searched the remaining rooms; the place was deserted Taking the envelope from her pocket, she looked at it for a moment, wondering what to do; whether to throw it on the fire, still smouldering beneath the cauldron hanging from a hook in the chimney, or keep it safe until she was able to contact Giorgio. Hearing the sound of a footstep behind her, Filomena attempted to return the envelope to its hiding place in her skirt..

"Give me that, you little fool." Mario's voice rasped in his anxiety. "I thought you might be coming here."

Frantically, she tried to throw the envelope on the fire, but Mario snatched it from her. Putting it away in one of his pockets, he said, in a more gentle tone,

"You silly girl, what am I going to do with you? ... This place is under surveillance."

Filomena looked at Mario calmly, he had the envelope; it was in his pocket. Could she trust him? A question that now tormented her. She had often dreaded the moment; wondering how she would react if caught and was surprised, that despite the doubts that now tormented her, she was not frightened. Her heart was pounding furiously as she contemplated making a dash for freedom. As if divining her thoughts, Mario stood, with his back against the door and said,

"Don't even think it, those men outside, dressed in black suits, it's almost a uniform with them, are Ovra poliziotti. Trust me ... on your own, you won't stand a chance, even my pass might not be enough to save you, but at least it is worth a try."

Almost tearful with frustration and disappointment over the failure of her mission, Filomena tried to smile; it was meant to be brave, but didn't quite work. Her lips only quivered. However, concern for Lucia overcame her feelings and she managed to say,

"Where is Lucia?"

"In a house with a friend, don't worry. She is safe." Then, taking Filomena firmly by the arm, he almost whispered, "Be as natural as you can."

It was only when Filomena saw the three men standing outside, that she remembered seeing them talking together, when she entered the house.

"Show me your documents," one of them said brusquely, digging Mario hard in the ribs.

Mario's reaction was immediate, he produced his lasciapassare and in a curt authoritative tone, said,

"Mind your manners and stand straight when you are talking to me."

Nonplussed, the OVRA officer looked at the pass; seeing who had signed it, he immediately smartened his stance and contented himself with saying,

"Who is that with you?"

"A friend," Mario replied, "I've been looking for her. She ran off when the killing started and was obviously in shock when I found her, standing looking lost, in the middle of the room in there."

Not satisfied with the explanation, the poliziotto turned his attention to Filomena and said,

"Who are you? . . . What were you doing there? . . . working with that spy, aren't you?" The questions were spat out in a staccato way that had all the brutality of machine gun fire.

Filomena looked at the speaker in silence, her eyes widening in defiance.

Filomena's interrogator, mistaking her defiance for fear, laughed. "So you are frightened," he barked, "and so you should be." Then, smirked maliciously and said, "You won't be so silent when we hand you over for questioning. The Gestapo men will see to that." Then laughed again, it was a nasty laugh; full of menace. Turning to one of his companions, he said something she couldn't quite hear, that brought a grin to his face and an angry exclamation from Mario.

"Mind your tongue you disgusting oaf. Nobody makes remarks like that in front of a girl when I am around, no matter who she might be, and this girl is a friend."

The three looked at Mario in surprise, then at each other and sniggered, but said nothing.

"That's enough of that," Mario's voice had the crisp note of suppressed anger as he added, "you are forgetting it is a friend of Roberto Farinacci you are talking to."

The mention of Farinacci, not only had an obvious effect on the three Fascist policemen, but also surprised Filomena.

"How can he possibly know Farinacci?" she asked herself

"Alright, you can go," a man who appeared to be the senior in rank said, then added, in a severe, yet polite tone; probably in an attempt to show his authority, "Be careful where you go in future."

Without answering, or making further comment, Mario turned to Filomena and taking care not to mention her name, said,

"Come girl, it's getting late, we've lost enough time already. Your father will wonder what's happened to you."

. . . .

Giovanna Cortesa, known as Favilla by her friends in the Partito d'Azione, gazed at the familiar walls of the room where they had put her. She could remember them covered in posters, with a large map of Italy and a picture of Mussolini holding prominent place beside that of the Pope; which had been replaced by one of Hitler. A large Nazi banner, formed a background for the new display. She remembered other pictures too, that had once decorated the walls; pictures, drawn and proudly displayed by various children of the school and a large poster, depicting 'The old women who lived in a shoe' that decorated the back of the, no longer there, piano.

The teacher's desk still stood on its raised platform in front of the blackboard, but the desks of the children were gone from the wooden terraces, which without them, looked like a wide flight of steps leading to the back of the classroom. Looking at the terraces, Giovanna recalled a small trapdoor on the top terrace, which gave access to a space the teacher used for storing books. Giovanna also remembered some loose planks on the outside of the wooden building; how she once squeezed through them when playing in the playground. The memory of the surprised faces of her tiny friends, when she appeared unexpectedly in the doorway of the school brought a fleeting smile to her face as she mounted the terraces to see if the trap door was still there.

The sound of a key turning in the lock broke Giovanna's reverie. The door opened and two men, dressed in civilian clothes, came in. One, she recognised as the man who had arrested her. The other, was taller and wore a Swastika arm band on his sleeve. Beneath that, there was another arm band bearing the legend 'Polizei'. Closing the door and locking it behind them, they approached the desk. While the man who had arrested her seated himself at the desk, the other remained on his feet and pushed a chair forward, motioning to her, to sit down.

Neither in haste, nor too slowly and taking care not to cross the eyes of the two men; in case they should read something in hers that she preferred they didn't see, Giovanna descended the terraces. Remaining where they were, one seated, the other standing, they watched her with a speculative air as she passed close to them and took the chair that had been offered.

The German put a seemingly friendly hand on Giovanna's shoulder, smiled encouragingly and said,

"My name is Otto . . . Otto Spach. If you behave yourself and answer our questions truthfully, you will come to no harm. Shall we start with your name?"

Amazed that she felt so calm, Giovanna looked at him in silence.

"Come girl, your mother's name then. Or your father's"

Giovanna's only response was to shift her position, so that she could watch the reaction of the Italian policeman, who was leaning back in his chair, pen poised, ready to write down anything she might say.

Still smiling, her interrogator pressed his point,

"Come now, silences won't help you. We have to know who you are and where you come from. That's reasonable. Isn't it?"

The line of questioning didn't surprise Giovanna, she knew her name had not been mentioned when being questioned by the poliziotti. The German's oily smile didn't fool her either. She broke her silence by saying,

"I don't come from these parts, I'm a refugee from Roccaraso. I don't know where my family is. In the mêlée of getting away, we became separated."

"What were you doing in that house?" The Italian barked out the words, as if by doing so, he hoped to jolt Giovanna into a confession. It only served to make her more defiant. Lying blatantly, she said,

"I was hungry. I saw the door open and went in, hoping to get something to eat,"

Getting up from his chair, the Italian came round the desk and strode threateningly towards her. In a voice that reflected his impatience, he said,

"Don't lie. . . . And, with that transmitter on the table, you didn't know you were in the house of a spy, I suppose. Do you take me for a fool?"

The Italian's words surprised Giovanna, she knew the poliziotti had searched the house, but didn't know they had found the transmitter beneath the boards, where it was hidden. She hadn't used it that day and for the first time the thought came to her, that, someone must have betrayed her. Trying to retain her calm, she said.

"What transmitter? I didn't see one."

"It was on the table," the Italian rasped out.

Giovanna shook her head. She knew the transmitter hadn't been found when she was taken away, and hoped that it hadn't really been discovered; that the odious man was trying to bluff her into a confession.

The Italian laughed harshly and turning to the German, said,

"She's lying, Otto. She isn't new to the area, I've seen her go in and out of that house before. Give me five minutes alone with her; that's all I need to get the truth."

"And kill her, as usual, no doubt, trying to get it. I know your reputation Alfredo. What good will that do?" Otto retorted. Then, turning to Giovanna, he said,

"Let's have the truth now, you don't really want me to hand you over to Alfredo. Do you?" His smile as he added, "Would you like a cup of coffee or a cigarette?" had a chilling quality about it.

Giovanna shook her head, there was a deathly cold feel in the pit of her stomach, as she saw how the German seemed to smile with his lips only; the eyes were like chips of ice and had a cruel look about them. 'Of the two,' she thought 'he is the most evil.'

"A glass of wine then?" As Otto spoke, he positioned himself behind the chair and placed a hand on her shoulder. Squeezing it gently, he added, "Can't we be friends. I'm sure you could do with some refreshment."

Despite herself, Giovanna shuddered, but said,

"A glass of water would be nice."

Otto smiled again and said,

"Of course, if that's what you prefer." Then turned to the Italian and added, "Alfredo, see to it, make sure it's fresh and cold."

As Alfredo left the room, Giovanna could feel the German's hand slowly creeping towards her breast. She tried to wriggle free, but the hand stayed there, relentless in its strength.

Giovanna tried to rise, desperate to escape the unwanted caress; the pressure was too great, holding her pinned to the chair. Bringing both her hands into play, she caught hold of his fingers in an attempt to prise the hand away.

Otto merely laughed, a brutal guttural sound. Taking a handful of her hair in his free hand, he jerked her head back against his chest, and tried to plant a kiss on her lips, but was frustrated as she twisted her head to one side.

"I don't like what you are doing." Giovanna protested angrily and she tried again to push away the hand that had now entered her clothing. She wanted to add, 'You are hurting me,' but pride and a determination not to submit, forbade her.

The German laughed again and said,

"You silly little girl, you would like what I can do to you, even less if you don't behave. . . . If we are friends, I can protect you; give you a Bescheinie[30]gung that will enable you to come and go, without hindrance, wherever you please."

As he finished speaking, the door opened and Alfredo entered, accompanied by an officer wearing the S.S. with four stars and bar insignia of Oberstubannfuhrer[31]. Otto immediately straightened up, clicked his heels and raised his arm in the Nazi salute. The oberstubannfuhrer acknowledged the salute with a perfunctory wave, stared at Giovanna's tormentor haughtily, while he took in the scene, but made no comment.

"Bring the woman to my office." he commanded. Then, turned on his heel and stalked out.

With a strange feeling of guilt, as if expecting to see her old head master sitting behind his desk, Giovanna entered the room that had once been his office. There was little change. The same strip of worn carpet in front of the desk. The same cupboard where *il Maestro* kept his cane. The same stool in the corner where she remembered sitting for an hour after classes were finished. Too often to remember how many times, or why. Even the big map of the world was still in its place; partly obscured by the Nazi regime banner, which hung over it. Seeing that map again. Giovanna wondered whether the defiant words she once scribbled on the border when Signore Giacobbi left her alone for a few moments were still there.

"It's no use pretending Favilla, we know who you are and that Favilla is not your real name. We also know who your father is."

Although the words were spoken in the dialect of the region, they had a strange nuance that told Giovanna the man wearing a fawn jacket, gazing out of the window was not born in Italy. Yet, there was something about him that was familiar. It was as if she knew him and she wished he would turn so that she could see his face. However, the statement brought a sigh of relief, Giovanna now knew for certain that he was bluffing. Her father had been dead for some years; killed in a mountaineering accident, when she was still quite a small girl. Suddenly, Giovanna remembered where she might have heard that

---

[30] German pass

[31] Lt colonel, (SS regiments)

voice before. For the first time since her arrest, she knew real fear, not for herself, but for the safety of her friends. It was an icy fear that clutched at her heart. She wanted to run, as fast as she could, as if by doing so, they would forget them and pursue her instead. But, the window was blocked by the man who had spoken and a piantone[32] stood between her and the door.

Panic stricken, eyes wide open, Giovanna stared first at one wall, then another, as she tried to convince herself, they were not closing in on her.

"So, now you are afraid."

Otto's harsh voice had a note of triumph which jolted Giovanna into reality. The walls receded. Reluctant to trust herself to speak, less her voice quavered, she fought for, and regained control.

"Who else are you working with?" Otto rasped.

"Come now, it's no use pretending Favilla is your real name. We have been watching you for some time, and have seen the coming and goings of your colleagues."

Something in the voice of the man at the window jolted Giovanna back to wondering who he was; where she had met him. On reflection, the thought that she had seen him talking to Giuseppina when she visited Michele after the snow melted, was unfounded. The man who had come to mind, could only talk a little Italian, and had a very foreign accent, whereas, this man was fluent and used the dialect of the area. She consoled herself by remembering that she had heard someone say spies didn't usually betray those that had given them lodging, not from loyalty, but, because by doing so, they brought themselves under suspicion. Remembering this, did much to allay her fears.

"Silence won't help you. . . . We can make you talk." Somehow the modulated tone of the Oberstubannfuhrer was more menacing than the threats of the other two.

The words grating in Giovanna's ears filled her with a loathing which drove out her fear. 'They won't find out anything from me' she resolved, as calm now and in complete control of herself, she glared defiantly at her interrogators.

---

[32] Orderly or guard

The small room they eventually shut Giovanna in had once been the domain of the bidella[33]; a kindly woman who looked after the cleaning and tried not to smile, when she berated the little ones for trampling all over her newly washed floor. The window had been fitted with bars and the door strengthened, which made the piantone an unnecessary extra and all hopes of escaping via the trap-door on the terraces in he classroom were denied. The absence of washing facilities dismayed her, and she asked,

"Can I have a bowl and some water to wash?"

The response she received from the S.S Oberschütze[34] who had escorted her, was accompanied by a snigger as he said,

"That isn't necessary."

. . . .

They woke Giovanna at dawn; having spent most of the night awake, it seemed to her, that she had only just dropped off. Two soldiers escorted her to the old school playground, she remembered it as a place of joy, bringing back memories of childhood friends in happier days. The fading stars in a clear sky gave promise of a fine day.

As they turned the corner of the school Giovanna halted and gazed with dismay at the scene before her. With wrists chained to rings set in the wall of the head-masters house, there were three men and two youths. One of her escorts pushed her in the back and said,

"It's no use struggling, we'll carry you there if you won't walk."

Although Giovanna had often contemplated the risks, that her work entailed; hoping, if necessary, she would meet her end bravely and with dignity, she had never really believed it would happen. Now that the time had come, Giovanna was pleased to realise that she felt calm and unworried as she walked, unaided to the wall and allowed them to chain her alongside the five already there. Pleased that no secrets had been squeezed out of her, Giovanna waited for the end.

Time seemed eternal before the firing squad, accompanied by an officer of junior rank, arrived.

The cry, *'For Justice and Liberty'* shouted by one of the men, was drowned by the brutal noise of lightweight machine gun fire.

---

[33] Female school janitor.

[34] First class private (SS regiment)

Unperturbed, the officer sauntered over, casually glanced at the bodies, now hanging by their wrists from the chains and deciding 'Coup de Grace' was not required, gave the order as he left.

"Clean up that mess."

CHAPTER SIXTEEN

"When we reach the bend, you shall have a rest" Ernesto promised, quietly urging his oxen forward.

It had been a long, hard day of toil on the slopes below La Villa and the animals were tired. With new found strength, the ageing pair of Maremmano lowered their horns, to strain at the shafts and haul the heavily laden cart up the steep gradient.

Satisfied that the wooden chocks were securely in position behind the wheels of the cart Ernesto lowered his weary body on to a log and contemplated the panorama spread out below. It all seemed so peaceful now that the soldiers had gone. The distant groups of workers returning from the fields and the chimneys of La Villa, peeping through a thin haze, tinted pink by the dying rays of the sun, gave such an air of tranquillity, that it was difficult to believe the stories of the previous day.

Anxiously, Ernesto switched his gaze to the distant motor road, just visible beyond the escarpment, as it entered Paese. A house on the edge of the road, just outside the small town was still burning and he wondered what happened to the people who lived in it. Too distant to make out, which house, he also wondered who the unfortunates were; 'probably someone I know,' he thought.

The shape of someone passing the end of the steeply rising path, sometimes used as a short-cut to avoid the bend in the track, caught his attention. It was only a glimpse; he was unable to see who it was. Ernesto hoped it wasn't one of the marauding Germans that had plagued the area that day; stealing the precious oxen for meat, and, for that matter, anything they could lay their hands on to supplement their meagre rations. Owners that protested were often pressed into labour camps. Deciding it would be safer to appear normal, he took an ancient clay pipe from his pocket and casually proceeded to load it with a mixture of tobacco and a fine, hair like growth, gathered from the top of maize stalks.

"Thank God you are safe."

Michele's normally jovial voice had a worried sound.

Alarmed by the tone and the grave expression on his employers face, Ernesto rose hurriedly to his feet.

Accompanying his words with a gesture, Michele said,

"Sit down, be comfortable." Then in a grave tone, continued with, "The Tedeschi have been to the house. Fortunately, they only took a few chickens and the rabbits. "He paused and despite the gravity chuckled as he added. "I'm glad, I sold the pigs last week."

Immediately concerned for the safety of Mario's horse, Ernesto said, anxiously.

"What about Nove? Did they get him?"

"I said, they only took some chickens and the rabbits." Michele paused momentarily before continuing with, "Nove is safe and the project I have been working on, which has so intrigued you, is ready at last."

Ernesto looked a little shamefaced, but, his employer was not only a friend, but also, since Lucia had said yes, his daughter's future father in law. The feeling of guilt passed.

Michele gave Ernesto an encouraging slap on the back and said.

"Don't worry, all the Tedeschi have gone, we can safely take your two friends home."

On arrival at the stable, a worried frown creased Ernesto's forehead. Although he knew that it was unlikely the horse would be outside, there was the possibility that one of the Germans might have come back. He went outside to have a look. There was no mistaking his anxiety as he said,

"Where's Nove?"

Scarce able to conceal the anticipation he was experiencing, Michele replied,

"Settle your charges down, and I'll show you."

When Ernesto, helped by Michele had groomed and fed the oxen, Michele said,

"First a drop of grappa, my friend, you deserve it, then I will take you to see Nove in his new home."

Hearing those words, Ernesto felt a surge of relief. His great and genuine love of all animals, was such, that when one of his chickens were needed for the table, the killing had to be done by Donnina, he couldn't bring himself to do it. Sipping with appreciation the grappa, which was even more potent than some of that which had been illicitly distilled, he said,

"Where is that then?"

"You'll see." was the only response.

Led by Michele, the two men followed an overgrown and no longer used path in the wooded area on the rising slopes above Casa dei Pioppi. It was a path used by long gone ancestors of the Zerella family which led to the old home. Built of stone, the house had survived the passing years and now stood a bleak relic in a remote area. Time had left it's mark. The forest had smothered it and brambles clambered over the walls and roof.

Bewildered, Ernesto looked at the old structure; scarce able to believe Michele was being serious. The entrance was obviously impassable. The door of the lean-too stable, was obscured by a growth of climbing vegetation, which clung to a sapling growing so close, that it blocked it. Transferring his gaze to Michele, he said,

"How do you propose to get Nove in there? There is no way you will get that door open. Where is he now? . . . It will take days to clear away that mess. The place is full of spines."

Michele laughed, delighted with the response. It was what he had hoped for; proof that the deception was effective. Then said,

"Not a problem."

Watched by Ernesto, he walked slowly over to the old stable and stood for a moment, enjoying the suspense he hoped he was creating, before pulling away a mass of dead brushwood; to reveal a small wooden tub bolted securely to the base of the stable door, in which the sapling, together with some of the wild growth, was planted. A trio of massive hinges had been fitted to the door, which enabled it to swing open with ease; revealing a clean interior, with Nove contentedly gazing out of the back. Happy with the effect he had created, Michele grinned and said,

"There is no way anything is going to get round the back and sides to see that head poking out."

In one of those flashes of absurdity, Ernesto said,

"What about mice or rabbits?"

Michele merely laughed and said,

"I'll treat that with the contempt it deserves."

At the far end of the stable, set into the wall of the house, there was a door, new in appearance; which seemed out of place. Michele saw Ernesto looking at it and, as if divining his thoughts said,

"That doorway had me puzzled at first, then I noticed the doorstep and remembered a painting I have. I'll show it to you when we get back to the house." Then, as he took a step forward, added, "The stable was evidently built on to the side of the house at some time after its original construction. We had considerable difficulty getting the old door open; I suspect it's the first time since my forebears added the stable. The whole place was blocked with undergrowth and the hinges so corroded with age, they wouldn't move. We ended up by smashing the old door, which wasn't easy, being thick and solid oak, and fitted that new one. Come in and see what we have done."

The door opened easily on new, well oiled hinges, to reveal the main room of the house, cleared of all signs of growth. A bunk type two story bed stood in one corner and a table with three chairs drawn to it was placed against one of the walls. Waving his arms in a sweeping gesture round the room, Michel said,

"Behold, accommodation for our guests. Safer for us and safer for them I would be surprised if any Tedesco would venture down that narrow overgrown path. If he did. He wouldn't see anything that matters."

. . . .

The tranquillity of the morning made it difficult to believe the horrors related by Nonno Ricci when, concerned by the non appearance of Gianni, who had promised he would spend a day out of the mountains with her, Carina returned to La Villa. Tales of convoys of lorries, loaded with unhappy victims and a rumour of forty people, shut in a barn, which was burnt down with them inside, increased her anxiety and made her wonder if Gianni was safe.

Carina had been reluctant to leave the church where she had been waiting, but Gianni's continued absence made her wonder if he had gone straight to her house. Now, praying she hadn't missed him, as she hurried back, she wished she hadn't stopped to say boungiorno to Nonna Ricci.

"Surely he would have waited." Carina told herself repeatedly; as if by doing so, it would erase the nagging doubt which troubled her.

Seeking solace in her faith, Carina entered the church and took a half burnt piece of candle from a pocket in her skirt, then, rummaged among the odds and ends she carried there for a match. Hoping the candle would light, she prised up the wick with the end of her match and lit it.

Having secured the candle in position with a few drops of melted wax, she watched it burn for a few seconds. Then, apologising for using a second-hand candle that didn't fit the only vacant candle stick, she knelt in prayer. Comforted by her devotions and in a happier state of mind, Carina returned outside to resume her waiting.

When the sun told her that mid-day had passed, Carina came to the conclusion that something had prevented Gianni from keeping his date, she made herself comfortable on a flat stone and with her back resting against the church wall, opened the pack that should have been a shared picnic. Firm in the belief that the candle she had lit and her prayers would protect the man she loved, her worries temporarily behind her, Carina tentatively bit the end off a pasty, inspected the cheese and tomato contents, then sampled the other end to see what sort of meat might be there.

Sitting in the warm early summer sunshine, her repast complete Carina found herself thinking of the times she had spent with Gianni, too few since he joined the ribelli. Talking to herself, her turkeys for the time being forgotten, she said,

"When I marry, it will have to be Gianni, only Gianni . . . Signora Battistero, has a nice sound to it, Signora Carina Battistero."

Carina was so absorbed in her dreams, she didn't notice a shadow had fallen across her, until she heard a chuckle and Gianni's voice saying,

"There you are Carina, sorry I'm so late. There is so much happening, I began to wonder if I would ever get away."

Blushing furiously and wondering whether Gianni had overheard her words, Carina jumped to her feet and stumbled into his waiting arms. Tears of joy in her eyes, she half whispered,

"It doesn't matter, you are here now, nothing else is important."

They stood there for several minutes, just holding on to each other; both reluctant to let the other go. Finally it was Carina who broke the silence, by saying, in a half guilty tone,

"Would you like something to eat? There's not much left, but there is a pasty and some pepperoni that I haven't eaten."

Gianni picked up the pasty, (one end had been bitten off) looked at Carina as he did so and tried not to laugh as he said,

"I'm not really hungry, but this pasty is tempting,"

Carina watched him eat taking in every detail of his being; happy, just to see him there. When he had finished eating, she said,

"Do you want to walk? We can stay here and chat if you would prefer it."

Happy to be with the girl he desperately wanted to marry, Gianni didn't mind what they did, so long as they were together.

"We must make the most of the short and precious time we have," Gianni said, as an opening to the more weighty matters he had in mind.

Carina watching Gianni's face as he spoke, couldn't help noticing how grave he looked. She had never seen him look so serious, scarcely able to conceal her concern, she said,

"What's the matter Gianni? You look so worried."

"Things are changing, and it looks as if the Allies are almost ready to move," Gianni replied. Taking both her hands in his, he smiled to reassure her. Then in a serious tone of voice, said, "You must promise me, that when the time comes, you will take refuge in the forest. Without delay; not even to collect cherished items. The deeper and higher you go the better."

Carina looked at him, but said nothing.

"Promise." Gianni insisted, planting a kiss, first on one cheek, then the other and another in the centre.

Carina laughed as she returned the kisses and said,

"Naughty! . . . Naughty!" Then, in sombre tone, "What's troubling you?"

"Let's stay here and enjoy each other's company while we can. It's pleasant in the sun and I have a lot to explain," Gianni replied. Putting an arm round Carina's waist, he led her to a hummock which offered more comfort than the wall of the church. Then, removed his jacket and spread it on the ground and grinning now, added, "Make yourself comfortable and I will fill you in."

For several minutes, the two of them, sat, sharing the jacket, holding hands and lost in the pleasure of being with each other.

It was Carina who broke the silence, when she kissed the hand that was holding hers and said,

"You were going to say?"

Gianni didn't reply immediately, when he did, he said,

"As I said before, we must make the most of this short and precious time together. Every-thing's changing." he paused to collect his thoughts, before continuing. "Small groups such as ours are beginning to bond with the larger organisations, it could mean that I won't be so independent."

"How do you mean Gianni?" Carina asked.

"Well if we bond with one of the three large groups..."

"Giustizia e Liberta, Matteotti and Garibaldini?" Carina interrupted.

"Well yes, no point in merging with one of the small Catholic or Monarchist groups. Like the Green flames, in Alta Italia or the Coccinelle. I don't know which way Donnola leans, but he is not an anarchist. With Partito d' Azione so strong in the area he is likely to go for Giustizia e Liberta. I hope so, I don't fancy serving with the socialistic Matteotti, or the communistic Garibaldini." Gianni stopped and laughed here. A twinkle came in his eyes as, thinking of the almost universal mistrust, at times amounting to fear, of carabinieri, held by the people living in mountain villages and remote areas, he added, "There are too many carabinieri in the Garibaldi brigades."

Carina, guessing what he was thinking, laughed and said,

"That shouldn't worry you, Lepre, lepri might look like rabbits, but they can run faster."

Gianni appreciated the joke around his nom de guerre and laughed with her. Then, becoming serious again, said,

"It would be advisable if we don't use that name, even when we are alone, someone might hear and make the connection."

Carina tried to look contrite, she knew he was right, but couldn't resist a giggle.

The giggle was infectious, and Gianni found himself laughing with her. The important matters on his mind faded and he drew her to him.

Time passed, with only a word or two said here and there, until, with the sun beginning to set, Gianni realised he hadn't finished what he wanted to say. Separating himself from her, but still holding one of her hands, he said,

"It's getting late, I'll finish what I wanted to say as we walk back."

Together, they tidied the area, and arms encircling each others waists started down the steep descent which led to La Villa.

"As I was saying," Gianni began, "We shall have to see what happens. One thing is certain. It is essential we come under one of the central commands, if clashes and duplications of movements are to be avoided. As things are, we tend to be acting as a lot of independent local forces."

"Will that make it more difficult for you to come and see me? . . . Is that why you said we must make the most of our time together?" Carina interrupted.

"Partly." Gianni squeezed her affectionately and continued by saying, "Don't worry, I'll find a way somehow. . . . All the signs are that the Allies by the River Sangro; and that sector between the other two rivers, the Foro and the Moro are preparing for a major offensive. They have been in that area for a long time now and can't stay there for ever. When they move, our task will be to make things difficult for the Tedeschi. Attacks in the mountain passes and sabotage; anything, that is, that will hinder them. You can see why we need a central command. Without it we are liable to hamper each other." He paused a moment to give her a hug. "If the offensive is successful, the Tedeschi will be in retreat, we all know what happens then. Destruction as they go. That is why I said you and you mother must take refuge in the forest at the first sight of them coming towards the village."

It was a long speech for Gianni, which Carina listened to with sinking heart. She could see the sense in what Gianni was saying and realised, that, through no fault of his, he would be away for much longer stretches of time than hitherto. Voicing the question on every-bodies lips, she said,

"Oh Gianni! When will this awful war end?"

"Soon I hope," Gianni replied. (Echoing the universal answer).

. . . .

Despite the early hour and the light mountain breeze, which gave a freshness to the air, denied to the valley, the heat of the coming day could be felt as Filomena skipped down the steep mountain path. Her light hearted gait belied the heavy thoughts that filled her heart. News of Favilla's fate had reached her ears and the presence of so many Germans in the valley worried her. Filomena also felt acutely conscious of the added risk for Gino, who hadn't yet returned from his mission and she uttered a short prayer that he wouldn't be back until the Tedeschi had completed their rastrellamento. Hearing a footstep behind her, she turned to see who it was, but the path was empty. It gave her an uncomfortable feeling of being followed.

By the time Filomena reached La Villa, the sky had lost the rosy tints of the rising sun and now blazed above in brazen splendour, The square, already crowded, seemed to buzz with a nervous undercurrent, as the various groups of people dotted about it discussed, nervously, the latest rumour voiced by Nonna Ricci. The fate of those forty souls burned to death in a barn not only filled their minds with horror, but also fear that it could happen to them. The embroidered story of five rebels and a woman, being executed, which had also been recounted by Nonna Ricci, didn't warrant much more than a mention, it was the sort of news that happened so often, it had become almost commonplace

Filomena looked about her, hoping to see Lucia, who she hadn't seen since that day in Paese. As she crossed the square, she saw Michele and her father, evidently on their way to Renzo's bar. She waved, but receiving no response, assumed they hadn't seen her.

"Was it only the day before yesterday?" she asked herself, "It seems an age."

"Filomena . . . Filomena."

The voice cut into Filomena's thoughts. She didn't have to look to see who it was, the boisterous laugh that followed the words was instantly recognisable.

"I was hoping to see you here, I have great news."

"Hallo Doninna," Filomena said, as Doninna approached, "How is Lucia?"

"Lucia is fine. She is in the house, I expect she would like to show you her ring."

Not wishing to spoil Donnina's joy in telling her, Filomena resisted the temptation to say she had already seen it and said,

"What ring? Has she said yes?"

Doninna laughed happily, and replied,

"Yes, yes, didn't you know? Of course, you wouldn't know, it was only the other day. Lucia is in the house; Gianni is there too, with Carina." Donnina paused a moment and in a more serious tone, added, "That girl really loves our Gianni, I hope he doesn't break her heart."

"I don't think there is much risk of that," Filomena commented, "I have seen the way he looks at her."

The happy smile faded from Donnina's face as she followed with,

"We see so little of our Gianni these days, he has to return to his group today. Why don't you come and find him before he leaves. I am sure he will be glad to see you and Lucia will be able to show you her ring."

Put the way it was, Filomena felt it would be churlish to refuse the invitation, so said,

"That will be nice, but I can't stop for long."

Taking Filomena by the arm, suddenly serious, Donnina's usual jovial expression faded, as she said,

"Be careful little one, I saw the Sicilian following you down the path . . . I'm sure he is a spy."

Then, with a wave of her hand and a cheery "Ciao," to one of her friends, Doninna bustled her way energetically between knots of people in the square as she led Filomena towards her home.

As they entered the house with a wolf for a knocker, Filomena gave a wave to Lucia, smiled broadly and said,

"I believe you have some special news for me"

Lucia's eyes lit with laughter. Guessing that Filomena had let Doninna believe that she was the one to carry the news, she turned to her mother and said,

"You've told her. Haven't you."

"Sorry darling, I was so happy for you. Did you want to tell her yourself?" Donnina replied, attempting, without success, to look contrite.

Trying not to reveal the laughter bubbling inside her, Lucia held up her hand, waggled her fingers and said,

"Look Filomena. What do you think?"

"Wonderful news, your mother did tell me, I hope you will be very happy . . . Isn't that ring lovely." While speaking, the thought that

Doninna might not know Lucia had been in Paese during the massacre, crossed Filomena's mind. Realising that Doninna would be worried if she knew, she halted and instead of asking where Mario had found it, said,

"Come closer, so that I can see it."

While dutifully examining the ring, Filomena couldn't help noticing the wistful look on Carina's face. Although thinking, 'It won't be long before you are proudly showing everyone your ring,' she wisely said nothing.

A knock on the door as it opened, brought a happy smile to Donnina's face. Greeting the mother of her son's girl friend and determined that no one was going to rob her of the pleasure in telling she said,

"Come in Concetta have a drop of wine. Lucia has news to celebrate."

Donnina's more than obvious determination to be the first to tell Concetta the joyful news, brought a peal of laughter from Lucia and Filomena.

On sight of Gianni, as she entered, the slightly annoyed expression on Concetta's face relaxed. It had been her intention to berate Carina for neglecting to take her turkeys out of the yard. The mood changed as she thought, 'No wonder she neglected her turkeys,' then, she laughed and said,

"I thought you were going back last night Gianni."

Gianni grinned happily as he answered,

"You don't get rid of me that easily," then, in a more sober tone, "I changed my mind. With all that activity yesterday, not only in the valley, but also in the foothills it seemed safer to wait for it to disperse. Had I left last night, there was a chance I would be followed. I didn't want to take that risk."

"And you would be with Carina a little longer," Concetta said, with a knowing wink.

"And you love her, you love her, you love her."

The sally, sung by Dora as she skipped round the table, coupled with the knowing wink from Concetta, brought a burst of laughter from Donnina.

Dodging the bobbing Dora, Concetta crossed the room to where Lucia stood, embraced her, before looking at the ring and with a look of genuine happiness, said,

"What a lovely ring; you are a lucky girl Lucia. I wish you all happiness. When is the happy event?"

"Too early to say, maybe not until this horrid war is over," Lucia replied.

"Carina tells me it might be a long time before you can spend a little time with us," Concetta said, turning her attention to Gianni.

"That's right. All the signs are that the Allies are preparing to move at last. Did Carina tell you her promise."

"About what to do if the Tedeschi come to the village, you mean?" Concetta asked.

"Yes, the same goes for all of you here." Gianni replied, glancing round the room.

"What's that Gianni?" Donnina queried.

"When the Tedeschi retreat, they destroy everything in their path. It is vital you get into the forest or mountains, at the first sight that they might be coming this way. You must leave without delay; the deeper and higher, the better.... I repeat, without delay."

CHAPTER SEVENTEEN

"What are you doing, coming out of that room?" Konrad's face was contorted with a mixture of anger and alarm. "You know it's absolutely forbidden."

Ida flushed, she was tempted to lie, to say she hadn't been in the room; that she was just closing the door, but habit asserted itself.

"Don't dare tell me what to do in my house," Ida retorted.

"You stupid woman, there is a reason you shouldn't go in there and that I . . ."

Konrad stopped abruptly; as if suddenly aware he had said too much and afraid his cousin and Roberto would become curious. Switching his attention to Roberto, he aimed a kick that the boy was quick to dodge, and snarled,

"Get out from under my feet you objectionable little brat."

Ida could feel a cold chill, like a tight band round her chest and her eyes felt hot. She wished she had never allowed Konrad to stay with her. Slow to anger and normally tolerant, the sight of her cousin mistreating her son brought all the resentment that had been building up in her to the surface. She exploded in a torrent of words.

"If you think I don't know about your radio Marco; that you have been spying on my friends, you are a fool. I have had enough of your ranting; of pretending you are not here. I don't want you under my roof any more. Get out! Get out!"

"Quiet woman! You've done enough mischief for tonight." Konrad replied angrily.

Catching sight of Roberto creeping out of the room, Konrad vented his anger on him. Shouting,

"Where do you think you are off to?" he grabbed the boy by the collar and cuffed his ears.

"No uncle! Don't," Roberto protested. Wriggling frantically in Konrad's grasp.

There was a rending sound as Roberto's shirt ripped and suddenly he was free, speeding for the comparative safety of the forest.

"*Gott in himmel!*" Konrad called blasphemously after him. The words, "You can stay out all night for all I care" were the last he ever spoke.

Blind now in her anger, Ida's maternal instincts came to the fore. Without even knowing what she was doing, she picked up the heavy iron cauldron suspended over the fire and brought it crashing down on Konrad's head.

Struck dumb with the shock of what she had done, Ida stood as in a trance, seemingly oblivious of the weight of the cauldron dangling in her hand. How long, she stood there, she didn't know. Unconscious of time, she became dimly aware that someone, with an arm round her shoulder was leading her to a chair. In her distraught state, she didn't know who. All she knew, was that someone was patting her face and a distant voice was saying,

"Don't be frightened Ida, we will look after you . . . Make some coffee Lucia, make it strong and see if there is any grappa or other spirit in the house."

Slowly, memory of what she had done, came back to Ida and she burst into tears.

"Where's Roberto?" she sobbed.

"Don't worry about him," Donnina replied, trying to sound encouraging, "he might be small, but he isn't silly."

"But he was so frightened," Ida managed to say.

"Did he see what you did?" Donnina asked.

"I don't know . . . I can't remember. I think I saw him leg it out of the door."

Relieved by the vague suspicion of a smile that crossed Ida's face as she replied, Donnina placed the cup of coffee Lucia had brewed in Ida's hand. Happy now that Ida seemed to be recovering, she said,

"Drink that while it's hot." Then, indicating Konrad, added, "Don't worry about the Sicilian, we have friends who will attend to that for you."

. . . .

Surprised out of his usual calm, Giorgio swore a silent oath and stared coldly at the small figure that had run blindly into him.

"What's a little man like you doing in the forest on your own?" He demanded.

Overcoming the fear of strangers, that Konrad had instilled into him and happy to have escaped a beating, some of Roberto's normal self-confidence asserted itself. He grinned impishly and said,

"Nothing."

"What do you mean? Nothing," Giorgio said, trying to look stern.

"Collecting snails," came the unexpeted reply.

"It will be dark soon, doesn't your mother worry?"

"She knows I won't get lost and is happy when I bring back plenty of snails."

Something about the boy, perhaps because he was so small, perhaps because he was obviously frightened, struck a chord of sympathy Giorgio didn't know he had. Without him realising it, his voice lost some of it's coldness. Instead of asking him what he proposed to collect the snails in, he asked him his name.

Reacting to the warmer tone in Giorgio's voice, Roberto relaxed. Concious of his Mother's repeated warnings not to give his name to strangers; the words *'They might be escaping prisoners of war or spies seeking those assisting them'* ringing in his head, he evaded the question by asking one of his own.

"Are you a Tedesco?"

"No." Giorgio shook his head as he replied.

Encouraged by the reassuring answer, Roberto became bolder he almost whispered,

"Are you a friend of the two Inglese who used to hide in il fosso[35]?"

Giorgio had not expected the talk to steer in that direction and for a moment he was nonplussed; it came as a complete surprise. Although several months had gone by since their departure, he could only assume the boy had seen Robin and Eric during their brief stay.

Intrigued by Roberto's curiosity, Giorgio contemplated the small face looking up into his. The fading light of the evening, which barely penetrated the canopy of leaves was reflected in a pair of eyes which dilated by the dimly lit setting, seemed darker than they really were. With an airy wave in the direction of the valley, he said,

"Over there under the escarpment?"

---

[35] A natural or artificial ditch or trench used for the distribution of water.

Roberto said nothing for a few minutes, then, seemingly forgetful of his mother's warning burst out with,

"They call me Robbo, what do they call you?"

"You can call me Giorgio if you like."

"Is that your real name?" Roberto asked.

Giorgio rarely smiled, when he did, it transformed his face. The boy's insistence amused him and he did so now, as he replied,

"What do you think?"

Spurred by thoughts of adventure and intrigue, his present problems forgotten, Roberto lowered his voice to a conspiratorial whisper, and said, with an air of daring,

"You are Inglese aren't you?" There was an almost imperceptible pause before he added, "I know where another Inglese is hiding."

Instantly alert, Giorgio chose his words carefully as he said,

"Do you really? I need a friend, can you fetch him for me"

Roberto shook his head and for several minutes remained silent; as if he was regretting what he had revealed and was debating in his mind whether he had said too much. Suddenly, his mind made up, he blurted in a rapid flow of words,

"He is not well, Mama has been looking after him. She says he might die. I mustn't let Uncle Marco know. You won't tell him will you? If I take you to him, promise you will keep it a secret."

"I promise." Giorgio responded.

Scared by his own daring, Roberto stared miserably up at Giorgio, his eyes widening with fear as tales of entire families who had been shot for harbouring prisoners of war came into his mind. Unable at first to move, he stood there, wanting to run, but his legs seemed to have turned to jelly, then he was gone; running as he had never run before.

Disappointed that he had not been able to learn more, Giorgio continued down the path he had been descending. Musing, 'I had better arrange a meeting with Filomena, she will know the lad's family,' he quietly made his way to the outskirts of La Villa.

The sound of the clock striking ten seemed unnaturally loud as Giorgio crossed the square and made his way down the steep steps to la fonte. Having ascertained that no one was collecting water, he crossed the intervening space that separated him from the communal fountain and stooped low over it as if refreshing himself with the cool water. Satisfied that the oak leaf he had lodged in a niche was secure, he straightened up and left as silently as he had come.

. . . .

Although, not yet seven o'clock, the sun was high in the heavens when Filomena met Giorgio in a secluded area of the forest high above La Villa. Bounding up to him, eyes aglow with the joy she always felt on the (in her mind) all too rare occasions, that he needed her assistance, she greeted him with,

"Salve Giorgio! Salve! Isn't it a lovely day."

Giorgio regarded Filomena solemnly as she approached. Then, unaware that he was always pleased to see her and was smiling, he greeted her with just a trace of enthusiasm.

"Salve!" Then, reverting to his usual manner added, "Do you know a little boy named Roberto?"

Disappointed, but not surprised, that Giorgio had not embraced her and thinking, 'no wonder they say the English are cold,' Filomena replied,

"It's a common name. . . . How little?"

With a wave of the hand, indicating the height, Giorgio said,

"About so high; possibly eight running up to nine years of age. Little boys all look the same to me. Said his name was Robbo."

"Seem friendly?"

Giorgio chuckled, Filomena wished his eyes would dance like that for her, as he replied,

"Very much so, a right little chatterbox, that's for sure."

"Sounds like Ida di Lorenzo's little boy," Filomena commented, "if so tread carefully, they say the Sicilian uses her house for a refuge."

"That clinches it." Giorgio's voice had an emphatic ring, "He did mention an Uncle Marco, I didn't connect it with that character at the time. Not even, when he said that Uncle Marco must not know about the man they were hiding. Which brings me to the point of why I want to see you."

Thinking, 'I might have known it wasn't for any romantic reason,' Filomena said,

"What's that then?"

Without replying directly to the question, Giorgio posed the question, "How well do you know Ida?"

"I haven't seen her for a long time, Babbo would know her better. My mother and Ida were very close, and I was quite a little girl then."

Giorgio found himself smiling at the use of the childhood name for father as he said,

"According to Robbo, he and his mother are looking after a refugee, who is so ill, he might die. I am hoping to make further contact. If the man is as ill as the boy said he is, we will have to use the Assisi people. I might want you to go to the Basilica di Santa Maria at L'Aquila; and if possible bring one of the friars back here."

"I suggest you have a word with my father, would you like me to tell him to expect you?"

. . . .

For a fleeting moment as he leaned across the table to replenish Giorgio's glass, Angelo relaxed.

Thinking, 'If this is what they call the mother of wine, I would sooner have the child,' Giorgio sipped the grappa Angelo had poured and raised his glass in the age old gesture.

"A Milano!"

Angelo's eyes twinkled merrily as he returned the toast with his usual pun. Then, becoming serious once again, said,

"If that lad is the son of Ida, and from your description, I am sure he is, we must be careful. We have known for a long time that the Sicilian visits Ida, always at night, and for all we know is living in her house . . . It could be that he has been relying on that lad to watch our movements."

"Somehow, I don't think so," Giorgio replied in a matter fact tone, "he was certainly scared of me and worried that I might be a German. You know the family, what do you think?"

Angelo didn't answer immediately, he just sat there, his brow corrugated in a heavy frown, toying with his glass with one hand, while the other drummed rhythmically on the table.

Giorgio waited patiently, for what seemed an eternity for Angelo to speak, when he did, it was as if every word had been carefully thought out,

"Ida was a close friend of my dear departed Anna. I seem to recollect that one of Ida's forebears married a German. Nevertheless, I feel, in my bones, Ida would not betray her friends. Donnina probably knows her better than I do, so it might be better if you have a word with her. Do you know her house?"

"The one with a wolf for a knocker," Giorgio grinned as he spoke, "Ernesto is very proud of that knocker."

"If that boy isn't having fanciful dreams and there really is someone he and his mother have been looking after, I am sure they wouldn't have let the Sicilian know." Angelo paused and added hesitantly, "I must admit that the presence of that man in Ida's house makes me more than a little sceptical."

"Nevertheless, if the boy is telling the truth, his mother will certainly know where the poor man is hiding," Giorgio said, before adding, with emphasis, "it is something we must check out."

"Perhaps Donnina could arrange for Ida to come to her house, you could talk to her there, without risk of the Sicilian seeing, or overhearing you. I could ask Filomena to have a word with Donnina." Angelo suggested.

"I don't think Filomena will be back here much before tomorrow evening." Giorgio commented.

Angelo looked at Giorgio sharply and in a curt tone said,

"How far have you sent her? She told me she was going on one of your missions and not to worry if she wasn't back until tomorrow or the next day. It had better not be as perilous as the last job you sent her on." Angelo's face paled, then took on a darker hue as he added, "If anything happens to her, you will have me to answer." Then, as if realising that it was an unfair comment, apologised by saying, "Sorry! That was uncalled for."

"No offence taken," Giorgio replied. Then, continued with, "She has gone to the monastery at L'Aquila. Roberto inferred that the man is not very well. It might be that we will need to get him away through the Assisi connection. Hopefully she will bring back one of the friars so that we can discuss the pros and cons. There is always the possibility of course, that the man will prove to be fit enough to go the usual way."

"Couldn't it have waited until we had seen him?" Angelo's frown was a clear indication of his state of mind.

"You know your daughter; wild horses couldn't have stopped her. The mere indication that the man was ill filled her with a sense of urgency. She insisted on going straight away."

Somewhat mollified and feeling very proud of his daughter, Angelo said,

"When is the next trip planned?"

"Nothing firm yet. We will see what Gino has to say when he gets back. Incidentally, did you know his trip nearly ended in disaster? According to Francesco," Giorgio continued, without waiting for an answer, "the Tedeschi surrounded the Safe house, capturing all except Gino, who was out scouting. I gather they shot Peter." Giorgio frowned and paused for thought before continuing. "Luigi and his band of ribelli rescued them. Oddly, although they found the body of Donna, did you know her by the way? There was no trace of Peter's body. . . . Francesco didn't say how Luigi knew about the crossing. Just happened to be in the area, I suppose. . . ."

"I can throw light on that," Angelo cut in, "when Tina visited Michele, with a message from Alan and Paul, she thought she recognised Peter as someone calling himself Gordon, who was in Francesco's party when he got surrounded. That coupled with one of the party, I think it was John, mistaking him for a friend called Charles, roused Filomena's suspicions. She went to Santa Stefano to ask Luigi to intercept if he could. Evidently, Tina had already voiced similar suspicions and Luigi, acting on them, had embarked on a plan of action before Filomena arrived. . . . To answer your questions, yes I did know about the rescue and no, I didn't know the lady at the safe house."

Giorgio, looked at his watch, the hands told him it was approaching seven in the evening,

"I have things to do," he said, "we shall have to talk to Filomena when she gets back."

"It might be better if I see Ida," Angelo suggested, "she knows me from the old days, if I drop in on Donnina this evening, it might be possible to arrange something."

"Sounds good, I'll contact you tomorrow, to see what developed."

. . . .

Although it was only a twenty five minute walk through the belt of trees, down the sloping path which skirted the church on its way to

La Villa, it was gone eight when Angelo lifted the wolf on the door of Ernesto's house and entered. Donnina, preparing the evening meal, turned to greet him, wiping her hands on her apron as she did so."

"Buon' sera! What brings you here Angelo? It's a long time since we had the pleasure of a visit from you."

"It is indeed," Angelo replied, "these are busy days. I hear from Filomena that Lucia has put Mario out of his misery by saying yes."

Donnina laughed as drawing a chair from under the table she said,

"That's one way of putting it, sit down be comfortable. Ernesto will be another hour yet. These light evenings, you know how it is."

Angelo nodded as he accepted the glass of wine that Donnina had been quick to pour and said,

"It's not Ernesto I've come to see, but he will have to know about the matter I want to discuss. Do you ever talk to Ida these days? I understand she is practically a recluse."

Jolted out of her usual calm, Donnina stopped what she was doing and gave Angelo a long hard look. She knew he couldn't have heard about the murder. Nobody knew except the two who had helped her dispose of the body and they wouldn't have talked. Wondering why he had asked, she said,

"I see her from time to time; as you say, she is practically a recluse, but when I do, she always has a pleasant word."

"What about the boy, he must be getting quite big?" Angelo had noticed Donnina's hesitation so gave a re-assuring smile as he spoke.

"Oh he is always around, you know what children are like, full of fun. He is a nice little boy," Donnina's smile was an indication of how much she loved children.

"I suppose you talk to him from time to time," Angelo said, trying to sound nonchalant.

Donnina gave him a quizzical look. Wondering where the conversation was leading, she hesitated before making comment.

"It would be difficult not to, that boy is a proper little chatterbox."

"Full of fanciful ideas, I suppose."

Donnina felt her heart jump, but quickly returned to normality as she remembered that Roberto wouldn't know about the events of the previous evening. It was late when he crept back home and Konrad's body had been hidden away. Unless Ida had told him; which seemed unlikely, Roberto wouldn't know that his Uncle Marco would not be seen again, so was quite happy and laughed as she said,

"Aren't all boys?"

Angelo was beginning to feel frustrated. Finally, realising that he was not getting anywhere, he said,

"Has he ever told you about his English friend hiding in the woods?"

Donnina compressed her lips and shook her head sideways as she murmured,

"No! Why do you ask? . . . Have you heard something?"

"A friend of mine has," Angelo replied, "He met a rather frightened little boy in the forest who said he was collecting snails for his mother. My friend was sceptical because, the boy didn't seem to have collected any, nor for that matter, did he have anything to put them in."

"When was this?" Donnina asked.

"From what my friend told me, I got the impression it would have been last night." Angelo replied.

"That being so, it probably was Roberto." Donnina hesitated. Then added, "Who is this friend? . . . Giorgio?"

Angelo couldn't help thinking, 'is nothing secret' as he said,

"Don't tell me you know about his work."

"Don't worry, his involvement with the guides and prisoners of war isn't common knowledge. I know about the evasion programmes. Anything Ernesto knows, I know. It stays in the family and that's all that matters." Donnina looked at the clock on the wall as she spoke and added, "It's not very late, Ernesto will be in any minute now, as soon as he gets in I'll take you round to Ida. I expect she will be glad to see you, she and Anna were such close friends."

"It's a beautiful evening Donnina . . . Oh! Salve Angelo, I didn't expect to see you here." Ernesto's quiet voice seemed louder that usual.

"Hallo Ernesto, have you had a good day?" Donnina said and stepped forward to greet him as he entered the house.

"Not so bad." Ernesto replied, then embraced her and added, "How was yours?"

"Not so bad." Like Ernesto, Donnina's response was always the same. As they parted from the embrace, she said,

"I am taking Angelo round to see Ida, it's a long time since he last saw her and he has something he wants to discuss."

"What's that then?" Ernesto asked, giving Angelo a shrewd look.

"It is something I hope to sort out," Angelo said, "Giorgio was asking about a boy he had seen in the forest. It could be anyone. . . . From Giorgio's description it did sound like Roberto."

"You will have to be careful," Instinctively Ernesto's voice dropped almost to a whisper. "the Sicilian has been seen entering Ida's house on more than one occasion. For all we know he is Roberto's mystery man. . . ."

"You needn't worry on that score," Donnina cut in, "he won't be there tonight or any other night."

"How do you know that?" Angelo and Ernesto queried simultaneously.

Donnina smiled, almost secretly and said,

"Never mind how I know, you can take my word for it."

Ida was obviously frightened, when Angelo and Donnina entered her home. She stood, pale faced by the fireplace.

"Perhaps you should have come round and prepared her?" Angelo said to Donnina, then followed up with,"Hallo Ida you remember me don't you?"

Ida relaxed and a brief smile curved her lips. Obviously relieved and pleased to see friends enter, she indicated some chairs and producing a flask of wine, seemingly from nowhere, said,

"Be seated, make yourself comfortable. Some wine perhaps." Then, in a re-assuring tone called out,

"You can come back in Roberto. It isn't Uncle Marco."

"Just the little man I want to see," Angelo said, beckoning Roberto over. "What's this about a friend hiding in the woods?"

Roberto stayed close to his mother and eyeing Angelo suspiciously, edged round behind her.

"I haven't said anything Mama. I haven't," he blurted.

Ida knew her son too well not to know he was lying; instead of rebuking him, she addressed Angelo,

"Is it true that you are involved with the evasion routes?" she asked, "Marco used to ask me that."

"Why? . . . Are you hiding someone?" Angelo replied, looking Ida straight in the face.

Nonplussed for the moment, Ida nodded and remained silent while she poured some wine. A mixture of relief and apprehension assailed her as she spoke, hesitantly.

"With my cousin staying here, we have not been able to bring him in the house. It's been a nightmare."

CHAPTER EIGHTEEN

It was late in the evening and two days had gone by when Giorgio found Roberto lurking on the path near the spot he had first met him. As it was nearly dark, Giorgio had expected to see Ida with him, but the boy seemed to be alone and had such an air of conspiracy about him that he burst out laughing.

"Hello young man," he greeted "Did your mother like the snails?"

Roberto grinned impishly, but didn't answer.

"Where is your friend? Is it far?"

Roberto shrugged his shoulders.

"There isn't anyone there? .. You are making it up aren't you?"

If Giorgio thought that by pretending he didn't believe him, it would stir Roberto in to action, he was mistaken. The boy made no attempt to move, he just stood grinning broadly at Giorgio as if the whole thing was a joke. Giorgio was beginning to feel exasperated but managed to smile encouragingly as he said,

"What's the matter young man, have you changed your mind?"

"He is waiting for me."

The unexpected voice, coming from the direction of a woodland path opening into the clearing startled Giorgio. Instantly alert, he put himself between the intruder and Roberto.

Roberto giggled and spluttered,

"It is Mama, she is coming with us."

"Buonsera, my name is Ida . . . Ida di Lorenzo . . . Roberto's mother. They will have told you about me." Ida crossed the intervening space rapidly as she spoke.

Giorgio took in the slim and attractive figure; judging her to be in her late twenties or early thirties. He had expected an older person. Responding to her greeting, he said

"It's a pleasure to meet you."

"Did Roberto tell you to wait for me?" Ida asked and cast a glance toward Roberto who was now standing solemnly by her side.

"No, he just kept grinning and avoiding my questions. The little rascal."

"I can believe that," Ida's eyes danced with laughter as she added, "it's all a game to him. Boys will be boys."

It took half an hour to circle round La Villa and climb a steep gradient through the forest. There was no path to guide them and Giorgio marvelled at Ida's dexterity as she navigated a route carpeted with pine needles, low lying grasses and moss through the closely growing trees. They eventually came to a halt by a charcoal burner's hut in the centre of a small clearing.

"He is in here I suppose" Giorgio said as he strode towards the refuge.

Ida shook her head. Then, stooping over a heap of gorse stacked against a large pile of logs, close by a charcoal burner's stove, she pulled some of it aside; revealing an opening at the base of the pile. and said,

"He is in here."

Giorgio eyed the opening dubiously. To enter, he would have to crawl on his hands and knees and would be in no position to defend himself if it was a trap. Thoughts of the Sicilian passed through his mind.

"Tell him to come out," he said.

"It's safe to come out Guino," Ida called softly, "We have brought the friend Roberto told you about."

"No, I hurt when I move. Bring him in."

There was no mistaking the Welsh accent. Giorgio's fears subsided.

As Roberto stooped to enter, he pointed to a length of string attached to the bundle of Gorse and said,

"We usually use that to pull the ginestra over the entrance, but with Mama here it won't be necessary.... Follow me."

The entrance seemed to be even lower than it looked. Giorgio found himself in a small chamber, about three metres long and two wide. Sufficient light came from between the logs for him to see a small figure seated on a log at the far end of the enclosure.

"We must get those changed pdq." Giorgio said, eyeing the Italian army breeches and British army shirt, Gwyn was wearing, with disapproval. "Everyone, German and Italian will know you for what you are if they see you dressed like that." he added scornfully.

"If I change into proper clothing, they can shoot me as a spy," Gwyn protested. "Anyway, the colour is good camouflage."

"Camouflage! Camouflage!" Giorgio snorted. "The best camouflage is to wear what everybody is wearing," Then added, with a trace of sarcasm, "You might just as well strut around in full dress uniform."

Ida, hearing the slightly raised tone of Giorgio's voice and suspecting some form of disagreement, called out,

"Is everything alright in there?"

"Everything is fine," Giorgio replied as he emerged from the tunnel, "Roberto is bringing Gwyn out now."

It was only when Roberto brought Gwyn out that, Giorgio realised how debilitated he was.

"Can you walk?" Giorgio asked.

"I think so," came the answer, "I hurt all over and my knees feel like jelly."

"It's a good thing your house isn't far," Giorgio said, addressing himself to Ida.

Ida looked at him, a faint frown creasing her brow,

"Didn't Angelo tell you we are not taking him to my house?" she asked.

Thinking, 'I wish Angelo had filled me in with the full picture,' Giorgio replied,

"No, I thought it had been arranged to take him to you. I hope it's not too far. The lad will never make it. As it is, I don't know how we are going to get him to our special refuge."

"Sorry, I thought you knew." Ida paused, then continued with, "We are taking Guino to a friend who cared for him through the winter months. It isn't safe in my place. Loriano, a high ranking Ovra officer calls regularly to see Konrad."

"Konrad? ... Who's that?" Giorgio's voice was sharp.

"A Cousin of mine, who pretended to be in trouble with the Gestapo and sought refuge with me. It was only later that I found out, that, in reality he was a German spy. You would know him as Marco or," Ida smiled as she finished the phrase, "the Sicilian."

"I knew he was a wrong one," Giorgio grunted.

"Sometimes they talked in Konrad's bedroom, and sent messages on a wireless transmitter. They thought I didn't know. Loriano is sure to wonder why he hasn't heard from Konrad and would think it strange if I didn't invite him in when he comes knocking."

"And if he does, what will you say?"

Giorgio was not surprised. He had already guessed what the answer would be when Ida replied,

"I will say that I haven't seen Konrad for a few days." Ida chuckled, "It wouldn't be a lie, would it?"

Giorgio chuckled with her, then, becoming serious, said,

"I have heard of Loriano, but have never, to my knowledge, seen him. What's he like?"

"You probably have." came the surprising reply, "He was staying somewhere in the area during the winter months, I don't know where; posing I believe as a released prisoner of war. We didn't see anything of him during that period. You remember there was quite a lot of snow. I heard Konrad ask Loriano why he wouldn't let him know who had been looking after him and he said if he did, it would put his cover at risk and he never knew whether he might want to use them again." Ida paused to collect her thoughts, "Medium height, with an athletic appearance, you know what I mean; broad in shoulder and lean in hips. Although he speaks Italian and the local dialect fluently, I don't think he is Italian. I don't know why, it's just an impression I get." Ida paused again, a slightly puzzled frown appeared on her forehead. Then, as if she had suddenly remembered something, added, "I don't know if it is important; I heard him tell Konrad he joined the baf in 1936, or was it buf? They were speaking English at the time, so I couldn't be sure, I got the impression it was some kind of club."

'Baf... Buf', reiterated through Giorgio's mind. It didn't make sense. 'Joined the Baf... Moustache? No, that is baffi and they were speaking in English, not Italian.' Then the phrase, 'Up the Buffs' came into his mind; it kept repeating itself, swamping collective thought. 'Was he a British soldier from the Buffs,' he wondered. Suddenly a thought came to him, 'More likely, Mosley's lot, BUF, British Union of Fascists'.

"Then he is from our Island." Giorgio said with emphatic certainty. "The BUF was a British Fascist group which has been disbanded. The name Loriano is not British, maybe Italian parentage."

"I don't know whether Loriano can speak German, or thought I might understand too much if that language was used, but he often spoke in

English when he wanted to say something they didn't want me to know."

"And could you understand everything they said?"

"Not very well, I know enough to talk to Guino. I learned it at school," Ida replied in reasonable English, "but have difficulty in following other people's conversation."

"All you need is a bit of practise." Giorgio responded, then added, "Where are we taking Gwyn?"

"Domenico. Do you know him?"

Giorgio shook his head, looked at the fragile figure of Gwyn and said,

"No.... By the look of our lad here, it had better not be too far."

Ida smiled re-assuringly as she replied,

"That's not a problem, Domenico's home is nearer than mine, it stands on its own just a little higher than here."

As Ida led the way along an ascending path exiting from a higher point in the clearing, she said,

"Domenico's House is only a short way along this path. He is a carbonaio. The logs and hut belong to him. He was a bit worried when Roberto found Guino, but was glad when I offered to help. He made me promise I wouldn't tell anyone." Ida smiled and a roguish look came into her eyes as she added, "I had to use a little subterfuge. Domenico would have been annoyed had he known that Roberto had already told you about Guino, so I said I had met a member of the evasion group."

"What did he say to that?" Giorgio asked.

"Domenico couldn't have been more pleased, he said it would be a relief to get Guino safe and on his way home. It was his suggestion that I bring Guino and you to his house where he could meet you in safety."

Ida had barely finished speaking when the path opened up to a large area paved with wooden blocks. On the far side of the clearing dim lights glowed from the shutters of a small house. Despite the low tones of Ida's speech, Domenico must have heard her; the door opened suddenly, throwing a subdued shaft of light across the intervening area.

Giorgio had to stoop to enter. The room he found himself in, lit by a single flickering oil lamp, was warm, almost suffocatingly so. A fire, evidently freshly made up blazed in the open fireplace; throwing into relief shadows of the sparse furniture and the occupants. There were two low openings, one on each end of the narrow room. Giorgio couldn't help thinking, 'I thought the entrance was low, but those. . .'

Domenico quickly made them welcome. Offering a chair first to Gwyn, then Ida, he pointed to two ancient crates, and said,

"Make yourself comfortable Giorgio. Do you like grappa?"

Giorgio nodded as he seated himself on the crate and said,

"Your own distillation I suppose."

"Of course, don't tell the Carabinieri." Then seeing Roberto climbing on the other crate, followed up with, "That seat is for me son, you can sit on the floor."

Roberto meekly obeyed.

From a dust covered shelf, Domenico took down three earthenware mugs, then, almost as if an afterthought, lifted another mug from its hook, glanced at Ida and said,

"You also? I know you enjoy it."

Ida smiled and nodded.

Blowing the dust off the mugs, he placed them on the table and reached for a flask. If the mugs were ancient, the flask was more so. Brown, with chips and age cracks in the glaze, it looked as though it was worthy of a place of honour in a museum.

Pulling off the stopper, a wooden bung, he half filled the four mugs. Leaving three on the table for his guests to help themselves, he raised one to his lips and with a happy smile, uttered the customary toast,

"Salute!"

While Giorgio and Ida returned the toast with the invariable,

"And to you."

Gwyn grinned, raised his mug and said,

"Bottoms up!" Then, emptied his mug in a single gulp.

While Giorgio and Domenico looked on in amusement, Ida's face was full of concern; Gwyn's eyes watered, then closed, and his face contorted in a grimace. Between coughing and spluttering, he managed to gasp,

"What on earth was that?"

"Would you like some more?" Domenico asked,

Gwyn shook his head and said,

"Maybe later."

Ida who had sampled Domenico's brand of grappa before, was more cautious and dipped her finger in her drink to test its potency before sipping to enjoy the flavour.

The climb through the trees to Domenico's house was more exhausting than Gwyn had expected.

He hadn't realised how weak his months of inactivity had rendered him and was glad to have a rest. He hoped the new refuge he was going to, wouldn't be far. Domenico, quick to notice Gwyn's condition, and aware it wasn't the effect of the grappa, wore a worried frown as he said, in halting English'

"Rest voglia rest . . . want rest?"

Gwyn looked a little uncertain, as if he hadn't quite understood.

"Do you want to lie down?" Ida supplied.

Gwyn nodded and stumbled towards one of the doorways.

Domenico's eyes twinkled as he said,

"He remembers where to go." Then, addressing himself to Giorgio added, "I know you won't be taking him to Ida's house, it wouldn't be safe. Have you far to go?"

"The other side of the valley," Giorgio, replied.

"He will never make it, he is too weak. It will be better if you take him tomorrow night. I will get Giuseppe tomorrow."

Seeing Giorgio's slightly perplexed look, Ida laughed as she said,

"Giuseppe is his donkey."

"I keep him in a friend's stable." Domenico explained.

It was well past ten when Ida and Giorgio left Domenico and his charge. Making their way back through the closely growing trees to the charcoal burner's hut, Giorgio marvelled again, at the way, despite the lack of a full moon, Ida was able to find her way.

"I don't know how you do it," he said.

"Do what?" Ida asked.

"Find your way so easily in the darkness."

Giorgio's answer brought a light, musical laugh from Ida and a giggle from Roberto; she stopped walking and said,

"All the trees have different shapes. This one for instance, I call it il Vecchio, you see the way the trunk is split at the bottom, making legs. The dead wood at the top are his wrinkles and the silver fungus an old man's hair. We must now go through that avenue to the right until we reach a fallen tree. You can see Domenico's hut from there."

Although Giorgio thought, 'what avenue, it all looks the same to me,' he said nothing.

Emerging into the clearing, Ida checked the entrance to Gwyn's refuge. Satisfied that the entrance was hidden, she said,

"I must leave you now, we will see you tomorrow, as arranged at Domenico's house. It will be sad, saying goodbye to Guino after so long. It's a relief though, to know he will now get the care he needs."

"Let me see you safely home," Giorgio said, "It's not far out of my way."

"Safer not to," Ida replied, "although it is late, there could be people about and it is better if we are not seen together."

"Then I will leave you at the edge of the forest." Giorgio said in a matter of fact tone that brooked no argument.

On arrival home, Ida found Loriano waiting outside the back entrance. He was clearly angry, when he said,

"Where have you been?"

"Visiting friends, what is it to you?" Ida retorted.

"Tell Marco I'm here." The tone was more an order than a request.

Ida could feel her blood rising, but kept her peace. Before answering she told Roberto to go to bed.

"It's getting late," she said, "I'll bring you a drink presently." Then, in answer to Loriano's query, "He is not here."

Loriano scowled, he was in a bad mood, having waited in the outskirts of the forest over an hour. He spoke abruptly.

"Where is he?"

Resisting the temptation to say you should know that better than me, Ida said,

"I really don't know. He goes off for two or three days, every now and then. Visiting friends, I suppose. I'll tell him you called when he comes back.... Now. If you will excuse me, I must look after my little boy and get to bed myself."

Disgruntled, Loriano bade Ida a curt goodnight and left.

Ida watched him go, then closed the door and dropped a heavy wooden bar in position to secure it.

. . . .

No news of the crossing had filtered through since Luigi's return and several days had gone by. The arrival of Gino, the evening before with the news that, with the exception of Peter, all were safely in Allied occupied territory was received, albeit with a tinge of sadness for Peter, with great relief. On hearing the news, Tina announced,

"I shall take the news to Angelo tomorrow."

Luigi wasn't very happy and it showed in his face as he said,

"I don't think that is very wise Precious, there has been a lot of activity over there during the past week. If you must go, then, take the route through the olive groves."

"I always do." Tina replied with a winning smile as she planted a kiss on Luigi's cheek.

Tania, looking on smiled broadly and whispered to Pamella,

"Cunning minx, she knows how to get round her dad."

Tina left early, shortly after first light, the following morning. Gathering together the few essentials she needed for the journey, she curtsied before the shrine by the door of the house, uttered a short prayer as she closed the door and set off down the steep and winding track cut into the side of the canyon. On reaching the bottom, Tina made her way upstream to a plank over the river, where she could cross without getting wet. Her brisk pace soon carried her to the mouth of the canyon where the motor road emerged. Acutely aware that there was a curfew in force and the Tedeschi passed along the road at frequent intervals, she stood, fearless, in the developing light of the dawn as she debated in her mind which of the two routes through the olive groves would be the best. Whichever way she went,

Tina knew that it would be dusk, if not dark, by the time she reached the track leading to Angelo's house.

With scarcely a glance at the village of Santa Stefano perched high above her, her mind made up, Tina made her way along the land-way at the base of the mountain. Passing the dilapidated house where she had made contact with Philip, reminded her of the letter her mother had given him. Tina tried to imagine the reaction of her uncle when he received the letter from his sister. A happy smile crossed her face, when she recalled Philip's promise to return after the war. 'I wonder if he really will,' she thought.

The sight of the distant bulk of the Gran Sasso towering high above the valley brought to mind the first time she had made the same long trek. In her mind's eye, Tina could see Filomena's warm smile when she saw the sycamore leaf in her hair and the shy way Angelo said, *'you are always welcome here'*, still rang in her ears.

When Tina reached Angelo's house it was in darkness. Perhaps, because she was tired she felt depressed. The path round Paese had seemed further and the gradient up the track steeper than she remembered. There was no smell of smoke from the chimney and the absence of even the smallest chink of light from the shuttered windows gave the place a deserted air. Tina knocked and listened, waited several minutes, then, satisfied that no one was at home, turned away.

Remembering that Filomena had told her that she was a frequent visitor to Michele's home, Tina wondered whether she could find the way. With renewed vigour she descended the track and crossed the valley. Resting on the same log that Ernesto had used a few days before Tina tried to remember the short cut Filomena had shown her. A path she had noticed on the way up seemed to go in the right direction, so she descended the track in search of it.

Tina found the path without difficulty. It was only a few metres below. Initially, she thought her guess was right, but, to her dismay, it quickly became almost impossible follow. When the path eventually petered out in a mass of tangled undergrowth, she burst into tears. Pulling herself together, Tina stared at the barrier, hoping, to see a passage through. Feeling utterly frustrated, she retraced her footsteps.

Tina had only gone a short way when she saw the silver birch. The tree was so close to the path and so clear, that despite the darkness of a night without stars, she wondered how she had missed it. It was then, that she remembered Filomena saying, '*If you ever need to use this path, look for that tree; it's the only one like it.*' She also remembered that the tree should be above her, not below. Testing the way forward with a stick and treading warily, less she spring a trap, Tina forced her way through a carpet of low growing brambles and peered through the trees beyond the silver birch. However, it was too dark below the canopy of leaves to see whether another path lay ahead.

Unsure, Tina looked back across the way she had come and tried to assess the direction she was facing in relation to the main track. Convinced that the path she hoped to find would be immediately ahead, she followed her instincts and made her way through the trees.

Undaunted by the heavy undergrowth and ignoring the way it clutched at her skirt and scratched her legs, Tina penetrated the forest until the ground fell away from her and she found herself at the top of a steep bank. A path that seemed to be the one she wanted, lay just below. It was narrower than she remembered and so close, she wondered how she had missed it. With a lingering look back at the silver birch, she picked her way down the bank. Although now sure the right path had been found, Tina broke off the top of a sapling to mark the spot in case she had to retrace her footsteps. Despite the memory of Filomena saying the route was steep, when the path abruptly changed direction and climbed so steeply that she had to steady herself by putting her hands to the ground, the feeling of uncertainty returned.

Deciding, on reaching the summit, that the path was going in the right direction and appeared to be one that was used, so would lead somewhere, Tina pressed on. When it turned again and dived so precipitously that she lost her foothold on the damp and slippery surface, she could have wept again in despair. Regaining an upright position, Tina looked around; a short distance behind, a woodland path emerged on to the track where she found herself standing. Ahead was an avenue of poplars. Confident now that she was on the track leading to Michele's home, she quickened her pace. The sudden appearance, little more than a light coloured blur, of Michele's dog trotting towards her, was a welcome sign that she hadn't far to go.

"Leone!" she called softly.

The dog stood still, and stared at the stranger approaching his territory. Then growled, a low menacing sound that seemed to well up from his paws.

Tina had inherited her mother's love of dogs, she called again,

"Leone!"

Taking care not to smile, less the dog see her teeth and think she was baring them in an act of aggression, Tina walked slowly forward.

Stiff legged and suspicious, Leone moved towards the intruder. Then crouched to the ground and lay motionless, nose on paws, watching Tina's every movement as she approached.

Tina was only a few paces away, when the night air was split with a cacophonous din, that startled the creatures of the forest and sent them scuttling through the undergrowth, as Leone leaped to his feet, wagging his tail and barking furiously. It happened so suddenly, it made her jump; she stepped back a pace and said, calmly,

"It's alright Leone."

Something in the tone of Tina's voice must have struck a chord of memory in the dog. Perhaps recognition of a visitor who had shared food with him several meals ago. Whatever it was, Leone stopped barking and cocked his head on one side. The silence lasted less than a minute. Without changing the still threatening stance, tail wagging faster as if its owner wasn't sure whether to hold Tina at bay or welcome her, Leone started barking again; but now it had a lighter, more friendly sound, mixed with shrill yelps.

"Who is out there Leone?"

Encouraged by the sound of Michele's voice, Leone barked louder than ever and stalked a few paces nearer.

Carrying a mattock for defence, Michele came into view and peered in Tina's direction.

"Who is it?" he demanded, "This is private property."

"Is that you Michele? . . . I'm Tina, do you remember me? I came with Filomena when she hurt her ankle. Is she here?"

"Stai zitto." Michele's simple command, silenced the dog, Turning his attention to Tina, Michele then said,

"Of course I remember you Tina, what are you doing here?"

"I'm looking for Filomena,"

"Filomena is not here. . . . Why did you think she might be?"

"She told me she sometimes stays the night at your house when Angelo is away."

227

"Why do you need to see her?" Michele lowered his voice and added, "Does it concern our work?"

Tina nodded.

"I assume you went to Angelo's house and found nobody at home, so came here. You must be tired," Michele said as he drew level with the now bedraggled looking girl.

"Yes, I am a bit tired," Tina admitted, I was planning to pass on some good and bad news and spend the night there, but the place was deserted. I waited a while for someone to turn up." She paused, then added a little lamely, "Then I remembered you."

Michele gave Tina a shrewd look and said,

"There wouldn't be, Angelo and George are on a special mission tonight, and Filomena is not expected home until tomorrow or the next day," Michele paused to stir the tobacco in an ancient terracotta pipe. Satisfied, it was now drawing sweetly, he continued with, "You had better come to the house, I am expecting both Angelo and Giorgio to arrive here within the next half hour. You can give Angelo your news then."

"So that is why . . ." Tina bit off what she was about to say as Michele interrupted with,

"You said you have good and bad news. These are perilous times . . ."

Tina looked at Michele gravely and said,

"Yes, they are. I'm sorry, but the bad news is about Peter, the party making the crossing were surrounded and we have been told that Peter may have been shot."

"That is sad news, it will upset Giuseppina, she was very fond of him," Michele said, then followed with, "what do you mean, may have been?"

Before answering the question, Tina said,

"The good news is that my father rescued the rest and they made the crossing safely." Then, followed with, "In answer to your question. After the skirmish with the Tedeschi my father and his sergeant major searched for Peter's body. They found Donna's, but there was no trace of Peter's."

When, as they entered the courtyard, Michele saw Vincensina and Giuseppina framed in the doorway, he came to a halt and lowing his voice, said,

"Don't say anything yet, it might be better if I get Vincensina on one side and ask her to tell Giuseppina about Peter, she will know how to break it to her."

As they reached the open doorway of the house, the opening words of a favourite piece of sacred music came floating through the air.

'*Ecco dunque peccatore, ecco salute la via . . .*'

Entranced by the purity of the voice, Tina stopped; she didn't think she had ever heard such a clear voice before, not even in the church at Santa Stefano. Reluctant to enter, less she break the spell, she placed a hand on Michele's arm, restraining him. There followed, in modulated volume, low notes which, with incredible smoothness, steadily increased, as the higher tones were reached, a rendition of Guono's beautiful Ave Maria.

"What a lovely voice," she whispered, "Who is it?"

Vincensina, who had heard the whisper said, with more than a hint of pride in her voice,

"It's my mother. Now you know who Giuseppina gets her voice from. Despite her great age, Caterina has retained her voice. If you think it's beautiful now, you should have heard her sing at our wedding; it was even better then. Such melody is not easily forgotten."

CHAPTER NINETEEN

Caterina greeted Tina like an old friend. Age had not impaired her memory, she recognised the voice.

"Come over here child, let me feel your face so that I know you."

"How are you Caterina? Well I hope."

"Not so bad," came the not unexpected reply. Then, as Tina approached, "you smell damp. It's not raining, where have you been?"

"In the forest, I used the short cut," Tina said, without mentioning that she had lost her way.

"And lost your way, I'll be bound," Caterina commented. "Don't say you didn't," she added with a cackle as she felt Tina's clothes. "Come and sit by the fire." Then, calling to Vincensina, "Get this child some clean clothes, she is covered in mud and her dress is torn. Giuseppina can wash and mend them."

Tina couldn't help laughing as she wondered how Vincensina and Giuseppina would take the peremptory orders.

Almost immediately, Vincensina appeared, she was laughing as she said, Mother still thinks I'm a child and won't think of these things."

"I heard that. I'm not deaf." Caterina's voice sounded slightly querulous. Whether she was peevish or not, there was no sign of it as she added, "Make the child some hot soup."

Vincensina smiled at Tina and winked as she said,

"Will do." Then, lowering her voice added, "Go into that room and change into the clothes on the chair."

Sitting by the fire in borrowed clothes, hunger assuaged by a platter of spaghetti laced with a dressing of tomato purée and chopped chicken, Tina tried to fight off a drowsiness that beset her as she listened to Caterina's tales of long ago. It is probable that she would have fallen asleep if Angelo hadn't arrived and greeted her with,

"Hallo Tina, to what do we owe this pleasure?"

As Gwyn, helped by Giorgio, entered a few minutes later, he looked around the room, taking in every detail. After the months of semi-confinement in his den and Domenico's small house, it looked spacious. The blazing fire in a large hearth, reminded him of his home in Wales; a large, rambling place, high up the slopes of one of the mountains. He tried to say how grateful he was of their help, but didn't know enough of the language to do so. Without waiting for one of the others to rise to the rescue, Tina said,

"Tell me what you want to say."

"Tell them, I will never forget the help they are giving me and God willing, I will come back to see them after the war has finished."

For the benefit of Vincensina and Caterina, she suspected Giuseppina knew enough to get the gist, Tina translated.

"You look tired," there was a note of compassion in Vincensina's voice as she said it. "A bed is already made up in your new refuge. When you have eaten, Michele will take you there.

Gwyn looked blank, Vincensina had spoken in Italian, Giorgio translated for him, and he managed to muster the word,

"Grazie."

Gwyn had barely finished eating, when the door opened and Mario breezed in. He was laughing and appeared to be in great spirits.

"Where did that donkey come from? Nove greeted it with great joy."

"The donkey belongs to Domenico, the carbonaio, we used it to bring our new refugee here." Michele stopped speaking for a moment and tapped his pipe on the side of the chimney. "I'll be glad when we can buy some tobacco that burns," he grumbled, then continued with, "The poor man is so ill, I don't think he will be able to leave for quite a while."

"We are hoping to make different arrangements for him," Angelo said, then, turning to Tina, followed with, "Have you come to see Filomena?"

Seeing Giuseppina hovering in the corner of the room, Tina answered with a simple,

"Yes."

From the corner of her eye, Tina saw Michele beckon Vincensina into an adjoining room and guessed he was going to tell her about Peter. When Vincensina re-appeared, her eyes were red. Tempted to comfort her Tina restrained. Young as she was, she knew that sympathy often had an unwanted effect. She felt it would be best to say nothing until Vincensina had broken the news to Guiseppina. She wanted to say Peter's body was never found, that he might have run away, but the time was not right. The cry that followed shortly afterwards told her that the two were grieving together.

Quick to pick up the signs, Angelo first looked at Tina, then Giorgio, then back at Tina who interpreting the enquiring glance, said,

"They are upset, Peter might have been shot, I will fill you in with the details as I know them, later." Then hastened to add, "The good news is, the group crossed over safely."

The hands of an ancient weight operated clock stood at five minutes past eleven when Michele said,

"We had better get this young man to bed."

"Do you want help taking him there," Mario said, taking in the debilitated condition of Gwyn.

"That won't be necessary," Michele shook his head as he replied.

When Gwyn saw the manger well laden with straw, he thought it was to be his bed. Had it been so, it would not have been the first time he had been offered shelter in a stable and slept in the manger.

"Looks comfortable," he said, "where are the animals?"

"We only use this stable when we want to hide them," Michele replied, "regular use would create a track, difficult to hide and there is always the risk of the beasts making a noise, which could attract unwanted prying." Michele didn't have Mario's expertise in the English language and was pleasantly surprised that he was not only able to construct the sentence, but also, Gwyn had understood what he wanted to say. 'Obviously,' he thought, 'talking with previous guests has made me more practical.' and smiled inwardly with self congratulation.

On his return to the house, Michele found Tina chatting happily to Mario. When he heard the words marriage and Lucia, he didn't have to ask what the pair were talking about. From the look on Tina's face, it was obvious that she had a romantic streak in her and was relishing the thought of wedding bells. It almost seemed cruel to interrupt them. But, interrupt them, he did.

"Now Tina, tell us more about this good and bad news, I'm sure Giorgio and Angelo are anxious to hear."

Both Giorgio and Angelo turned their heads sharply, looking first at Michele, then Tina. Mario stopped talking about his forthcoming marriage and said,

"What's this about good and bad news?"

"I expect," Tina began, "Filomena told you about my father's rescue of Philip's party."

"No, what rescue?" Angelo asked, "I know of course that she went to see Luigi, because she was worried the Tedeschi might know about the venture."

Tina, surprised at first, that Filomena hadn't told Angelo about the rescue remained silent for a moment.

"Of course," she said, on reflection, "Filomena wouldn't know, she left us before Papa returned. I think you know, Angelo, she was so worried about something she overheard when the party was assembling that she came to see us."

"That's right," Angelo concurred, "it is why she went to find Luigi and ask him to watch for them. I believe, from what she told me on her return, that by the time she arrived Capitano Vincenzo had already left with a squad of his men."

"Briefly," Tina continued, "Filomena remembered I was disturbed when I saw Peter here, I kept him talking, because he looked like someone called Gordon, who was in the party when Francesco got hurt. Remember; all except Francesco and the guide were captured. When I told Filomena about Peter looking like Gordon, she laughed it off, said I was imagining things. I gather that something happened at the assembly point that made her re-think. Whatever it was, she became convinced that Peter might be a spy and came to warn us. Since I too had the same, what seems now an absurd idea, I had already persuaded Papa to watch over them."

"Filomena has never said anything about this to me," Giorgio, put in, "Do you know what it was Angelo?"

"John thought that Peter was someone named Charlie. Peter seemed quite cross, I don't know why. Mistaking someone for somebody else is a common enough." Angelo explained.

"Why do you now think it absurd?" Mario asked.

"Tina tells me that when the party was captured, Peter was shot." Michele supplied.

A stunned silence, broken only by Giuseppina's sobbing, fell over all present,

"Oh Pietro, my Pietro," Giuseppina murmured.

"Papa couldn't find his body, so he might have escaped and run off," Tina hastened to add.

The hopeful look on Giuseppina's face was unmistakable.

Giorgio's brain as he listened to the dialogue was racing. 'Too many coincidences', he told himself. 'too many unexplained happenings.' One by one odd snatches of conversation passed through his mind as he tried to recall pieces that seemed irrelevant at the time. 'Who was Gordon?' he asked himself. 'Released prisoner of war who had joined a band of rebels operating near Assergi, the other side of the Gran Sasso, and had decided he wanted to join Francesco's group on an evasion route. Presumably, when they were captured he would have been taken, with the others to a transit camp.' Giorgio had never met Gordon, but knew from what Francesco had told him that he was fluent in Italian. Since, in addition to this, although Peter's Italian was reasonable, it was by no stretch of the imagination fluent, Tina's suspicions seemed unfounded.

Giorgio's reverie was disturbed by Michele standing over him, a bottle in each hand,

"What is it sambuca or grappa?"

"Grappa please," Giorgio's response was immediate.

It was turned one in the morning, when Angelo announced,

"Look at the hour, it's a good thing tomorrow is Sunday. I must get away home. Are you coming with me Giorgio?"

"I can walk part way with you, but have some loose ends to tie up; I need to think about them and can do so while I am walking...." Giorgio said, without explaining further.

Caterina had long since gone to bed and Tina was sound asleep in her chair. Vincensina and Giuseppina were not only still there because it was the custom not to retire until the menfolk did, both of them also had Tina's clothes to attend to in mind.

Instantly alert, Vincensina said,

"Tina had better sleep here, she is too tired to walk across that valley. Michele will bring her over to you tomorrow."

Evidently, hearing her name, Tina stirred and looked vaguely about her. She gave a half smile to Vincensina and said,

"Did you say something?"

Vincensina, without making a direct reply, took her by the arm and saying, "You don't mind sharing a bed with Giuseppina tonight," she led her to the ladder like structure that was the stairs, turned to Giuseppina and said,

"Take her with you, I'll look after that little job."

. . . .

Suddenly, Tina was awake. She had no way of telling how long she had been asleep. Wondering what had disturbed her, she looked at the square that was the window and tried to judge the time from the amount of light that was coming in. Swinging her legs to the floor, she glanced at the sleeping Giuseppina, then crossed to the window and looked out.

The clouds that filled the sky the evening before had dissipated, giving place to a star studded splendour that lit the courtyard below with an ethereal subdued light. Nothing moved and the air had a stillness about it that seemed to tell her she couldn't have been asleep very long. Tina stood at the window, breathing in the cool night air for several minutes; just listening to the small sounds of the night and enjoying the serenity of the star lit sky before returning to bed.

Laying in bed, staring at the dim shape of rafters supporting the roof, the gentle breathing of Giuseppina sounded louder than it really was as Tina tried to woo a sleep that wouldn't come. She tried to relax, to dismiss the torrent of thoughts running through her brain. Thoughts that drifted in and out of her mind as she went over every detail of what had happened over the last two weeks.

Tina must have dozed off; in a vague way, she was aware that the church clock in La Villa had sounded the hour, and marvelled at the distance sound travelled during the stillness of the night. She didn't know how many times it had struck and vowed, if she was still awake, to count the chimes next time. When they came, she only half heard them and couldn't be sure whether it was three or four.

The close by crowing of a cock woke her. It was dawn, and the sun was already rising. Taking care not to disturb the still sleeping Giuseppina, she poured water into a small metal bowl and splashed her face.

Refreshed, Tina looked out of the window. Michele was moving around the yard.

"Buongiorno!" she called softly.

Michele waved to her and returned her greeting.

"If you are awake, you can come and help me," he suggested with a roguish grin.

Returning his grin. Tina said,

"Not before I am dressed."

The clothes she had borrowed were gone. In their place on the chair where she had left them, neatly folded and ironed, were her own clothes. Even the tear had been mended. Tina dressed herself quickly and scurried down the steps to join Michele.

"Oh no you don't, he'll have you working till you drop," Vincensina said as she barred Tina's way. "Not before you have eaten."

Carving a massive slice of bread from a freshly baked loaf, Vincensina sprinkled it with olive oil and salt, then stood by to make sure that Tina ate it.

Tina was surprised how hungry she was and didn't hesitate when Vincensina carved a second slice.

"Oh! You are kind," she said, thank you for looking after my clothes. How did you manage to get them dry so quickly?"

"That wasn't a problem, I washed them last night, and hung them near the fire." Vincensina replied, without adding how difficult the jagged tear had been to mend in a way that didn't show.

During the walk across the valley to Angelo's house, Tina chatted happily, she was amazed by the extent of Michele's knowledge. He seemed able to converse on every subject under the sun. The way he interposed silly, but amusing anecdotes every now and then kept her entertained. 'How nice,' Tina thought, 'it is to talk about something different to the state of the crops or this horrible war.'

When they arrived at Angelo's house, shortly after mid-day, there was no sign of Angelo. Surprised they looked in the stable. There was only Forli, who looked at them expectantly, as if to say, are you taking me for a walk or feeding me?

As they left the stable, Tina glance up the hillside.

"There he is," she said.

Seeing them, Angelo beckoned them up. As they came abreast, he pointed to the distant track leading to Paese and said.

Filomena is on her way, it looks as though she has one of the friars with her."

"Did Giorgio spend the night here?" Michele asked, more as a point of interest than a need to know.

"He had things he said he needed to think about and would do so while he was walking. He didn't say to where, you know what he is like. Nobody knows where he stays. The man's like a willow-o'-the-wisp. He comes and he goes."

"A bit like the Scarlet Pimpernel, you mean," Michele said, with a grin, then more seriously, "I got the impression last evening that he wanted to talk to Filomena."

"That's right," Angelo confirmed, "he asked me to try and remember precisely what John said to Peter, that made him annoyed. . . . I said I wasn't close by so didn't catch all of it but whatever it was, it started Filomena thinking. Giorgio said he will make contact today or tomorrow."

"It shouldn't take much more than half an hour for them to get up here," Michele observed. Then added, "providing that friar isn't a slow walker."

Far from being a slow walker, Filomena had to use all her energy to keep up with the young man who accompanied her. Taller than her by a head, with long legs, he had set a brisk pace that almost had her running, so that as she said later,

"We broke all records coming back," Filomena made the remark with a laugh, "didn't we Abbondio?"

Abbondio's eyes twinkled as he nodded.

"He thinks I should marry the church," Filomena continued, "he is so devoted to his calling, I don't think he can understand why we like a fuller life." Filomena tried not to laugh as she said it.

"Let us meet this young man I've come to see," Abbondio said, as he swallowed the remainder of the wine Angelo had poured for him. "Where is he?"

"He is not here." Angelo said,

"What do you mean, not here?" Abbondio's voice was crisp; there was just a trace of annoyance in it.

"Don't worry, he is in a safe place," Michele said, "We will take you to him after dark."

If Abbondio was disappointed, he didn't show it when he said,

"What's wrong with now? I haven't time to waste"

"It's too risky. You will have to wait," Angelo retorted as he refilled Abbondio's glass.

Mollified, Abbondio gulped a mouthful of wine and embarked on a flow of questions relating to Gwyn, his religion, state of health and reason for needing assistance from the church.

Without knowing, whether it was true or not, Michele felt no qualms as he told Abbondio that Gwyn was a good Catholic.

Having regard to the amount of wine Abbondio had swallowed, both Angelo and Michele were amazed that he appeared unaffected as they made their way across the valley to the house named Casa dei Pioppi.

"I reckon he does five Kilos to the Litre," Michele joked, speaking in the local dialect, which he hoped Abbondio wouldn't understand; if he did, Abbondio didn't make comment.

Although not yet dark when they climbed the track to the avenue of poplars, Michele said,

"I think it's late enough to go straight to the refuge, the Tedeschi don't prowl around much at this hour."

So saying, he led the way round the back of the house to the place which used to be the family home.

Without uttering a word, Angelo and Michele watched Abbondio's face for his reaction when he saw the only doorway, apparently blocked by a tree.

If they expected to see bewilderment, they were disappointed. Abbondio's expression didn't change. It looked calm and expectant and showed no sigh of surprise when the door to the stable swung open, complete with the attached tree. However, when he entered and looked around the stable, obviously expecting to see Gwyn, he did then, look a little puzzled as he said,

"Where is our friend? I thought he would be in here."

"Open that door at the far end and you'll find him," Michele said quietly.

Clearly pleased to see them, Gwyn rose to his feet and left the table where he had been sitting engrossed in a book. Doing so was obviously an effort.

Angelo was amused to note that the book was a child's version of *Arabian nights*, and wondered how much of the Italian Gwyn had been able to understand. 'Probably just looking at the pictures' he thought.

Abbondio, in passable English said,

"Sit down my son, you are not well. I can see that. It will take a few days, but I will get you in the care of our sisters. After that, when you have recovered your strength, other arrangements can be made."

"Gwyn looked first at Angelo, then Michele and said,

"Will it be safe in a hospital? Don't the Germans go into them from time to time?"

"They are sacred houses, attached to the monastery, even the Germans wouldn't dare to desecrate them." Abbondio said, with a note of firm conviction.

Angelo winked at Michele, and read in his face the same thoughts as his own, 'If only I had that same faith.'

Producing, from seemingly nowhere, a bottle of holy water, Abbondio sprinkled a few drops on Gwyn's head and said,

"Let us say a little prayer for our friend and give thanks to Mary, our Madonna, who loves us."

Later, refusing Michele's invitation to spend the night under his roof, Abbondio said,

"I will keep our friend company tonight, he could do with someone to talk to."

"I doubt whether there will be anyone about, nevertheless, keep your voices low and make sure the shutters are tightly closed. It wouldn't do for any light to show." Michele said as he and Angelo closed the door behind them.

· · · ·

When Filomena saw the oak leaf lodged in a crevice by the fonte, she was mildly surprised; this was the second time within a short time that Giorgio had made contact this way. For a while now, ever since, in fact, he had discovered that Angelo now knew about her involvement with him and the Partito d' Azione, he had tended to contact her at her home. It was a more reliable method than the oak leaf signal; there had been more than one occasion when the leaf had become dislodged. She resolved to ask him why he had reverted when they met.

The position of the leaf's stalk, indicated that she was to meet Giorgio at two pm and the crevice the leaf was lodged in told her the place; one of three. While, nearing the appointed time, Filomena made her way along a secluded path high above La Villa, the song she was singing was evidence of the joy inside her. Forgotten for the time being that the reason he wanted to see her was not a romantic one she skipped happily along towards the rendezvous.

Giorgio was already waiting when she arrived. The shadow of a smile crossed his face as he greeted her with the words,

"Salve! Thank you for coming, I need to talk to you. Urgently."

The words were formal. Filomena knew they would be, she hadn't really expected them to be otherwise. Nevertheless, a pang of disappointment slowed her rapidly beating heart as she said,

"Hallo Giorgio, why have you reverted to contacting me in the old way, instead of coming to the house? I thought, when Babbo found out that I was working with you, it was agreed it was more reliable. What do you need to discuss?"

"It is becoming increasingly obvious there is a spy watching our movements and I don't want to attract too much attention to you and Angelo. From what was being said the other evening, I got the impression that something was said that made you suspect it could be Peter. What made you think that?"

Remaining silent for a few minutes, while she cast her mind back to the evening in the assembly house, Filomena tried to remember the precise words that were said. Only when she was satisfied that as near as possible, she had them right, did she say,

"As I remember it when Papa introduced Filippo and Peter to John, John grasped Peters hand. He greeted him like an old friend and said haven't seen you since that party at Maud's place. What a night that was. Confident now that she had recalled the precise wording, she couldn't help thinking, I wonder why, English phrases stay in my memory better than those said in my own language. Part of the process of learning I suppose, before continuing: "Peter looked a bit vague and sounded annoyed when he said 'I think you must be mistaken, I don't think we have ever met. I don't know anyone named Maud.'" Filomena paused a moment while she watched a woodcock strut down the path behind Giorgio, "It was only then that I realised Maud was the name of someone. Anyway it got me thinking, I remembered Tina's doubts. The more I thought about it, the more worried I became"

Wondering what had caught her attention, Giorgio found himself looking at her and thinking 'I've never noticed before what long eyelashes she has.' When he spoke, he tried hard not to reveal an odd feeling welling up inside him, but his eyes betrayed him.

"That's a common enough mistake," he said, "thinking you recognise someone you haven't seen for a while. I've done it myself. What did you think Maud meant?"

Filomena managed a laugh as she answered.

"I thought Maud's place was a place in England."

Trying to ignore the subtle change in Giorgio's eyes and quell the emotions they raised in her, Filomena hoped her voice hadn't let her down when she answered. For a brief moment grey eyes locked with brown; then the magic was gone, as suddenly as it had begun. Bemused by the strange protective urge that beset him Giorgio looked away. Filomena could feel her cheeks getting hot and hoped that if she was blushing, it didn't show. To her great relief, her voice was steady when, in response to Giorgio's comment she said,

"In itself, no. But, as I just said, it reminded me that Tina was sure she had met Peter before. She couldn't think where. Initially though, she thought he was Gordon. It seemed too much of a coincidence. I didn't hear all the conversation, because I went out to prepare some food. John was laughing and talking about a party where someone called Giorgie hung from a rafter by his toes until he dropped off on his head." Filomena smiled broadly in amusement at the memory. "As I came back with the food, I heard John say something, about mostly Blackshirts, I can't say precisely what it was, because I only caught a snatch of it, and assumed they were probably talking about the Decima."

CHAPTER TWENTY

When Abbondio returned, accompanied by another friar, he was leading two donkeys. A full week had flown by; a week during which Gwyn steadily improved. The ability to move around in his refuge and the company of someone to talk to had done much to restore his morale. The gentle walk to the house, or short stroll, after dark, accompanied by Ernesto or Mario in the surrounding forest when safe to do so, was beginning to bring back the strength of his legs.

It was late afternoon, when Abbondio knocked on the door of Casa dei Pioppi and held out a tin mug to receive the customary donation of grain.

"Isn't it a bit early for that," Michele said as he opened the door.

Abbondio grinned roguishly and said,

"It helps the deception. let us say it was an early harvest."

Michele took the mug and filled it with grain reserved for the flow of monks, who at the height of the season would be calling in a seemingly never ending stream, from a cask near the door of the house. Abbondio took the mug and promptly emptied it into one of two sacks hung across the back of one the donkeys.

"How is our friend?" he asked.

"Greatly improved." Michele replied, adding, "put your beasts in the stable and come in and rest a while. I will bring Gwyn to the house when it's safe to do so."

"Can't we go to him now? Nobody is going to take any notice of a couple of friars," Abbondio said, with a hint of the impatience which seemed to be a trait of his.

"Nevertheless, it will do no harm to wait till evening." Michele replied sharply. "You don't intend to leave straight away, surely."

Abbondio, looked at his partner, who nodded and said, in an authoritative tone,

"Do as Michele says. It can wait."

Deducing that he, and not Abbondio was in charge, Michele led one of the donkeys to the stable and said,

"Come in to the house, by the time my wife has a meal ready it will be safe to bring the young man here. . . . What is your name Brother?"

"Don Pezza . . . just call me Pezza. . . . You must excuse our brother, he is young and still a novice."

"All is forgiven, he is keen," Michele commented, adding, "presumably you will stay the night here, I assume you have bedding."

"Naturally," Don Pezza replied, as he pointed to a bundle on the back of the donkey without the sacks of grain, "and that is a habit for your friend to wear. . . . I expect we will have to shave his head to achieve the usual tonsure. I understand he doesn't know our language, so it will make sense if we say he has taken the vow of silence."

"I don't suppose he will mind that and his hair could do with a good cut; it's almost as long as Samson's." Michele tried hard, without success, not to laugh as he spoke and was relieved to find that Don Pezza also found it amusing.

When the evening meal was cooked and ready to serve, Michele brought Gwyn to the house so that he could spend his last evening in the comfort of a home and the companionship of a family.

There followed an evening of conversation and prayers, during which Gwyn proudly spoke of his home on the slopes of Snowdon, where his father owned a sheep farm. The distant mountains, he said, although not so green reminded him of his beloved Wales. The evening ended, when Don Pezza said,

"It's time we called it a day. We must make an early start tomorrow. Where is the . . ." he paused and grinned, "Priest hole?"

"It isn't far. I will take you there." Michele replied.

Unable to sleep, with thoughts of the risk involved when he left the safety of his refuge clouding his mind, Gwyn lay on his bed, hands clasped behind his neck. One of the slats in the half open shutters caught his eyes, it seemed to be a different colour to the rest. He tried to forget it and closed his eyes, but the sleep he so desperately needed didn't come. The slat was like an obsession; every time he thought about it he felt compelled to open his eyes and have a look.

Suddenly it was daylight, Gwyn knew he must have been asleep, but didn't know how long. Abbondio was standing by the bed, a bundle of clothing in his hands.

"Get dressed in these," he said.

Helped by Abbondio, Gwyn dressed in the coarse habit. The cowl felt strangely bulky on the back of his neck and he fumbled with it as he tried to draw it over his head.

"You will soon get used to it." Abbondio chuckled as he adjusted the huge cross which hung awkwardly from its sash and added, "I wouldn't put the hood up if I were you, it will be cooler left down."

As Abbondio spoke, Don Pezza, who had slept in the manger, entered the room, he gazed at Gwyn critically and said,

"It's fortunate you are small. Except for that hair, you look a typical Franciscan. Sit on that chair, Abbondio will soon put that right."

"Is it very far to the monastery?" Gwyn asked as Abbondio produced scissors and prepared to cut his hair.

"Our monastery is near L'Aquila," Don Pezza replied. "we won't be going there, it is too far out of our way."

"Where are we going then, is it a long way?"

"Not really," Don Pezza replied, "we could be there in three days, but expect to be on the road for a week to ten days. A fit man going over the hills could do it in two."

Gwyn's face reddened.

There was a merry twinkle in Abbondio's eyes as he commented,

"You can't hurry a donkey." The twinkle developed into a grin as he added, "The peasants are generous to a fault. They often invite the brothers in for refreshment while they prepare their gift of flour or grain." Then paused and winked as he added, "Try to avoid the wine, we have to call at every farmstead between here and Ass . . . the monastery," he corrected himself hastily.

"That's right," Don Pezza cut in, "do as he says, not as he does." Then, turning to Abbondio, "If you are going to progress in our service to God, you must curb your thirst."

"I can't speak Italian," Gwyn said dubiously. "Won't they guess . . ."

"You won't have to speak, other than to say *ego te benedicat*, it's a phrase you must learn. They will believe that although you have taken the vow of silence, you are allowed to utter that blessing."

From the window of her room, Guiseppina watched the two friars load the bags of grain and their bed-rolls on to the back of one of the donkeys. Speaking to Vincensina who stood beside her, she said,

"I don't like it Mama."

"What's worrying you?"

"We know now that Pietro wasn't a spy. I always knew he wasn't, despite what Tina said to Filomena."

"And?" Vincensina gave Giuseppina a quizzical look.

"I know there have been problems and the Tedeschi knew about the party that Pietro was in," Giuseppina paused and blinked to clear the moisture forming in her eyes before continuing, "How can we be sure they don't know about Gwyn?"

"We can never be sure, it's the risk we take," Vincensina replied.

"What worries me is that he came to us from Ida di Lorenzo. She used to look after the Sicilian. Papa says he is a German spy who has now gone back to Germany."

"Giorgio knows more about that than we do," Vincensina said, with a re-assuring smile. He wouldn't have brought Gwyn here if he wasn't sure that Ida can be trusted."

Vincensina had barely finished speaking, when Gwyn, accompanied by Michele and Giorgio emerged from the wooded area behind the house. As they came into sight round the end of the house, Vincensina said,

"What a difference a week makes, Gwyn is walking quite well now."

Together, they watched Gwyn, helped by Abbondio climb on to one of the donkeys.

"We should go down and bid him a safe journey," Vincensina said as, followed by Giuseppina, she hurried down the steps.

Now that the time to leave had come, Gwyn found himself beset with a strange reluctance to go. Although his stay had been short, it was like parting from his own family. Thinking, as he wondered whether he would ever return to thank them, 'It would have been nice, to spend just one more evening round the fire,' he swallowed the lump forming in his throat and thanked them for their help.

They were already out of sight down the avenue of poplars when Ernesto joined the group by the door. He was smiling broadly as he said,

"I liked the smaller of those two donkeys, that little brown one was such a friendly soul. He really took to me."

"Are you sure it was you and not the tit-bits you offered," Michele said with a knowing smirk.

Ignoring the comment, Ernesto returned to the stable. Talking softly to his beloved oxen, he led them out and prepared them for the days work ahead.

That day, developed into the hottest day of the year. By ten o'clock a brazen sun sent its scorching rays over the valley. As Giorgio, seemingly indifferent to the heat, strode rapidly towards the track that would take him to Angelo's house, his mind was racing with conflicting thoughts. 'Who was in that assembly, fluent enough in Italian to be the spy?' he asked himself. 'Only the S.A.S. man, Geof, it would be easy enough for him to return, but he wasn't in the party when Francesco was nearly taken prisoner. Was it Francesco?' Dismissing the thought as ridiculous, Giorgio went over everything Filomena had said about the conversation between John and Peter. He wished Angelo had overheard it as well. Try as he might, he couldn't get the idea out of his mind that there was a connection between that conversation and the snatches of talk that Ida had overheard, but couldn't reconcile them. He resolved to have another talk with Filomena.

Spurred by a sense of urgency, Giorgio quickened his pace. Climbing the track as quickly as he could he arrived at Angelo's house, knocked on the door and gave it a push. When it failed to yield, he realised that both Filomena and Angelo were away from home. Hoping to see Angelo at work on his section of ground, Giorgio ascended to a point where he could survey the valley. The only sign of life was a figure, too far away to recognise with certainty, just leaving the base of the escarpment.

Disappointed, he decided to call on Ida and ask her to repeat precisely what she had overheard Loriano say about joining the Buf. Grateful for shelter from the sun and relishing the relative coolness of the forest; the feeling of urgency no longer with him, Giorgio followed, at a slower pace, a path Roberto had shown him, that would take him to the rear of Ida's house.

The way the door swung open at a touch was reassuring, it was an indication that Ida had overcome her initial fears that Loriano would return unexpectedly seeking Konrad. Nevertheless, not knowing what to expect, Ida was startled and turned swiftly when she felt a gentle flow of air and heard Giorgio's footsteps behind her.

"Sorry, did I make you jump?" Giorgio said.

Ida's apprehensive expression was replaced by a radiant smile as she recognised the intruder and turned back to attend to the task that was occupying her before Giorgio entered.

"I am just preparing pranzo. Are you hungry? . . . Of course you are. You must join me." she said; as she turned to face him, the look on her face brooked no refusal.

Nodding his thanks, Giorgio accepted the chair Ida pulled from beneath the table. Despite being well used to the seemingly insatiable desire Italian women invariably had to feed their guests, he had not expected to be fed.

With a deftness born of habit, Ida spread a film of polenta on the bare wooden table. Using a wooden spatula she covered it with a dressing of pesto, added a sprinkling of crushed pork crackling and divided it into four equal parts. Inviting Giorgio to eat, she went to the door and called,

"Roberto, come in."

"Why?" came the answer.

"Eat your polenta." Ida was inwardly laughing as she looked at Giorgio and said "He'll come for that."

Roberto's re-action was instantaneous, he appeared at the doorway.

"Where is your girl friend?" Ida asked.

"I don't have a girl friend," Roberto replied indignantly.

Grinning now, Ida, without raising her voice, said,

"You can come in and have some if you like Rosa."

A little girl, possibly a year, not more than two, younger than Roberto, appeared. Smiling happily, she made for the table.

Pointing to one of the portions, Ida said,

"That is yours Rosa, eat it and don't let Roberto raid any of it."

The reason for the warning became obvious, by the time Ida seated herself, Roberto, at incredible speed, had almost finished eating his portion.

The table scrubbed and the children gone, Ida produced glasses and the inevitable bottle of wine. Knowing that she could ill afford such hospitality, Giorgio was reluctant to accept and made a mental resolve to find an excuse to bring a gift of some of Michele's excellent product. Thanking her as he made the customary toast, he said.

"Have you seen any more of Loriano?"

"No," Ida replied, "he did say he would be coming back because he must talk to Konrad, but I haven't seen him since."

"Let me know if he does. . . . Next time you see him, look for any distinguishing marks that might help me to recognise him."

"Scars or tattoo?" Ida asked

"That's right. Any little thing, pierced ears, balding patches, colour of his eyes. Little habits, like scratching his head. Does he swing his arms when he walks or hold his hands behind his back?"

"Nothing that I have particularly noticed. Unless . . . ." Ida stopped abruptly.

"What were you going to say? "

Ida didn't reply immediately, it was as if what she was about to say seemed silly. Giorgio waited patiently for her to speak, when she did, she said,

"It doesn't seem important now."

Giorgio smiled encouragingly and said,

"Let me be a judge of that. . . . Tell me what you remembered."

"He only came a few times, after dark, but although one of the times he came it was one of those hot humid nights, he wore a jacket. Thinking back I never saw him when he wasn't wearing it."

"That could be quite important. Even in town, jackets are not often worn on warm evenings. Habitually, is even rarer. Was it always the same jacket?"

Ida shook her head, frowned and speaking so quietly, that it was difficult to hear her, said,

"I think so, a sort of fawn colour. Oh! . . ." she frowned, but didn't continue. There followed a period of silence. Watching Ida's face, Giorgio got the impression she was thinking hard, so said nothing. Eventually, Ida shook her head again, and with an almost apologetic look, "No! Sorry, I can't think of anything; except, sometimes Konrad called him Carlo. He didn't seem to like it." Ida paused again before saying, in a dubious tone, "Although he speaks in the local dialect, I think he might be German . . . which reminds me when they were speaking English, Konrad mentioned someone called Nummer drei and something about her living in the village." Then, more positively,

"Yes, there is something else, he always had the collar of his jacket raised, as if it was cold."

"What makes you think Loriano might be German?"

Ida shrugged her shoulders, and looked a little shamefaced as she replied,

"I don't know, it might be imagination, something in his accent I suppose."

"Don't let it worry you," Giorgio said, then looked at his watch and added "I must be getting away. If you remember anything, no matter how trivial let me know." He paused and his voice took on a serious note as he continued, "Place a leaf from that ash tree by the church in a crevice below the Madonna."

Ida looked surprised,

Reading the question in Ida's eyes, Giorgio said,

"Be careful you are not seen, even the forest has eyes."

"Konrad used to speak to Nonna Ricci sometimes."

"I know," Giorgio said. "He never gave himself away, she only knew him as the Sicilian. I suspect the only thing he would have ever heard from her would have been some tale that everybody already knew."

With a note of apprehension in her voice, Ida asked,

"Do you think it could be her? Did she know Konrad was living in my house?"

Giorgio shook his head and made a move towards the back door, "Nonna Ricci once told me she suspected Marco might be a spy and tried to find out where he stayed, but she never got more than here and there."

Ida looked relieved and said,

"Sounds like him. . . . Wait I'll check there is no one about."

With a quick wave, and brief "I'll be in touch." Giorgio left the house, his long legs carrying him rapidly out of sight as he disappeared in the wooded slopes above.

Wondering whether to retrace his footsteps to Angelo's house or leave his visit till the following day, Giorgio debated, in his mind, the best course to take. He looked at his watch, it indicated the time was approaching four. He could hardly believe he had spent so much time with Ida and inwardly cursed himself for having wasted the afternoon, then, paradoxically, decided it wasn't really wasted, he now knew that Loriano was probably the family name; his Christian name being Carlo. He also knew that Ida would be visited again. The only problem being, when? His mind made up, Giorgio decided to see whether Angelo or Filomena had returned.

As Giorgio turned away from the still locked door of Angelo's house, he heard the rustle of light footsteps coming from the direction of the woodland path. Cheered by the prospect of one of the two returning, he waited.

Almost immediately, Filomena, who had seen him through the encircling trees, came in sight carrying a basket; her face telegraphing her pleasure, she greeted him with a wave of her hand. Giorgio waved back.

"Have you been waiting long?" Filomena asked as she turned a colossal key in the door.

"Only just arrived." Giorgio replied, without mentioning that he had been there earlier.

"Babbo shouldn't be long. He went to Paese this morning and said he would be back home about five. As he is not working today, we don't have to wait till sundown. Come in and make yourself comfortable," Filomena said as she took hold of a hand and guided him to a chair.

"I am glad I have found you in, it is important that I talk to both of you regarding what was said that evening at the assembly point," Giorgio said, gratefully accepting the proffered chair.

Without saying a word, Filomena held up a bottle of wine and smiled.

Feeling he had had enough wine already that day, Giorgio shook his head, half rose from his chair and said,

"Perhaps later, I would prefer water now."

"Don't get up, I'll get you some, it's been hot today, I expect you are thirsty."

While still speaking, Filomena dipped a ladle into the Conca and hurried over to give it to Giorgio. Then, with a happy smile lighting up her face, watched him drink.

"Are you still thirsty? Would you like some more? Will you stay for Cena?" The three questions came in quick succession.

Before Giorgio had time to answer, she was dipping the ladle into the Conca. It made him laugh,

"No! No!" he said with a wave of the hand, "I've had enough."

Filomena dropped the ladle and picked up the basket she had been carrying. From its depths, she produced some ample cuttings of sirloin and a bundle of small cane sticks.

"Do you like Rosticcini?"

"Who doesn't?"

Watching Filomena chop the meat into small pieces, Giorgio felt an urge to help.

"Give me a knife," he said, "it will give me something to do."

Filomena answered by pushing a bundle of canes towards him and saying, "You can thread them on the sticks if you like. Two lean, one fat, like this," she demonstrated how to do it.

Having finished chopping the meat, Filomena plunged into the basket once again and produced a bundle of vegetation which she had collected from the country side. Fascinated by her apparent lack of concern in respect of how much water was used, Giorgio watched her change it so often he found himself wondering whether the supply would run out. When satisfied at last the verdure was clean enough to prepare she set about trimming away the unwanted parts, Giorgio who had finished assembling his sticks of meat said,

"I will give you a hand with that if you like," then without waiting for a response took a knife from a drawer in the table and proceeded to help.

Working together, time passed so swiftly, that they scarcely realised it was nearly six when the door opened and Angelo walked in. First he looked at Giorgio, then Filomena, then back again at Giorgio, smiled broadly and without saying why he was so much later than expected, said,

"She has you working then, I had better prepare the charcoal before she finds something for me to do."

The sight of Filomena sprinkling olive oil and salt over the huge pile of greenery reminded Giorgio of the salad meals his mother used to serve in the garden when he was a boy. Days that would never be forgotten. He saw again the swing his father had built and the little vegetable patch that was his pride and joy. The words *home grown tastes so much better* came into his mind and he wondered nostalgically, what Pop as he called him would have said about country weeds.

251

The evening was spent under a serene sky, enjoying the cool air and indulging in small talk. Forgotten for the time being all thoughts of the war and the reason for his visit. The bright light of day had given way to the silver rays of a full moon when Giorgio, with a note of reluctance, said,

"Can you take your minds back to the evening when Philip's party was being assembled?"

Almost simultaneously, Angelo and Filomena answered,

"Yes." Then, Angelo added "Is there a problem?"

"Not really," Giorgio replied. "I want you to remember precisely what was said about Blackshirts."

"I didn't hear it" Angelo said.

Giorgio looked at Filomena and said,

"You heard something about Blackshirts and thought they might be talking about the Decima. What made you think that?"

"Mention had been made earlier about those poor souls that were massacred in that village near Gubbio . . . San Remo. It was still fresh in our minds and I had heard that the Decima was involved."

"Can you remember precisely what was said?"

"*Prevalenza delle Camicie nere.*" Filomena replied.

"No say it as you heard it, in English."

"Mostly Blackshirts."

Giorgio's heart gave a great leap. "Is there a connection?" he murmured "Mostly could easily be confused with Mosley" and he remembered Ida saying she heard Loriano say he joined the BUF In 1936. He also remembered thinking that Loriano could either be English or an Italian living in pre-war England. The idea that Peter and Loriano were one and the same seemed absurd. According to Ida's description, Loriano was lean of hip and broad of shoulder; whereas Peter, while lean of hips, could hardly be described as broad of shoulder.

Filomena, who had seen his lips move but only half heard the words 'connection' and 'Loriano', guessed he was speaking his thoughts aloud so didn't ask him what he had said. She looked at Angelo, who had also heard the murmur and waited for Giorgio to voice his thoughts.

There followed several minutes of silence, broken only by the sound of Angelo stirring the dying embers of charcoal and the small sounds of the night. The shadow of an owl, as it dived silently on its prey, sped across the open area was followed by the cry of its victim. From somewhere in the distance a fox barked. When Giorgio eventually spoke, it was slowly, as if he was thinking carefully of every word before saying it.

"If Loriano is Peter, and Peter is Gordon," he began, "the Scolopendre will want to put him before the Tribune. Even though Gordon was taken prisoner with the rest of the party, he could be the one that betrayed them. Because the Tedeschi surrounded their H.Q. so soon after Gordon left and seemed to know the precise position of all their look-outs, Migale has always said he suspected it was him."

Filomena looked surprised and said,

"I thought that everybody in that little group of ribelli was massacred when the Tedeschi swooped on their stronghold."

Most of them were," Angelo began, "a few escaped. Since then, Migale, with the help of Grillo has managed to recruit a few more, I believe you will find they have now merged with one of the larger formations. I don't know whether they still call themselves Scolopendre, but both Migale and Grillo will want to see justice done through the media of resistance groups."

"As will the other three survivors." Giorgio commented.

"I'll have a word with Alberto, that young boy has a remarkable knowledge of everything that goes on in the groups of ribelli." Angelo laughed as he said it, "All the rebels; or should I say partisans, trust him. If anyone can find out where Migale is, he can."

CHAPTER TWENTYONE

It should have been one of Lucia's happiest days of her life; it was the day Don Umberto confirmed that the wedding fixed for only a few weeks hence would go ahead on the day planned. It would have been if Alberto hadn't brought the news that it was very unlikely Gianni would be free for the day of the wedding. The increasing activity of the Allied forces, now under fifty kilometres from La Villa, had brought a steady build up of German troops into the area, which kept the various groups of partisans busy making things difficult for them in the passes. Scarcely a day now went by without news of a skirmish in which all too often a loved one had been killed and she feared for the safety of her young brother.

Reprisals, particularly against those found to have given succour to released prisoners of war, were rapidly becoming commonplace. Too many now had friends or relatives who's home had been blown up, the occupants dragged out so that others may see the shooting of the women after they had watched their men folk hung. The bodies were invariably displayed in the street or village square, or suspended from a tree as an example to those who would defy the Fascists and their Nazi masters. There also seemed to be, a more active presence of the hated Decima Flottiglia; a Fascist force under German command, which seemed to delight in carrying the law which said, *anybody seen to be carrying guns or suspected of being a partisan may be shot on sight*, to the letter. They were said by many, to be even more ruthless than the German Storm troopers and often shot, on sight, without checking first.

Alberto who had been in the hills, on one of his many visits, carrying messages and items of food to loved ones from their relatives at home, had been asked by Lucia to seek out Gianni and tell him the proposed date of the wedding. Having, already been asked by Angelo to find out what he could about Migale and Grillo, it was a good opportunity to do so. Alberto knew the changing conditions were making visits to the ribelli more and more dangerous with each passing day, but it didn't deter him. He also knew the long climb up steep gradients without the company of his little friend Francesca would be lonely; with a wisdom beyond his years he refused to allow her to accompany him on the mission.

Alberto's foresight proved to be well founded, even though Gianni was with him most of that day, he had met suspicion from many of the partisans; particularly those who had come into the area to support the groups already making life as difficult for the hated Tedeschi as they could. It was as if, with the increased numbers of Germans in the valleys, they had become more wary.

They eventually located Migale in a small group high above La Villa. When, surprised that Migale was not still in the same area as his previous group, Gianni said, "We expected to find you over Assergi," he was told the groups there are mainly Matteoti.

"Although still independent, I have bonded with one of the larger monarchist groups because I prefer to work with them or Giustizia e Liberta" Migale explained.

With the locating of Migale the day's effort had been even more successful than Alberto had hoped and he was looking forward to passing on arrangements made, to Angelo. Nevertheless, notwithstanding his eagerness to be on his way, he had no hesitation in accepting Donnina's offer of a meal.

The sight of the young boy sitting at the table enjoying a plate of pasta brought a jocular comment from Mario as he entered the house with a wolf for a knocker.

"But you are always eating."

Then noticing the woe-begone look on Lucia's face, Mario kissed her on the cheek, then took her hand in his and kissed that as well.

"Is everything O.K? . . . Umberto confirmed our day, I hope" he said.

"Oh yes." Lucia's expression changed to one of joy as she spoke.

Still holding her hand, Mario drew her close and took her in her arms as he said,

"That's better. . . . Why the glum look?"

"Gianni might not be able to come."

"How disappointing! . . . never mind, it's only a might not." Mario tried to look convincing as he said it. Then, seeking to change the mood, added "Oh this horrible war. Let's go for a walk, it's a lovely evening."

Lucia glanced towards her mother, who smiled and nodded.

"It will cheer you up."

Alberto was tempted to tell Lucia that Gianni might be accompanying Migale or Grillo when one or the other came out of the hills to meet

Angelo, but decided that if Gianni couldn't get permission the disappointment would depress her even more.

The light breeze which came with the sinking of the sun added a welcome freshness to the end of a hot day and did much to lift Lucia's spirits. By the time they reached the square, she was chatting happily and completely her usual self. Inevitably, her talk centred on the coming happy occasion. Mario, content to just listen to her excited chatter, apart from the occasional yes or no, remained silent.

Mario and Lucia had barely left the house when Alberto, who, despite being tired was determined to take his news to Angelo that evening, announced that he would have to leave. As he also wanted to let Carina know that Gianni was safe and well, the thought of leaving his news until the following day, didn't even enter his head. Having finished his meal, he looked at an ancient twin belled tin alarm clock, which hung, suspended on a length of string from a hook on the wall and thinking. 'By the time I've seen Carina, Angelo will be home,' said, without saying why,

"Thank you, I can't stop now."

Donnina laughed boisterously, the speed in which Alberto had cleared his plate, followed by a seemingly no longer interested in being there attitude amused her. She contented herself by saying,

"On your way then, would you like some fruit?"

Alberto didn't say no, with the fruit in one hand, a wave from the other and scarcely a glance back, he went on his way.

The look on Alberto's face as he hurried out of the wooded area surrounding the house, told Angelo, standing at the door, that the mission had been successful. As did the words, blurted out in a breathless gasp,

"I found Migale."

Feeling very manly, now that he was eleven, sipping and enjoying the watered down glass of wine Filomena had poured to accompany the plate of food that lay before him, Alberto was careful not to mention the meal he had devoured less than an hour before. Twirling an overloaded fork of spaghetti, he said,

"I was surprised how big Migale is. Nothing like the little spider his name suggests." Then, giggled and added, "But just as hairy."

"Has he a beard then?" Angelo asked.

"Yes," Alberto giggled again and choked on the food in his mouth as he spluttered, "and he has long hair ... it's all over his arms as well."

"Did you meet his second in command, Grillo?"

"No, he was away on one of the forays, but Migale is going to speak to him as soon as he returns."

"What did Migale say about Gordon?"

"He didn't seem to know who I was talking about at first," Alberto replied, "It wasn't until I said we thought that someone named Gordon who claimed he had been a partisan with the Scolopendre, might be the traitor, that he became interested."

"Did you tell him, it was only a suspicion, because as far as we know, Gordon was captured with the rest?"

"Yes. But he was a bit doubtful. . . . He said the partisan who left the group was known as Lori. He also said he had never heard him called Gordon and as it was unusual for Englishmen to adopt a nom de guerre, because they didn't have families at risk in Italy, they never suspected him of being other than Italian." Alberto paused and giggled, "I asked Migale whether Lori had a long tail and big eyes." then giggled again as he saw the laughter in Angelo's eyes when he said,"

"What did Migale say to that?

"I think he was laughing at me. He said that kind of primate might have big eyes, but it doesn't have a tail and asked me what made us think Gordon might be the traitor."

"What did you tell him?" Angelo asked.

"I said I didn't know for sure, that it was something about someone looking like Gordon; that you would explain everything when you meet."

Filomena, who was bustling round finding something to do here and something to do there, overheard the last comment and said,

"Be careful Papa. Can we be sure it was Migale Alberto found?"

"Both Gianni and Donnola know Migale and Grillo. Gianni was with me when we found Migale." Alberto cut in.

"How was Gianni?" Filomena asked

"He seemed alright, if everything goes to plan, you will see him soon. Migale wants to meet Angelo on Sunday and has asked Gianni to accompany him." Then, he turned to Angelo and said, "Gianni suggested that a good place to meet would be Renzo's bar, if that was alright with you. I said that if you preferred to meet somewhere else, I would be outside the locale at mid-day to let them know where."

"No, that is reasonable, the villagers are used to seeing the odd stranger come into Renzo's bar and when they see Gianni, they will guess Migale to be a rebel. We need to talk and if the locale is crowded, we can use Nicoletta."

"They don't like to be called that," Alberto cut in.

Angelo's smile looked far from contrite as he said,

"Partisan. . . . Point taken," then in a serious tone, added, "be careful where you use that word."

"What about Giorgio?" Filomena said, "Won't he want to be in on it?"

"I can fill him in later, as he wasn't at the assembly, he didn't hear John greet Peter as Charlie . . . I wish we knew more about what happened to Peter when the Tedeschi surrounded the party. Everything we know is second hand; even Guido can't help us. All the others are now safely in Allied occupied territory; Luigi and Guido only know what Philip told them."

"Tina is the only one that has seen both Peter and Gordon; it was her, that first made me suspect that they could be the same person," Filomena reminded Angelo. "You remember Babbo, it was why I wanted to ask Luigi to look out for Guido and his charges," Filomena pointed out, oblivious for the moment that young ears were listening to everything that was said. Realising her omission, she turned her attention to Alberto and reminded him that anything he heard must not be repeated outside. Not even to friends.

"I know that," Alberto said feeling slightly affronted that Filomena might not have trusted him. Then he grinned and added, "I already knew that anyway. Who is Nicoletta?"

Both Angelo and Filomena laughed; it hadn't occurred to them that Alberto might not know the name of a room behind the bar used for private functions such as family gatherings, when the home was too small to accommodate more than a dozen guests.

. . . .

Sunday proved to be another hot day, with a sun that bore relentlessly down on La Villa. Leaving Alberto, who had insisted in accompanying him, outside Renzo's Bar, to watch out for the arrival of Migale and Gianni, Angelo entered and bought a bottle of sweetened water for the lad.

"What do they make this with, melted gold?" he asked, when told the price.

"It's the war, you know how it is. *Lavorare lavorare, Fascisti mangiare.*" Renzo said, quoting the slogan, Work work Fascists eat, so often repeated.

Alberto accepted the gift with great glee, it was a rare luxury.

Because it was a difficult item to acquire, Angelo had visions of Alberto taking the empty bottle home for his mother, so he said, with a grin,

"Don't forget Renzo will want the empty bottle back."

Alberto, already sampling the contents, nodded and mumbled a barely audible Grazie.

It was exactly mid-day, although the hands indicated approximately the correct time, the village clock struck two, when Gianni and Migale came into view. Alberto waved to them as they came abreast and said,

"Angelo is inside waiting."

Gianni greeted Alberto with,

"Hallo Alberto, you got back safely then, how is your little friend Francesca?"

"Not so bad." The classical response was followed by,"She isn't little, she is eleven now, like me."

Both Gianni and Migale tried not to laugh at the proud way Alberto said it, but the laughter was there on their faces.

"Angelo says he will be with Nicoletta."

Migale looked sharply at Gianni and said,

"I thought we were only meeting Angelo, can Nicoletta be trusted?"

Trying to look serious, Gianni replied,

"I would imagine so, Nicoletta is a private room."

Even if Gianni hadn't been with him. Angelo would have had no difficulty in picking out Migale when they entered the room. Alberto hadn't exaggerated when he said Migale was a big hairy man. Although, not over tall, he had a barrel chest, thick neck and wide hips. The dark hair, almost black, together with the very hirsute arms gave an appearance of great strength. His voice, in contrast had an almost gentle sound about it when he greeted Angelo with a formal shake of the hand and said,

"So you are Angelo, it's a pleasure to meet you."

Taking the hand, Angelo was quick to note that, notwithstanding the man's obvious strength, the clasp was firm; not the crushing display some strong men seem to delight in. He returned the greeting with.

"And I you."

"Grillo was unable to come," Migale said, reading the question in Angelo's eyes "I am told you might know the whereabouts of Lori. You will understand, we prefer to deal with these matters ourselves."

"I realise that, it's the reason we sent for you," Angelo replied, then added, "nobody can be sure of these things and the man we believe to be him arrives at a house we know about, without pre-advice. So, difficult as it might be, we will need to have someone easily accessible who can not only confirm his identity, but also take charge if necessary."

"How do you suggest we do that? We can't afford to have someone away from the formation, on standby, for indefinite periods." There was just a trace of steel in Migale's voice as he spoke.

"The reason he goes to the house is to meet Konrad, a German spy who has been disposed of." Angelo's eyes twinkled as he said disposed of. "We have asked the person who lives there . . ." Seeing the question in Migale's eyes and interpreting it, Angelo paused momentarily to say, "yes she can be trusted," before continuing with, "to give our suspect a definite date that he will find Konrad at her house. She will then advise us and we can let you know when to go visiting."

"That arrangement sounds workable but I gather the person you refer to is a woman. If spies meet at her house, how can you be sure she can be trusted?" It was obvious from the way the question was asked, that Migale was not happy.

"Believe me, I know what I am doing," Angelo replied. "Konrad was a German relative by ancestral marriage to the lady in question. He tricked her into looking after him by saying he was in trouble with the Nazi regime and needed somewhere safe. He no longer exists."

"You mean, he is dead?"

Angelo nodded and said,

"Her friends disposed of the body."

"We don't know whether the traitor was Lori, so it is essential he has a fair trial," Migale said, the faint trace of steel that had crept back in to his voice, didn't pass unnoticed by Angelo. "Because he spoke Italian so well, we believed him when he told us he had left the army, because he didn't want to fight his anti Fascist brothers. It was only when he heard of the opportunity to cross the line with an evasion group that he confessed to being a released prisoner of war. Even then, he didn't tell us his name was Gordon."

"Although Gordon told Francesco, he had been serving with partisans, as far as I know he never said which group." Angelo paused a moment to replenish the glasses on the table, looked at the bottle, still half full and continued with, "Not even when we heard of the attack on your formation following so soon after the capture of Francesco's party did we think the two events might be related."

"What makes you think the man you have in mind might be Lori?"

Angelo shrugged his shoulders and didn't reply immediately, when he did, he said,

"A series of happenings and snatches of conversation overheard seem to link four individuals together. The man we have in mind, Carlo Loriano is one of them. We know him to be a member of Ovra and although as far as we know, one of the four, named Peter has been shot and another calling himself Gordon was taken prisoner. We suspect that Carlo Loriano is not only the partisan you knew as Lori, but also the two ex prisoners of war that we knew as Gordon and Peter..."

"That Peter, Gordon and Lori are names used as aliases for Loriano?" Migale cut in.

"Precisely. The only people we know that would recognise Gordon are Tina and Francesco. When Tina told us about a chance remark, made to her by Gordon, about the Scolopendre, we began to wonder if it was your group he had served with."

"Capitano Vincenzo's daughter?" Migale asked.

"Yes, do you know her?"

"We were on the Maiella for a time and shared a couple of operations with Luigi. I met her briefly when we were assembling for one of those. Lori was still with us then, but I don't think she met him." Migale frowned, it made his abundant eyebrows seem even more of a bush than they were before, before continuing with, "So we still don't really know if Gordon was an alias for Lori."

"That's right," Angelo said as he replenished Migale's glass again, looked at Gianni's and emptied the remains of the bottle into it. Then, placed a note on the table, winked and left it to Gianni to interpret what to do before continuing with, "the only way we can be sure is for you or Grillo to be present when we arrest him."

Laughing, Gianni picked up the bottle and the note, strode over to the mini counter and tapped on the small door above it.

"If Carlo Loriano is Lori and your theory is right, we will put him before the Tribunal; it's Partisan Law. If not, it will be your decision what to do."

The talk between Migale and Angelo went on for much longer than Gianni had expected. Feeling more and more exasperated he listened to and joined in occasionally, the small talk which followed; impatient to get away and visit his girl, it seemed never ending.

When, eventually Gianni was able to leave, his visit to his mother was much briefer than either Donnina or Lucia would have liked. Alberto had told them that Gianni was in Renzo's Bar with Angelo and another and they had waited, for what seemed a far longer period of time than it really was, for him to arrive.

After the initial embrace, Donnina stood back to look critically at the son she now saw at such infrequent intervals.

"You are not eating enough," she accused him.

Gianni just laughed and said,

"Oh Mama! We do very well up there."

"Then why are you so thin?" Donnina retorted.

From the corner of his eye, Gianni could see that Lucia was trying to hide a grin. Partly because she was so happy to see him safe and well and partly because Donnina's comment had amused her, the grin was as broad as a barn door.

Gianni glanced at the tin time piece on the wall; it indicated six-forty, looked at the watch on his wrist, (a relic from his first posting near Milan, when there was still plenty to purchase in the shops) then, without warning, hugged his mother, kissed her on both cheeks, turned to his sister and did likewise to her before opening the door with a wolf for a knocker.

"I've been given permission to stay overnight, but have to return first thing tomorrow morning. See you later." he call out over his shoulder and scurried away.

The house where Concetta lived with her daughter was only a few steps, nevertheless, Gianni was close to running as he passed the houses that lay between. When he arrived, they were dressed in best clothes and on the point of leaving. Carina had a piece of paper in her hand on which was written '*we are at church.*'

Uncaring whether it crushed her frock, Carina left Concetta's side and rushed towards Gianni, holding him close, she showered him with kisses,

"Oh there you are Gianni, Alberto told us you are here. I was just saying to Mama, we must leave a note so that you will know where to find us."

Gianni looked at Concetta, smiled but didn't leave Carina's side to embrace her mother, then, although he knew the answer would probably be no said to Carina,

"Shall we go for a walk?"

"We can't go now," Carina answered ruefully, "I promised Mama that I would go to Mass with her this evening."

Gianni looked hopefully at Concetta, whose face lit up with a radiant smile as she suggested,

"Why not come with us."

Gianni looked at his rough and not very clean clothing; he had been so impatient to see Carina it hadn't occurred to him to change from the every day gear he wore as a partisan to something more suitable. Rather hopefully, he said,

"I can't go to Mass dressed like this."

"Don Umberto will understand." Carina said, giving him a squeeze and finding it an excuse to kiss him yet again, she did so.

"But I haven't been to confession for a long time," Gianni answered rather lamely.

"All the more reason for you to come with us," Concetta said, taking his arm and dragging him away from Carina. "I am sure Umberto will take your confession after the Mass. Hurry now, we are already late."

Holding Carina's hand, Gianni reluctantly followed the determined Concetta as she strode towards the village exit and the path that would take them up the grass covered slope to the church.

"And, after the Mass?" Gianni whispered, slipping an arm round Carina's waist.

"We shall see," Carina said, with an almost secretive smile.

Entering the church through the already open door, the sound of voices singing a hymn, was a clear indication that the service had already started. Concetta closed her eyes and covered her face with her hands. It was almost as if she was thinking if I can't see Don Umberto, he can't see me; that he wouldn't notice her late arrival. If so, she was mistaken. Don Umberto's voice boomed across the heads of the congregation.

"Come in Concetta, we have only just started. . . . I will see you later Gianni."

The gentle cooling breeze which ushered in the evening was a welcome relief to the oppressive heat of the day; even in the church it had made itself felt. With the service over and Gianni, having been persuaded to enter the dark cubicle, back with her, Carina was at last able to enjoy the unshared company of her loved one. Words seemed superfluous as they walked silently hand in hand up a gentle rising slope above the belt of trees that hid La Villa from view; just being together was all that was needed to make life complete. Frowning above them loomed the great jagged crests of the summit.

Suddenly, when high up the mountain side, Gianni stopped walking and gave Carina a hug, then left her side and said,

"Wait here a moment my dearest one. I won't be long."

Carina watched him hurry over the loose shale of fallen rocks surrounding the bottom of the jagged crests. Heart in mouth, barely able to breathe, she saw him scale part way up the smooth rock face and balanced on a precarious foot-hold high above the base, with no apparent hand-hold available, lean to one side.

"Be careful Gianni," she called out in trepidation as he stretched an arm out. Then, held her breath until he reached the safety of the rock strewn ground below. Only then did she give a sigh of relief.

When Gianni returned, he was holding one arm behind his back. Full of concern, as she wondered if he had hurt himself, Carina crossed the shale surface to meet him.

"Have you hurt yourself Gianni?" she asked on arriving at his side.

Noting the look on Carina's face, Gianni laughed; he had a mischievous twinkle in his eyes as he produced from behind his back a small white flower and sang the first line of a popular love song, *Non te scordare di me, quella bianca stel'alpina*, a ballad of two lovers who while alone together, heart to heart, picked the little mountain flower.

"Of course I'm not hurt." he replied as he handed her the gift he had risked his neck to collect.

Laughing now, eyes still moist from a mixture of emotion and anxiety, Carina took the little flower, fastened it in her hair and said,

"Oh Gianni! You darling man, in that song, they sing, *cogliemmo la matina*, (we gathered in the morning.) and it's evening now."

Gianni looked at her and thought 'she is prettier than that flower.' Unable to resist the temptation, he kissed her nose and said,

"Does it matter?"

Carina returned the gesture with a hug and murmured.

"Thank you Gianni, thank you."

Reluctantly, Gianni and Carina broke away from the hug that had been sustained for several minutes and without saying anything began the descent that would take them home. Both knew, that although still light, the sun had long since disappeared behind the towering mountain and it would be dark within the next half hour.

Not much was said on the way down, as each tried to avoid the subject on both their minds; a subject they didn't want to discuss. But it couldn't be avoided. Eventually, as they approached La Villa, Gianni said,

"I don't know Darling, when I will see you again. Hopefully at Lucia's wedding. I have to return first thing tomorrow."

Carina just looked at him and gave the hand that was holding hers a squeeze. Her heart was in her throat, which prevented words coming out.

Gianni was determined not to tell her the real reason he had to return so soon, was that the Allies had asked the Partito d'Azione to organise an operation that would severely hinder the Germans in one of the passes. Briefing was set for the following day. According to Intelligence, the Germans were expected to bring considerable reinforcements for the forward area through the pass on either Tuesday, or Wednesday at the latest. Every available partisan was necessary if the intended ambush was to be successful. He lied by telling her it was his turn to be on watch.

Concetta's outline framed in the doorway of her home betrayed the anxiety that she had experienced while waiting for the return of her daughter. Even though she knew Gianni was with her, she was worried about the possibility of wolves or bears; which were still occasionally seen on the higher mountain slopes after dark. They weren't usually a threat, nevertheless it didn't stop her worrying; she was worried, in fact, about everything she could think of. Recognising the signs, Carina left Gianni's side and hurried forward to comfort her mother.

It was close on mid-night when Gianni eventually arrived home, Donnina, Ernesto and Lucia were playing cards in the dim light of a flickering flame shed by the tiny oil lamp they used. Even Dora was still up, obviously trying to stay awake as she busied herself combing the hair of an almost bald doll.

"You've left it late Son," Ernesto said as Gianni entered.

Gianni nodded, he knew from the tone of Ernesto's voice that his father wasn't grumbling. That it was just a comment. He crossed the room, smiled at Lucia and embraced his mother. Then, feeling Dora clutching at his shirt, swung round, lifted his little sister high enough for her head to touch the ceiling and said,

"My you're a big girl, I won't be able to do this much longer."

Dora giggled with pleasure, pulled his hair, then, with her hands beneath his chin, leaned over until she could press her face against his.

"You are a bad lad Gianni," Lucia said, shaking a finger at him, "you said you have to leave early tomorrow. You are going to be tired out."

"I'm used to short hours in bed Lucemun. Don't fret, I only need a couple of hours sleep to be bright and perky." Gianni said with an impish grin as he used the house name, he knew Lucia hated.

"You can forget your birthday when it comes round," Lucia said with a laugh as she handed him the wine she had just poured.

Despite the early hour Carina was outside waiting, when Gianni, loaded with a supply of victuals Donnina had insisted he take with him, emerged from the house.

"These are for you to eat on the way back," she said as she handed him a small basket laden with, still steaming pasties.

Gianni looked at the over generous supply. Packing them into his haversack, he was tempted to say even an elephant couldn't clear that lot in a day, but resisted the temptation and thanked her instead.

"I can come part way with you, Mama's looking after my turkeys." Carina said as she took back the basket and put it on her head, leaving her hands free to hold his.

"Only as far as the shepherd's refuge. You could easily get lost finding your way back from beyond there." Gianni said, in a tone that brooked no argument.

Watched by the group at the door and Concetta, who stood on the threshold of her house with the turkeys gathered round her, Gianni and Carina made their way to the exit. Pausing only to wave, they disappeared from view.

Only Donnina remained when, twenty minutes later, they came into view over the roofs of the houses. Although she knew, the two indistinct figures high on the grassy slope above the trees could not see her, Donnina waved and with tears in her eyes turned back into her home.

The sun was already high in the heavens and the hands on Gianni's watch stood at a few minutes before six when they reached the little stone hut used by shepherds when required. They knew the time to part had come and both of them tried to look cheerful as they clung to each other, neither wanting to say goodbye.

Shedding the tears she hadn't wanted Gianni to see, Carina watched Gianni make his way along a barely discernible path until he reached a miniature pass, which he turned into and was lost from sight.

CHAPTER TWENTYTWO

Tuesday morning started with a heavy mist which enveloped the foothills and obscured from view the two narrow roads they wanted to watch. To the small group of partisans gathered on a premonitory which jutted out high over a chasm, the lack of visibility was both a curse and a blessing. The two passes which could be used, each with its own bridge which crossed the chasm at different points were invisible. It had been decided that neither bridge should be destroyed until the leading vehicles of the expected German convoy were on it; not only because more damage would be done, but also because they didn't want to alert the hated Tedeschi by the sound of explosions. Migale, patiently waiting for a report from Guerriero, peered through the mist and said,

"If this mist doesn't lift soon, we won't be able to see our targets."

"It works two ways, they won't be able to see us either." Il Tiranno said with a throaty chuckle.

Carlo Bartolino was intensely proud of the name, Guerriero, given to him by Luigi and he insisted on being known by it. He had been put in charge of the young scouts sent out the previous night to watch the roads below the foothills. This was his first real active assignment and he was feeling very proud that he had been trusted with the mission. As he looked out over the wide valley beyond the foothills, the inability to see clearly which of the two routes would be used and the lack of any sign of the expected convoy disappointed him.

Slowly, during the course of the morning, the mist lifted; by eleven even the tops of the mountains could be seen. Guerriero's eyes were beginning to get tired and the glare of the sun was making them ache; nevertheless he continued to gaze into the distance. Finally, at around two in the afternoon, he spotted a cloud of dust and guessed it would be the long awaited convoy.

Turning to a young lad beside him, he said,

"Run Alfonso, tell the sergeant major the Tedeschi are on the way and I will come as soon as I know which route they are going to use. After that, tell the other watchers they can stand down."

When Guerriero saw the column of dust split in two, he guessed rightly that the Tedeschi were taking no chances and intended to use both passes. His guess was confirmed, when one half of the convoy took the eastern route round the mountain and the other, the west. Only when he was satisfied that this was so, did he leave.

Il Tiranno received Guerriero's report with dismay. He had hoped to wait until half the vehicles had crossed the bridge before blowing it up; thus destroying whatever was on the bridge and at the same time splitting the force. Now, it would seem he would have to split his own forces. He pondered over the problem which now presented itself. Voicing his thoughts, he turned to Migale and said,

"That eastern route is much shorter than the western. The section using the eastern route will be across their bridge and well into the pass long before the others arrive. If we blow the bridge while the leading half is still on it, the Tedeschi on the western route will be alerted and all chance of an ambush lost."

Carlo listened carefully to the sergeant major and waited patiently for him to finish speaking. Then, seizing the opportunity he said,

"Excuse me Sir. I have sent two of my men to get details of the convoy on the west side and one to do the same on the east. Have I your permission to join him?"

Il Tiranno, smiled quietly to himself as he answered; the term, my men, in some idiotic way pleased him,

"Good thinking Guerriero. Let me know what you find out as soon as you can. Run along now."

As Carlo left, Il Tiranno said to nobody in particular,

"That young lad has the makings of a good soldier."

"Sounds a bit war-like, that name. . . . Gad! He's like a mountain goat. What a whizzo jump," a man wearing the uniform of a British officer commented as he watched Carlo speed down the slope and leap across the chasm at a point high above the road where an overhang that jutted out over the chasm reduced the width to a bare three and a half metres.

Il Tiranno nodded and replied,

"Guerriero? It is; it means warrior. Capitano Vincenzo gave it to him and he is very proud of it."

The ability to run the gauntlet of a comparatively short, but narrow loop road which had been cut in to the bare rock to join the road coming round from the west could not be ignored. Providing there were no large vehicles it would enable the two halves of the convoy to conjoin. Turning to the British lieutenant standing beside him, Tiranno said,

"Have you enough of that plastic to blow both bridges Sir?"

Lieutenant Cyril Flood, who had been sent by the Allies to assist the partisans and train them in the 'gentle art', as he called it, of demolition, had a working knowledge of Italian and was not embarrassed if the occasional English word had to be used, replied,

"Call me Sandy, they all do. I have already set charges under both bridges; that man you sent to help me, he's like a limpet." The admiration showed in Sandy's face as he spoke."

The word limpet spoken in English bewildered Migale, who said,

"Limpet . . . Limpet! What do you mean Limpet?" then, deciding it was not important, shrugged his shoulders.

"Who helped him?" Luigi asked as he joined the group, then, in answer to the question he had overheard as he approached, added almost as an afterthought. "Limpet . . . *Patella*."

Acknowledging the interpretation with a nod, Migale replied,

"Lepre?"

"He is just joining us," Luigi remarked, then added, "I don't think, Migale you've met the man with him; he is Donnola, the head of one of the small bands that are helping us." Then, turning to Il Tiranno, "What's new?"

"Who's taking my name in vain?" Gianni said jovially as the two came abreast.

"You have good ears Lepre, worthy of your name." Luigi commented as he waited for Il Tiranno to answer his question.

Il Tiranno didn't answer immediately. It was a feature of him, he liked to choose his words carefully, particularly when the subject was important. When he did, no detail was left untold.

Luigi listened carefully, ticking off in his mind everything that was being said and making mental notes of a possible plan of action. Only when Il Tiranno came to the end of his lengthy report, did he speak.

"What do you propose to do about the prospect of two columns instead of one?" he asked, casting his eyes around the group.

Sandy picked up the answer and replied:

"The time element is the major problem. If I blow the first bridge when the first party of Huns are half way over, the others, who are still on their way, will hear the bang and the surprise element will be lost; the Hun is not daft. The last thing we want is to have them form a defensive position in an open area where we can't attack them easily."

"There is not much danger of that up here," Il Tiranno broke in to Sandy's discourse. "the road is narrow, but it is pretty certain that any of the Tedeschi who haven't reached the bridge when it is blown, will make a dash round the loop road to join the other half of the convoy. With the exception of our sharp shooters, we are only armed with Stens, which are mainly close quarter weapons. Even with men posted among the rocks overlooking the chasm we can't hope to get more than a few."

"Precisely what I was going to say," said Sandy. "If we let the first half through in to the pass, how far do you think they could get . . ."

"Before the other contingent arrives?" Il Tiranno, forecasting what Sandy was about to ask, finished the question for him, then he added in answer, "Not too far, we have already made it difficult for big vehicles to get through the eastern pass by placing large boulders in strategic areas."

"Might I point out," Migale began, "the road on the west runs through foothills and mountains, which is partly the reason that those on the eastern route will be here first. It is Scolopendre territory, so I know it well. There are not many open areas they could use in the way Sandy suggests. It is possible that with a few men, I might be able to make the Tedeschi hurry along. The confusion created by being attacked will mask the sound of any activity here and hopefully force them to make a dash for the pass. Whichever way you look at it, it would be a gamble."

"Your suggestion has possibilities, Migale, but I don't like gambles" Luigi commented. "They are certain to have machine guns mounted on some of the trucks. I think it better if we keep our force concentrated on the two passes and the approach area as originally planned. If we let the early arrivals cross the bridge, we can deal with them in the pass. Both bridges can then be blown up when the other half of the convoy arrives."

The heat, forecast by the morning mist, though not as oppressive as it was in the valley, could be felt even in the high region where the group of partisan waited patiently for the leading vehicles of the convoy to appear. It was turned three o'clock; much later than they had expected, when a staff car appeared on the road below. They were not surprised that there was no sign of the expected convoy, because Carlo had sent one of his helpers to tell them that the column had come to a halt in an open area a short distance away from a bend in the road that hid it from view.

"It looks as though fortune favours us," Luigi remarked, "hopefully, they intend to re-form before going through the pass. The question is, which pass?"

The words were hardly out of his mouth when another staff car came in sight round the other bend and came to a halt at a passing point mid-way between the two bridges, where the other car was waiting. The watching partisans saw two German officers descend from each car, exchange salutes and stand in a small cluster. While talking they formed an easy target; the temptation to open fire was difficult to resist.

The German officers must have talked for twenty minutes to half an hour before they returned to their cars and moved off. There was no way they could turn round, so both cars drove forward and turned on to the respective bridge ahead. It seemed they intended to reconnoitre the passes beyond. However, to the relief of the watchers, both cars halted. Then one reversed off the bridge and returned in the direction from whence it had come. The other waited till it had gone, then did likewise.

"Why didn't they just swap cars?" Sandy remarked.

The others just smiled, but said nothing.

Minutes after the two staff cars had left, Carlo came running up the steep slope towards them. His eyes alight with excitement, he gave his report.

"Both halves of the convoy are similar," he began, then glanced at notes he had made before continuing. "The half I saw had one staff car, three low loaders, each carrying a tank, two armoured cars and six of those large vehicles they use for carrying troops. I sent Florio to look at the others and from what he tells me, the two halves are identical. While I was watching, the staff car left."

"*Cazzo!*" Il Tiranno swore audibly and gazed at the sky as if seeking inspiration. "We have seen the staff cars. There is no way low loaders carrying tanks can pass along that loop road. They have to be intending to use both passes. How was the convoy disposed?"

Carlo looked bewildered for a moment, as if he wasn't sure what Il Tiranno meant. He looked at Luigi, who nodded in encouragement and said,

"What was their formation? . . . What were they doing and where were they?"

"They were resting and seemed to be preparing a meal," Carlo replied, happy now and more sure of himself as he continued. "The lot I saw were parked about two kilometres from here, where there is still grass on the inner edge of the road. Some of the men were walking about stretching their legs."

"The convoy stayed on the road I suppose," Migale said, stroking his beard, which appeared to be a habit of his.

Carlo nodded and glanced at his notes; his voice developing a note of excitement as he said,

"Oh yes, the grass where they are isn't wide enough for them to get off the road. They are only just beyond the place where the road narrows to climb in to the pass. . . . The formation is, the staff car at he head of the convoy, followed by one of the armoured cars. "He looked at his notes again and continued with, "One of the low loaders carrying a tank came next, then three of those big lorries and another low loader with a tank. Behind them, were the other three lorries, the third tank and an armoured car; in that order."

Obviously, we can't stand and make a fight against the gunfire of armoured cars and tanks, but we can make life difficult for them," Luigi began, "With that tank at the rear end of the column, there is no way on this side that the convoy can turn back easily. The road is much too narrow for a low loader to reverse quickly. What idiot decided to trap everything except the armoured cars and the two staff cars between the tanks like that I wonder."

"What about the convoy on other side?" Sandy asked.

"That road passes through quite a wide area and there are not many places where it is overlooked by the higher levels," Migale replied.

"So, they can turn back quite easily," Sandy said.

"Yes", said Migale. "But with the pass blocked, it will take at least one day longer, if not two to get back on their route." He paused, stroked his beard and then grinned, "If you still have any of that plastic Sir, I know plenty of places where I can make it awkward for them" and with a chuckle added "they will wish Migale had never been born."

"Not much, but I do have some. "What are you proposing?" Sandy asked.

Migale looked at Luigi, he didn't need to speak, Luigi could read the question on his face.

"The lieutenant will be needed here to blow one of the bridges," he said, without waiting for the question to be asked.

"I could do both of them, Sandy has shown me how." Gianni volunteered.

"I know that Lepre," Luigi replied, giving him a disapproving look. "nevertheless I think it wiser to stick to our original plan until both of the bridges are destroyed. It will take the Tedeschi a while to sort themselves out. Migale can take the British officer and carry out his plan afterwards. There will be plenty of time."

"That's whizzo by me," Sandy said, then, the thought occurred, 'how do we get across with the bridges down?'

Reading his thoughts Luigi gave a tight lipped smile and pointed to the gap where Carlo had leaped across.

Sandy's immediate thought was, 'what am I doing here?' but kept it to himself.

They didn't have long to wait before the drone of running engines told them the convoy was now within earshot. Gianni crouching close by the bridge he had been assigned, felt a surge of expectancy. The earlier doubts he had experienced were now replaced by a confidence in his ability to carry out the task allotted to him. If he had any worries, they were for Donnola, who, with four of his men and one of Luigi's sharp shooters was waiting in the pass for the arrival of the staff car. The decision to wait until the first of the low loaders was on the bridge meant that one of the armoured cars would be close behind the officers in their car. He wondered who had been allotted that task in the other pass, then grinned, as he recalled the look on Sandy's face when he realised he would have to leap across that awesome drop. The appearance of a car approaching his bridge broke Gianni's reverie. Almost, as if he was dreaming, he watched the car, cross the bridge; it seemed to be moving in slow motion. This was not the first time he had experienced that sensation every soldier who has seen action knows, and he knew it would not be the last. When eventually the low loader arrived with its tank, the delay between setting off the charge and the subsequent explosion seemed an eternity. Meanwhile, the distant sound of shots was evidence that Donnola and his companions were at work.

Slowly, almost gracefully, the bridge trembled, then dipped, stayed for a moment, one end suspended in air, then tilted steeply and hung there. The tank barely hesitated before it dived into the depths of the chasm, followed almost immediately by the low loader.

Happy with the success of his mission, Gianni made a discreet retreat into the hills.

From a prudent distance, behind friendly rock cover, Gianni saw the leading lorry in the convoy attempt to make its way along the loop road, but when its offside wheels slipped over the edge of the chasm, it only succeeded in completely blocking the road. The intention, Gianni assumed, had been to tell the officer in charge of the contingent coming round the western route about the blowing of the bridge and warn him that they would not be able to follow his section because of the acute bend that would have to be negotiated. This combined with the narrowness of the road meant that the drivers of such large vehicles would have to pass the bridge, then reverse across. Gianni grinned as he pictured the driver wondering where he would find a spot in the pass where he could turn round. The prospect of such a manoeuvre by the following vehicles was too ridiculous to contemplate. While he watched, the distant sound of sporadic bursts of rapid fire, intermingled with the occasional sharp crack of a rifle came to his ears. Happy with the success of his efforts and the unforeseen blockage of the loop road, Gianni decided to stay where he was until the other bridge, which was visible from his side of the chasm, had been successfully destroyed.

From their vantage point, Luigi and Migale watched the sequence of events below with pleased satisfaction,

"It couldn't have turned out better," Migale observed, "do you think the others will be able to see the wrecked bridge when they arrive?"

"No, I don't think so," Luigi replied, "I would imagine the curve in the road will hide it from view. When you think about it, when standing in the centre of one of the bridges, it is only possible to see a small part of the other. With luck, when the other staff car crosses, the officer in it won't notice the other bridge has disappeared. They might see that truck though. I must admit to being surprised that nobody was sent forward to warn them."

"Too much discipline, nobody is allowed to think," Migale commented, then added, "It would have been easier for the driver and his gefreiter to go forward than it was to do that crazy act of climbing over the roof of the cab. I suppose, because they weren't very far along the loop when they slipped over the edge, they preferred to rejoin their comrades, rather than risk the unknown dangers ahead."

"That truck must be wedged against the rock face, leaving no room to squeeze through for them to try a stunt like that. The way the vehicle is canted over the edge must have made the roof of the cab slope too steeply in the wrong direction for comfort." Luigi said, in a matter of fact voice.

"The others probably heard the explosion and will be on the lookout. . . . I know I would." Migale chuckled, "If they aren't, they are in for a shock."

Luigi allowed himself a brief smile, turned to Carlo and said,

"Run to the British officer Guerriero, tell him, if the staff car and the accompanying armoured vehicle go across the bridge, he is to allow them to cross and wait for the arrival of the low loader with its tank. If it doesn't arrive, then use his own judgement."

Migale watched Carlo run off, then looked at Luigi, he was obviously surprised by the decision. The original plan was, that if the two bridges could not be blown up at the same time, because the two halves of the convoy arrived at different times, the first bridge would be destroyed while the first of the leading low loaders was on it; the timing of the second would depend on the subsequent events. He felt sure the distant sound of battle would alert the Germans and the opportunity to deal another blow would be lost. However, Luigi's reasoning was that while the Tedeschi may have heard the explosion, it was more than probable that the noise created by moving vehicles would mask it.

"I know you don't like gambling Sir, but I think this one is worth a try," Migale began, then continued by saying "I suspect the Tedeschi heard the noise of the bridge being blown up, but not the subsequent sound of battle that followed. Hopefully, if they did hear it, they will assume we are only in that pass. If so, they are in for a shock."

The distant sound of battle had stopped and ten minutes had gone by before the long awaited staff car, with its accompanying armoured vehicle arrived. Without even a pause, they sped across the bridge and out of sight."

Migale stroked his beard grinned broadly and said slowly,

"It looks as though the gamble might come off."

The words were barely out of Migale's mouth when the first of the low loaders appeared round the bend.

"I don't think they will able to see the other bridge, or rather what there is left of it, from there," Migale commented. Then, when almost as if he had been overheard, the turret on the tank swivelled, pointing its gun first in the direction of the stranded vehicle, then high above the bridge towards the promontory where they stood, he added, "the crew in that tank aren't taking any chances, I wonder if they have seen us."

"I shouldn't think so, more likely they have spotted that lorry and are being cautious." Luigi remarked.

. . . .

Sandy, poised and ready for action smiled quietly to himself as he watched the manoeuvring of the huge low loader. The road was so narrow and the angle so tight, that he wondered whether the driver would succeed or, like the lorry get itself wedged against the rock wall. He waited until a mixture of perseverance and skill brought all six wheels of the vehicle on to the bridge before setting off his charges. To his amazement, when the bridge collapsed, the lorry didn't slide off; somehow it had hooked a back wheel round one of the stout posts supporting the railings. The bridge meanwhile, remained firmly attached to its moorings on the side opposite to him. The tank, miraculously held on the transporter by its retaining chains, stared forlornly into the depths below. Sandy stayed only long enough to see the crew of the tank and the two men in the drivers cab of the low loader make a desperate scramble to safety before he melted into the background.

The thought of shooting the desperate Germans didn't enter Sandy's mind; if he had been asked why he had not taken the opportunity to kill them, he would have replied 'It wouldn't have been cricket dear boy.'

Such sentiments were far from Il Tiranno's mind as, accompanied by a selected six, he watched and waited for an officer to leave the stationary staff car and walk over to the armoured car in order to tell the crew to clear away the large chunks of rock, which had been scattered on the road in a narrow section of the pass and prevented them from proceeding. Il Tiranno's guess that this would happen, proved correct; the ensuing massacre was inevitable. The strict order to hold fire until the men were at work proved effective, the Germans were mown down, without mercy, with little or no chance of reaching the sanctuary of their armoured vehicle.

With the road ahead cluttered with boulders and the armoured car behind blocking the way, the staff car was trapped. Realising the soft metal structure of their car was no protection, the three officers in it made a dash for safety behind some massive boulders under an overhang below the area where Il Tiranno and his men were stationed. Armed as they were with pistols only, the Germans had no chance of survival in the hail of bullets from the Sten guns of the two men waiting there.

The western pass, being considerably wider than the eastern, could not be blocked in a similar manner to its counterpart so Donnola found himself confronted with an active and mobile armoured car. Dispatch of the officers in their car was swift and easy, but even if he had more than the six men with him, there was no way, without suitable weapons, of dealing with an adversary already raking the area with heavy machine gun fire. He and his men disappeared quietly into the foothills and climbed the slopes to rendezvous with Luigi and Migale. Gianni and Sandy were already there when they arrived; a few minutes later, Il Tiranno and his men made an appearance.

Satisfied that all had gone to plan, Luigi cast a critical eye over them, checking nobody had been hurt and was keeping quiet about it and said,

"Well done! It's time we joined Grillo and Alan."

Each alone with their thoughts, nobody spoke as they made their way to the gap across the chasm and jumped; that is all except Sandy, who, to the amusement of all, shouted Geronimo as he leaped over the fearsome drop.

Heavily outnumbered the two groups, headed by Alan on the west and Grillo on the east were already actively engaged when Luigi and those with him joined them. The battle that followed was long and bloody with losses on both sides. Armed, as they were, with only Sten guns and rifles, there was no way of dealing with the heavy machine gun fire from the armoured vehicle at the rear end of each of the two columns. However, because of the difficulties involved in reversing the two low loaders, Luigi's sharp shooters managed to inflict a considerable number of casualties as the Germans strove to reverse their columns into a wider area.

. . . .

The smoke filled bar of the locale hummed with the low murmur of voices as the villagers discussed the news narrated by Nonna Ricci. Tales, laced with Nazi propaganda, told, in varying gruesome detail. Her story of a battle between the ribelli and the Tedeschi in the passes a little south of Sulmona was on everybody's lips. They spoke with pride as they told each other how the ribelli had attacked a large convoy of the Tedeschi on its way to the forward area; how all but a few had been slaughtered when aeroplanes bombed them; how those that had been taken prisoner were now in Sulmona waiting public execution. There wasn't a soul in Renzo's bar that night, who didn't have either a friend or relative in one of the local bands and their hushed voices, often masking a sob, expressed their sadness.

Mario's immediate reaction when Michele followed him in and related what he had just heard from Nonna Ricci was to think of Lucia. Without delaying long enough to pick up the drink Renzo had served, he hurried out of the locale.

When Mario saw Donnina and Lucia holding hands and staring into each other's faces, he knew that Nonna Ricci's news had reached their ears.

"Don't believe everything you hear," he said, "These rumours are often started by Tedeschi alarmists. They are meant to frighten us into submission."

"Others have come with similar stories. I spoke to one who saw the planes," Donnina replied.

"Gianni said he had to go back because he was needed. My little brother, are you safe?" Lucia stared out of the window as she spoke, it was as if she was scared of what the others would read in her eyes.

Mario didn't know what he could say to comfort Donnina and Lucia; he was thankful that Dora was not in the room. Feeling more than a little embarrassed he put an arm round both of their shoulders and said,

"Would you like me to fetch Ernesto?"

Donnina shook her head and said,

"Don't worry, we will be alright." Then, as she separated herself from Mario, added, "That poor girl. Carina will be on her own. . . . Concetta has gone to Paese. . . . You stay with Lucia while I go to her." The words came out in a torrent of disjointed sentences as she went out of the door.

Tight lipped and determined to appear cheerful, Donnina hurried along to Concetta's house The one thought in her mind was to comfort the girl friend of her son. When she found Carina staring with red eyes at the *Stella Alpina*[36] that Gianni had plucked, she knew that Nonna Ricci's version of events had reached her. Thinking that giving the girl something to do might ease the pain and guessing that the little flower had been plucked on her last walk with Gianni, she said,

"Isn't it a pretty flower, are you going to press it?"

A shadow of a smile crossed Carina's face as she picked up an exercise book, a relic from her school days. Then, carefully spread the petals of the flower on one of the pages, gazed at it fondly for a moment, then shut the book and pressed the covers firmly together.

"I'll always keep . . ." Carina began to say, then burst into tears.

Somehow, as she comforted Carina, the pent up emotions which had been tormenting Donnina evaporated, she began to think more positively. 'After all,' she told herself, 'not many of the rumours passed on by Nonna Ricci are accurate. Many have come to her second or third hand and stories relayed in this way are often distorted beyond belief.' With more than a trace of hope in her voice, she said to Carina,

"We don't know yet whether Nonna Ricci's story is true. Gianni is probably alive and hiding out somewhere."

Carina looked at the mother of the man she loved. There was a glimmer of hope in her eyes as she said,

"I hope so, I do hope so. . . . Please God make it happen."

---

[36] Small white mountain flower.

CHAPTER TWENTYTHREE

With only a few days to the wedding, Lucia and her mother were kept busy. There was so much to do and so little time to do it. They tried not to think of the stories circulating as they bustled around preparing the food that kind neighbours and various friends had generously donated from their own scant stocks.

Two days had passed since Donnina had watched the distant shapes of Carina and Gianni as they came into view on the grassy slopes above the village. Two days that seemed an age as she anxiously watched Lucia, who, despite the proximity of the long awaited wedding day, scheduled for the following Saturday, went about her tasks with a straight face. For a girl so full of life and laughter Lucia's demeanour filled her with foreboding. When she said, "Mama, we shouldn't be celebrating." Donnina was fearful that her daughter would follow with the suggestion that the wedding should be called off. To her relief, if Lucia had such a thought in mind, she didn't broach it.

Seemingly unperturbed, Ernesto carried on as though he hadn't a care in the world. Determined not to reveal the ache in his heart, he contrived to smile when, in his usual quiet way, he recounted the little incidents, often repetitions of happening on previous days, that had occurred during his day's work. With only two days to go, he went to his cellar, as he called it, actually a corner in the coolest part of the house and took out one of the bottles of wine he had laid down in the year of Lucia's birth.

"That was a good vintage year," he murmured as he withdrew the stopper. Happy with the bouquet, he poured a thimble of the wine in to a glass to sample the taste. "Even Michele couldn't better this," he told himself as he replaced the stopper. Taking care not to disturb the sediment, he replaced the bottle in the rack.

. . . .

Hours of scrubbing and inspection were spent preparing the cart (that had been built for Mario's grandfather) for the wedding and at last it was ready. A seat, padded with folded blankets covered with a white sheet had been fitted into the rear and fold-away steps were provided on one side of the cart.

Washed and groomed till fit for entry in a show, Bruto and Bella stood patiently between the shafts as they waited by the door with a wolf for a knocker. Cherished white ribbon, saved from a wedding many years before, had been used to decorate their heads with magnificent bows; further lengths of the ribbon were stretched between their horns and the cart. Michele drew a huge turnip watch from his waistcoat pocket, glanced at the time and said,

"They won't be long now."

The words were barely out of his mouth when the door opened and Lucia, on the arm of her father appeared.

First Lucia, helped by Michele, mounted the cloth covered steps and took her place on the seat in the cart. Then Ernesto followed. When he leant forward to close the small door that had been fitted, Michele shook his head and closed it for him. Then, having made sure his passengers were happy, took up the reins and followed by a number of friends and well-wishers, started on, what should be, Lucia's last journey as La Signorina Battistero Lucia.

A gentle breeze, bringing the cool air of the mountains to La Villa was a gentle relief for the well wishers that packed the church on the hill. Despite the otherwise oppressive heat, several of the men proudly wore their cherished and well preserved wedding suits. Others contrived to find a tie and jacket. The women, almost without exception, were dressed in the clothes they reserved for Sunday Mass.

All heads turned as Lucia, on the arm of her father, made her way down the aisle. Smiling bravely, she tried not too look at the empty space in the pew reserved for immediate family. Dora proudly holding the train of the bridal dress followed discreetly behind.

The dress Lucia wore would not have disgraced a society bride and brought a gasp of admiration from the congregation. Made from parachute silk, it represented an uncountable number of hours of painstaking work; during which the material had been washed and bleached repeatedly until even Donnina's critical eyes were satisfied with the purity of its whiteness. Caterina, notwithstanding her poor sight had made a veil with a net, so fine it could have been spun by a spider. Embroidered with tiny florets and edged with delicate lace, it was a thing of exquisite beauty.

Praying that the unexpected and uninvited Antonio, who she had seen occupying a seat at the rear of the church, would not speak out when the question about just impediments was made, Lucia waited for Mario to join her.

Mario would have liked to wear his Alpini Officer's uniform, but settled for the still serviceable, if a little tight and slightly short in the length of the sleeves, suit he wore on the day of his inauguration. His arrival at her side steadied Lucia's nerves and for a brief moment she forgot her fears.

From the woods above the church, a figure wearing service trousers tucked in to the top of stout boots, and a faded shirt emerged, glanced cautiously around, then quickened his pace as he made for the church. The six day growth of beard rendered him almost unrecognisable as he hurried down the aisle and filled the empty space in the pew reserved for the family.

The low pitched murmur, combined with the rustle made by the turning of many heads that Lucia heard, when the time to make her vows and exchange rings came, renewed the fears that had been clutching at her heart. Wanting to turn her head and look, she forced herself to keep her eyes on Don Umberto. 'Had Antonio stood up ready to denounce her?' The question raced madly round her brain, swamping coherent thought. To her relief, the vows were said and rings exchanged without interruption. Deciding to thank Antonio for attending the ceremony and tell him he would be welcome at the reception, she looked at the place where he had been sitting; it was empty. Then, she saw Gianni.

Happy now, all her fears behind her, Lucia resented the unavoidable delay as friends gathered round her while en route to sign the register. Delay which prevented her from reaching Gianni to hug him. To her disappointment, when, at last she was free, there was no sign of him. She looked for Carina, but the girl Gianni loved was nowhere to be seen.

Because the stair like street which led from the high end of the village to the square was not only too narrow, but also had a surface which prohibited the passage of wheels, Michele took the cart and its passengers round the circuitous mule track. By the time Mario and his bride arrived, the room known as Nicoletta was packed with guests.

Immediately on arrival at the reception, Lucia looked for Gianni; he was not there. Donnina, quick to note the straight face of her daughter, who should be smiling, guessed the reason and hastened to be by her side.

"Gianni has gone home to clean up and change his clothes." Donnina gave Lucia a motherly hug as she spoke, then, with a twinkle in her eyes, added, "He said he wouldn't be long; Carina has gone with him, so I don't know how long that might be." and laughed.

Donnina's laughter, was heard by Gianni, who with Carina by his side had just entered the square. There was no mistaking who it was.

"Your mother sounds happy" Carina said. The laugh that followed her words was a more musical sound.

When Gianni entered Renzo's bar, all eyes turned towards him. One and all, would have liked to ask him if the tales they had heard were true. Circumspection being the order of the day, 'such question should be asked in private' was the ruling thought in their minds.

The Bride forgotten, the guests at the reception swamped Gianni and Carina as soon as they were seen, frustrating Gianni's attempts to reach his mother and sister. They were rescued by Ernesto and Michele, when Michele said,

"Your boy needs help."

Together, they threaded their way through the mass of guests surrounding the new arrivals. On reaching them, Ernesto called out,

"È pronto il pranzo[37]," and pointed in the direction of a long table, groaning under the weight of food at the other end of the room.

Heads turned but, it seemed, the thirst for news was stronger than the desire to eat.

. . . .

Filled with pleasure over the success of the reception and flushed with the pride a father has for a beautiful daughter, Michele's congratulations on the quality of his wine still ringing in his ears, Ernesto watched Lucia and Mario depart in the wedding carriage.

The heat of the day had given way to a serene night as Lucia and Mario sat close together contentedly talking in low tones and watched the horns of Bruto and Bella sway in the silvery light of the moon. Walking at their side, Michele grinned happily as he heard Lucia murmur,

"*Signora.*"

Late as it was, Michele didn't mind the long walk across the valley to Casa dei Pioppi. He had steadfastly refused to allow Ernesto to return with him to attend to the animals. When the thought was broached by Ernesto, he laughingly said,

---

[37] The dinner is ready, (In this sense the wedding meal is ready)

"Whatever next? A father can't escort his daughter on the way to her wedding suite."

There had been talk of clearing away the woodland surrounding the old home of Michele's ancestors so that the young married couple could use it, but Mario had insisted that it remain a refuge until such time as hiding places were no longer required. The apartment that they had prepared was simple, but adequate, consisting of a small room where they could be private and a larger room where they would sleep. Kitchen facilities would have to be shared with the family; a point that didn't concern Mario and didn't worry Lucia.

The guests at the reception didn't stay long after Mario and Lucia left. A few remained to help leave the room known as Nicoletta clean and tidy, then they too were gone. As Donnina looked round the now empty room, she was assailed by a sensation that was a mixture of relief and happiness. Relief that everything had gone well, happiness that her son was safe. Her happiness showed in her face as she said,

"Your being here made the day Gianni, you have no idea how it was for Lucia."

"I know," Gianni said, then added, "Didn't she look lovely in that dress, I have never noticed before, how beautiful she is. I suppose, because she is my sister, I never really looked."

As Gianni finished speaking, he felt a tug at his shirt and heard Dora say,

"Do I look pretty in my new frock?"

Gianni looked down, saw the roguish look in Dora's eyes and couldn't resist the temptation to tease her. He waited a few minutes before answering, then said,

"What frock?"

Her eyes bright with laughter, Dora smacked the back of one of his hands and said,

"Oh you're horrid Gianni I hate you," then stretched up on tip-toes to deliver a kiss.

Walking back to the house with a wolf for a knocker, holding Dora's hand in one of his and Carina's in the other, Gianni felt at peace with the world.

Pleased to see Gianni relaxed, Donnina took hold of Dora's free hand and uttered a sincere prayer of thanks. When Ernesto joined the chain, which now stretched across the entire width of the street, she truly believed her prayers had been answered.

During the few minutes taken walking back to their home, Dora, keeping a firm clasp on Gianni's and her mother's hands, kept up an incessant flow of chatter as she skipped along between them.

Sipping the grappa, Ernesto had poured for him, Gianni stretched out his legs and leant back. He had expected to be tired, but felt wide awake and ready for the barrage of questions he was sure would come and hoped with all his heart that those with answers locked in his brain, would not be asked. Seeking to delay the moment when the barrage of questions would begin, Gianni placed his now empty glass on the table and said,

"That grappa was too good to gulp down without tasting, What did you do to it Papa?"

Ernesto took the hint, topped up Gianni's and his own glass, beamed his pleasure and said,

"Nothing, the grappa and the wine were a gift from Michele. What did you think of my special red?"

"Like nectar," Gianni replied and fumbled in his pockets for the pack of tobacco that should be there. When the thought came to him that it would probably be in the pocket of his other trousers, he remembered that Donnina had been through to the back of the house and was gone for several minutes. Praying that she hadn't put his trousers in soak ready for washing in the morning, he said.

"I hope Mama you haven't put my dirty clothes in the wash."

When Donnina saw the look of trepidation on Gianni's face, she found it difficult to control the laugh bubbling inside her as she said,

"Why not? They were disgusting."

An awkward silence followed, which Donnina was determined not to break until she reached the chimney breast. Taking the missing roll of tobacco from a niche in the wall, the laughter she had been fighting to control came to the surface as she spluttered,

"Is this what you want?" and between fits of laughter, added," Surely you didn't think I would wash your clothes without emptying the pockets first."

Feeling a little sheepish, Gianni took the pack, murmured his thanks and deftly rolled a cigarette. Then, offered the makings to his father.

Ernesto shook his head, produced a blackened terracotta pipe from a pot on the hearth and proceeded to stuff tobacco into it as he said,

"I prefer the pipe."

Gianni watched with amusement as his father fiddled with the stem, a short length of cane like material cut from a shrub which grew in the area. He had seen the performance so often before; it was almost a ritual.

Not happy with the way it was drawing, Ernesto first removed the stem and blew through it. Then tried sucking. Holding the offending piece before the flickering light of an oil lamp, he tried to peer through it; deciding it was clear he refitted the stem to the terracotta bowl. Still not satisfied, he threw the stem on to the fire and replaced it with a fresh, ready prepared, cutting taken from a selection kept in the same pot that he kept his pipe. Grunting contentedly, Ernesto poked and stirred the tobacco until it was burning to his liking, then posed the question they all wanted to ask.

"Were you in that action we have heard talk about? Is it true that a group of ribelli, sorry! Partisans was completely wiped out?"

Gianni hesitated a moment before replying, then said.

"You don't have to believe half the stories that have been told about the skirmishes on the slopes of the Maiella, . . . yes I was there."

Carina drew her chair a little closer to Gianni's. Put a hand on his shoulder and in a tone that expressed her concern said,

"Oh Gianni, you were there. How awful." Carina's concern was more than a little obvious as she turned her head to gaze into his eyes.

Words were unnecessary, Gianni nodded and seized the opportunity to hug her.

Donnina looked at Gianni, it was the sort of look a mother gives her son when she wants to ask him something, but doesn't know how to without causing him sadness. After a few minutes hesitation, she said,

"What about your friend, Donnola? We heard that all but a few of you were killed."

"As I just said to Papa, you don't have to believe half the stories bandied about, especially those passed on by Nonna Ricci; I wonder where her sympathies lie sometimes. Donnola is fine and asks to be remembered to you." Gianni was aware of a surge of emotion as, in low tones and speaking slowly, he said, "We lost a few," then, with words tumbling over each as if anxious to be spoken, he added, "Nobody you would know."

"But friends of yours," Donnina said sympathetically. It was not the sort of comment Gianni wanted, he could feel a lump forming in his throat and took a larger sip than usual from his glass.

Ernesto, quick to recognise the signs, reminiscent of twenty five years before, hastened to refill Gianni's glass and in an attempt to change the subject, said,

"I don't know where that old lady gets her stories from."

Something in the timbre of Ernesto's voice struck a chord, Gianni and his father's eyes met momentarily, each knew what was in the others mind.

Without commenting on Ernesto's remark, Gianni went on to tell about the way the two bridges had been blown up. His account of how the Germans scrambled over the cab of the lorry, when it was stuck on the loop road brought a light stir of amusement from his audience. Deliberately keeping his account low key and encouraged by the occasional murmur of laughter, Gianni went on to tell them his impressions of Sandy's face when confronted with the leap across the chasm. Although Gianni's much exaggerated description brought a peal of laughter from all, there still remained a subtle air of tension until they heard a voice say.

"Oh Gianni" did he really look like that?"

The voice came from behind an open door where Dora had been hiding.

"Why aren't you in bed?" Ernesto demanded, using the sternest tone he could muster.

Dora hung her head, but she didn't look repentant.

Using a softer tone, Gianni beckoned Dora over clasped her to him and said,

"These tales are not for you, be a darling and go to bed."

Although Dora was reluctant to go to bed, she didn't show it as she went round the room delivering goodnight kisses to all and sundry.

Dora's appearance of non contrition as she moved towards the stairs, brought a burst of laughter which filled the room. Hopefully, as if she was thinking, 'they might relent and let me stay up a little longer,' Dora stopped momentarily and looked round the room. Ernesto, without saying a word waved the back of his hand towards her in that age old gesture indicating, go on, and she meekly climbed the stairs.

The interruption eased the tension that had been there; Gianni was even able to laugh a little as he recounted the story of the series of small skirmishes that had been played out on the slopes of the Maiella and the surrounding foothills. He told of how the Tedeschi had struggled, under repeated sniping from the men who wore the black feather, to reverse the low loaders down the steep and narrow road. How Migale on the western road didn't have an easy target, the road and area through which it ran being much wider. Explaining that because he was on the eastern section, he didn't know much about what happened on the west, Gianni chuckled as he told them how, by the time the Tedeschi brought their machine guns into play, Migale and his men had disappeared and added that they watched the Very lights[38] and shadowy figures carrying stick bombs from a safe distance before they too melted away. He finished off by saying,

"In a way, I feel sorry for that lot of Tedeschi."

Surprised by the comment, Carina lifted her head from his shoulder and looking him straight in the face, said,

"Why feel sorry for them? they are horrid."

"After all that effort getting their stuff down to level ground, Allied aircraft came in the morning and bombed them out of existence. Their dead lay everywhere, we let those who survived make their way to Sulmona."

"They wouldn't have done the same for you," Carina commented.

Gianni shrugged his shoulders and planted a kiss on her nose.

By the time Gianni finished talking, the first grey streaks of dawn were making their appearance in the sky. Ernesto looked out of the window and said,

"Another day begins, I'm glad I don't have to go to work today. By the way, did you see anything of Alan and Paul? I believe they both joined Luigi's formation."

Gianni looked surprised and said,

---

[38] Very lights (named after E. W. Very, 1847–1907, US inventor) were signal flares, fired from a pistol (flare gun).

"The two Englishmen? I didn't know you knew them. . . . I saw Alan briefly, Paul was with Migale. By all accounts, Alan is a very brave man. I didn't see what happened and so don't know what he did, but Il Capitano told me that had he been in normal service with the Italian army, he would have received the Silver medal."

Ernesto's weather-beaten face became a mass of wrinkles as he grinned knowingly and said,

"Your old father often knows more than he admits." Taking his pipe from his mouth, he gazed at it for a moment, looked at his son and added, "I never actually met them, they stayed with a friend of Giorgio's and were supposed to meet one of Topo's guides, who didn't turn up and has never been seen since. They decided to make the attempt on their own, met some of Luigi's lot and joined up with them. I heard about it a few days later when Tina brought a message from them."

"I expect Michele will be pleased to have news of them. I shall be around for a few days, so will make a point of visiting him," Gianni said.

There was no mistaking the happiness glowing in Ernesto's eyes when, on hearing this bit of uninvited news he said,

"Your mother will be pleased to hear that you are not going back for a few days."

"I heard him say it. Of course I'm pleased," Donnina's voice rang out as she re-entered the room and added almost accusingly, "Why didn't you tell us before?"

"Gianni grinned and said, "Didn't think of it." Then added, as he stiffly rose from his chair, "Migale has asked me to contact Angelo. Something to do with a suspected spy."

Ernesto took his pipe from his mouth, looked at it momentarily, then switched his gaze to his son but said nothing. Meanwhile, Carina rose from her chair and clutched at Gianni's arm. She was trembling as she said,

"Oh Gianni do be careful."

"I'm sure he will be," Ernesto said, with a forced smile that wouldn't have come naturally.

Gianni drew Carina close to him, looked fondly at the head of dark chestnut coloured hair now lying on his chest and said,

"I always am. Come you are tired, your mother will wonder what has happened to you."

"She knows where I am," Carina said as she snuggled up against him.

It was turned four o'clock in the afternoon, when, beneath the shade of interlocking branches Gianni made his way along the remote woodland path that would take him to Angelo's house. Dressed as he was in clean trousers and shirt and wearing light weight sandals instead of the stout mid calf length boots he wore in the hills, he bore no resemblance to the shabby figure that had emerged from the forest the previous day. The purple bandanna worn by the followers of Donnola was stuffed in his pocket lest it betray him as a partisan. Somehow without it round his neck he felt half naked. Alone with thoughts that switched repeatedly from the mission confronting him to tender reflections of the girl he loved, he half regretted refusing to allow Carina to accompany him. He knew in his heart though that his decision was right.

Wondering whether he would find Angelo at home, he crossed the stream before following it down the hillside to the place where it formed a pool and became two entities, each taking its own route down the hillside.

As he approached the boulder that divides the stream, he thought he could hear someone speaking, then, hearing the words, *'Bella figlia del' amore'* he realised that someone, who he guessed to be Filomena, was quietly singing a snatch from a popular song of the day. Grinning roguishly he peered round the boulder.

Filomena was sitting on the edge of the pool combing her luxuriant tresses. Despite the silence of Gianni's approach the faint rustle of his movement reached her ears. Hoping it was Giorgio, she stopped singing, gave one last long stroke to her hair and smiling happily turned to face the boulder. Nobody was in sight. Vaguely disappointed, she picked up a brush to give the final touches to her hair.

"*Salve* Filomena, is Angelo at home?"

The voice, coming as it did from behind the boulder, startled Filomena. Dropping her brush on the ground, she leaped to her feet. Then as Gianni came in sight, she smiled in relief and said,

"What brings you here Gianni?" gave a musical chuckle and added "I know it's not to see me."

Laughing with her, Gianni said,

"Why not, you are pretty enough."

The flirtatious remark made Filomena blush. Recovering her composure, she said,

"Babbo will be home soon. I believe he wants to see you."

Together, Gianni and Filomena descended to the house. It was cool inside, a pleasant relief from the heat of the day. Gratefully, Gianni helped himself to a ladle of water from the conca; relishing its freshness.

Filomena pleased that he felt at home, watched him replace the ladle, poured a glass of wine and said,

"You enjoyed that, now have a glass of wine, Babbo won't be long. You will stay and have a meal with us, won't you?"

Had Gianni wanted to say no to the invitation, he would have found it almost impossible. Taking his answer for granted, Filomena embarked on a barrage of small talk as she bustled round the table, preparing places for three.

"I saw you at the wedding yesterday, Lucia was so pleased you were able to be there. Didn't she look beautiful in that dress? It must have taken hours to make. . . . That horrid man Il Mareschiallo was . . ." Suddenly aware that she was talking about Gianni's grandfather and feeling a little embarrassed, Filomena stopped in mid sentence and attempted to change the subject by continuing with, "Something must be happening on the Allied front, there has been so many of their planes flying over in the past few days. Nonna Ricci says . . ."

"Don't take any notice of what Nonna Ricci says," Gianni interrupted, "half her stories are propaganda and bear no relation to what is really going on."

It was then that the door opened and Angelo walked in. "What's the old lady been saying now?" he asked as he cast his eyes around the room. Seeing the three places set at the table, he embraced Gianni and followed with, "It gives me great pleasure to see you at our table. Do have an aperitif while you are waiting."

Gianni watched Angelo take an ancient earthenware flask from the shelf where it was kept and pick up the now empty glass that had been used for the wine Filomena had given him.

"You must be an honoured guest," Angelo said as he rinsed the glass preparatory to pouring a generous serving of grappa into it. Taking a mug from a hook on the shelf, he poured himself an equally generous helping. then looked at Filomena, who shook her head. Smiling at some secret thought, he replaced the flask on the shelf. Becoming more serious, he added, "When I saw you yesterday, I guessed you might come to see me. Have you brought word from Migale?"

Gianni nodded.

"Time for talk later," Filomena said in a firm voice as she ladled steaming spaghetti on to the plates. Saying "the *sugo* is *dell'arrosto*," she placed a large bowl of the condiment in the centre of the table and watched them start eating before she sat down.

When the meal was finished, Angelo rose from the table and said,

"It will be cooler outside Gianni, we can talk safely there."

Seeing Gianni and Angelo head for the door, Filomena started to clear the table and called out,

"I will be with you as soon as I have cleared away these things. Do you want me to bring you a refreshing drink?"

"The wine left over in the bottle will suffice," Angelo replied.

Although the sun had lost its height, it was still high enough to throw lengthened shadows of the two men across the small courtyard as they approached a crude table beneath the shade of a massive oak tree. Indicating one of the rush bottom chairs set beside it, Angelo said,

"Make yourself comfortable, Filomena won't be long." Then, almost as an afterthought, added "You can safely talk in front of her."

Despite the lack of a breeze, there was a pleasant freshness in the shade below the oak tree and the proximity of the surrounding woodland endowed the air with its fragrant aroma.

True to her word, Filomena cleared the table in record time and appeared, carrying the bottle of wine in one hand and two mugs in the other. Gianni managed to stem the chuckle he wanted to make as the thought 'she is not risking her precious glasses outside,' entered his head. Placing the mugs on the table, she shared the contents of the bottle between them and while doing so said,

"I'll get another mug and some water. Do you want another bottle Babbo?"

Angelo looked at his daughter and responded to the hint, he knew Filomena liked the sweet liquor he was going to suggest. The knowledge brought a glint of fond humour in his eyes as he said,

"No, bring the grappa. You can pour yourself some rosolio if you like."

For a period of approximately half an hour, the three sat in silence, each alone with their own thoughts. Not even the almost obligatory toasts had been uttered as they sat enjoying the serenity of the evening. The only sounds were those made by tiny animals moving and the faint rustling of leaves in the trees.

"Migale asked me to see you." Gianni's voice broke the silence.

"I suspected that was the reason you were here, about Loriano I suppose." Angelo's voice was modulated to a level which could not be heard more than a few feet from the table.

Speaking equally softly, Gianni said,

"He didn't mention that name, only that I had to make some arrangements with you about a traitor, who he believes could be a partisan calling himself Lori." Gianni paused a moment to think, "I suppose Lori could be short for Loriano"

Angelo pondered for a few minutes before he spoke. When he did, he said,

"The same idea had struck me. I'll arrange a meeting with Giorgio. Did Migale say why he sent you instead of coming himself?"

"If the man is to be arrested it will be best to have someone at hand. As I live in La Villa my being around will not cause the speculation that his presence would. Also he believes I might have met Lori using a different name, that of Peter. If Loriano looks like both Peter and Lori, if you get my drift, then the names Lori and Peter could be aliases for Loriano." Gianni explained rather awkwardly before adding, I find it difficult to believe that nice young man I met last Christmas is a spy."

Angelo nodded sagely and said,

"Nevertheless it makes sense, I'll get in touch with Giorgio. How long will you be around?

"As long as it takes," was Gianni's laconic reply.

Filomena emitted a low pitched trill of laughter and said,

"That will please Carina."

CHAPTER TWENTYFOUR

Oberschütze Maxmilian Gunter, who preferred to be called Max, had lost the lower half of one of his legs and was waiting to be repatriated. He knew from personal experience that the war was not going well on the Adriatic front and was glad to be out of it. Four years of active service with a Panzer division had destroyed any enthusiasm he might have had.

Leaning heavily on crutches and gazing across the valley at the distant multicoloured roofs of La Villa, Max felt the rest on one of the stone 'dragon's teeth' that bordered the road was well earned. The path he had started on with the intention of crossing the valley began as a gentle gradient and he had been confident that he would be able to keep a promise made to friends that he would visit Hannah di Lorenzo if he was ever in the area.

Glancing at the watch on his wrist, Max was amazed to see the hands stood at twenty minutes past three. He couldn't believe how long he had been sitting there, just staring at the distant village nestling in the hills on the other side of the valley. Max had been warned by a German friend, not to trust a man who lived in one of the narrow streets in the outskirts of the oldest part of the town. When asked why, his friend said that there was a rumour that he was English by birth, but because he adopted Italian citizenship a few years before the outbreak of war and had friends in high places, he escaped being interned. Having been told this, Max was reluctant to accept the man's offer of help, when, on being introduced during a visit to the dopolavoro, he claimed to know Hannah. Feeling confident he could manage, Max decided to cross the valley to La Villa on his own. Disappointed by his lack of ability to reach the village, so tantalisingly near and yet so far, he turned to his companion and said,

"Time to go home Bruno. We will try again tomorrow."

Moving awkwardly as he tried to balance on his good leg, Max reflected bitterly on the days, not so very long ago, when he would have crossed the valley in a fraction of the time it had take him to reach his resting place. Thinking he was still talking to the dog belonging to the people who lived in the house where he was billeted while waiting his transfer home, he said,

"Could have been worse Bruno, I'm lucky to still have a leg and the pain will go when the wound is fully healed." then realising the dog was out of sight, he called out, "Come Bruno, time to go home."

The dog came out of a dense woodland area some fifty metres from the road and, looked at him, tilted his head to one side; then disappeared again between the trees. Max grinned, Bruno reminded him of his own dog at home; he could almost hear his mother saying 'Otto has more important things to do than obey you.' Although Max had only been billeted in Paese for a couple of weeks, a strong bond had been forged between him and his four legged friend.

"Come here you disobedient rogue," he shouted, more in amusement than in anger.

Bruno made a brief re-appearance, wagged his tail. Then, instead of obeying, went back into the cluster of trees.

Moving awkwardly over the uneven ground, Max made his way to the edge of the copse, Bruno was nowhere to be seen, but the sound of rustling gave evidence that the dog was somewhere in the tangled undergrowth. Peering between the trees, he could only just see Bruno digging furiously on the edge of a small clearing.

Despite the pain in his groin, which laughter provoked, Max couldn't help doing so. The frantic antics of Bruno were so similar to those made by his own dog when an illicit object had been found. Taking from his pocket a piece of hard black bread, Max tried to tempt the dog, but to no avail. Bruno only lifted his head, wagged his tail and resumed digging.

"What have you found that is more interesting than food?" Max said as he tried to ease himself through the thick undergrowth that separated him from the dog.

Before he had taken even one cautious step into the copse, Max realised that his handicap would not allow him to reach the place where Bruno was digging. Feeling certain the dog would follow or if not, would know his way home, he gave up the attempt.

The conjecture was right, Max had barely covered half the distance to the road when the dog, head held high and tail waving gaily came bounding by carrying something that looked like a field cap in his mouth. Hoping Bruno wouldn't dance away as he was inclined to do when he wanted to play, Max called to him,

"What have you found?"

Bruno looked at Max and wagged his tail, but didn't come any closer.

"Come on, be a good dog, let's see what you've found," Max said encouragingly and offered him the piece of bread.

Bruno trotted towards Max and reluctantly dropped his prize, then snatched the piece of bread and with eyes bright with excitement, stood back waiting for the prize to be thrown.

His every movement watched by Bruno, now dancing in anticipation, Max balanced himself carefully on his crutches and stooped to retrieve the mud splattered object. It was as he had already suspected, a forage cap, similar to the one he was wearing. Although examination was difficult, while trying to retain balance and at the same time ward off the dog, who was making desperate efforts to snatch back his stolen booty, Max could see that the mud and blood spattered cap had not been worn for long. Wondering what to do about it, he stuffed it in his pocket.

Feeling betrayed, Bruno barked hopefully, then apparently satisfied with the full slice of black bread Max threw as a substitute, pounced on it and darted up the slope with the unexpected gift clamped firmly in his jaws.

The first tentative steps on the slippery grass that covered the steeper slope at the edge of the road were difficult and Max cursed himself for leaving the road at a place where there was no track. Ignoring the pain, he persisted. Resorting to hands and knee plus stump, he eventually succeeded in clawing his way to the edge of the road and gratefully, sat again on the stone 'dragon's tooth' that he had left half an hour before.

The shadows were already getting long when Max finally reached the door of the house where he was billeted. It had been a slow painful walk back, with muscles crying out in protest at each step. Nevertheless, he was happy in the knowledge that he had achieved something.

"Make way for me you lazy devil," he said to Bruno who had gone ahead and was lying on his back blocking the entrance to the house. Stretching over the dog to help himself to a ladle of water from the conca kept just inside the door, he chuckled and added, good humorously, "you have four legs, I only have one and a . . ."

The rest of the sentence was left unsaid as Petra, the wife of Sergio Ferucci who owned the house, came to the door and said,

"Sit out here and enjoy the fresh air."

Placing a chair in a shady spot near the door, she bustled round him in a motherly way.

Max's grasp of the Italian language was practically nil but the offer of the chair made understanding of Petra's words unnecessary. He knew from experience, that no amount of adjusting would prevent the chair from rocking on the uneven surface of the cobbled street, so didn't try to find a level patch. Smiling his gratitude, he seated himself and leant forward to pat Bruno, who immediately seized the opportunity to invite more affection by placing his head on Max's lap.

"Don't let her do that, she's dirty." Petra remonstrated.

Although Bruno was a dog, Petra always referred to him as she. Her previous dog had been a bitch and the habit formed over the years of ownership prevailed. Max hadn't understood what Petra had said and assumed it was something to do with making himself comfortable, so smiled his thanks and patted Bruno who wagged his tail and settled himself at Max's feet. Shrugging her shoulders and thinking, 'these Tedeschi are terrible people, yet he seems to be a nice boy,' she went back into the house.

The time passed swiftly, as Max relaxed and idly watched people pass by while reminiscing over events that happened long ago. It seemed an age since he was last home, yet recollections of almost insignificant things were still clear in his mind. Petra calling him in for the evening meal woke him from his day-dreams. Smiling over one of the memories his dreaming had evoked, he rose to go in.

As he crossed the threshold, Bruno nuzzled at his pocket. Remembering the cap, Max pulled it from his pocket and tried to read an embroidered label he had seen inside the sweat band. It was only then he realised how the light had faded.

The sight of his lost prize brought a gleam of joy into Bruno's eyes and he leaped up almost knocking Max over in his efforts to regain possession.

"*Va fuori*" Petra shouted raising a hand as she ordered the dog to go out.

Knowing it was best not to disobey, Bruno gave one last hopeful look at the cap and scuttled outside.

"What have you there?" Petra asked as Max returned the cap to his pocket and settled himself at the table.

Max looked at Petra and gave her an enquiring look, he wished his knowledge of Italian was more than a few words.

Sergio, who had just entered, having returned from a days work in the field repeated the question in halting German.

"Something the dog found," Max replied.

"Let me see it." There was a note of anxiety in Sergio's voice as he spoke.

Thinking, 'these people seem to get worried over the slightest thing,' Max handed the cap over and said,

"It's a German forage cap."

Wrinkling her nose in disgust, Petra said,

"It looks very dirty, would you like me to wash it for you?"

Even though Petra had spoken very slowly, Max didn't understand what she said, so looked at Sergio, who repeated the question in hesitating German. Nodding his thanks, Max handed the cap to her.

Petra took the cap and scraped a portion of the encrusted mud from it with her finger. Taking no notice of the still damp flakes which fell to the floor, she frowned at the residual stains and said,

"These stains look like blood, then turned up the band to read the label.

"*Hans Wenzel. Fur Gott und Vaterlandsliebe,*" she murmured, stumbling over the unfamiliar words as she read them.

Sergio snatched the cap from her and frowned as he read the label and said,

"I have heard that name before, it means trouble. Where did you find it?"

Sergio's brow furrowed as he tried to remember why the name meant trouble. He knew he had heard it, but couldn't think where.

Max looked at him blankly and shook his head.

Realizing Max hadn't understood, Sergio repeated the question in halting German.

Max only partly understood what Sergio wanted to say, but it was sufficient to enable him to answer. Speaking slowly in German and using simple words so that Sergio would understand what he was saying, he told him how Bruno had found the cap in the little patch of woods near the motor road.

While Max was speaking, Sergio continued to search his brain for the reason he remembered that name. Then, as Max mentioned the patch of woodland, memory came flooding back. He remembered Hans Wenzel was the name of a missing recruit who had disappeared the previous year. With it, came the memory of intensive searches and reprisals. Every available man had been used to comb the valley and foothills; even the distant villages had come under scrutiny. The soldier was never found and was posted as a deserter. Snatching the cap from Petra, he threw it on the fire.

Anxiously, as he watched the cap burn, Sergio wondered if the body of Hans Wenzel was lying in the soil where the cap had been found, he looked at Petra, who's face had paled as if she too had recalled the terrible events of a year ago. Not daring to voice his thoughts, he decided that no matter what the risks were, he would visit the copse that night and if the recent rains had brought a corpse into view, bury it. His mind made up, he said to Petra,

"Don't worry if I am late home from the dopolavoro. I will be setting a few traps."

With womanly intuition, Petra guessed what Sergio had in mind. She had a superstitious terror of the copse at night and could feel an icy band squeezing her chest as she said,

"Must you?"

Sergio gave a reassuring smile he didn't feel and said.

"Meat stocks are getting low and there is no curfew at the moment."

Listening to the exchange of words, which followed the burning of the cap and noticing the changes of expression as they were said, Max knew that something to do with the cap had upset them and wished he could understand what they were saying. Why? He wondered had Sergio been so disturbed and thrown the cap on the fire. Then, grinned inwardly and murmured to himself,

"What possessed me to put in my pocket? I don't think, even washed I would have fancied wearing it."

. . . .

The dopolavoro was alive with laughter when Sergio entered the smoke filled bar. Courteously refusing offers of a drink from various friends, he pressed through the crowd at the bar to reach the man he wanted to see. On reaching him, he said,

"Hallo Pietro, I haven't seen you for a long time," then lowering his voice as he spoke, "we must talk, it's a matter of urgency."

Pietro gave Sergio a shrewd look, he knew from the opening phrase, 'I haven't seen you,' that Sergio wanted to discuss clandestine matters. Following a leak, the group that both he and Sergio worked with had been inactive for several weeks. Nodding his understanding, he led the way to a table in the far corner of the room.

"We shouldn't be heard here, but be careful," he warned.

Speaking as quietly as he could, Sergio said,

"Briefly, the man billeted with me found a cap, which I believe belonged to that soldier who went missing last year. You remember there was quite a fuss at the time."

"Does he still have it?" Pietro's voice was sharp, "Where did he find it and when?"

"Today . . . my dog found it in *Il Bosco dei Vivente Morti*[39] when Max was taking him for a walk. It was very dirty and I threw it on the fire."

"That was a silly thing to do, was, . . . what's his name? . . . Max? annoyed?"

Sergio thought a moment before answering, then said with a note of conviction,

"I am sure he wasn't, if anything, I think he was glad to see it go."

Pietro's face paled, the thought of entering that copse, known as the woods of the living dead at night was daunting. Without revealing his superstitious fears, he said,

"Nevertheless, I think we should take precautions," he paused while re-filling the empty glasses, "I suggest we check out the copse tonight, if that soldiers body was buried there and has surfaced, the sooner it is re-buried the better."

"It's one of the reasons I am asking for your help. I don't mind burying it, but I will need a look-out that can be trusted."

Relieved that he wasn't being asked to enter the copse, Pietro said,

"You said one of the reasons, what was the other?"

"I can't speak German well enough to convey my thoughts to Max."

---

[39] Woods of the living dead.

"Which are?"

"I was thinking of asking him not to mention the finding of the cap to anyone, especially Loriano." Sergio replied in a not very convincing tone.

Pietro shook his head and frowned. It was obvious that he was not comfortable with the idea. Sergio looked anxiously at his friend who had risen from his chair and although the bottle on the table was still half full, was heading for the bar. When Pietro returned, now smiling, he was carrying two small glasses of grappa. Seating himself back at the table, the smile broadened into a grin as he said,

"I think better when I'm walking and getting this seemed a good excuse."

Sergio emitted a throaty chuckle, emptied the contents of his glass down his throat and said,

"Who needs an excuse?"

For a while after Pietro seated himself. The only sound was that of the hum of voices in the background and an almost inaudible rattle from the glass he was twirling on the table. When Pietro finally spoke, he began by saying,

"Not a good idea, the least said about Loriano, the better." there followed another long silence which Sergio was unwilling to break, lest it would disturb Pietro's thoughts.

"As I see it," the words came suddenly, "we must be careful not to rouse the man's suspicions. The suggestion that if the wrong people hear about his finding of the cap, it might raise enquiries, which would delay his repatriation, might be the way to proceed."

Sergio, lit a cigarette then without making comment, waited for Pietro to proceed. Very nearly seven minutes passed before Pietro spoke again, when he did, he said

"When I heard that Max was making enquiries about a woman, who lives in La Villa. I began to wonder if she was behind the leak that has been plaguing us. It was a suspicion that seemed to be backed up when I heard Loriano claim to know her." Pietro paused and rummaged in his pockets for the wherewithal to roll a cigarette. Then added, with an almost malicious grin "I wondered if she is the reason he is often away from town for several weeks at a time."

"Have one of these," Sergio said, offering him a crumpled pack of *Tres Stella*.

Pietro gladly accepted the offer which he lit with a minute wax match. Expelling the smoke slowly, he watched it curl its way to the ceiling before continuing with,

"I decided to visit friends in La Villa and pose a few discreet questions. It seems, she is probably Ida di Lorenzo. According to my sources, although Loriano visits her from time to time, she can be trusted."

Sergio's brow furrowed as he took in the information, he didn't say anything, but reading the expression on his face, Pietro, said in a serious tone,

"Believe me those sources are impeccable."

Somewhat relieved, Sergio took another cigarette from the pack he had laid on the table and bent forward to accept a light from the cigarette that Pietro was smoking. Murmuring his thanks, he said.

"You said something about not rousing Max's suspicions, what had you in mind?"

"I will explain later, . . . before making up my mind, I will have to talk to Max. Try and keep him in the house until I have done so. I'll come round first thing in the morning." Pietro said as he stubbed out the end of his cigarette and stowed it carefully away in a small bag he had taken from his pocket. Then, glanced out of the window and added "It's dark enough to set those traps, finish your drink and we will get moving."

Fortune favoured, there was no moon to light up the area. Hoping that the dark blur of trees ahead would cancel out the vague shapes of their bodies a star studded sky could reveal, the two men approached their target. Motioning to Pietro to stand close to the edge of the copse so that his outline could not be seen, Sergio studied a patch of undergrowth that appeared to have been disturbed.

"I think this is where Max tried to enter," he whispered.

Taking care while parting the tangle of growth not to snap any twigs, Sergio succeeded in reaching the disturbed area where Bruno had been digging. Apart from a patch of loosened earth, everything seemed normal. Using the shovel he had with him, he started spreading leaves and rotting vegetation over the patch. As he did so, the shovel caught on something that offered resistance, then he saw it; the tip of a boot. Deciding that to rebury the body would take too long and create a section difficult to conceal, he shovelled earth and leaves over the boot and hid his handiwork by dragging the roots of a fallen tree over the area. Repairing the damage he had done took time, and the first grey streaks of dawn were in the sky when, tired but triumphant he emerged and said with a grin, "Nobody is likely to go in there looking for firewood."

....

The distant sound of a clock striking the half hour warned Pietro that it was well past seven in the morning and he hoped it wasn't too late to stop Max from taking his morning exercise. With Sergio words, '*I will try and keep the young man in. He is determined to get fit and goes out every morning on his crutches; he is nearly always away for forty minutes or so. He is so keen, he doesn't even have a cup of coffee first.*' ringing in his ears, Pietro quickened his steps and cursed himself for sitting down for five minutes and falling asleep. His intention had been to have a quick wash and change of clothes only.

"I should have known that would happen" he muttered.

Pietro needn't have worried, Max was still in the house when he arrived and greeted him with the words,

"It's a pleasure to meet you Pietro, my friend Sergio says you can speak my language. That is good. Will you tell him how grateful I am for the way he and his wife have been looking after me."

As Pietro translated the words and passed them on, Petra came in to the room and motioning them to sit at the table, said,

"You are early, Pietro, Sergio told me you were coming. Have you eaten? Of course not, there wouldn't have been time. We are about to have our *prima colazione*[40], (It was typical of Petra, who liked to be precise, to use the full term for the morning meal rather than the usual abbreviation) you must join us."

Smiling his thanks, Pietro poured olive oil on one of the massive slices that Petra had cut, sprinkled it with salt, then, turned to Max and said,

"Do you like our bread?"

Max nodded, and said,

"I quite like the way you put oil and salt on it." Then added with a grin, "Not as much as black pudding and sausages though."

---

[40] First meal of the day (usually abbreviated to colazione.)

The comment brought a laugh from both Pietro and Sergio, who had picked up the word sausages and guessed the rest, and a look of interrogation from Petra, who said,

"What did he say?"

"He said he likes the bread, but prefers black pudding and sausage," Pietro explained.

Following on from his comment, Max said,

"I will bring some if they like,"

Pietro waited until the meal was finished before broaching the reason for his visit. He started by asking about Max's home in Germany, and chatted generally about the comforts of home and how sad it was that so many young men could not be with their families. When he felt he had gained the young German's confidence, he said,

"Sergio tells me Bruno found a hat in the copse, but it was so dirty. he put it on the fire. A bit naughty of him wasn't it? I hope you didn't mind."

Max laughed, it was a high pitched sound, almost girlish and said,

"I had already regretted bringing it home, I don't know what possessed me, but you know how it is; you do things on the spur of the moment, without thinking."

"That's true," Pietro agreed,

Pietro was pleased with the way things were developing; he was even more pleased when Max said,

"On second thoughts, I realised that if found to be wearing a cap with someone else's name in it, I could be accused of stealing it."

Quick to seize the opportunity, Pietro said,

"The last thing you want is an enquiry that would delay your repatriation."

Max put a hand on Pietro's arm and in a vaguely anxious tone, said,

"I hadn't thought of that. If word gets about that I found a cap and didn't report it, I could be in serious trouble. You won't say anything, I hope."

Pietro smiled disarmingly and said,

"Of course not, we are friends aren't we?"

Max breathed a sigh of relief and glanced towards Sergio. Divining his thoughts, Pietro said,

"You don't have to worry about Sergio and Petra, they won't say anything."

Hearing her name mentioned, Petra gave Sergio an enquiring look, which, engrossed in trying to follow the conversation, he failed to notice.

Exasperated by his lack of attention and assailed by pessimistic thoughts, she said sharply,

"Sergio. What did he say?"

Surprised by the tone, Sergio stopped listening, to answer and missed the suggestion made by Pietro,

"Sergio tells me you have a friend in La Villa that you would like to visit. I can borrow a donkey if you don't mind riding one."

Max chuckled as he pictured himself astride the animal and said,

"She is not a friend, I don't even know her. People she met when visiting some relations of hers asked me to pass on their regards if I was ever near that village. I hope to be home soon, so it would be nice to be able to tell them that I met her." Max paused and smiled as he added, "Of course I don't mind riding a donkey, five legs have to be better than one and a bit."

"What's that about five legs?" Sergio asked, with a puzzled frown."

Max and Pietro looked at each other and both of them burst out laughing.

Irritated by her inability to understand what had been said that caused such merriment, Petra started clearing the table. The short quick movements she was using, sent a clear message, not only to Sergio but also to Pietro, who guessing she might be thinking they were laughing at her quickly ran through the gist of what had been said. Then followed with an a outline of the arrangements he had been making with Max.

Somewhat mollified, Petra made a mental measurement of Max as she looked him up and down and said,

"You can't go into that village in uniform. Even if you have Pietro with you, they will think you want to arrest her. I can fit you up with some clothes, they might not fit very well, but small clothes on a big man is not such an uncommon sight, so nobody is going to take any notice. If they do, they will probably think you are a refugee from a Concentration camp."

Max cast an enquiring look at Pietro who translated what had been suggested.

Smiling his thanks, Max said,

"That sounds a sensible idea."

CHAPTER TWENTYFIVE

The arrival of Max in La villa brought exclamations of sympathy from all who saw his handicap and a worried frown to the brow of Giorgio. A few days earlier Angelo had brought him news that Ida was expecting a visit from Loriano during the coming week and the presence of a German when he and Gianni tackled the OVRA officer was the last thing he wanted.

"Why didn't Angelo's contact put the man's visit off till next week?" He said to Gianni, who stood beside him, "It wasn't much to ask."

"Perhaps he is hoping to be on his way back to Germany by then," Gianni commented as he stepped out of the fringe of trees on the edge of the forest area that overlooked La villa and the grass slope beyond the houses, so that he could see the street that fronted Ida's house.

Together, they watched Pietro tether the donkey and help Max dismount. Then both were lost to view. Since the door to Ida's house was not visible, it was reasonable to assume that Pietro and Max had gone inside.

"Not much point in going down there," Gianni said, with a wry smile, "we'll have to hope our suspect doesn't come today."

"If he does, we'll cross that bridge then," Giorgio replied as he settled himself on a log large enough for them both to share.

Making himself comfortable beside Giorgio, Gianni pulled out a packet of Players and said.

"I expect it's a long time since you saw one of these, would you like one?"

"It is, but no thank you, I haven't smoked for a while now, so don't tempt me."

When darkness fell, there was only the thin sliver of a new moon to cast its rays on the unlit street. The vague dark shadow of the donkey against the wall of the house was the only indication that Pietro and Max were still inside.

"They are leaving it late," Giorgio said, glancing at the luminous dial of his watch.

The words were scarcely out of Giorgio's mouth when a faint ray of light, partly obscured by vague moving shadows appeared on the paving. When a brief glimpse of Max on the donkey and Pietro leading it as they passed through the area lit by the open door, indicated that Ida's visitors were leaving, Gianni gave a sigh of relief and said,

"I wouldn't think Loriano is likely to come now. I wonder why they left it so late, it's inviting trouble."

"Not really," Giorgio replied, "You forget Max is a German soldier on convalescent leave and would have the documents to prove it. He only has to tell them he is visiting family friends and Pietro is helping him, to keep Pietro out of trouble."

Three days passed, three days with no appearance of Loriano. Giorgio was beginning to wonder if he had been given wrong information until he saw the broad shoulders of a figure wearing a light coloured jacket slip quietly across the grass slope behind Ida's house.

"Didn't Ida say that Loriano doesn't worry about being seen; I hope he hasn't been warned that we are on the lookout for him." Gianni said.

"If he has, he is not the man we are looking for. I must admit he doesn't look a bit like the man I thought it would be."

"Which means we must look for someone closer to home, you mean," A note of suspicion crept into Gianni's voice, "do you think it could be ..." Whatever he was about to say was left unsaid.

Thinking if he really believes whoever he has in mind is guilty he will tell me, Giorgio gave Gianni a shrewd look and said,

"Think about it Gianni, remember suspicion is purely conjecture. Meanwhile, I suggest we carry on as originally intended." Then, with a broad smile, added, "you had better tell your friends to get ready for action. I will be behind the houses a few doors away from Ida's house."

Without voicing his surprise that Giorgio knew about the secret arrangements he had made with Donnola, Gianni sped up the woodland path that led to the charcoal burner's hut.

Waiting in the shadow of the houses for Gianni to return seemed an eternity to Giorgio. Actually less than ten minutes had gone by when Gianni, accompanied by two men wearing a purple bandanna to mask their faces. joined him. That Gianni had also pulled his bandanna over his face, didn't surprise Giorgio. The importance, if reprisals on the village were to be avoided, of the abduction of Loriano being attributed to the ribelli, had been discussed at some length with Donnola, who finally agreed that since Loriano was not a resident of La Villa such knowledge would not alienate the villagers.

A few quick strides took Giorgio to the back door of Ida's house, which he opened without knocking. Ida and Roberto were nowhere to be seen and Giorgio assumed they were probably upstairs. A man was standing with his back to the room gazing through the window. Giorgio wondered if some movement had caught his attention. The figure he presented was a little shorter than it had appeared to be when seen flitting across the grass towards Ida's house. Broad in shoulder and slim of hip was as Ida had described Loriano, but the shoulders were unnaturally broad. The padded shoulders reminded Giorgio of the jackets worn by American gangsters during the years of prohibition; as depicted in films he had seen in his younger days.

Giorgio had barely taken a step into the room when Loriano, with a cat like lithe movement, swung round. Mutual recognition was instantaneous. With the speed of light, Loriano's hand drew a pistol from a shoulder holster hidden beneath his jacket and fired a shot. With equal speed, Giorgio performed a flying double somersault which would have been the envy of a professional all in wrestler. The bullet tore through the loose sleeve of Giorgio's shirt; barely missing Gianni, who, followed by his two companions, had just come through the door. At the same time as the bullet hit the wall, bringing down a small shower of stone chippings, before ricocheting and burying itself in the wooden beams of the ceiling, Giorgio's feet landed on Loriano's chest. The force of the contact slammed Loriano into the front door, and caused him to drop the gun.

Quick to recover, Loriano aimed a kick at Giorgio's head (which failed to reach its target) and cast a glance around to see where his gun had landed. Seeing the three partisans rapidly crossing the room, Loriano realised the futility of resistance and made a desperate attempt to flee through the front door in to the street. The three partisans stationed outside, Sten guns ready, stopped him in his tracks. He put up his hands in surrender.

....

The Tribunal, presided over by a governing member of the *Partito d' Azione*, who, in happier days had been a judge, was assembled in a deserted house high on the slopes of Monte Corno. Defending Loriano was a partisan, calling himself Volpe who claimed to have been training as a lawyer (in reality he was a junior filing clerk in a solicitors office) when dragged into the army. He was not very expert, but it sufficed to satisfy the judge that justice was being done; even though all they had for a jury was seven partisans.

Opening the proceedings as Prosecuting Counsel, Giorgio said,

"There are two charges. The first charge being that while posing as a released POW you served with a group known as the Scolopendre. Using the name Lori, you betrayed them. We will seek to prove that after you left the Scolopendre to join a party attempting to cross the line to Allied territory you contrived to reveal the location of the Scolopendre head quarters to the enemy. You also betrayed the men who thought they were helping you. How do you plead?"

"The betrayal of the party crossing the line is not relevant to the charge presented." Volpe objected.

There was a moments silence, then the Judge said,

"Your objection is upheld. Watch your comments. Prosecutor."

"My apologies *Signor'*," Giorgio replied as he tried to hide a feeling of satisfaction.

The Judge looked at Loriano and said,

"How do you plea?"

"Not guilty. I don't..."

The judge raised his hand to silence him and said,

"You can have your say later."

Continuing his indictment, Giorgio said,

"The second charge is that while posing as a released prisoner of war, named Gordon, you joined a group, or groups attempting to cross the line and betrayed them. For some time now, the activities of the evasion groups have been plagued by betrayals, and you Loriano are accused of being the perpetrator. We will seek to prove that on two known occasions while claiming to be a released prisoner of war you joined a party of personnel attempting to cross the line and enter Allied territory, then revealed their location to the Germans. Do you plead guilty or not guilty?"

Loriano didn't reply immediately, when he did, his plea came in a firm and clear voice.

"Not Guilty."

The first witness to be called was the partisan known as Grillo.

"Do you recognise the prisoner in the dock?" Giorgio asked.

"Yes" came the reply, "he is the partisan, Lori."

"Are you sure?" Volpe cut in without waiting to see whether Giorgio had further questions.

The judge frowned but did not comment,

"Of course I'm sure, partisans are a close group, living together, practically a family." The resentment to the question Grillo felt, was obvious in the way he added, "If you did your duty in the mountains, you would know that."

"I am a serving partisan," Volpe replied hotly, his face a picture of indignation.

"Then you should know better," Grillo retorted.

While Giorgio turned his head so that the grin he knew was on his face would not be seen, the judge, ignoring the titter of amusement from the Jury, coughed and covered his mouth with a handkerchief.

Receiving a nod from his look of enquiry at the judge, Giorgio continued his questioning with,

"What makes you believe that Lori as you knew him was the man who betrayed you?"

"Our secret location was raided so soon after he left. . . . We were quite a small band, and nobody other than our comrades would have known where it . . ."

"What about the Staffettini?" Volpe almost shouted.

"Those children can be trusted, but even they only know where to find a look-out," Grillo retorted.

"That is not proof," Volpe butted in again."

This time, the judge spoke sharply,

"You must not interrupt Counsellor. I will not warn you again."

Resenting the rebuke and red faced with embarrassment, Volpe sat down. As he resumed his seat, he muttered something uncomplimentary under his breath.

"Speak up Counsellor, what did you say?"

"My apologies *Signor'*," Volpe lied.

Dismissing Grillo, Giorgio said,

"I have no more questions for you at this stage Grillo, you may go. If necessary, we will call you again. I now call upon Guido."

Guido, an athletic looking young man in his mid twenties seemed to glide into the room, taking up his position and not waiting to be asked, he pointed to Loriano and said,

"That is Gordon, he is the man who betrayed us."

"Ignore that remark Jury," the judge said, then addressing Giorgio added, "please proceed."

"Do you recognise the man in the dock?" As he posed the question, Giorgio couldn't help thinking this question is superfluous but it has to be asked.

"Yes," came Guido's prompt reply. "He is the ex-partisan named Gordon who was with our party, he was missing just before the Tedeschi surrounded us."

"Where were you at the time? . . . Why weren't you taken prisoner with the rest?"

"Francesco, our escort and I were reconnoitring. We saw what happened, but could do nothing about it. When the Tedeschi saw us, they started shooting; it was then that Francesco was wounded."

"That is all for now," Giorgio said then, turned to Volpe and followed with, "have you any questions?"

Quick to seize his opportunity, Volpe sprang to his feet.

"You say you are a guide called Guido. Is that your real name?"

For a moment a hush fell on the courtroom, all were amazed that such a question should be asked. Then, before Guido could answer the question, using terse tones the judge said,

"The witness is not on trial, you needn't answer that Guido."

Somewhat exasperated and feeling frustrated, Volpe sat down.

"As further evidence that the man in the dock has been spying on our activities, I now call upon another guide, who is also known as Guido."

In answer to the question, 'do you know the man in the dock?' Gino said,

"He is Peter, one of the men in a party I was guiding; which was surrounded by the Tedeschi." Gino hesitated for a moment before resuming. "I am surprised to see him here . . . we all thought he was dead."

"Why aren't any of the men in the group being called to back up your statement?" Volpe asked when given the chance to question Gino.

"Bringing them back from Allied territory would be a little difficult."

Gino's reply brought another titter of merriment from the jury and a note of authority from the judge who, assuming a severe aspect, he didn't really feel, said,

"Let's have a little less levity."

When Luigi's sergeant major was called, he had no objection to his name, Ricardo Florio di Tirane being revealed and volunteered it. Answering all questions thrown at him first by Giorgio and then by Volpe, he gave a clear account of Tina's suspicions as being the reason they tried to intercept the group Gino was guiding and were on hand to effect the rescue. Confirming that the personnel in the group could not be called, he commented that although Il Capitano and himself were told that Peter had been shot, an intensive search failed to find any trace of his body. When asked if he recognised the man in the dock, he replied,

"Not to be certain . . . I couldn't swear to it. I only met Lori once when he was with the Scolopendre and the man named Peter he is accused of being was missing from the group we rescued"

When it was his turn to ask questions, Volpe rose from his seat. With an expression of anticipated triumph on his face he strode quickly across the floor and confronted Florio at close quarters.

"The only thing your evidence confirms, Tirane, is that you were on hand to rescue the party. On your own admission you didn't see the man on trial when you rescued the group. The suspicions of Tina are nothing more than hearsay," he almost bellowed, bringing his face close to that of the sergeant major.

"Tina is here if you wish to call her," Ricardo said in a cold matter of fact voice."

Volpe looked at the judge, who, while nodding his head in assent, said,

"This isn't a theatrical play . . . you must not try to intimidate the witness."

Having confirmed that her name was Vincenzo Tina, Tina said,

"I first saw that man when delivering a message to the Scolopendre. I commented that he looked like an Englishman and was told that he was called Lori. A few weeks later, when he was in a group being assembled by Francesco, he told me he was Private Gordon Spink, that after he was released from a Concentration camp, he spent a while in the mountains with a band of partisans, but now wanted to get home.

"What made him give you that information?" Volpe's tone was full of disbelief.

"Part of my duties as a staffetta[41] working for Francesco and other agents is to record the names of personnel being assembled. Before you ask," she added with a saucy grin, "no I don't have a horse."

The judge hid a smile and busied himself with some papers then whispered something to the clerk taking notes of the proceedings.

Continuing her statement, Tina said,

"Some time later, I thought I saw that man in the dock while visiting friends and believed it was Gordon. He was introduced as Peter, a released prisoner of war spending the winter under their roof. I knew, from what Francesco told me, that Gordon was missing just before the Tedeschi arrived and had probably been taken prisoner with the rest of his group; the man staying with my friends was so much like Gordon, they could have been twins. When he told me he didn't have a brother, I began to suspect he might be a spy so spent some time talking to him under the pretence that I wanted to practise my English. On my way back to the house where I was staying, I mentioned my thoughts to Filomena. At the time she laughed them off. Later however something happened to change her mind. Filomena isn't here, but her father is."

Giorgio taken by surprise, pondered a few minutes over Tina's statement, '*I thought I saw that man in the dock while visiting friends.*' Then, with more than a note of disappointment in his voice, said,

"Why do you now say you thought you saw him? What made you change your mind?"

"I spent a long time talking to Peter that evening, and would have noticed that mole."

"Did Gordon have a mole on the neck?" Giorgio said, hopefully.

"I don't know, he was wearing a Scolopendre bandanna tied round his neck," came the disappointing reply.

Before Giorgio could continue his questioning, Volpe sprang to his feet; almost shouting in his excitement he declared,

---

[41] Adult courier. (Derived from horse riding messenger carrying dispatches etc.)

"That proves the man is innocent," then addressing the judge, "You should bring in a no case to answer verdict."

The judge, obviously ruffled glared at Volpe and said,

"Don't tell me what to do. Sit down and behave with more decorum."

At that point, Grillo rose to his feet, bowed to the Judge and asked permission to speak.

After a interrogative look at Giorgio and Volpe, the judge nodded.

"Lori had that mole, it is the reason I could be so certain that the man in the dock is him." Grillo turned to face Volpe and added contemptuously, "The witness saying the man called Gordon was wearing our emblem is proof that Lori and Gordon are one and the same person."

"Ignore that comment, it is not necessarily proof," the judge instructed the jury.

The last to be called was Angelo, who gave evidence that the 'Safe House' used for the assembly was destroyed two days after the party, with Peter in it, had left. His account of the conversation overheard by Filomena was challenged as hearsay by Volpe and upheld by the judge.

During his summary, the judge pointed out to the jury that hearsay evidence should be ignored, he also said that they should give careful consideration to the statements made relating to the similar brief periods of time that elapsed, after Lori left the Scolopendre and the group that Peter was with left the 'Safe House' where they assembled, before the Germans arrived. He also pointed out that both parties being surrounded and taken prisoner could be coincidental. He then reminded them that evidence given indicated that Peter had been shot when the group was surrounded. The fact that Peter's body couldn't be found was not proof that he hadn't been shot. When finalising his instructions to the jury, he finished by saying,

"Think carefully when reviewing the evidence about that mole on the neck. If you have any doubts re the identity of Peter, you must bring in a verdict of 'not guilty or not proven.' on the second charge."

The jury was gone for barely ten minutes before returning a verdict of guilty on both charges.

. . . .

Gianni felt sick, he had spent a sleepless night and his hands trembled as he tried to fashion a cigarette from foul smelling, recycled cigarette butts. He was not a newcomer to killing and there had been times, when it seemed there was only the war, the wounded and the dead. But this was different, he had never fired at an unarmed person before, least of all someone he might have met and drank wine with; he didn't relish the thought. Having been a caparol maggiore in the Italian army he knew orders had to be obeyed. What had to be done, had to be done. The judge in passing sentence had ordered it.

Finally succeeding in rolling his cigarette he struck a match on the steel tip of a boot and drew gratefully on the cigarette. Breathing in the acrid smoke, his nerves calmed.

"Are you ready Lepre?" The voice of Migale sounded unnaturally loud.

Gianni rose stiffly from the rock where he had been sitting, smoothed his well worn army jacket, which still bore the insignia of his rank and crossed the small area that separated him from the hut where Loriano was being held. He was joined a few minutes later by Migale, wearing the ochre coloured bandanna with its embroidered millipede, worn by members of the Scolopendre, tied round his neck. Behind him was Grillo also wearing the bandanna of the Scolopendre and another, who Gianni didn't recognise, but knew from the green bandanna and black feather in his cap that he was one of Luigi's sharp shooters. Together, in silence, they entered the hut and led Loriano out.

Blinking with the strength of the rising sun on his face, Loriano angrily tried to shake off the hand that was gripping his arm and said,

"Let me walk free, I am not afraid of being murdered."

Ignoring the protest, Grillo tightened his grip and forced Loriano to quicken the pace.

Standing stiff legged against a tree, Loriano tore the blindfold from his eyes, raised his arm in the fascist salute and shouted,

"*Viva Il Duce*," then, in English, "Long live Mosley and the . . . "

The hollow, rapid cackle of two lightweight machine guns mingling with the sharp crack of a rifle, cut short what he was going to say; his blood, blending with the dark red bark of the beech tree behind him, he sunk to the ground.

Migale grim faced and solemn, walked quickly over to administer the coup de grace, turned and said,

"Bury him deep, so that the wolves don't get him and mark the spot well, his folk might wish to move him."

CHAPTER TWENTYSIX

The long hot summer was drawing to its close and stories of the activities in the forward areas brought by the ever increasing flow of refugees were as varied as their frequency. All told of ferocious and prolonged battles with the Tedeschi on the losing end. Stories that brought hope of a finish to the war, accompanied by the natural fear of what would happen if where they lived became a battle ground.

Two weeks had passed since the trial and execution of Loriano, two weeks of intensive activity for the partisans who were constantly on the move, harassing the German forces at every conceivable opportunity. In contrast, with most of the occupying forces hurrying to the forward area a feeling of peace and tranquillity (despite the now daily passage of allied aircraft flying north) reigned over the valley and surrounding areas.

With operations on hold for the section of the Partito d'Azione involved in the evasion programmes, there was time to relax, a luxury they couldn't usually afford. Notwithstanding this, Giorgio was kept busy with all manner of duties many of which were only remotely connected with his work of organising the crossings. So, it was with unexpected delight that Filomena saw his tall figure heading for the track that led to her house. Resisting the temptation to run down the track to meet him, she rushed indoors and changed the dress she was wearing for one she didn't normally use for every day wear. After a quick brush of her hair and a glance in a mirror to make sure it was tidy, Filomena reached the door of the house as Giorgio came into view across the tiny courtyard.

"Hallo Filomena," he said in his usual straight faced way, "is Angelo about?"

"He is in the fields, its the vendemmia, but he shouldn't be long." Filomena smiled hopefully and added, "will you be staying with us tonight? The spare bed is ready."

"If I may."

Filomena was irrationally pleased to see just the hint of a smile on his face as he replied.

....

Giorgio's business with Angelo concluded, the three relaxed in the fresh air of the evening. With the almost obligatory flask of wine and bottle of grappa on the table, talk inevitably turned to the recent trial and verdict.

"I don't altogether agree with the verdict on the second charge," Giorgio commenced, "I must admit that I was somewhat taken aback when Tina said that about the mole."

"Does it really matter?" Angelo commented and looked at Giorgio, who raised his eyebrows and said,

"I suppose not, but carry on."

"Originally I was sceptical, when Filomena came to me with her theories about Gordon and Peter being the same spy using two different aliases."

A ripple of laughter, drowned Angelo's voice as Filomena, her eyes bright with amusement said,

"Oh Babbo, you were more than sceptical, you were scornful at first and said I was talking nonsense."

Angelo gave his daughter a benevolent look and said,

"If you say so. . . . After talking with Migale, I had no doubt in my mind that the man calling himself Gordon was the spy that betrayed Francesco. But, because of the reports that Peter was shot when the group was captured, I still had my doubts about Gordon and Peter being the same man using different pseudonyms. However, when I saw Loriano in the dock, I changed my mind. There certainly was an extraordinary likeness. Without that mole, only intimate friends could have told the difference. The thing that then puzzled me is how the Tedeschi knew about the movements in time to muster the raiding party. It had to be someone in the party or a watcher able to pass some sort of signal, it's been done before."

"The Sicilian was still around then and we know, from Ida, he had radio facilities and was in regular contact with Loriano." Giorgio said, then added. "What worries me now is that even when I knew Loriano was north, conferring with the Salo government, false leaks I arranged were followed up so quickly and still are, even though Loriano is dead . . . I can only think there must be another spy with radio facilities in the area."

Giorgio was up early the following morning, refusing more than a slice of bread and a cup of black coffee, he said,

"I have things to attend to which will keep me busy for several days. All the signs are that the Allies are ready to make a push. I think you will be safe enough here, it's well away from La Villa. Nevertheless, although it is unlikely any of the retreating forces will come up this far, it would be wise to get in to the hills and stay out of sight."

Watching Giorgio drink his coffee, Filomena couldn't help wondering how he could drink the large cup of watered down black coffee with no sugar which he seemed to prefer to the tiny cup of strong, syrupy coffee that both she and Angelo liked.

There was only the smallest sliver of sun showing over the horizon when Giorgio rose abruptly from the table and with a cheery, "Take care." was gone.

Tears in her eyes, Filomena looked at her father and said,

"Babbo . . . I have a horrid presentiment we will never see him again."

Angelo hugged his daughter to him and in a bid to comfort her, said,

"Giorgio knows how to look after himself. He will be back before you know it . . . trust me."

. . . .

All was busy with expectation in the Transit camp on the outskirts of Sulmona. Orders had been given to assemble in the outside pens ready to leave, and the inmates; some still in uniform, others in civilian clothing, deduced that it was a clear indication the German forces were anticipating a retreat.

Reluctantly, boots were carefully marked for identification and handed in. There wasn't a prisoner of war watching the footwear loaded on to a lorry, that really believed he would ever see his own boots again. Mid-day came and mid-day went, as one by one, the men answered the roll call and walked through a gate in to the main compound. The roll call took time and seemed an eternity before eventually, all names had been called. Even then, the men had to wait in the open compound for close on an hour before canvas covered lorries arrived and they were ushered aboard. Sitting on the floor and packed like sardines, they knew the journey over rough roads was not going to be comfortable and the uncomplimentary comments made were many and varied. However, typical of their kind, their spirits remained high.

It was turned three in the afternoon when the convoy of ten lorries left the already deserted camp and took the road running north for Popoli. If, when the convoy turned off and headed for Capestrano, those who had been free for a while and knew the area, thought they were going to the camp at L'Aquila, they were mistaken. Nightfall found them at Teramo, where they were offloaded and crammed in to a number of small cells in what had at one time been a prison. Some of the graffiti on the walls were clear evidence that the cells had been occupied at one time or another by British Tommies and brought hoots of laughter from most of those who read, the not always repeatable, comments scrawled on the walls.

Despite the late start on the following day, the convoy was within a few kilometres of Guilanova, when shortly after mid-day it became a target for a squadron of aircraft which suddenly appeared in the sky.

The convoy ground to a hurried halt and the orders to take shelter were barely necessary as guards and prisoners alike sought refuge below or behind the solid structures of the vehicles. Within moments the squadron turned and swooped down towards the convoy, strafing it with a deadly hail of bullets.

Crouching below one of the vehicles and watching the spurts of dust as the bullets hit the ground one of the prisoners of war, said,

"I wish our boys weren't so bloody accurate."

His companion, who lay flat on the ground beside him laughed and said,

"Never mind that, Jack do you see what I see?"

"Nothing I want to." Jack grunted.

"You will this." The other said, as he rose to a crouched position and pointed to a rise in the ground which partly obscured a house around 100 metres away. Adding, "be ready to run as soon as this fly past is over." he started to run.

Jack, without stopping for thought, followed. The two men ran as they had never run before; each so intent on reaching the sanctuary offered before the planes returned that it didn't occur to them that they might be shot from behind by one of the guards, so ran in a straight line.

Reaching the top of the rise, they tumbled over each other as they rolled down a bank and out of sight from the convoy. Laughing, despite being out of breath, they rose to their feet. It was then that a man appeared in the doorway of the house. Smiling, to show his friendship, he beckoned and said,

"*Vieni* ... come." and held the door open for them to enter.

Having, before being re-captured, both experienced the helpful friendliness of the *Contadini* they didn't hesitate to accept the offered hospitality. Having sat them down he told them that he was called Enrico and his wife was named Fiora.

"I am Jack and he is Peter," Jack said by way of introduction.

. . . .

As the flow of refugees subsided, an air of freedom descended on the area around La Villa. For the first time in an age the marauding German groups out to steal what they could find were absent; for the first time in many months people felt able to relax. Even the increased frequency of aircraft flying north failed to disturb their new found peace of mind.

It was a dark night when flashes of gun-fire were first seen on the horizon. It was also the night that Michele heard a knock on the door. Since friends would normally knock and enter, he wondered who it could be and called out,

"Who is there?"

Receiving no answer, Michele picked up a stout cudgel, and cautiously opened the door. At first he could see nothing except the blurred outline of Leone wagging his tail and gazing at someone, or something out of sight. Thinking, whoever it is must be a friend or Leone wouldn't be acting that way, he stepped out into the open and looked towards the barn.

"Hallo Michele." The voice came from behind him.

It was a voice Michele recognised, a voice he had never expected to hear again, there was no mistaking the accent.

"Pietro! . . . We thought you were dead," he shouted as he warmly embraced, a thought to be dead, friend.

The shouted greeting brought Guiseppina hurrying to the door, closely followed by Vincensina; even Caterina rose to her feet.

"Pietro . . . Pietro." Tears in her eyes - tears of joy, not sadness; Giuseppina pushed past Michele in her eagerness to embrace Peter. Such was her emotion, she couldn't speak as she hugged him to her. In the background, she was dimly aware of her mother saying,

"Come in Pietro, be comfortable, have you eaten, are you thirsty? Look at your feet, they're bleeding. Where are your shoes? I'll bring a bowl of water and dress them, hurry now, it's a cold night, you can do that inside." The words came tumbling out in rapid, disjointed succession as Vincensina pushed the pair over the threshold and through the door.

Michele smiled broadly as a silly thought struck him, 'how can she dress and wash his shoes?' then threw a log on the fire and rushed to fetch a bowl, which he filled with warm water. Sprinkling a little salt in it, he placed the bowl under the table, drew a chair close and said,

"Soak your feet in that Pietro, it will ease them, Vincensina will bind them later."

With remarkable speed, a steaming plate laden with boiled maize tagliarello and black beans was placed before Peter. Having not eaten that day, he lost no time in breaking the bread lying in the centre of the table and dipping a spoon into the mixture.

The heat of the fire, a substantial meal and the effects of a long day had the inevitable result.

Peter could feel his eyes drooping and fought to keep awake. Dimly aware that Giuseppina was pressing a pillow behind him his eyes closed.

Peter didn't sleep long, barely more than an hour. He woke, feeling amazingly refreshed. While sleeping, Vincensina had smeared his feet with a soothing oil and swathed them in aromatic leaves before lifting them on to a low stool. Michele, fiddling with his pipe by the fireside didn't realise that Peter had recovered, until he heard Giuseppina say,

"Hallo Pietro are you awake"

Raising his head, he looked at Peter, who was now sitting upright in his chair and without voicing his thought, which were 'silly girl; she can see he is,' said,

"Are you comfortable Pietro?"

Peter nodded and reached out for a mug of water that had been placed on the table beside him.

Just then, Vincensina came bustling in from outside. Seeing that Peter was now awake, she said,

"I have prepared a bed for you in the stable, you can sleep there for tonight. Tomorrow, Michele will take you to a special safe place."

As Vincensina finished speaking, the door opened and Mario, closely followed by Luciana walked in.

"What are you doing here" Mario demanded, giving Peter a suspicious look.

Seeing the look and guessing the thoughts, Michele said,

"Of course, you have been away, so won't have heard the results of the Tribunal, Peter is not a spy. His innocence has been proved beyond any doubt."

Somewhat mollified, but still mildly suspicious, Mario said,

"I hope you're right," then turning to Peter added, without embracing him. "Glad to see you. So you are not dead after all."

The statement caught Peter by surprise, he gave a puzzled look to Michele, who said,

"We were told you were taken outside and shot."

"I always knew you were alive and weren't the spy." Giuseppina cut in, looking fondly at Peter and placing a hand on one of his arms.

This time it was Michele's turn to look surprised as in a tone of disbelief, he said,

"I thought our suspicions had been kept from you."

Giuseppina just smiled, almost secretively, but made no comment.

"I think I know how that came about," Peter said, "It's a long story, but I will be as brief as possible."

"But you are tired, you should rest," Vincensina's voice was full of concern.

Ignoring Vincensina's words, Michele produced a bottle of sambuca from seemingly nowhere and placed it beside the almost obligatory bottle of grappa already on the table. With the impish grin, he knew how to make, he pointed to the two bottles and said,

"Not too tired for this," then looking at his wife and the two girls, he grinned even more broadly and chuckled as he added, "and you three won't say no to sambuca.

The customary toasting over, Peter began by saying,

"As I said, it's a long story so I will just give you the outlines." He paused to collect his thoughts, then continued in a mixture of English and Italian, which his listeners found difficult to follow, until Mario suggested that he should speak in English and he would interpret. Starting again, he said, "You obviously know we were surrounded and all in the group with the exception of our guide Guido were captured.

I suppose he told you about it. What puzzles me is how he could have known about me being taken out of the house . . . I've never been more frightened than when I was led out with a gun stuck in my back, it made me desperate enough to make a dash for it. The man fired at me, but missed, I'm glad he only had a pistol and wasn't very expert. By the time he had taken aim again I was in the bushes. There was a little path which I raced down, it ended in an open area, which I crossed as fast as I could. There was a barbed wire fence the other side; don't think I've ever seen that before in Italy. Any way I crossed it and kept going.

When Peter paused to take a drink of water from the mug at his elbow, Michele rose to his feet to replenish glasses and said,

"A group of partisans rescued the others who had heard a shot just after you were taken outside and thought you had been killed."

For the first time that evening Peter laughed,

"So that's what the rumpus was about, I hard it from a distance. Believe me, I wasn't in the mood to turn back to see what was going on . . . I spent the night under a tree." Peter laughed again. "It proved to be a colony of pigs favourite truffle source. They woke me in no uncertain manner. Anyway, to cut a long story short. Having decided to attempt the crossing on my own, I was nearly home and dry when I ran in to a group of Germans reconnoitring the area and ended up in a small Concentration camp near Sulmona. We were being transported further North when the opportunity to make a bid for freedom presented itself . . . and here I am."

The following morning Michele took Peter to the converted house and left him there. It was a fine morning with a clarity which enabled even the tops of the mountains to be seen. Michele looked about him, relishing the almost unnatural calmness that seemed to be in the air. Suddenly the calm was shattered by the sound of aircraft flying south as if returning home. When they dived, and the distant sound of bombs being dropped came to his ears, Michele stared into the distance and saw that the fighting planes had been joined by bombers. Remote from any motor road as Casa dei Pioppi was, Michele had no fears that a retreating army would come near his residence. Nevertheless, he was taking no chances, hurrying back to the house, he looked quickly in the stable to see if Ernesto was still there. He wasn't surprised to see it empty, in fact, the reverse, he would have been surprised if Ernesto had not already left for work in the fields.

With his womenfolk safely ensconced with Peter in the converted old house, Michele joined by Mario stood on the cliff like edge of the escarpment and watched a distant cloud of dust slowly develop into a mixed medley of lorries, tanks and armoured cars; that was a retreating army.

Across the valley, on the grass slopes above La Villa, several groups of people could be seen heading for the mountain paths beyond the belt of woodland. Anxiously, Mario scanned the area through a powerful pair of binoculars as he desperately tried to locate Donnina and Dora.

"Can't see a sign of them," he said.

Michele lowered his glasses and said,

"If you mean Donnina and Dora, I think they are in that small group to the left and just above the church. Lend me your binoculars, they are stronger than mine.

As he handed his binoculars to Michele, Mario gave a sigh of relief and said,

"You are right, Ida and her little boy are with them, I'm not sure who the other two are, they look like Carina and her mother."

Michele adjusted the glasses to suit his eyes and said,

"I can see them better now, you are right, the other two are Concetta and Carina."

"Let me see . . . is Papa there?"

The words came from behind them. Mario swung round; although ruffled because Lucia had left the refuge, he felt proud that she was putting her concern for her family before her own safety. Without showing his feelings, he pointed first to the distant church then to the valley and said,

"Your mother and Dora are a little to the left of the church and Ernesto is down there just bringing the beasts back here."

"I can see them, I can see them." Lucia's voice was quivering with relief. It was a relief short lived as the thought occurred that her father would hurry home to look after the safety of his family. "I will intercept Papa and tell him Mama and Dora are safe."

Lucia turned to go; quick as she was, Mario was quicker, he grabbed an arm and said, curtly,

"No you won't." then, as Lucia struggled to free herself, he laughed and added, "Don't worry you little vixen, I'll do that for you. Go back to the refuge and stay there."

By mid afternoon, the distant rumbling of the passing army's vehicles had subsided and only the occasional small cluster of trucks were to be seen as they passed along the distant road. Across the valley, a few small groups could also be seen as they returned to La villa. Michele frowned and said in a worried tone,

"I think those returning to their homes already are taking a risk it's too early to be sure they won't be raided. If all I've heard is correct. It has happened before."

Well over an hour had passed without any movement on the small stretch of road visible from the grass covered slope above Angelo's house when Filomena said,

"I think that's the last we will see of them. It should be safe now to check the fonte."

"I am not happy about you going in to La Villa today, Giorgio won't have left a signal," Angelo said, giving her an anxious look.

Filomena laughed and displaying an air of confidence as she tidied her dress and secured her bandanna with a knot below her chin, said,

"Don't worry Babbo, I will be careful. If there is any sign of trouble I will get out of sight."

Angelo made a grab to stop her, but she was too quick. Deftly avoiding the attempt she skipped down the slope and out of sight. Angelo knew he stood no chance of catching his daughter; that if he tried to follow, she would run.

. . . .

Happy that Dora and Roberto were safely ensconced in the refuge once used by Gwyn, Donnina and Ida were content to stay where they were on a rocky ledge above the belt of trees. However, Concetta and Carina were anxious to return and care for their turkeys and wanted to leave.

"There has been nothing on that road now for well over an hour," Concetta said forcefully, "we can't stay here all night." Then, pointing to the scattered groups that could be seen returning to their homes, added, "Everyone else seems to be . . ."

Concetta's words were cut short as Ernesto, who had joined them earlier in the day, pointed to a solitary truck that had appeared on the distant road. Together they watched the truck veer off the road on to the track that would take it to La Villa. As it drew closer, six German soldiers, could be discerned sitting like marionettes in the open rear of the vehicle.

Across the valley, Mario, who had also seen the truck, said to Michele.

"I hope that doesn't mean trouble."

From her point of safety, Donnina watched the approaching truck with bated breath and without knowing it, as it passed out of sight behind the houses, echoed Mario's words as she said,

"I hope that doesn't mean trouble."

Before the truck had ground to a halt at the bottom of the narrow street that was the entrance to La Villa the six Germans leaped out, and with their lightweight machine guns firing indiscriminatingly, ran up the steps in to the square. It was a horrific scene with men running, women running, children running and even dogs running as each strove to escape the deadly hail. The Death's head helmeted Germans were only there five minutes; five minutes during which incendiaries were thrown through windows and doors; five minutes which left death and destruction everywhere.

The arrival of the death squad coincided with that of Filomena, who was walking down the main street when she fell. Arriving in time to see it, Giorgio broke into a run; before he could reach her, he felt a searing pain and dropped.

. . . .

When the first contingent of Allied soldiers arrived, most of the surviving inhabitants were still on the mountain slopes. A few, Ernesto amongst them had descended to man the hoses attached to the fonte's three pipes, in a desperate attempt to quell the large number of blazing fires. They were joined by several willing hands with foam extinguishers. Others, immediately became busy attending the many fallen.

Standing at the top entrance of the square a Royal Army Medical Corps Doctor turned to the Sanitatstruppe Personal Doctor, who stood beside him as they surveyed the scene. Nonna Ricci caught his eye, a pathetic sight slumped in a chair, the spun wool at her feet stained with blood. Clutched in her hand was a strip of tape, bearing the last message she would ever receive from the German high Command. Around her, dead, wounded and dying lay everywhere. Hardly able to believe what he was seeing, the British officer, turned to the German and said,

"Come Kurt, there is work to be done."

Together they walked to a large marquee and entered.

THE END

EPILOGUE

Giorgio could not remember a time when he had felt so tired, he tried to sit up, but couldn't even lift his head. Dimly as in a dream he was aware of someone lying on a stretcher. Of dark lashes curved against pallid cheeks and a hand on the ground, with fingers stretched towards him. Mustering all his strength, he reached out over the edge of the stretcher on which he lay and succeeded in touching them.

"I love you," he whispered.

Filomena's eyes opened and her lips curved in the faintest of smiles as she said,

"I know dear man, I know."